Ralph Gibson

Richard Price is the author of seven novels, including *Lush Life, Clockers, Freedomland,* and *Samaritan.* He has received an Academy Award in literature from the American Academy of Arts and Letters and shared a 2007 Edgar Award as a cowriter of HBO's miniseries *The Wire.*

Also by Richard Price

The Wanderers

Ladies' Man

The Breaks

Clockers

Freedomland

Samaritan

Lush Life

Bloodbrothers

Richard Price

Picador

—

Farrar, Straus and Giroux

New York

www.picadorusa.com

Picador® is a U.S. registered trademark and is used by Farrar, Straus and Giroux under license from Pan Books Limited.

For information on Picador Reading Group Guides, please contact Picador.
E-mail: readinggroupguides@picadorusa.com

ISBN-13: 978-0-312-42869-3
ISBN-10: 0-312-42869-3

First published in the United States by Houghton Mifflin

First Picador Edition: March 2009

10 9 8 7 6 5 4 3 2 1

For John Califano, a true Bloodbrother, in love and friendship, "you know how we do . . ."

To Sabrina Di Benedetto

To Ellen Joseph and Carl Brandt for their enthusiasm and encouragement

To Cubby

To Lord Buckley

who am I

I rather think about bein Mighty Mouse and flyin through the air an like that. But now . . . they askin me questions — what I dream about and what I think about and what about my mother my father an like that. Man you start thinkin about things like that an it give you the sweats like a junkie . . .

Man — you ask Why should I be me — how I get to be me — why am I me here and not someplace else — and you just end up scared like you was walkin down a empty street at night. So scared it running out you ears . . .

The Cool World
by Warren Miller

Bloodbrothers

1

A WARM SOUR CLOUD wafted across to Tommy's side of the bed as his wife rolled over in her sleep. Tommy De Coco lay on his back smoking a Marlboro and staring at the green metal venetian blinds. One of the slats was bent and let in some early-morning sunlight. 7:30.

"Tommy, don't . . ." He turned his head. Marie was talking in her sleep again. She lay on her stomach and he stared at the brown and white freckles that made her back and shoulders look like salami. Tommy ditched his cigarette and put his arm behind his head. He absently massaged his dick under the covers. Four blocks away church bells rang.

Sunday. Family day. No matter what he did six days a week, on Sundays Tommy De Coco was a family man. And this Sunday he had a big surprise for his family.

His hand smelled from that oily shit inside Trojans. His pubic hair was still damp. He debated getting out of bed and taking a shower before Marie woke up and got a downwind whiff. Tough titties. What could she do? Yell? Scream? He'd crack her so goddamn hard she'd shit teeth for a week. Tommy sniffed his fingers. Fuck it. He rolled out of bed and headed for the shower. Goddamn stuff stinks anyway.

~

Seventeen-year-old Stony De Coco woke up to the hissing of the shower on the other side of the wall. Raising himself slightly he saw that his brother, Albert, was still sleeping, his head obscured from Stony's vision by the chest of drawers between their beds.

He pulled a Marlboro from beneath his pillow. Sunday. Shit on toast. Family day. His old man would make everybody get in the goddamn car and he'd drive around the whole goddamn Bronx looking for a G-rated movie. And Stony couldn't bitch either because his old man had thumbnails as big as clam shells and if he gave Tommy any bullshit he would get a flick behind the ear that would sting like a bastard.

~

Eight-year-old Albert De Coco lay in bed listening to his older brother smoking. He was afraid Stony was going to get lung cancer if he kept smoking every morning. Albert was nauseated like every time he woke up. The idea of eating made him even more queasy and he hoped Marie wouldn't force him to eat like last Sunday. Then he remembered she threatened to feed him like a baby if he didn't start eating more. A chill settled over his skeletal body.

~

Marie De Coco was dreaming about her mother again. This time Marie was a little girl and her mother was very old and shriveled like she looked before she died and she was caressing Marie's cheeks with fingers of cold blue wax and crooning to her, "Pretty, baby, pretty, baby, see how pretty, baby," and ran those bloodless fingers down over Marie's eyes and across her lips and Marie shut her eyes and rested her cheek on her mother's marble-smooth palm. Then her mother took her hand and led her through a long hall. "Come see how pretty, baby, come see how pretty." And Marie saw a mirror at the end of the hall. "Look how pretty, baby, see?" She pointed a finger at the mirror. Marie looked to see how pretty she was and screamed — she had no reflection.

She awoke with a start, but she couldn't move beyond that initial jerk. She knew she was awake but every muscle in her face and body was frozen. She couldn't move and she couldn't breathe. She could hear the bells from Immaculate and she could hear the shower in the bathroom. She was paralyzed. She couldn't even open her eyelids and her lungs were collapsing. She tried not to panic. She knew by now she had to concentrate. Relax. She had no breath in her lungs and couldn't open her mouth to scream. Then with a great inner wrenching she bolted upright in bed. Her lilac nightgown was damp with sweat. Marie was a kid when she first got these attacks. Her father had them also and he told her that if anybody touched her when she was awake and paralyzed like that she would die of a heart attack. Marie rubbed her nose, grunted and lit a cigarette.

~

When Tommy stepped out of the shower he heard Marie banging around in the kitchen. He cursed. He liked the dinette to himself for a few hours Sunday mornings so he could read the *News*, have a few smokes, a few cups of coffee, listen to the radio. He dried his blue black hair vigorously, wrapped a purple towel around his waist and leaned close to the mirror to inspect his new Fu Manchu. In the last year he had grown six different kinds of face hair including muttonchops and a real handlebar, but he liked the Fu Manchu best of all — it extended down each side of his mouth to his jaw in two thick black lines. He had to smile. That chick last night said, "Oooh, look! It's Jack Palance!" Chubby got jealous until she said *he* looked like Jack Palance too. Chubby looked like Jack Shit as far as Tommy was concerned. Jack Palance. He touched his high cheekbones, his rocky chin.

"Daddy, can I get in?" Albert's voice on the other side of the bathroom door jolted him out of his reverie. "I gotta pee."

Tommy opened the door and brushed past his son without looking at him.

~

"Hey, Thomas Junior!" — Tommy winked at Stony — "pass me the salt." Stony's fingers were greasy with butter and the shaker slipped onto his father's plate.

"I don' wanna eat any more." Albert had three Lucky Charm cereal bits glued with milk on his chin. He had only taken three spoonfuls.

"What?" Marie stared at him severely. "Don' wanna eat any

more, hah?" She nodded and narrowed her eyes. "Don' wanna
eat any more?"

Albert stared at his cereal.

"Where'd we go yesterday?" she demanded, not looking at him.

"Doctor Schindler," he answered meekly.

"What?"

"Doctor Schindler."

"I can't hear you."

"Doctor Schindler."

"I . . . can't . . . hear . . . you!"

Albert shut his eyes, lightly opened and closed his hands, his
fingertips touching, then springing away from each other. Stony
was about to jump up and smash his mother in the face when
Albert blurted, *"D — Doctor Schindler!"*

Tommy looked up surprised for a second, then returned to his
eggs. Marie lit a cigarette. Albert looked up at her mascaraed
plumpness through the snaky haze of smoke.

"And what did Doctor Schindler say?"

"I weigh too little."

"How little?"

Albert's eyebrows were raised and his lips shaped words that
wouldn't come. His stomach spun viciously. Tommy got up from
the table, grabbed the *News* and split for the john.

"Where the hell you goin'?" Marie barked.

"I gotta take a crap. You mind?" Tommy shot back. She
dismissed him with a disgusted wave of her hand. "Why don't the
hell you leave the kid alone!" Tommy shouted, his face turning
black. He held the paper in a giant fist.

"You know how much he weighs? Do you *give* a shit?" she
shouted back. They were both standing. Albert started crying.
Stony touched his brother's shoulder, made a funny face at his
parents and winked at him. Albert rubbed away some tears with
the heel of his palm. "Tell your father how much you weigh," she
demanded.

"Fif — fifty-five."

"You're goddamn right." She glowered at them both. "And

what am I gonna do with you this summer if you don't gain twenty-five pounds by June?"

"Puh — put mum — me in-na hospital."

"And what do they do to skinny boys in a hospital?" she pushed.

Tommy stormed out of the room and a second later the bathroom door slammed. Marie forced out two funnels of smoke from nostrils taut and arched with rage. She dropped her cigarette into her coffee and started clearing the table without looking at either of her sons.

Stony nodded to Albert to get lost. Albert got up, went to his room and turned on some Sunday morning cartoons.

~

Tommy sat on the toilet lost in thought. He thought about Marie and what a vicious cunt she had turned out to be. He thought about cracking her and then remembered what happened the last time he hit her after she kicked his brother, Chubby, out of the house when he burned her coffee table with a cigarette. He remembered coming back from Banion's that night and seeing her feet sticking out of the bathroom into the hallway. At first he thought she was drunk. Then the doctors. The fucking stomach pump. Her goddamn mother (may her soul rest in hell). How many times can you say you're sorry? Tommy thought of Albert. He was so skinny that he made Tommy think of Mahatma Gandhi in those big diapers and sheets, although he wished Marie would lay off the kid once in a while. Stony. Oh, Stony. A son-and-a-half. Thomas Jr. Fuckin' A. He thought about Stony coming in with the electricians. Tommy could swing him in easy. Maybe they could even work the same job. He imagined bringing Stony into the electricians' shanty and introducing him to the guys. Stony'd do great. He was strong as a goddamn bull. Yeah. Stony. Chubby. Fuckin' jibone. Tommy laughed. Jack Palance all right. He remembered the look on Chubby's face last night when he was balling that girl. He looked like Yogi Berra in heat. That *girl* was a bit all right though.

~

"How come we gotta wear suits?" Stony protested.

"Just do it, awright?" Tommy said.

"Sheezus." Stony almost said shit as he took off his dungarees.
"All we doin' is goin' a damn movie."

"We not goin' a damn movie," Tommy mimicked.

"Aw . . . we goin' visitin'?" Stony groaned.

"Just, just do what I say, hah?" Tommy turned from the door
and whistled at his wife, who was wearing a hot pink pantsuit.
She ignored him, still pissed off from this morning. As she walked
by she laid down a cloud of perfume. Tommy loved heavy
perfume. Her face was almost furry with rouge and powder.

"Hey, Marie." Tommy smiled like a little boy and stood before
her with his arms extended palms up.

She exhaled heavily through her nostrils, glowered at him and
shook her fist in front of his nose. The fight was over.

~

"Where the hell are you taking us?" Marie asked as Tommy
turned the car onto the George Washington Bridge.

"Keep your draws on." Tommy smiled. Albert sat in back
chewing on his fingernails and staring at some sailboats. Stony
was playing basketball in his head, doing weaving, whirling
lay-ups in slow motion against a whole team of six-foot-ten
spades. Then he started running numbers in his head. Cheri.
Under their new agreement they were both free to play. Last
week after graduation the Mount rented out Club D'Artagnan for
a shit-face and Cheri started coming on to Mott the Bear. Stony
went berserk and Butler had to shove him into the john to stop a
fight. If she wanted to play, she didn't have to be insulting about
it. Mott the Bear, Christ. Tommy. His old man was starting to
break his chops about the union. His only alternative was college.
Stony wasn't in love with the idea of more school, and more
school wasn't in love with the idea of Stony. The only place he
could get into his counselor had to find with a magnifying glass.
Purdy Free Normal, Purdy, Louisiana. Hot damn. He didn't

have anything against construction work. It was healthy, good bread, but . . . but . . . but. Marie. His old lady was coming down hard on Albert these days. That scared him. The kid had a constitution like a dandelion. If he wasn't careful he'd get loved to death.

A few miles into New Jersey Tommy swung the car into a cemetery driveway and drove up the narrow, steep lane for a quarter of a mile until he came to crosshatched blocks of graves. He stopped the car and took a scrap of paper out of his jacket.

Marie turned white. Afternoon sun glinted off the cellophane strips keeping the lacquered black curls in place by her ears.

"Tommy . . ." She pressed her fingers to her lips. Her eyes were wide. "This ain't funny."

Stony sat up and stared in puzzlement at the endless tombstones. Tommy read directions from the paper and continued driving, making sharp rights and lefts for a mile more through the heart and into the outer regions of the cemetery that were more sparsely populated. He drove with his head out the window reading names on headstones.

Marie lit another cigarette. Her hands were shaking so bad she had to use the car lighter instead of a match.

"Lucca!" Tommy shouted, and slammed on the brakes. "Everybody out!" He jumped out of the car, studied the paper again and walked to a grassy headstoneless twenty-by-twenty plot slightly uphill from a headstone marked Lucca. Tommy turned around and waved impatiently for his family to join him.

"What the hell is goin' on, Tommy?" Marie fumbled in her purse for a yellow pill. "Shit," she winced. She couldn't take pills without water.

"This is weird." Stony gawked. "Whatta we doin' here?"

"Well how d'ya like it?" Tommy beamed.

"What?"

Tommy extended his arms over the patch of grassy earth. "That's ours."

"What're you talkin' about?" Marie frowned.

"I bought it through the union. It's a benefit. I figure we gonna all die some day, right? So we need a place. You know, so we can stay together. The union got this burial committee. Frankie Jacobs is on the board so I ast him to get me a good deal."

Nobody said anything. Albert looked worried. Tommy walked onto the center of the plot and stared at the ground around him. "I figure I'll be here. Marie, you'll be next to me. Then Stony right under me and Albert next to him under you, over there."

"I wanna be next to Stony," said Albert.

Tommy lay down on the ground, put his hands behind his head and crossed his legs. "Not bad," he laughed. Marie ran back to the car. Albert walked over to his father and lay down next to him. He crossed his legs and put his hands behind his head like Tommy.

~

Going home everybody was silent. Tommy was angry that nobody was crazy about his present. Stony thought about Mott the Bear. Albert wondered if dead people had to eat.

"Tommy?" Marie looked at him.

"Yeah?" he sulked.

"Long as we're here, could we see Mama?" Marie's voice was thin and sad, cutting off any wisecrack Tommy wanted to make.

"O.K.," he said, after he'd driven half a mile. He turned off the highway at Paterson and drove through a residential area until he hit the entrance of Saint Ambrose Cemetery.

"Stop a minute." Marie got out of the car, walked into the monument and flower shop and came out with a small cross of lilacs and tiger lilies. Tommy drove into the cemetery past clusters of gravestones that jutted out of the earth like rotten teeth.

"I'm gonna stay in the car," Tommy mumbled. Marie didn't answer but got out and walked to her mother's grave. She was weaving slightly like a stunned cow. Tommy watched her for a while, then turned around to his sons. "Go with your mother." He nodded in her direction. Albert was sleeping with his head on Stony's lap. Stony pretended to be asleep. Tommy sighed and lit a cigarette.

Marie walked to the gray headstone and carefully placed the floral cross on the earth at the base. Her head was spinning as it

did every time she came here. She knew her mother was watching
her in heaven. She touched the carved lamb on the top of the
stone and read the epitaph for the millionth time in the last six
months:

> Farewell my husband and daughter dear.
> I am not dead but sleeping here.
> As I am now you soon shall be.
> Prepare for death, and follow me.
>
> Jeanette Scalisi
> 1908   1973

Marie sank to her knees in the soft earth — grass staining her
hot pink slacks. Her face contorted into a trembling pout. She
raised her fingers to her lips as if in prayer. "Oh, Mama." She
closed her eyes.

Fifty yards down the path Tommy De Coco sat restlessly,
wishing his wife would hurry the fuck up.

~

Sunday afternoon sunlight splashed the walls and furniture as
Chubby De Coco lay on his back like a beached whale in his
blue-striped boxer shorts on the sheetless king-size bed. He was
wearing enormous headphones, listening to the best of Henry
Mancini. His eyes were closed and he was smiling. A frosty mug
of beer sat on the night table within easy reach. Phyllis was at her
mother's and would be gone until dinner. He was happy.

He took off the headphones after a while and pivoting himself
on his ass swung his legs over the side of the bed. He reached for
the mug, finished the beer, yawned and made his way to the
bathroom. The bagginess of the boxer shorts made his legs look
even thinner than they really were but the elastic waistband was
taut.

He stood over the toilet and pissed, holding his dick with both
hands. He hated the way Phyllis decorated the john with gold
Florentine wallpaper, gold ceiling paper, a gold furry toilet cover,
a fake brown wood sink, a shower curtain with brown, gold and

crystal beads like a Chink whorehouse. The whole house looked like a whorehouse as far as he was concerned. Like his brother, Tommy, they lived in Co-op City so he only paid $200 rent including utilities for a four-and-a-half-room apartment with air conditioning in every room. He figured for that price he could afford to let Phyllis splurge on furniture and wallpaper and crap. He himself could give a shit what the place looked like as long as he had that air conditioning but she liked what Marie called "Jewish Renaissance." She couldn't buy goddamn lamps — she had to have chandeliers. Jungle-thick rugs all over the house so you couldn't touch anything without getting twenty-five volts up your ass. Plus you had to take your goddamn shoes off like you were entering a Dutch church. And the stuff *he* liked, like the purple velour couch and the red leather Barcalounger, she had wrapped in what looked like big Glad Bags — giant plastic slipcovers — so that he couldn't even relax and watch TV in the living room without leaving half the skin on his back stuck to the plastic every time he wanted to get up to make a sandwich or go to the bathroom. He was surprised she didn't put a slipcover over the color TV.

Chubby wandered into the kitchen for some eats. He peered into the refrigerator, took out a bowl of tuna salad, two Schaefers and a hard-boiled egg. He hummed the theme from "Peter Gunn" that was on the Henry Mancini album. That was the other thing he liked in the apartment besides the air conditioning. That stereo with the headphones he got himself. He could spend all day with those headphones on listening to Tony Bennett and Frank Sinatra. He was fixing himself a tuna sandwich and wondering what the hell ever happened to Perry Como when the phone rang.

"Yo."

"Chub."

"Tommy, how you doin'?"

"Chub, lissen. I met this chick." Tommy was whispering. "Chubby, I'm tellin' you, she got a tongue like a anteater."

Chubby snickered, scratched his belly.

"I thought I was gonna die, Chubby. I hadda *beg* her to stop."

Chubby lit a cigarette. It looked as thin as a kitchen match between his stubby fingers.

"I swear to Christ, baby."

"She a blonde or a brunette?" Smoke slipped and curled over the tip of his slightly protruding tongue.

"Neither, orange."

"Orange! Jesus Christ. Cuffs and collars?"

"Cuffs and collars."

"Tommy, I gotta meet this bitch. You know that, don'cha?"

"How 'bout tonight? I tol' her all about you. She's gonna be waitin' at Banion's."

"Oh my heart." Chubby closed his eyes and let his tongue hang out.

"I tol' her what a steed you was." Tommy laughed.

"Oh shit." Chubby turned pale. "Tommy, I can't do it tonight."

"Whatta you talkin'?"

"I tol' Phyll I'd take her to a movie."

"Bullshit! Take her tomorrow."

"C'mon, Tommy, I promised."

"You pussy."

"Hey, Tommy, c'mon now. It ain't right."

"What time's the movie?"

"Eight-thirty."

"So, come after."

"What am I supposed to say to her?"

"You know you sound like a fuckin' teen-ager, Chubby. I tell everybody what a goddamn stallion my brother is and set 'im up with a million-dollar mouth an' a pair a jugs what belongs in the Museum a Modern Art an' he can't even get away from his wife."

"Hey." Chubby grinned. "You really tell everybody what a stallion I am?" He ran a thumb around the elastic of his boxer shorts.

"Chubby, you know what they call you down at Banion's now?"

"What?"

"The Prick."

"Tommy, pick me up at the gas station." Tommy neighed like a horse. Chubby was about to hang up. "Hey, Tommy! Tommy, what's her name?"

"Sylvia."

~

"Lissen, I tol' Tommy I'd meet him for a drink in a half-hour," Chubby said to his wife as they came out of the movie theater.

She shrugged. "So go."

"You not mad?"

She shrugged. She looked tired, with deep eye sockets and a bony face. There were always deep swaths under her eyes. She looked dehydrated.

"You sure you ain't mad?"

She shrugged again.

" 'Cause if you want I won't go." She didn't answer.

"O.K. I'm goin' now." Chubby took a few steps. "You sure? You don't wamme to watch Johnny Carson with you?"

~

Banion's was a bar up in Yonkers where Tommy and Chubby liked to hang out. It was long and dark with yellow lights and wood paneling. Banion was the bartender as well as the owner. He was paralyzed from the waist down and worked in a motorized wheelchair. Behind the bar was a three-foot-high platform with a ramp at the end so Banion could be eye level with all his customers. He knew the De Coco brothers from the time he was a construction electrician with them and they were all working on Freedomland back in 1957. In 1960, a steel beam fell across his back when he was working on the Albert Einstein Medical Center. Disability paid for the bar.

~

Tommy let Chubby off in the parking lot and sat in the car for a half-hour smoking cigarettes.

"Then I had this dream . . ." Sylvia delicately scratched her nose with a long red pinkynail. "I had this dream where this man comes to my door and gives me two jugs of wine . . ."

In the almost brown, subdued light of the bar Chubby looked interested. He looked sincere.

". . . and I went to this old Jewish lady in my building, and you know, I told her the dream because she knows about things like that and the old lady asks me if I got children and I said yeah I got two boys in Vietnam and then she said the man in the dream was God and the two jugs of wine were my boys and God was giving them back to me safe and sound from Vietnam."

Chubby smiled, motioned for another seventy-seven for the lady, rested his hand on hers and looked into her eyes. She squeezed his hand. He was in.

"An' your boys are awright, right?"

Sylvia started weeping into a pastel Kleenex. "Larry died three days later."

"Aw shit! Hey that's terrible!" Looking at the bar mirror he saw Tommy finally walk in. Chubby caressed her veiny fingers and cursed himself silently. "The *other* one's O.K. though, right?"

She blew her nose and sneered. "He comes back and in two weeks he marries a Puerto Rican."

"Aw Jesus!" Chubby said with real feeling.

"She'll break his heart. They don't know from faithfulness, those animals. All they know is this." She shot her middle finger through a ring of her thumb and forefinger moving it back and forth rapidly.

Tommy sat at the far end of the bar. His eyes met Chubby's in the mirror. They both stifled laughs.

"He'll come crawling back to me" — her face turned ugly — "but I won't be there."

Chubby took in her jugs again. Nice big hangers. Come in Rangoon. She was about fifty he figured. Frosted orange hair. Wrinkle cream. He wanted to change the subject.

"So now you live alone, hah?" He extended a lighter under her unlit cigarette, caught Tommy's eye again and smiled.

"Just me and Shaintze."

"Ha?"

"Shaintze my Siamese."

"Oh, haha."

"Do you like cats?"

"Oh yeah, haha, I love 'em to death."

"Nat loved cats too."

"Your husband?"

"He died two years ago. He died of cancer," she said, raising her chin and tapping her throat. "Right here."

Chubby automatically swallowed and felt a half-dozen painful lumps as the saliva went down his gullet.

"They put in a rubber tube," she said, still tapping.

"He's prob'ly happier where he is now," he offered.

"How do you know?" she asked. She cupped his hand between her palms and lowered her head to light another cigarette, forgetting the just-lit one in the ashtray. The dry warmth of her fingers gave him a hard-on. He motioned to Banion for another drink.

"Cancer's a real bitch," he said.

"My whole family had cancer," she said. "My father had lung cancer, my mother had ovary cancer, my sister had stomach cancer." She counted off on her fingers. "And me . . ." She stopped counting and stared at him. "I got cancer of the rectum."

Chubby closed his eyes and felt himself falling off the barstool. He saw the walls rushing past him and the floor zooming up into his face. When he opened his eyes a second later he was still sitting on the barstool, his cigarette between his fingers. Pearls of sweat formed at his hairline.

"They just keep cuttin' and cuttin' and cuttin' . . ." Sylvia droned on.

Chubby jumped as he heard the whine of Banion's wheelchair. Sylvia touched Chubby's hand. He jerked away from her touch. He looked into the mirror for Tommy. The bar was deserted. He jumped off his stool and looked around frantically. Sylvia's face managed to look sharp and cold in the soft shadowy light. "Motherfuckin' bastard!" Chubby clenched his teeth, looking for his brother.

"It's not contagious," Sylvia said in a weak yet bitter voice not even directed at Chubby.

Chubby kicked open the "Gents" door and saw Tommy doubled over with laughter by the urinal. Tommy tried to whinny but he was laughing too hard. Chubby took a swing at him. Tommy caught Chubby's fist with his own big hands but the force of the punch knocked him down anyhow.

Tommy kept laughing. "You — you shoulda seen your face." He pointed at Chubby.

Chubby pulled back his leg to kick him in the ribs. Chubby's skin was gray and his hands were trembling. Tommy saw the kick coming and rolled away. Chubby suddenly smiled. The color came back to his face and he turned, moving swiftly into a stall, and emerged two seconds later with two sopping-wet balls of toilet paper that he threw at Tommy, hitting him in the face with one and in the crotch with the other. Tommy jumped up and ran into the other stall. Chubby ran back into the first stall. In less than a minute they were laughing and yelling, having a toilet paper war, covering themselves and the walls with gray clots of wet tissue until they were both exhausted. Laughing weakly and panting, they staggered from the bathroom, through the bar, ignoring Sylvia, who stared rigidly at her hands, and out into the street.

~

"Did you really ball her, Tommy?" Tommy cruised slowly down Central Avenue, Chubby sprawled in the shotgun seat.

"Nah." Tommy popped a piece of Dentyne that was on the dashboard into his mouth. "I was talkin' to her Friday night. She tol' me like she tol' you. I almost fell through the floor." Tommy never took his eyes from the road. Chubby stared at the swaying brown-beaded rosary knotted and dangling from Tommy's mirror.

"She ain't never gonna get picked up tellin' guys *that* shit about herself." Chubby yawned.

"Banion's is startin' to give me the creeps, with Sylvia there startin' to hang aroun' an' Banion in his goddamn wheelchair," Tommy said.

"Maybe we should find some new place."

"How about this here?" Tommy slowed the car as they approached a low, rambling roadside discotheque — the 88 Club. More than a hundred cars were parked across the road. Tommy pulled the car over by the parking lot on the shoulder of Central Avenue. Six teen-age girls came out along with a blast of live rock and roll music. The girls trotted across Central Avenue to the parking lot.

"Oh Jesus, look a' that one!" Chubby gawked.

"Hey, Miss! Hey, Miss!" Tommy yelled out the car window. All six of them turned their heads.

"You need a ride?" Chubby leaned out his side.

They kept walking.

"Jesus Christ, look a' that one." Tommy pointed to the tallest one, who had a skirt up to her crotch. "I'd eat a mile a shit if it led to *her* asshole."

The girls piled into a Mustang twenty feet in front of Tommy's car. When the tall one bent over to crawl into the back, her skirt hiked up, flashing flowered panties in Tommy and Chubby's direction. Chubby grabbed Tommy's arm. Tommy flicked his brights on and off. One of the girls shot them the finger as the Mustang backed out onto Central Avenue. Chubby jumped from the car, whipped out his cock and started running after them, yelling and laughing.

"Looks like a prick, only smaller!" one of the girls shouted out the window as the driver shifted into forward, burning rubber.

Chubby stood on the shoulder of the road wiggling his dick in the wind, laughing and shouting. More kids left the 88 Club. Tommy started the car, drove to Chubby and pulled him inside.

"Oh, Tommy, that one likes me!" Chubby was out of breath. "Le's follow 'em!"

"Nah, c'mon, they're kids." Tommy pulled onto the road.

Chubby tried to catch his breath.

"You wanna get pneumonia?" Tommy asked.

"Hah?"

Tommy looked over at Chubby's crotch. Chubby looked down. His dick was still hanging out.

"Shee!" Chubby arched himself, lifting his ass out of the seat, and shoved his dick back in. "That's a nice place there, that 88 Club." Chubby zipped up his fly.

"Too young," Tommy said. "That's for Stony, not us."

"Stony," Chubby chuckled. "He gettin' any a this?" he asked, making a loose fist and shaking it like he was going to roll dice.

"What, a' you kiddin'?" Tommy laughed. "He got that hot little girlfriend a his."

"That little blonde with the big tits?"

"Cheri," Tommy said.

"I wouldn't mind a piece a that myself," Chubby said.

"Hey, don' tell Stony that, he'll tear ya heart out."

"He got it bad, hah?" Chubby lit a cigarette.

"I think she cheats on him too." They passed an open diner. "You hungry?"

"Nah. So she's a little tramp, hah?" Chubby nodded sadly. "Poor fuckin' Stony. I love that kid. He deserves the best."

Tommy cruised through a red light on the deserted road, and turned left up a hill into an expensive residential section. "Every time I go through here," Tommy said, maneuvering the car on narrow winding curves and peering at the darkened brick and stone mansions, "every time I go through here I feel like a fuckin' kid, you know? I feel like sayin' . . . when I grow up *this* is where I'm gonna live . . . an' then I remember I'm fuckin' forty-five an' I ain't never gonna live here. I live in fuckin' Co-op City an' that's straight life." He stopped the car in front of a fortresslike house with a widow's walk and lead castings on octagonal windows. "Here, this is my fuckin' favorite." Tommy winced. "I would give anything to live here."

"Hey, you know what kinda land taxes this guy must pay?" Chubby said.

"When you got a place like this you don' fucking care about no land taxes."

"Bullshit. These guys are all prob'ly up to their asses in mortgages." Chubby flicked his cigarette out the window.

Tommy started driving again.

"I dunno." Chubby squinted. "I like Co-op City, no hassles, no utilities, you got a Chinese restaurant right there, air conditioning in every room, you can take yogi classes in the community center, no niggers."

"You got plenty a niggers."

"Yeah, but they're the ones that moved outta the old neighborhood because of the niggers movin' in, they're almost like us."

Tommy turned onto the Parkway going to the Bronx. "You know, I bet Stony's gonna have a house like that one back there," he said, flooring the accelerator on the deserted, unlit Parkway. "If he comes in the local in July, you know? He puts in his four years apprenticing he'll be . . . lessee twenty-two when he turns journeyman, right? Four years from now journeyman's base'll be up to ten an hour I'll figure . . . so that's like maybe . . . with time-and-a-half after twenty-five hours . . . it'll come to . . . I dunno, fuck, let's say twenty grand a year, O.K.? I give him two years he'll be straw boss 'cause he is one smart bastard that kid. So I figure at twenty-four, he'll, say twenty-five, he'll be makin' twenty-five grand. Another five years he'll be a goddamn foreman pullin' down forty a year like Artie Di Falco. So figure when he's thirty I come an' visit my son in fuckin' Scarsdale, New York."

"I thought he was gonna college?"

"Nah. He got into this dipshit school in Louisiana. Cracker State or somethin'. He'll go into the union. He don't need college. What'll he do? He'll fuck aroun' down there four years, then get a job jerkin' off a pencil for eight grand?" Tommy turned on his brights. "He's too smart to go to college. He knows where the action is."

2

9:30 FRIDAY NIGHT, Stony stood bathed in the soft red light of
D'Artagnan's, leaning against the bar. The walls were white
stucco with crosshatched beams of dark wood. Over his head was
a black-light poster of a voluptuous nude chick with an enormous
Afro standing spread-legged in a jungle clearing. Her eyes,
nipples, the lush vegetation around her and the legend "Lilith"
gave off a sinister phosphorescent gleam.

Stony was waiting. Every once in a while he glanced at the
tables to his right. Three guys sat there checking out the scene.
One of them, Mott, kept staring at Stony. When Stony looked
over that way, he would lock eyes with Mott for a second, then
they would both feign disinterest and look away. Stony kept
clenching and unclenching his fists. His gut was rippling. He was
chain-smoking and chugging seventy-sevens. The slick mixed
crowd of whites, blacks and PRs shook the floor to Al Green's
"Love and Happiness." Stony heard the music as if it was three
rooms down. At the end of the song, Butler staggered off the
floor, his silky flowered shirt sopping wet. He stood beside Stony,
wiping away a bead of sweat from the tip of his nose. "Mother-
fuck!" He gasped and collapsed hunched over the bar. "If that
bitch can hump half as good as she can bump . . ." Stony
ignored him, staring grimly at Mott. Butler looked at him. "You
hear what I say?"

"Huh?" Stony turned as if just noticing Butler's presence.
Butler looked over at Mott. He punched Stony in the arm. "Hey!
You gonna do a number tonight or what?"

"Nah . . . nah." Stony's gaze turned back to the table.

"Hey look, I'm not gettin' in a fight tonight . . . you know? You promised."

"No sweat."

Manu Dibango's "Soul Makossa" played over the PA. Butler took a deep gulp of air and plunged back onto the dance floor. Stony finished his drink as Cheri walked in dressed in tight dungarees and a white silky blouse, the shirttails pulled up and knotted under her tits. Stony dropped a load. He could see her nipples stand out from ten yards off. She came up to him, ran a hand up his rigid arm and kissed him on the cheek. He didn't respond. She saw Mott and smiled. Her teeth glowed ghostlike under the black light. Stony wanted to crack her in the mouth.

"Whadja do, burn your bra?"

She looked at him, her face collapsing in exhaustion. "Stony, gimme a break."

"Where do ya wannit?" He sniffed.

She started walking away. Stony grabbed her arm. "Where you think you goin'?"

"I wanna dance, you mind?"

"Then dance with me." He pushed her to the dance floor. They both danced in a rage, out of rhythm, stiff. Halfway through the number, Cheri walked off the floor. Stony stood there, panicked. He pushed through the dancers after her, grabbing her arm again back at the bar.

"I love you, Cheri." Sweat streamed down his face. Her features relaxed for a moment.

"I love you too, Stony, but you promised," she pleaded.

"I know, I know." He winced. He stared at her thin, dark face bordered with long plaits of black hair. Her huge brown eyes searched his face for parole. He let go of her arm. She smiled, kissed him lightly on the nose and walked over to Mott's table. Stony watched in horror as she sat down next to him, kissing him full on the mouth. Stony clutched his forehead and staggered blindly away from the bar.

Butler stopped him. "What happened?"

"I'm gonna kill 'em both."

"What?" He looked at Mott's table. "Oh Christ, Stony, I knew this was gonna happen."

"I'm gonna kill 'em both."

"Stony, give her some slack. You can fuck around too, you know."

"I don't want to. I don't *need* to. She don't need to either, fuckin' cocktease." He was panting, staring off wildly.

"C'mon, let's go to the Third Rail."

"I wanna stay here!" He stabbed a trembling finger at the floor.

Butler exhaled wearily. Suddenly his eyes lit up. "Hey, Three-Finger Annette said she was goin' to the Camelot tonight. Let's go ov — "

"I don't need no town *pump,* Butler, all I need's right in that corner." He pointed.

"Hey, Stony! Howya doin'?"

Stony grunted a hello to the bouncer, a tall black guy with long bow shoulders and a high Afro. "Butler, what's shakin'?" He slapped Butler on the back.

"Jump back! Don't give'm no flak! The man with the tan! It's Chili Mac!" Butler slapped palms with Chili Mac. Stony turned away annoyed.

"What the fuck's with him?" Chili Mac jutted his chin in Stony's direction.

"Ah, Cheri's breakin' his balls."

"Whada you mean?"

"She started swingin' with Mott."

"Mott the Bear?"

"In his underwear."

"B.V.D.s?"

"Gimme a break, please."

"Nice an' easy?"

"Don' make me queasy."

"You guys are real fuckin' comics. Yah oughta be on Broadway," Stony spat.

"Uh! The man don't joke," Mac said to Butler.

"Hey, Mac, howdja like a crack?" Stony asked.

"In front or in back?"

"Will you cut that shit!" Stony looked as if he were halfway between tears and murder.

Chili Mac eased off.

Stony shook his head sadly. "Her funeral an' my trial."

Mac raised his eyebrows. "Whyncha go over to the Camelot tonight. I heard ol' Three-Fingers is gunnin' for you."

"You fuckin' guys got a one-track mind. Whyncha both go over yourselves."

"I would," said Chili Mac, "except she only got eyes for you."

"Yeah?" Stony said, trying to keep his interest down.

Barry White's "You're My Everything" started playing. The bar drained of people.

"Bet . . . on Annette," Mac said.

"She does it with Gillette," said Butler.

"She does it with a razor?"

"It don't even phase'r."

Butler and Chili Mac slapped palms. Mac did a quick about-face, and, extending his hands behind his back, slapped palms with Butler again.

Stony laughed for the first time that night. Butler and Chili Mac looked at each other relieved. "Fuckin' clowns," Stony snickered.

As the song ended, the tide shifted again, the bar crowding up. Then Carl Douglas' "Kung Fu Fighting" came on, the tide moving out.

Chili Mac danced absently at the bar, his eyes spanning the floor for any trouble. He was only eighteen but he lifted weights and studied karate. He never saw the man that could take his ass. Frankie Bones, the other bouncer, danced on a chair at one end of the floor overlooking the crowd. All night, every night, he stood on that chair dancing unless there was trouble. Frankie was thirty, Irish and big. He and Chili Mac hated each other with a passion. Chili Mac dreamed of the day they would finally lock assholes in the parking lot. He wanted a big crowd there too.

Stony felt better. Relaxed. He dug the Mac. He forgot about Cheri. He wasn't even looking at her, but as the three of them lounged at the bar Cheri and Mott passed by arm-in-arm on their way out the door. Stony fell back against the bar.

"He a *ugly* sucker," said Chili Mac.

"Do ya think he'll . . ." Butler didn't finish the rhyme.

"Do ya think he'll *what!*" Stony grabbed Butler's shirt, his eyes crazy-man blind.

"How do I know?" Butler grinned nervously, looking to Chili Mac for help.

"Well, if you don't fuckin' *know*" — Stony stabbed Butler in the chest with his finger — "don't fuckin' *say.*" He stabbed him again.

"Hey, mah man." Chili Mac laid a hand on Stony's shoulder. Stony violently shook it off, still staring at Butler. Chili knew when to give slack and didn't get pissed.

"You know you're a big fuckin' help, Butler."

"Hey, Stones." Butler managed a smile. "Look, I didn't mean nothin' by that." He tentatively put an arm around Stony's shoulder, and when Stony didn't resist, gently turned him toward the bar.

"Two seventy-sevens, straight up." Butler still had his arm around Stony's hunched shoulders, and when he reached into his pocket for money, Stony's body started trembling. He fell against Butler's damp chest and cried like a baby. Chili Mac was almost relieved when a fight broke out on the floor and he had to split. Butler patted Stony's back awkwardly. Stony straightened up, wiping his eyes.

"Ah bullshit." He wiped away some tears. "I feel like a jerk. I need this, right?"

Butler took a napkin off the counter and dabbed at Stony's face. Stony grabbed the napkin from him and laughed. "C'mon, what're you . . . my mother?"

"Not yours." Butler shivered.

Stony blew his nose in the napkin and dropped it on the floor. "Hey lissen, gimme the keys to the short, I wanna drive over to the Camelot, check out Annette."

"I'll go witcha."

"Nah, I wanna go myself."

"You ain't gonna go over to Cheri's?" Butler looked skeptical. "Whatta' you crazy?" Stony smirked.

Butler held out his car keys to Stony, then pulled them back. "You sure?"

"Gimme the fuckin' keys." Stony grabbed them from Butler's hand. "I'll be back in an hour. I gots to cop me some haid, bawh!" He winked.

As he left D'Artagnan's, La Belle belted out "Lady Marmalade." "*Voulez-vous coucher avec moi, ce soir?*" He drove directly to Cheri's house.

At Cheri's, Mott was shitting a brick. He was caught between his lust for Cheri and his fear of what Stony might do to him. Not that he couldn't take care of himself — he was over 200 pounds of mean meat, but you could never tell what a guy would do if you fucked around with his woman.

Sitting next to Mott, Cheri was silent. If his cock was as big as his gut it might be a bit all right. Stony was such a putz sometimes. He was the only guy she ever balled with. Every time he went down on her she would come a river, but she would never come from fucking. Inez used to date Mott and she came all the time. Cheri was pushing seventeen and she didn't want to see life pass her by. Stony would sulk for a while, but whatever. It was funny. As much as a yo-yo as Stony could be, there was something about him that really had her hung up on the boards. She just needed more experience. Romance-wise Mott was nowhere city. This was for science. Maybe if Stony checked out Three-Finger Annette tonight tomorrow would be less of a hassle.

Stony drove along White Plains Road under the el tracks. His heart was pumping Kool-Aid. He imagined Cheri nude except for knee socks, blue ones, going down on Mott. Mott coming all over her face. Mott hoisting her up, her knees wrapped around his rib cage, lowering her on his cock. Mott standing spread-legged, her arms wrapped around his neck. Mott's hands lifting and lowering her ass on his dong. Cheri biting his neck. The moans, the squeals, the oohs, the ahhs. Stony's boner gave him a hard time with the clutch.

"You wanna drink?" Cheri got up and fussed around in the kitchen.

"Nah . . . thanks." Mott sat sprawled on the green-and-white-striped sateen sofa. Something felt off. He smelled danger.

Cheri poured herself a gin and tonic. "You sure?"

"I'm fine." Mott tried to concentrate on Cheri's nipples, but he felt like he was in Vietnam. "Where ya parents?"

"They went to Puerto Rico for a week." Cheri walked carefully into the living room as if her drink was filled to the top of the glass.

Mott had heard Cheri only came from eating out. This freaked him. The only girl he'd ever made come was Inez, and she was the type of chick that once she started moaning you could get up, fix a sandwich, watch the eleven o'clock news, take a piss and when you got back in bed she would still be moaning like you were never gone. A very intense personal experience.

Cheri sat down beside him.

"I'm thinkin' a becomin' a T.A. cop," he said.

"Fascinating." She gulped down the rest of her drink, swallowed a belch, shuddered and clutched Mott's thigh to brace herself.

Mott put an arm around her neck, thumb raising her chin, and lowered his face to hers. She moved her hand to his crotch. He slipped a hand in her blouse and the doorbell rang four times. Mott jumped up, almost sucking Cheri's tongue out of her head.

"What the fuck!" Cheri fumed as she strode over to the door. "Yeah?"

"Cheri, let me in."

"Oh Christ, Stony, come back tomorrow."

"Lemme in or I'll kick down the fuckin' door."

She walked back to Mott and took his clammy hand.

"Let's go in the bedroom. He'll go away."

Mott stood rigid. Stony started pounding the door. Cheri tugged on Mott's arm.

"Let 'im in." He was scared shit, but he would be more scared tomorrow if Stony split.

"What the hell for?"

"Just . . ." The door exploded inward, the chain lock flying into a mirror. Stony stood hunched in the foyer hissing in pain, rubbing his right shoulder.

"You!" He pointed to Mott. "Get the fuck outta here!"

"Now look . . ." Mott started. Stony lunged at him, both tumbling down on the couch. Cheri screamed curses at Stony, holding her temples, her face turning red. They held each other in bear hugs cursing, spit flying. They rolled off the couch onto the rug, snarling with frustration.

"Yah fuckin' homos!" Cheri bent down over them as she screamed. Mott kicked Stony away and scrambled to his feet.

"I'll kill ya!" Stony charged again, swinging wildly, accidentally catching Mott with a backhand across the bridge of his nose. Mott fell down, blood all over his shirt. Stony was startled by the blood and stood over him as if trying to keep his balance.

Cheri slid down next to Mott. "You fuckin' prick!" she yelled at Stony, one arm around Mott. Mott sat dazed. The pain from his nose made his eyes tear. Gingerly he touched his nose, stared fascinated at his bloody fingers.

"Ya broke it." He glared murderously at Stony. Stony didn't know what to do with his hands. He started to apologize, stammering. Mott pushed Cheri away, stood up, shoved past Stony and stormed out of the apartment, slamming the door.

Cheri sat on the rug crying. Stony didn't know whether to go after Mott or Cheri — stood nailed to the spot.

"I wanna thank you for a wonderful evening," Cheri spat with her head down.

"Me!" Stony sputtered, pointing to himself.

"Oh, get outta here." Cheri got up, slapped away Stony's hand and marched into her bedroom, slamming the door. Stony felt panicked again. He ran to the locked door. "Cheri, lemme in."

"Whyncha break it down."

Stony rested his head on the wooden door. Suddenly the door swung open and he almost pitched forward into the room. Cheri walked past him into the bathroom, slamming that door.

"Cheri, I love you," he whined.

"Do me a favor, don't love me so much."

He heard running water and gargling.

"I got jealous," he offered to the closed door. More gargling. "I'm sorry," in his best puppy tone of voice. "I'm goin'." He lingered at the bathroom door. "Hey . . . Cheri? He's fulla shit. I didn't break his nose. I just tapped it. You remember that time I thought I busted my nose? You remember that game against Power? That guy rammed me with his helmet? I thought I was dead. All I got was a nosebleed." The only response Stony heard was running water. He went into the kitchen and poured himself some orange juice. Cheri came in five minutes later wearing a red bathrobe.

"Stony, get out of my house."

"Just answer me one question. Then I'm gone." Stony carefully placed his glass on the counter. "Did you fuck with him?"

Cheri put her hands in the deep pockets of her robe, tossed her head to snap the hair out of her face. "Yes."

Stony's insides frosted over. He stared at her. Her expression was set. No backs. No penny tax. The end. Stony lifted the juice glass, put it down. Walked into the living room. Walked back. Picked up the glass, put it down. Walked into the bathroom, brushed his teeth, came back into the kitchen, picked up the juice glass, stared at her immovable face, her get-out-of-here eyes. He wheeled and with a yell flung the glass against the far wall. The smash stung his ears. Orange rivulets dripped down the wall to the counter, flattening out, heading left and right along a strip of chrome behind the faucet. Cheri didn't move. Stony picked up a chunk of glass at his feet, dropped it in the plastic-lined trash can and left the apartment.

3

STONY HIT the streets, hands in pockets, nose aimed at the pavement. He walked half a block before he heard shouts. Mott was running toward him, bloody handkerchief to his face, followed by two Mott-sized guys brandishing baseball bats. At first he thought they were chasing Mott, but when one of them pointed to Stony — "There he is!" — Stony turned and tore ass back to Cheri's. He took the stairs four at a time up to the third floor.

"Cheri!" Stony pounded on the door for fifteen seconds until he heard shuffling slippers.

"What n . . ."

He pushed past her indignant face, slammed the door. "Mott's comin' up the stairs wit' two guys." He leaned spread-eagled against the door, panting.

"What!?" Cheri didn't know whether to be angry or scared, settled on stunned.

A commotion in the hall. Stony almost jumped into Cheri's arms as one of Mott's friends decided to play home run derby with the door, the resounding boom rattling the dishes in the kitchen.

"C'mout, De Coco, yah cocksuckah!"

"Right away!" Stony shouted back.

Another explosion of wood and metal. Cheri stood catatonic, eyes as big as half dollars. She made a halfhearted grab at Stony's arm as he raced into the living room, lugged and yanked the couch back into the hallway, jamming it lengthways between the door and the near wall. Two bats going at once like the Fourth of July.

"I'll kill yah, De Coco!"

With every smack on the door Stony took one step in a different direction, making a full circle after five shots, his hair a nest of sweaty ringlets. After every smack Cheri twitched convulsively as if she was warming up for an epileptic fit. Stony finally shoved/ushered her into her bedroom, slammed the door, ran into the kitchen and grabbed the phone. After six rings: "Ma!"

"Stony?"

"Where's Pop?"

"He's out. You think I ever know where . . ."

Stony hung up and dialed again.

"Yo."

"Chubby!"

"Hey, Stones, wh — "

"Chubby! You gotta help me! Three guys are after my ass wit' bats. I'm gonna get creamed. Hurry!"

Stony slammed the phone down, walked in little circles. "Shit!" He grabbed the phone again. Chubby picked it up on the first ring. "I'm at Cheri's. Three-two-o-one Bainbridge. Hurry!"

Stony ran into Cheri's bedroom. From the sounds at the door Stony guessed the two lummoxes were trying to shoulder-butt the door down. Cheri started crying. Stony sat her down on the bed, squeezing her shoulder. "Chubby'll be here in ten minutes." His hand strayed down to her tit. Her nipple was erect. He was pretty erect himself. She didn't seem to notice, just stared at the far wall. He debated laying her down on the bed, but a renewed barrage of bat blasts had him on his feet. He ran into the foyer, the door trembled with each blow, but the couch held it shut. He high-jumped the couch into the living room and hung his head out the window scanning the empty street for Chubby's car. After five minutes, an orange-and-cream Impala careened screaming up Bainbridge, coming to a rocking stop in front of the building. Chubby burst out of the driver's side, carrying a five-foot-long broom handle.

"Chubby!" Stony almost fell out the window. Chubby looked up, saw Stony on the third floor waving his arms in desperation like a woman at the window of a burning building. Chubby swung his weapon over his head, let out a battle cry and charged into the building. Stony did a little war dance in the living room, laughing gleefully, ran into the kitchen, grabbed a wax applicator, took a few practice swings smacking the kitchen door. Cheri screamed, running from the bedroom into the bathroom, slamming the bathroom door. Stony stood in the foyer, waited until he heard the stairway door burst open, shoved the couch out of his way and stood poised at the locked door holding his pole like a bayonet.

"What the fuck?" one of them said.

When Stony heard Chubby yell in the hallway, he unlocked the door and came out swinging, his first blow hitting Mott squarely between the shoulder blades with the applicator. Mott fell on his face in the dimly lit sea green corridor. Twenty feet away Chubby dueled with the two other guys. Mott jumped up, bulled Stony backward and ran like hell down the stairs. Stony smacked his head on the wall, sank dazed to a sitting position on the red cement floor and through blurry eyes watched Chubby hold the other two at bay like Little John versus the varlets. Cheri opened the front door and peeked into the hallway. Chubby tightened his grip on the stick, eyes wide open. Suddenly he moved forward a step, stomping his foot with an echoing slap. The two guys jumped back, their bats protruding from under their arms like jousting lances. Chubby laughed.

"C'mon, yah fucking creeps, ya know how to use those things?" Chubby licked his lips, inching forward, raising the stick to his shoulder. He blocked one of the two exits. Stony sat three feet from the other exit, trying to clear his head, still feeling too dopey to stand up. "I'm gonna bash ya faces in . . . you know what that feels like? . . . hah? . . . you know what that feels like?" Chubby taunted.

Unblinking, Chubby inched forward. They inched back toward Stony and Cheri. "I once killed a guy in the service. It felt good . . . you know that? . . . hah? . . . it felt *real* good." Chubby made a weird whining noise in the back of his throat. Stony got frightened by it — a one-note high-pitched whine — because it seemed that Chubby didn't realize that he was making it. Chubby took a vicious cut, lunging at one guy's face with all his beef. The stick made a ringing slap against the wall. The guy dropped his bat, quickly stooping to pick it up. "Hey, shithead, how'd the Yankees do today?" Chubby took another swing, a murderous arc missing chins by inches. One guy screamed, the other retreated within five feet of Stony. Stony cautiously lifted the wax applicator between the guy's legs and gave him a stiff goose. He squawked, dropped his bat, turned around, leaped over Stony and ran down the stairs.

"Jus' me an' you." Chubby grinned wolfishly at the remaining flunky. "What's yah name? Hah?. What's yah name?" Chubby stomped his foot again.

The flunky whirled around, running toward Stony and the unblocked exit. Stony ducked and at the same time thrust his stick between the retreating legs. The stick spun out of his hands, as the guy fell headfirst into the door, belly-crawled/scrambled to the stairs and was gone. Chubby stood triumphant, panting in the corridor, his stick hanging loosely from a relaxed fist. He exhaled noisily. Stony struggled to his feet, using the wax applicator as a support.

Chubby laughed. "Yah lazy fuck. I hope yah dug the show."

Cheri stood gawking in the doorway, staring at Chubby. Chubby wiped the side of his face with the sleeve of his T-shirt, smiled at her.

"I'm goin' to bed now . . . when I wake up . . ." Cheri dumbly nodded her head and closed the door, locking it with a terminal click. The outside of the door looked like the hood of a car after a minor head-on — a riot of scratches, dents and craters from the bat barrage. Chubby and Stony stared at each other. Chubby nodded at the door and wordlessly urged Stony to stay with her. Stony dismissed the idea with a shrug, propping the wax applicator beside the door.

"I was pretty fuckin' good tonight, hey?" Chubby draped an arm around Stony's shoulder as they headed for the elevator.

Stony wanted to ask Chubby if he knew he was singing like a crazy man during the fight but the memory of the sound weirded him out.

"You were a fuckin' lifesaver, Chubs."

"What's the story?"

"Huh?"

"What was happenin' here?"

"Ah, nothin'." Stony gingerly touched the back of his head.

"Oh, nothin', yeah, O.K." Chubby smirked.

"Ah, I had a fight with Mott over Cheri, busted up his face a little an' he came back with those two lames."

"Hey." Chubby grinned. "Howdja like that thing I did with the foot-stompin' number, hah?"

"That guy almost jumped back in my lap," Stony snorted. The elevator opened with a groan. "Hey, Chubs, you really kill somebody in the service?"

Chubby screwed up his face with a "whatta-you-kiddin'?" expression. "Nah, I got shell-shocked though."

"Really?"

"Yeah, I ate too many peanuts." Chubby guffawed and held his gut until he started wheezing, motioning for Stony to slap him on the back as he leaned over, hands on knees, trying to catch his breath.

~

Chubby ushered Stony into a bar, Buddy Love's, replete with huge shamrocks pasted on either end of a long mirror, crossed I.R.A. and American flags and an all-Irish juke box. They sat in a dark back booth lit by a red-tinted, wax-filled squat glass sheathed in plastic fishnet.

Stony rested his forehead on the corner of the table as if he were looking for something on the floor.

Chubby sat with his arms crossed, elbows on the table. Smirking, he surveyed the bar. "Hey, Stony, you know what they call a faggot Irishman?"

Stony weakly shook his head from side to side.

"A Gay Lick," Chubby cackled.

"Hah," from under the table.

"I hate Irish bars," Chubby muttered. "I'd rather be in a fight in a nigger bar. The Irish got no sense of humor."

"Who does?"

"You know, that's the first sign a somebody goin' crazy. They lose their sense a humor."

Stony raised his head and rubbed his eyes. He looked like he was sleeping.

"I used to know this guy once, about ten years back. We used to call him Joe Sick." Chubby leaned into the aisle to catch the waitress' eye. "He was a steamfitter. This guy was a beast the likes a which I never seen since. He used to be a wrestler. We'd go to a bar and he'd open beer bottles with his teeth." Chubby pantomimed snarling as he ripped the cap off an imaginary bottle. "This fuckin' guy could piss a Dixie cup off a fire hydrant at twenny feet. He went to jail for two years for throwing his foreman through a plate-glass window. Broke his back."

Stony winced. "Was he Irish?"

"I dunno."

"What'll you be havin', boys?" The waitress stood over them. Her long, black hair hung down her back. Her eyes were crystal blue.

"Tequila," Stony mumbled.

"We don't have tequila." Her brogue was thick as stew.

"Give us two shots of Jameson's." Chubby winked. She left. "Tequila!? Where you think you are, Tijuana?"

She brought two filled shot glasses and left again.

Chubby leaned across the table and whispered to Stony, "Lemme give you some advice. Don't ever fuck around with an Irish woman."

"Temper?"

"Temper nothin'. They don't know their ass from their elbow in bed. That fuckin' church thing got 'em so uptight. They all got twenny-nine priests as brothers. When I was a kid I had an Irish girlfriend. Kathy Conroy. She useta think eating out meant not having any dishes to wash. The first time we fucked she complained of having this weird feeling all over. She went to the doctor. He told her it was an orgasm." Chubby laughed. He noticed the knuckles on Stony's right hand were scraped. He nodded at Stony. "Hey, what'd you do to that guy? He looked like he got hit in the face with a bag a nickels."

"I went berserk . . . ah dunno." Stony lowered his head to the edge of the table again. Chubby stared at him for a while before reaching over and slapping him on the shoulder.

"Ah, yer all right, kid, yer all right, you take after yer uncle. You ever hear what I did with Phyllis once? Two months after we was married I walked into the house an' she's sittin' on the couch with this guy I never seen before. I take one look at both a them and I grab this clown by the front of his shirt. I'm just about to put him through the wall and Phyllis says, 'Chubby, I'd like you to meet my brother Larry.' " Chubby downed the shot of whiskey and smacked his lips. A liquor-scented belch reached Stony's side of the table. "The cat never visited us again. You know, there ain't nothin' like jealousy to get the ol' juices flowin'.' "

"I think it sucks." Stony took a sip of whiskey and shuddered.

"Granted it ain't the most divine feelin' in the world, but let me ask you something, an' I want you to answer me straight. When you belted that guy tonight" — he finished off Stony's shot — "when you smacked that clown tonight, didn't you feel jus' a *little* good?" Chubby held up his thumb and index finger slightly apart. "Be honest."

"Nah, whatta' you kiddin'?"

"Nah, whatta' you kiddin'?" Chubby mimicked.

"Well . . ." Stony shrugged, fighting back a smile.

"Yeah, just a little, right?" Chubby eyed him slyly.

"A little." Stony smiled.

"Lemme tell you somethin' . . . when you're gettin' ready to break some joker's legs 'cause he's been fuckin' around with Mary Lou, you feel like fuckin' King Kong and John Wayne. God's on your side an' everything. You feel like a man. Am I right or am I right?"

Stony laughed. "You're sick, Chubby."

"Yeah, I'm sick." He motioned for the waitress, held up two fingers.

"Ninety-nine percent a the time a woman cheats, she does it to get her man jealous. Women love violence. Especially when it's over them." Two more shots were brought to the table. "How many times you think Cheri came tonight watching you guys duke it out?"

Stony was horrified. "You're really outta your tree, you know that?" His face was flushed. "You don't even *know* Cheri."

"Yeah, well I know that look she had on her face. There was four guys fightin' over her ass. That was prob'ly her first gang bang. An' I'll tell you something else, you're a schmuck for not hangin' around after it was all over. You prob'ly missed the greatest lay of your life."

Stony groaned and banged his head on the table.

"You got a lot to learn about women, kiddo. They're killers." Chubby lit a cigarette and chucked Stony on the chin. "You got time."

"Maybe I should go back?"

Chubby wrinkled his nose. "Too late. You gotta have timing with things like this. Chalk it up to experience."

"Experience means mistakes." Stony took a cigarette from Chubby's pack.

"So chalk it up to mistakes." Chubby reached for Stony's drink. "You know, don't get me wrong, Stones. I don't mean you gotta be like an animal all the time. Women dig tenderness too. The trick is to know when the recipe calls for garlic and when it calls for sugar. You know? You gotta use psychology. You gotta get 'em to relax, you gotta get 'em comfortable, you know? Put on some nice music, dance a little, make 'em a drink, get 'em to take a bath with you. You know, get *in*timate . . . like they don't even know they're gettin' laid, but don't make 'em *too* comfortable. Girls like to be a little scared. It's more exciting for them. You know, like I said, garlic and sugar . . . a little, a little."

Four men at the bar burst into laughter.

"Fuckin' green niggers." Chubby sneered. "I'll tell you something else, Irish *men* are the lousiest lovers. They like to cross themselves right before they come."

"Hey, Chub?"

"Italians and Jews are the only good stickmen around. All niggers know is to stick it in until they come."

"Hey, Chub?"

"Greeks aren't bad if you can get 'em out of the restaurant before they drop dead from washin' too many dishes."

"Hey, Chub?"

"Krauts like to do it to marching music an' Polacks got foreskins like pup tents."

"Hey, Chub, slow down."

"Huh?"

"Lissen, I wanna ask you somethin'. How many chicks you racked with?" Stony bit his nails and raised his eyebrows.

Chubby shrugged his shoulders, suppressing a smile. "In my whole life?"

"In your whole life."

"Oh Christ, three, or maybe four."

"C'mon, will you be serious?" Stony began bending his plastic swizzle stick at different angles.

"Whatta you drivin' at, Stones?"

Stony concentrated on the straw, inserting one end into the other. "Uh . . . like . . . every time you ball with a chick, does she come? I mean . . ."

"Nah." Chubby frowned. A bunch of middle-aged women took the booth in front of them. The waitress stood there joking and laughing with them.

"Well, what percent did?" Stony made an octagon with the swizzle stick.

"What kinda question is that?"

"About what percent?"

"Stony . . ." Chubby took the straw from him. "What's on your mind?"

The waitress stopped at their table. Chubby motioned for another round.

"Well." Stony picked up the straw. "Cheri . . ." He tossed it aside.

"She don't come?"

"Oh no, it ain't that. Yeah, she don't come, I mean she comes, but not when we're balling."

The waitress brought another round. Chubby sipped his drink thoughtfully.

"I mean I try all different ways. I go slow, I go fast, I do it from the back, from the front, from the side. Nothin' works."

"I don' know what to tell you. If it'll make you feel any better, I been married to your Aunt Phyllis for twenny-three years. I think she came three times, but I'll tell you one thing though, it don't do any good to worry about it."

"Three times?" Stony looked pained.

"Look, some women come more'n that in one fuck, others go to their *graves* without coming." He shrugged.

"Don't that drive you crazy?" Stony squinted.

"Well, look. Somebody can still dig sex without coming. That don't make 'em lesbians. But like I said, it don't help anybody to worry about it, you know, you just gotta hang loose."

"Hang loose." Stony nodded, picking his teeth with the mangled straw. "Lissen, Chub, I got Butler's car. I gotta go pick 'im up at the club. It's gettin' late."

Stony stood up. Chubby sat playing with his pack of Marlboros, slowly stripping the cellophane wrapper.

"Ah lissen, thanks for helpin' me out tonight."

Chubby gave a short salute off the top of his head.

"Hey, Stones? Also, stay away from PR women. They got two million boyfriends and brothers. They'll tear yah heart out."

~

Stony got back to D'Artagnan's about midnight. Butler was standing at the bar where Stony left him. He was talking to Chili Mac.

"Stones, you missed some fuckin' fight." Butler was drenched with sweat.

"Oh yeah?" Stony ordered a seventy-seven.

"So how's Cheri?" Butler smirked.

~

"Well, I'll tell you one thing, mah man, she can fuck Mott, Pot, Snot, Twat and half the fuckin' Marine Corps from now until doomsday, she ain't never gonna find a better stickman than me and *that's* the goddamn truth."

They sat parked in White Castle. Stony scarfed down half a hamburger and exhaled through his nose as he chewed. Butler had stopped listening to Stony's bullshit hours ago. He stabbed a straw through the center of the plastic top on his orange drink and eyed the middle-aged carhop ladies scurrying around the parking lot in royal blue slacks, blue short-sleeve tops and little blue Dixie cups on their heads. Some of them wore blue scarfs under the Dixie cups to keep their ears warm.

"My mother would dig that get-up," Butler said.

"Because not only am I a good fuck physically, Butler, but I know all that psychological shit about scoring pussy too." Stony crumpled the hamburger wrapper into a ball and rolled it lightly between his palms.

"I mean, you know, how to make them, how to get them relaxed." He dragged out his words. "You know how . . . how to get them to trust you, you know? So they don't even know they're gettin' laid."

"You know what my ol' man got my ol' lady for Christmas?" Butler challenged. "Ankle socks! A fuckin' dozen pair a *ankle* socks." He paused for the news to sink in, reaching for his cigarettes on the dash. "She *asked* for them." With his thumb he bent a match onto the carbon and flicked a light.

Stony ignored him and went on. "First I get 'em a drink, see? An' then I put on some music, you know somethin' nice, right? An' we'll dance." Stony shut his eyes and dreamily swayed his head. "I won't even grind, maybe just a little bump like . . . unh!" Eyes still closed, Stony licked his lips, arched his pelvis off the seat and rotated his hips.

Butler raised his eyebrows and making a noise like a garbage disposal sucked the last drops of orange drink from the crushed ice.

"And now they're startin' to breathe a little funny, right? So I dance just a little closer, not grindin' or anythin', just enough to brush them with my meat, you know? Give them a hors d'oeuvre."

Butler unwrapped a hamburger.

"They try to act like they don't feel it, you know? But let me tell you something, Butler, you gotta be dead not to feel my piece — "

"I don' *wanna* feel your goddamn piece." Butler started in on some french fries.

"Anyways, I only do that once, one time, then we keep dancin'. They can think about it an' then like maybe two minutes later I say to them . . . 'You wanna take a bath?' Very casual, you know? If the chick says 'sure!' you know that bitch is *mine!*" Stony tossed the crumpled wrapper on the tray hanging from the half-open car window. "Except one time I ast this girl to take a bath an' she got insulted. She thought I was sayin' she *needed* a bath."

An orange GTO with an idle like a dragon with asthma pulled in beside them on Stony's side. Butler squeezed Stony's knee. Two girls were in the front seat. Nice blondes with hard eyes and thin lips.

"Hey!" Butler smiled, leaning across Stony's lap. "What's happenin'?"

The driver and her friend stared straight ahead.

"You wanna take a bath?" He laughed, looking at Stony. Stony elbowed him back to his side of the car. The driver turned away and said something to her friend. Stony leaned out the window, winked at the driver and drummed his fingers against the car door.

"Hey" — his smile was right out of a Crisco can — "your name Carol? You look like a girl Carol I know. Your friend's name Carol?" No answer. He shrugged.

Butler bolted over Stony again and hung out the window. "How 'bout a shower?" Stony cracked up, seeing it was a lost cause.

The girl on the passenger side lit a cigarette. In the brief light of her match Stony could see that her skin was ice white smooth and she plucked her eyebrows. His gut wrenched.

"Maybe you just wanna wash up a little?" Butler continued. Stony didn't laugh. He wanted the bitch with the plucked eyebrows.

Butler tried to say something, but Stony held him back.

"What's your friend's name?" Stony asked in a calm but intense tone that made the driver at least look at if not answer him.

"The girl name is Gelia . . ."

Both Stony and Butler spun half-around at the sound of the deep Jamaican voice. Slowly the rear-seat window rolled down with an electric hum. The impassive black face was almost invisible behind steel-rim shades and a salt and pepper goatee.

". . . an' she go for thirty bills."

~

"You work outta this place mainly?" Stony tried to sound cool as he took off his shirt. Gelia didn't answer. They were in a clean but boring motel off the highway on the Bronx side of the Mount Vernon border.

Gelia pulled off her green turtleneck. A plump pale tit fell out of her peach-colored bra. She hadn't looked at Stony once since the deal. Stony eyed the curve of her belly. She didn't bother to put her tit back. Stony sucked in his gut and casually tensed his biceps. She could have cared less. She slipped off her tartan plaid skirt but left on her brown leather knee-high boots. Stony sat down on a wooden rocking chair to pull off his shoes. He stared intensely at the opaque outline of her pubic hair through the lacy mesh of her white panties. When she turned around to pull down the bedspread, he imagined fucking her in the ass. The skin of her back was milky, and he followed the line of her spine up to the nape of her neck. Her yellow hair fell on either side of her neck. He could see the darker roots fan out from her part. With her back still to him she bent down and slipped off her panties. Stony stared at the scalloped curve of her ass for a minute. He was afraid he was going to come too fast so he got up and locked himself in the john. He tore off the blue and white sanitary seal on the toilet seat, took out his throbbing hard-on, straddled the bowl and started jerking off. When he came, his first feeling was of crushing loneliness and wishing that Butler was out there instead of the bitch. He imagined getting shit-faced with Butler, then cruising in Butler's car and scoring some pussy. Then he realized that's exactly what they did. He opened the bathroom door a crack and watched her standing naked except for the boots. Her bush was brown, soft and flattened against her slightly arching belly. Her nipples were smooth and untaut. Her eyes were narrow snaky green, devoid of emotion. Her nose was long, thin and freckled. He started getting another hard-on. Absently he pulled on his dick before returning to the bedroom.

"A blow job's ten extra but I don't feel like it tonight anyhow. I don't do ass fucking. I gotta fuck on my side cause I got a bad back and if you shit in bed or do anything funny I'll cripple you for life."

This was the first time she'd said anything to Stony. He sat on the bed and tried to say something amusing. "You tongue-kiss?"

Ignoring him she walked around to the opposite side of the bed and lay down on her side facing the wall. She left the boots on. Stony stared at her spine, noticing little bumps all the way up.

He lay on his side in the same position, his nose touching the back of her neck, his prick flat against her buttocks. He could sense that her eyes were open. The overhead light was still on. She lifted her left leg so that he could slip it in. Stony lowered himself a little so his lips were kissing her shoulder blades and taking his prick in his hand he tried to get inside. He couldn't do it. Death Valley. When he pushed harder she winced in annoyance. He froze, afraid she was going to do something like she threatened. He stared at the overhead light for a second, absently kissed her back.

He wanted to lightly run his palm along the hills and curves of her side, but he was afraid. Her leg was still up in the air. Thinking that she might be getting impatient he tried once more to get in. No dice. He spit in his hand and rubbed the saliva over the mushroom tip of his dick. That made it easier. A little. A little, a little more, soon he was all the way in but still was afraid of stroking her belly or touching her tits. He held his breath as he fucked. He liked rubbing his crotch against her buttocks every time he went in deep. Raising himself slightly on his elbow he could see her profile. She was absently chewing on her thumbnail and spacily staring at the red on red fake brocade wallpaper.

"How you doin'?" Stony ventured as he kept it moving around. Leaning slightly forward, not enough for him to fall out, she clicked on the plastic ivory-colored radio on the night table. Frankie Crocker's low-key riff filled the room. He stopped moving inside her, his guts felt like spilling water.

"You come?" she asked. Stony started moving again, though he was losing his hard-on.

"Almost." He stared at her back, her shoulder, the wallpaper. Frankie Crocker chuckled. He started feeling angry, and he fucked harder and faster, but she didn't move.

> Tell me somethin' go-o-od
> Tell me that you love me . . .

She laid her arm against her side and patted her thigh in rhythm with the song.

~

When Stony came downstairs to the lobby he found Butler sprawled out on a narrow sky blue couch with metal rods for legs. One arm lay across his eyes, a foot rested on the linoleum floor. Above him on the wood-paneled walls hung a Woolworth's painting of a kid fishing near a barn. When Stony got closer to the painting he realized the wood paneling was contact paper. Stony lightly kicked Butler's foot. Butler raised his head, eyes dazed, arm still shielding his face. "Hey! How'd it go?"

"Fantastic," Stony monotoned. "Let's go."

"You wanna go home?" Butler leaned over the rear of the front seat as he backed out the driveway.

"Let's have a drink. How'd it go for you?"

"Ah, for shit. That black bastard said thirty bucks, right? Well, I get undressed. I'm layin' on the bed nude, right? She takes her clothes off, sits between my legs and whips out a bag. Awright, I prefer bareback, but it's for my protection too, you know?

Anyways, so there I am with this ski glove on my cock and she starts jerkin' me off. I'm gettin' nice and hard and I figure she'll jump on when it gets to her likin', but all of a sudden I'm feelin' like if she keeps it up I'm gonna come so I says, 'You better hop on now before you miss the show,' and she says, 'For thirty bucks all you get is a hand job, if you wanna get laid it's an extra twenty.'" Butler punched Stony on the arm. "Mother*fucker!* So I said, 'I don't *have* an extra twenty,' and she says, 'How about your friend? Can you get it from him?' I said, 'Ahh, just finish what you're doin',' an' I came." Butler shrugged. "It was all right."

"Dunsky," Stony laughed.

Butler pulled into a roadside bar with a bright orange "Topless Dancers" sign in the window.

"Butler, please." Stony gestured at the sign. "I just ate."

Butler backed out to the highway. "That didn't happen to you, hah?"

"Are you kiddin'? She was makin' so much noise we had to turn on the radio so the cops wouldn't come in."

Butler shifted into forward.

"I swear I was gonna ask *her* for thirty bills."

"You know, Stony, if I didn't think you was lyin' through your teeth I'd be jealous."

"I ain't lyin'." Stony shoved his fingers under Butler's nose. Butler sniffed without removing his gaze from the road.

"Smells like hamburger to me." He pulled into Roland's, a nice, quiet, empty bar. "C'mon, I'll treat you to a Dunsky's Delight."

An hour later, Butler almost carried Stony back to the car. "Butler, this tequila is makin' me sick. I can't explain to you about Cheri. I would come in her mouth, and she would make one little motion, wiping her lips with her pinky, and I would get a hard-on all over again right then and there, and later I would fall asleep and wake up thinkin' all my crotch hair was burned, and I would feel the crispy burnt stubble and fall back on the pillow sweatin' like I was gonna die, and you don't understand. I *want* to feel this . . . this shit I'm goin' through now. Like all my skin is peeled and any way I turn it hurts. Don't you understand, you stupid prick, you motherfuckin' bastard with your goddamn thirty-dollar hand job. Cheri, you cunt of a lifetime, I love her, I can't breathe. Butler, you bastard; you stupid . . . let's go home. I saw her put her goddamn lips on that pig's *mouth.* Butler, do you love your prick? You should. I love my prick. It's like nobody else's. I don't understand how she could touch anybody else's when she got mine. Butler, open the goddamn windows, go faster. I need air. My dick is like my left hand. It got grace. Butler, open the goddamn window *more.* My hand can dance. Butler, you pinhead, I'm never alone. My hand is a goddamn ballerina. I'm never alone. When I was a kid I would lay in bed and my hand would dance for me in the dark. Butler, what's she doin' now? I want Chubby. Butler, be Chubby. Do you know how scared Albert is all the time? Do you know Mott, that motherless bastard, must got a prick like a dead twig? All fat guys except Chubby got small dicks. That's the law. Can you imagine what it must stink like when he takes a dump? She's a fuckin' hoowah, Butler. I wake up and my crotch is burnin'. I can smell the burnt hair an' she's sleepin' like nothin' happened. Butler, where we goin'? I don't wanna go home. There's nothin' there." Stony slid down in his seat, his cheek resting on the window.

"Stony, I just got one question." Butler removed a fleck of tobacco from his tongue. "If I came runnin' into your room at the motel there tonight an' told you I needed another twenny to get laid, would you've given it to me? Hah?"

Stony slept.

4

"YOU WANT SOME COFFEE, Tommy?" Phyllis stood before her husband and brother-in-law, almost kowtowing in her pale green housedress.

"No thanks, dear." Tommy dangled one leg over the arm of the Barcalounger.

"Chubby?"

"No thank you, sweetheart." Chubby sat on the edge of the couch, elbows on knees, biting his nails.

Phyllis smiled nervously. "I'm going to bed now."

"I'll be in later, sweets." He turned to Tommy. "Hey, Stony tell you what happened last night?"

"Yeah, I heard, yah beast!" Tommy smiled.

Chubby got up. "You want some coffee, Tom?"

"Just a little."

Chubby fussed around in the kitchen and came out with two cups and a pastry box of cannoli. They sat in the dinette and dug in.

"You hear anything about the union?" Chubby picked out a cannoli.

"What about the union?" Tommy turned the box toward him and picked out the biggest one.

"You know, about Stony."

"Any time he wants, he's in." Tommy wiped his mouth with a napkin. "The fuckin' kid's breakin' my chops though. He keeps stallin', yes, no, yes, no."

"Give 'im slack, he's goin' through a rough time."

"Rough time, my ass. That kid's got it made. He ain't workin', he ain't goin' a school. He hangs aroun' gettin' laid an' jerkin' his bird. He's gotta start pullin' his own weight or I'm gonna kick him out on the street."

Chubby snorted. "Right, I can see you doin' that. Who you think you talkin' to, Indians?" Chubby picked up another cannoli. "You don't let that kid go to the john with less'en twenny bucks in his pocket."

"Well, that's all gonna stop right away."

"Uh-huh, hey, I gave Stones some pointers last night on how to handle women. The kid's awright, but sometimes I think he walks around wit' his head up his ass. Din't you ever tell 'im the facts a life?" Chubby licked some cream off his fingers.

"Hell, no! Let 'im learn it the way I did . . . in the gutter." Tommy laughed. "Nah, really, what am I supposed to tell 'im? How to stick it in?"

"Nah, you know . . . just . . . he don't know how to handle things. I don't think he got any problem knowin' *how* to stick it in, he just don't know *when* to stick it in. An' I also think he don't know when to pull it out. That Cheri girl got him doin' a hurtin' dance."

"Hey, you know what Pop said to me when I was twelve? Here's the facts a life for you. I ask him how you do it, you know? He says to me, 'Don't worry, when the time comes, you'll know, animals can do it, you can do it.' " Tommy slurped his coffee.

"You're lucky. When *I* ast him, he answered wit' the back of his hand."

"He was a motherfucker, wasn't he?"

"Yeah, Pop was somethin' else again."

"He really smacked you, hah?"

"You should remember, Tom, that's when I was gonna leave home."

"Oh yeah! That's when I came at you wit' . . . ."

"Yeah, remember? You was ten. I was packin' my knapsack an' I told you I was runnin' away. You left the room an' come back wit' a friggin' butcher knife. You says to me, 'If you ever do anything to break Mom's heart, I'll kill you.' "

"Holy shit! I remember that! Yeah! I was a cunt hair away from runnin' you through."

"I saw it in your face. You were one fuckin' sick puppy that day."

"You know, it's funny. I didn't get scared standin' there with that knife, until I saw *you* was scared. You started unpackin' right away, remember?"

"Do I remember! I didn't leave the fuckin' bedroom for a week, you sick fuck!"

"Pop was a fuckin' bastard with us though. Hey, you remember that whistle a his? Any time I was playin' in the street an' I heard that whistle, my heart would jump into my mouth. No matter what I was doin' I would stop everything and run upstairs, an' half the time he was callin' me to whip my ass for somethin' or other. Din't make no difference cause I knew if he had to whistle again I would just get beat worse. Till the day I die I won't ever forget that whistle." Tommy put his thumb and middle finger on his tongue and let loose with three shrill blasts — the first two short, followed by a long, higher-pitched third.

Chubby winced at the memory. "You know, Tom, about six years ago I heard a guy on a job give Pop's whistle. I almost shit on myself."

"We were like trained dogs. One time I was fingerin' Sally Rudnick in the hallway. Pop whistles, I almost ripped out her box."

"Yeah, but he had his moments though. I mean, he wasn't the greatest, but he did what he had to. We never starved, he always had a roof over our heads an' we always had a little coin in our pockets. He useta say alla time a man's only worth what he got in his wallet. An' he shoulda known too. I remember one year in the thirties he was holdin' down three jobs. He would come home at five from the construction site, eat dinner an' go down to the *Times* plant on Forty-sixth Street and load papers on the trucks until midnight an' on the weekends he was the bouncer at Gianelli's. You remember Gianelli's?"

"Pop was a bouncer?"

"Yeah. You was really little at that time. He did it for about six months until one Saturday night when he eighty-sixed some punk. The guy came back with some friends after closing an' they bushwhacked him outside the club, broke his fuckin' arm. Old man Gianelli fired him on the spot. What good's a bouncer with a busted arm? An' they din't have compensation in those days either."

"I never knew that."

"It's the truth. An' it took six months for that arm to heal because he wouldn't take time out to rest. He was probably the only guy doin' construction an' loadin' trucks in New York City with his arm in a sling."

"Hard-nose bastard."

"Give 'im his due, Tom."

5

MONDAY MORNING Marie and Phyllis did their weekly shopping together. After unpacking the groceries, Phyllis walked to Marie's to shoot the shit.

Marie foraged in the refrigerator for the Half & Half. "I went to Schindler Friday."

"For Albert?" Phyllis sat at the kitchen table, two cups of steaming black coffee and a box of marble cake in front of her.

"For me." Marie shut the refrigerator door and sat down, putting a quart of milk on the table.

"For what?" Phyllis lightened her coffee with the milk.

Marie shrugged. "I still got those cramps."

"I thought they went away." Phyllis picked at the cake.

"They did. They came back. And I started bleedin' a little too." Marie extracted a cigarette from her red plastic case. "Schindler said it's from aggravation."

"Aggravation?" Phyllis repeated incredulously. "He's a goddamn horse doctor. How come you don't use Schwartz?"

Marie shrugged.

"What Schwartz forgot is more than Schindler'll ever know."

"I dunno. He gave me some tranquilizers."

"He's a quack," Phyllis said contemptuously.

"At least he's better'n Marcus. Remember Marcus?"

"Marcus, even if Marcus *was* a horse doctor, he'd still be a quack."

"Remember when I was in Parkchester with Albert?"

"Oh, with the tubes?"

"The tubes?"

"Yeah. The thing with the tubes, you remember."

"Oh that. I almost forgot that. God, *that* was something, but I wasn't thinkin' about the thing with the tubes, I was thinkin' about the thing with the blood," Marie said.

"What thing with the blood?"

"You know, with the needle?"

"I don't remember."

"Maybe I never told you . . . when Marcus took blood?"

"No."

"Remember, I was in Parkchester two days before I had Albert? The night before I had him Marcus had to take blood from me. One of the big needles that they take from here." She tapped the inside of her elbow. Phyllis made a face. "You know I'm not squeamish or anything. When Stony opened his head on the wall that time I was the only one that could stand there with the ice cubes," Marie said.

"I remember Tommy fainted." Phyllis raised her eyebrows.

"Yeah, big tough guy. Anyways, so you know, I'm not afraid of a little blood. But what Marcus did . . . I was sittin' in a wheelchair. They had me in a white smock, and you know how Marcus always had the shakes?"

"Yeah, well, he was shootin' up all the time," Phyllis said offhandedly. "That was the only thing that kept him going. I saw him do it once in the bathroom. He came over one time when Chubby had the flu. He walks in the house and goes straight to the bathroom and shoots up. It was probably speed," Phyllis added knowledgeably, "that's the only way that old bastard could keep goin'. He wouldn't take on a younger doctor to help him. I saw him shoot up and I said forget it, that's it. I don't need a junkie doctor for me an' my own. You remember I called you that day? You didn't believe me."

"If I called *you* then, would you believe me?" Marie shrugged. "Whatever . . . anyways . . . I'm sittin' on a chair in my room. It's night; Tommy just left, and I was reading a *Life* magazine." She flicked the ash of her cigarette. "This nurse comes in with a wheelchair and wheels me down to this lab or something and there's Marcus waiting for me with this big needle to take blood and I see he's into his "Shimmy Like Kate" number. The nurse gets me up on this table, ties one of those rubber things around my arm and Marcus goes in with the needle. I was scared because he was shakin' like he just got religion. But it don't hurt much, it's over real quick and he starts injecting the blood into this test tube. The nurse starts takin' the rubber tube off my arm and she must've bumped a tray or something off the table but all of a sudden there's this crash. Marcus . . . Marcus jumps twenty feet in the air and spills all the blood in the test tube all over me, all over my white smock, and I look down and I'm drenched with my own blood."

"Oh my God!" Phyllis covered her mouth. "What you do?"

"I fainted. I woke up. I was in bed with a clean gown on. For a while I thought the whole thing was a dream, until I saw the look on Marcus' face the next morning."

"Disgusting." Phyllis shook her head.

"I should've known then that Albert was gonna be heartache. It was a bad omen."

"Oh stop, Marie."

"Everybody has a cross to bear in this life, Phyllis, and Albert's mine."

"Marie, don't talk like that." Phyllis flinched. "He's such a sweet baby. All he wants to do is please you."

"Ten years between babies . . . why'd I do that?"

"You tell me."

"Thirty-seven's too old . . . with the diapers, the screaming, the sickness all over again. I used to wake up with him crying and whining and I would have this fantasy . . . this thing . . . I would imagine getting up, putting on my coat, taking the Christmas Club money, one suitcase, and grabbing the first bus out of Port Authority to wherever it's going. One time I actually got down there, suitcase and everything. I remember that night. Albert started crying about two in the morning. Sometimes I would just lay there forever until he stopped crying. That night I lay there an hour. He wouldn't stop. Finally, I just got up, put on that green dress I had, threw some underwear and jewelry in a suitcase and walked out of the house. I had about seventy-five dollars on me. I took a cab down to Port Authority and I got in line where they got that big map of the country with all the cities lit up. When I got up to the counter the man said, 'Where to?' I looked up at the map and said, 'Buffalo'; then he said, 'Round trip?' and I felt like I didn't understand him and he said, 'Round trip?' again. I just said, 'What?' Then he got pissed and looked at me like I was a Puerto Rican or something. I got so embarrassed I ran away from the counter. I remember sitting down in the waiting room and crying for about half an hour. Some nice fella came over with a cup of coffee from a coffee machine and sat down next to me. A very good-looking tall guy. He gave me the coffee and offered me his handkerchief. He said he was meeting his wife in half an hour. She was coming in on a bus from New Jersey. She was a singer in a club there, but they lived in the city and he was trying to get a better job so she wouldn't have to keep up this schedule and she could sing at only the clubs she wanted to. He asked me if I was coming or going. I said I wish I knew. Anyways, we talked and talked and talked and I felt terrific, like I totally forgot everything and then his wife came over. She was very beautiful with dyed red hair and this guy introduced us. At first I think she was sizing up the situation but then she saw I had been crying. Anyways, the three of us went into a place for coffee and we talked for a long time. Her name was Francine Etter but she sang under the name Marlena King. She did that hoping that some people would confuse her with Morgana King. His name was Larry Etter. He worked in the post office as a foreman but he was going to night school at Bronx Community College to be a mechanical drafts-man. I never seen two people so much in love in my life. I got all sorts of excited and I told them about that time I was on Ted Mack's radio show with my girlfriends Maureen and Felice and we sang 'Boogie Woogie Bugle Boy' and 'Hold Tight' and the program director told us we sounded just like the Andrews Sisters even though we didn't win and the next day when we went back to James Monroe we were celebrities and all the kids heard us the night before on the radio and our pictures were on the front page of the school paper." Marie stared past Phyllis. "Anyways, we exchanged phone numbers and promised to get together over the

holidays and I was talkin' about everybody going up to the
Neville Country Club in Ellenville for Memorial Day . . . real
crazy things like that. And they both kissed me goodby and I felt
like they were my best friends in the world. But the minute they
left I started thinkin' about the baby, about Tommy, about the
apartment and I got this feeling like I couldn't breathe. I wound
up cryin' again and I took the subway up to my mother's place on
the Concourse. It was six-thirty and the sun was just comin' up
and everything looked really quiet and peaceful and I remember
wishin' that the Bronx could always be like that. I go up to my
mother's place and I didn't want to wake her so I just lay down on
the couch in the living room and next thing I know somebody's
shakin' my shoulder. My mother's standing over me yellin' in
Italian. I see it's ten o'clock. I got in a panic and I jump up, run
downstairs and grab a cab back to the house. I run into the
bedroom and there's this godawful stink and I see there's shit all
over everything. Stony was standing over the crib trying to
change Albert's diaper. He was ten years old, can you imagine
that? He even fed Albert a bottle. He couldn't figure out how to
heat the formula so he filled the bottle with cream soda. I tell you,
I could've had ten kids like him."

Phyllis looked at Marie incredulously. "Marie, you're outta
your mind. How come you never told anybody about that night?"

"What was I supposed to say? I ran away from home like a
kid? It's over . . . it's ancient history."

"Did you ever get in touch with those people?"

"What people?"

"The singer and . . ."

"Oh . . . oh . . . nah."

~

"Heya, Chub."

Stony opened the apartment door to make way for his uncle.

"Hey, Stones." Chubby faked a grab for Stony's nuts and
walked in through the ivy-vine-wallpapered foyer and headed for
the kitchen.

"Where's your dad?"

"He got the lobster shift."

"What! It's Monday. Thought Carmines got it on Monday."

"Carmines's sick."

"Ah shit."

Stony walked into the kitchen. The top half of Chubby's body was obscured by the open refrigerator door.

"You were gonna do somethin'?"

Chubby stood up holding three hard-boiled eggs. "Nah, just go to Banion's or somethin' . . . what're you doin'?"

Stony shrugged. "Hangin' around."

Chubby regarded him for a minute. "You wanna get shit-faced witcher uncle?"

"Sure." Stony smiled.

~

"Whassamatta?" Chubby asked. Stony was playing with the swizzle stick in his Scotch, staring at the table and not drinking.

Stony shrugged. He wouldn't look at his uncle. "That's good fuckin' Scotch, Stones, you don't want it . . ." Chubby reached for the glass. Stony grabbed it and downed the shot in one gulp.

"Woo!" Stony smiled in spite of himself, but he still wouldn't look up. Somebody played the juke box:

> two faced woman an' a jealous may-on,
> thas how awl the trouble in th' worl' be-gay-on.

Stony snickered. He had taken the shot a little too fast.

"You like that nigger shit?"

"What?" Stony finally looked up. Chubby nodded toward the juke box without taking his eyes from Stony's face.

"What's that? James Brown, right?"

Stony shrugged again, still smiling, looking down now.

"Yeah, I ain't that old." Chubby grinned.

"I didn't say nothin'," Stony mumbled.

"I seen that guy once on Ed Sullivan. If I could make all that bread screamin' like a momo faggot pimp I'd quit work tomorrow."

Stony imagined Chubby on TV dancing like James Brown. He chuckled.

"That's funny, hah?" Chubby downed his Scotch, then nodded to Banion for two more. Banion zoomed down in his wheelchair.

"Mikey." Chubby grabbed Banion's hand. "You know who this is?" He nodded at Stony, who studied his reflection in a small puddle of liquor on the bar. "Guess who's kid this is."

"Tommy's?"

Chubby cackled. Banion squinted at Stony, who wouldn't look at him. "You goin' in?" he asked Stony.

"Hah?"

"You goin' in? The 'lectricians."

"I dunno." Stony turned to him. He focused on the network of red veins in Banion's nose.

"You got a good uncle," Banion said, still squinting, his mouth slightly open, "and a good father." He pushed a button and the wheelchair glided backward, away from Stony.

"I'll tell you about nigger music." Chubby sipped his drink. "It died wit' Nat King Cole." He paused, waiting for that fact to sink in. Stony gulped half his Scotch during that comment. "I used to say Johnny Mathis, then I read he was queer. Stony, what the fuck is goin' on wit' you?"

Stony was startled. "Nothin'," he answered in a cracked voice.

"Stony, don't bullshit a bullshitter, it's Cheri, right?" Chubby grabbed Stony's wrist. "She got you doin' a hurtin' dance. I know the fuckin' signs, baby. The first sign is you don't talk to your fuckin' favorite uncle when he takes you out for a good time."

Stony shrugged and halfheartedly tried to remove his hand from his uncle's beefy grip.

"It's Cheri, hah?" Chubby squeezed.

Stony rubbed his other hand across his eyes. "Chub, you don't know."

"Stony, I remember when you was born. I remember the shit smell of your diapers if you wanna be honest. Baby, I remember stuff about you that you ain't gonna wanna know for a million years."

"Like what?" Stony freed his hand. He felt a little looser.

"Like you don't wanna know." Chubby finished his drink. "Take my word for it."

"Like what?" Stony persisted.

"Like that time when you first got a piece?" Chubby laughed.

Stony remembered that night when he was fourteen and drunk doing somersaults in the living room and accidentally kicking in the screen of the three-week-old color TV. Tommy went to belt his ass but Chubby got his old man in a bear hug until he cooled down. Chubby had poured them all a victory Scotch. For a second Stony was flooded with a feeling of love for his uncle. He flushed and felt a corny lump in his throat.

"You remember that, hah?" Chubby lightly punched him on the biceps. "So don't tell me I don't know."

"Every time . . . every time I think about her, Chub, I get so sick. I love her so bad. She puts out like her cunt was spare change, and it hurts me, like I wanna break somethin', you know? She used to be so . . . so innocent." Stony's face was twisted with grief. He searched his uncle's eyes for some kind of answer.

"I get this . . . itch . . . this hunger in my head when I'm around her like I got poison ivy inside me and I can't scratch it. I feel really clutchy, like I can't have her out of my sight . . . out of my *arms* almost. I keep driven' her crazy. Sometimes it feels like anything I say comes down to 'Do you love me?' in some way or another. An' when we're screwing an' I feel like that I feel like I weigh six hundred pounds on top a her. I don't know what I *want* from her. It makes me so crazy sometimes. When I'm home alone I feel so lost in space I gotta put on some record that's real familiar to me, some Sly, some James Brown, an' I gotta sit down an' lissen to the music an' let it hook me back to Earth . . . like I'm stoned or something. I can't swing it no more. Somethin's gotta give."

Chubby stared at the ice cubes in his drink. He wasn't laughing. He looked Stony in the eye. "Stones, you're seventeen now . . . in my book that makes you a man. You're still a kid in a lotta ways but in the heart you're a man."

Stony frowned at Chubby.

Chubby chewed on his thumb and stared beyond his nephew.

"O.K. I'm gonna tell you somethin', Stones. I'm gonna tell you a
story that only me an' your old man know about."

Stony felt better for telling his uncle about his grief.

"I wanna tell you about Sooky."

"Who?"

"Lissen, lemme ask you something. Whatta you think a your
Aunt Phyllis?"

"Whada you mean?"

"You know." Chubby shrugged, pouting. "You know." He
curved out a female form on the bar. "Whada you think?"

Stony was embarrassed. "I dunno."

"Yeah, bullshit you don't know. She got a nice ass, hah?"
Chubby smiled.

"I dunno." Stony blushed. He didn't think so.

"I dunno," Chubby mimicked in a moronic bass. He downed
his Scotch and the rest of Stony's. "I seen you lookin'." Chubby
made a jerk-off motion. Stony started to protest. "Screw that."
Chubby waved his hand. "Sooky . . . Sooky made Phyllis look
like a *rag*." Chubby nodded his head. "Twenty-fuckin'-eight
years ago." Banion brought another round. "Met her in Surinam
in the war. I was fuckin' twenty years old." He looked astonished
at the thought. "God, I was a *sleek* stud!" Chubby banged the
bar, then screwed his face in disgust. He grabbed Stony's hand.
"I made you look like a goddamn pissant *faggot* then!" Stony was
too scared to be insulted.

"She was Java*neese*, Stony, you know what that means?"

"A Jap?"

"No, lissen, Ja-va-nese."

"I dunno."

"A *Dutch Chink!*" Then to himself in a slow whisper, "Naked."

Stony conjured up an Oriental face bordered with flaxen bangs.

"Naked." Chubby clenched his teeth and closed his eyes.
"Ooh, baby, that fuckin' smoky bitch. God, she had nipples,
Stony, those were friggin' *jungle* titties." He threw down the rest
of his drink.

Stony flashed on green shimmering jungle. The flax turned wet
black in his mind.

"I just *took* the bitch!" Chubby whispered, "Soft . . . Sooky." Banion brought another round of drinks. Chubby gulped his. "Fuckin' . . . cunt . . ." He was weaving on the barstool. Stony got scared. He didn't know whether to steady his uncle. He raised his arm to catch him if need be. Stony had the vague fear of being punched.

"Blackest . . . sweetest," Chubby trailed off.

"She was black?" Stony asked amazed.

Chubby opened his eyes. "She was *gold* . . . *took* the bitch! First time." His head started bobbing. "She had a cunt like a wet black rose . . . loved her so bad."

Banion caught Stony's eye and winked. Stony didn't know what the wink meant.

"Cat face . . . cat . . ." Suddenly he stopped and straightened up. "She never fuckin' said nothin', ever. Big slanty eyes, but she would never never say nothin'. I would ram her right up . . ." He cut himself off and motioned for another Scotch. "Phyllis don' mean shit."

Chubby stared at the bar top tight-faced. He looked at Stony and for an instant Stony knew exactly how his uncle would look in his coffin. "You only get one shot, Stones. Don't fuck it up."

Stony got up from the bar. "I gotta go home, Chubby."

Chubby rested his head on his folded arms. Stony walked out. After a while Chubby struggled to his feet and staggered to the john, supporting himself on the shoulders of the men sitting along the bar. The last shoulder he grabbed was Sylvia's. Startled, she spun around, saw Chubby and quickly turned back to her drink. Chubby stood weaving for a second before going into the bathroom. He slouched over the urinal, his forehead pressed against the cool wall, his body gently rocking back and forth, his dick in his hand.

6

SATURDAY, 5:30 A.M., Stony moved under the covers like a shifting mountain range. Only his hair was exposed like a small black shrub. Albert had been up a half-hour, teeth brushed, hair combed, shoes tied. He sat on the edge of his bed watching Stony's sleeping shape. Every time Stony's snoring pattern changed or he rolled over or he scratched himself, Albert jumped up, and when Stony settled into sleep again, Albert plopped down on his bed in anguish. Between five-thirty and six-thirty he changed his shirt five times. At a quarter to seven he brushed his teeth again. At seven the sound of cartoons and the shifting silver reflections of the TV screen had Stony sitting up in bed dazed blind and fuckfaced.

Albert sat cross-legged on the rug in front of the TV. He turned when he heard Stony struggling. "Is it too loud, Stony?" Stony grunted and coughed. His eyelids were sealed with crud. "You want some coffee, Stony?" Stony coughed again, a noise like some prehistoric bird in a Japanese monster movie. He groped under his pillow for his Marlboros. Albert's stomach twisted when Stony lit up but he was afraid to bug his brother this particular morning so he didn't say anything.

"Wha' the fuck time 'zit?" Stony mumbled.

"It's about eight o'clock, Stony. We gotta go soon." He moved toward the kitchen.

"Wait wait wait." Stony waved him back with a clumsy motion. Grabbing his clock he held it in front of his face. "Aw jeez fuckin' Christ, Albert, it's fuckin' seven a clock." He ditched the cigarette, fell back on the bed. Albert started twisting his fingers anxiously. He felt a lick of panic under his skin.

"Stony? Stony, we gonna be late, we gotta go soon."

Stony exhaled heavily through his nose, rubbed his hands over his closed eyes but made no motion to sit up again. "Hey, Albert, the fuckin' movie don't start till noon, O.K.? That's five fuckin' hours. Gimme a break, O.K.?"

"But they could get sold out." Albert fidgeted and squirmed in his insistence.

"Hey, the goddamn box office don' open until eleven-thirty, O.K.? Look, lemme sleep till nine o'clock. Nine o'clock, and we'll go right down there an' buy tickets, O.K.?"

It wasn't O.K., but before Albert could respond Stony was snoring away. Albert went into the dinette and opened the Friday New York *Post* to the movie section for the sixteenth time since Stony told him last night he'd take him to a movie today, and studied the red-tinted ad for any minute detail he might have missed. Across the top of the ad in letters of broken bamboo read THUNDER PUNCH — KUNG FU THRUST OF DEATH! Under that was a gigantic bloodstained fist smashing through what looked like the paper the ad was printed on. Over the fist was the face of its owner. A long-haired head-banded Chink with eyes clenched shut in rage and a mouth frozen open in the middle of a kill-shriek. On each side of the fist were two more Chinks locked in mortal kung fu combat. At the bottom of the ad, two eyeballs lay in a pool of blood staring up at the fist. Albert knew every drop of blood by heart.

Stony got up at nine like he promised. At eight fifty-five Albert was standing in the doorway like a servant with a cup of coffee.

At nine-thirty they were standing in the foyer. Stony was checking his dough. They heard Marie getting up. Stony stared at his parents' door, feeling an angry tightness in his gut. When he looked for Albert, Albert was gone.

While they were waiting for the train, Albert unselfconsciously slipped his hand into his brother's. Normally Stony would consider this a stone faggot action, but Albert was his little brother. Besides, he liked the feel of Albert's hand — it was always warm and dry. He also liked to smell Albert's head for some crazy reason. Whenever they were wrestling or fucking around he would always try to stick his nose as close to Albert's head as possible, even if it meant getting Albert's hair up his nostrils — Albert's head always smelled like baby powder. Stony guessed he loved his brother, stone faggot action or no.

The subway exit let out in the middle of a dozen sleazy movie theaters. Albert was bug-eyed with excitement. He had never been in Times Square without his parents. Stony was blown out by all the lowlife. Dudes in dresses, young dirty stud hustlers jiggling their balls in their pockets and staring down old guys in front of movies, tall skinny black guys in imitation pimp lime greens and emergency yellows, alkies, junkies, lonelies. It was ten o'clock on a Saturday morning and the place was jumping.

"Holy shit!" Stony stood there gawking. He hadn't been down here in years.

Albert laughed and clapped his hands. "Look at the movies!"

"Who needs movies? I never saw so many fuckin' creeps in my life." Stony stared in fascination at the thirteen-year-old Puerto Rican kid standing in front of an Orange Julius. He had long greasy black hair tied flat with a red bandanna. He had a dark slit-featured face and was dressed in dungarees and a dungaree jacket. Suddenly Stony realized that the dude was staring back at him. Stony made a vague "not-me" motion with his head and grabbed for Albert's hand. The kid snickered. Flustered, Stony quickly disengaged Albert's hand. "He's my fuckin' brother!" Stony grabbed Albert's hand again and beat it around the corner.

They got to the movie an hour before the box office opened. Albert wanted to stand in line but Stony pulled him away. "C'mon, I'll take you to the automat."

Inside, Stony gave Albert a fistful of silver and told him to get anything he wanted. Fifteen minutes later Albert came back carrying a tray with orange soda, a corn muffin and a hot dog resting in an oval bed of baked beans. Stony had coffee and a prune Danish. "You ever come here before?" he asked.

"Once with Mommy when I was six. I threw up." He drank the orange soda.

"What were you doing here with Mommy?"

"She was gonna be a secretary and had to see a man and she didn't have a baby sitter."

"What she do when you threw up?"

"I got punished." Albert took the hot dog off the baked beans and broke off pieces to pop in his mouth.

"She don't fuckin' let up on you, does she?"

"What?"

"Nothin'. Eat up, I wanna play some pinball."

Albert left the beans and the corn muffin untouched. They went to a pinball arcade next to the movie house and walked down the lanes of machines amid a din of exploding torpedoes, screeching tires, ringing bells, whooping sirens and monotone groans from a robot cowboy.

"I wanna play this!" Albert stopped in front of a pinball machine with the legend HOOTENANNY — all the characters from "Hee-Haw" were painted on the scoreboard. Albert didn't do so hot. He kept flipping the flippers too late and was losing all his balls.

"Hold it, hold it. I got an idea." Stony slipped another dime in the machine. "You take that flipper and I'll take this one." He manned the left side of the machine and Albert took charge of the right flipper plus springing the balls into play. They played six games, each final score higher than the last. "We're regular fuckin' pinball wizards, huh?" Stony nudged his brother on the way out.

"Yeah!" Albert laughed. "Boing boing boing boing ding! ding!" He laughed again. "Hey, Stony, look!" Albert pointed in amazement to a row of red and white buttons hanging on a rack of gorilla masks, corny T-shirts and rubber chickens in the window of a novelty shop. On the sidewalk a small mechanical rubber porpoise was swimming in a pan of water and every few seconds spouting a thin schpritz. "Look a' that button!" He pointed to the first button in the row with ALBERT on it. "An' that one!" Albert pointed to a button marked TOMMY. "We can get two a them, one for you an' one for Daddy." Before they went inside Albert saw MARIA. "We can get one for everybody."

~

The movie was a real slam-bang smack-fooey with more methods of dealing death than Heinz had kinds. Pajamaed Chinks jumped forty-two feet in the air to rearrange each other's faces. Blood poured, spurted and dribbled from every human hole imaginable. Albert sat through the whole thing eating popcorn, his eyes as big as half dollars. Stony dug it too, nailed to his seat, sitting on his need to piss through the whole movie.

"I dug the part where Ting Ping pulled the guy's nose off." Albert extended two curled fingers, stuck them up an invisible opponent's nostrils and yanked.

The afternoon sunlight blinded Stony. He blinked, trying to get his bearings. "You want some Chinks?" They walked uptown on Broadway until they hit the Hunan Star.

"Hey, Stony." Albert peeked around the huge red menu. "You think they know . . ." He made a short karate chop in the air.

"Only the ones from New Jersey."

They sat next to a four-foot-high partition in the center of the restaurant. The partition was topped by a strip of heavy-duty plastic green shrubs. The far walls were covered with blowups of the Great Wall. Stony and Albert were the only customers. Chinese waiters scattered among the tables, silverware in hand, setting up. A tall skinny guy in a red jacket splotched with food and a six-inch-high shiny black pompadour asked for their order.

"Ah, number nine with egg drop soup. Albert?"

Albert looked up at the waiter, closed one eye and stroked his chin. Stony had a horrible premonition and covered his eyes.

"Do you know kung fu?" Albert asked.

"Ah! . . . Bluce Lee!" The waiter smiled.

"Albert, don't." Stony hid behind the menu. Albert jumped up from the table and affected kung fu position number one. Hunched over, one hand palm up, fingers curled, pulled back to his chest, the other arm extended rigidly, hand in a fist. The waiter laughed and yelled something in Chinese. The other waiters stopped what they were doing, looked over and started laughing.

"Albert, please." Stony wouldn't uncover his eyes. His face was redder than the menu. One of the waiters near Albert, a fat guy with a six-foot smile, stepped forward and assumed Albert's stance. Then he let out what passed for a kung fu shout. Albert attacked, making up his own kung fu shouts and windmilling karate chops. The waiter tried to look serious as he fended off the featherweight blows, but finally he fell on his ass laughing. All the waiters were howling, staggering around the empty restaurant holding their guts.

"Stony! Stony!" Albert tugged on his brother's arm. "I beat him! I beat him!"

After Stony finished his shrimps in lobster sauce and Albert his hamburger, the fat waiter whom Albert defeated brought a bowl piled with ice cream, Jell-O, kumquats and pineapple to their table. A half-dozen toothpicks with parasols protruded from the pineapple. He set the dish in front of Albert. "Dis for Bluce Lee!" He tousled Albert's hair. "You one tough customer!"

~

"Hey, Mister Bones!" Stony removed his jacket and threw it on his bed. "For a guy who don't eat much you know what you had today?" He counted on his fingers. "You had a hot dog, a Coke, popcorn, a hamburger, ice cream, pineapple, *another* Coke . . ."

Albert smiled triumphantly, then all of a sudden his face turned green and he bolted for the john.

~

Saturday afternoon Chubby drove up to Banion's. The day was hot and sticky and he relished the thought of some cool drinks and lazy conversation in the air-conditioned bar.

"Hey-y, Ban-*yon!*" Chubby walked in, hands in pockets, and swung a leg over a barstool.

Banion poured out a Scotch.

"Chub, you missed somethin' here las' night." He wiped the counter in front of Chubby. "We had the fuckin' cops."

"You get held up?"

"Nah, you know Dave Stern?"

"Big Dave?"

"Right, the fireman."

"Yeah?"

"The cops were after him. They dragged him outta here last night."

"Big Dave?" Chubby sipped his drink. "What the hell for? He's one a the quietest guys I ever seen. He start a fire or somethin'?"

"Nah, nah. See, his kid, he got a twenny-year-old kid. He ran away from home last week. Just packed up and split. Yesterday, Dave gets this letter from him. The fuckin' kid joined a Jesus commune down in Arkansas, right?" Banion raised his eyebrows. "He writes this letter like, 'Dear Mom and Dad, I've found God blah, blah, blah.' Now get this — 'I have changed my name. I am no longer Michael Stern. My name is *Matthew*' — O.K.? Dropped the family name, the religion. Dave's Jewish, no word where he is, when he's comin' home, *if* he's comin' home and the fuckin' kid has the balls to sign the letter: 'Smile, Jesus loves you. Matthew.' "

"Oh Christ."

"The kid dropped outta New York University. Not a word, *nothin'*." Banion poured himself a drink. "You know that goddamn kid was only a junior and got accepted to dental school awready? Can you believe that? He's so goddamn smart he got accepted a year early. All he had to do was finish up his junior year an' he was in. Full scholarship, Chubby, *full* scholarship. You have any idea how he broke his parents' hearts? Dave's wife had a nervous breakdown. Dave's older kid, Ronnie, drove off to Arkansas to find his brother and drag his ass back home. Dave was in here last night. Drinkin' like a fish. The poor guy's whole life fell apart. He runs outta here, an hour later comes runnin' back in, his shirt's all ripped, pantin' like a bull, ten minutes later three cops come in, they take him outta here at gunpoint, poor guy's cryin' like a baby. One a the cops tells me what happened. You ever see those Harry Krishner creeps that dance around in fronna the shoppin' center on Central Avenue? Seems like Dave was drivin' around, saw them and went nuts, you know Harry

Krishner, Jesus Freaks, what's the difference? Dave jumps outta his car, grabs a crowbar. Three a them wound up in the hospital. The cops chased him all the way back here. A couple a the guys went down to the station, explained to the judge what's been goin' on, the judge set bail at fifty bucks. They chipped in an' took him home."

"I tell you, Banion, these days, I thank God I don't got kids. Poor Dave. How's his wife?"

Banion shrugged. "Hard to say, I think she'll be O.K." He poured Chubby and himself another. "It's a knife in their hearts, Chubby, a knife in their hearts."

"Big Dave," Chubby muttered. "Don't you feel the same way?"

"What?"

"About havin' kids. Don't you feel glad you don't got any?"

Banion looked grimly at Chubby. "I got a kid, Chubby."

"You do? How come you never say nothin'?"

"Nothin' to say . . . kicked him out three years ago." Banion busied himself washing clean glasses.

"How come?"

"Paul's a fag," Banion said offhandedly. "He's a fuckin' fag."

Chubby felt a rush of dizziness like he'd felt with Sylvia that night. His hands and feet tingled and his eyes wouldn't focus. "What . . . uh . . . how you know?" His voice sounded weak.

Banion glared at him. "Don't fuckin' ask me how I know. I know, I know, is all." Chubby walked to the john. When he came out Banion was sitting behind the bar, his back to Chubby, his hands resting in his lap. He wheeled the chair around. "You're right, though, Chub. These days . . . these days people without kids should thank God."

They sat in silence through three more drinks until Chubby eased himself off his stool and headed for the door.

"Chubby?" Chubby turned around. "Don't say nothin', O.K.?"

7

STONY GOT UP early Monday morning. He and Butler had promised Chili Mac they'd help him move into his own place near D'Artagnan's. When Stony got out of bed Albert was already watching cartoons. His old man had split for work and his mother was still sleeping. When he passed her bedroom she was tossing and turning, making weird moaning noises in her sleep. Stony shrugged and left the house.

~

Marie dreamed that she was sitting naked in her mother's house on the brocade piano stool. Her parents were standing in back of her laughing hysterically. She was glad they were happy and started laughing along with them. Her mother said between guffaws, "Don't worry, Marie, Doctor Marcus will be here any minute." Marie got scared. She hated Doctor Marcus. "Why is he coming?" she asked.

"Because look!" they both cried, pointing to her back. Then they doubled over with renewed laughter. Marie reached behind her back; her fingers touched something soft and sticky. She ran to the mirror and screamed. Her spine had split open from the base of her skull to a point above her buttocks, revealing a huge white pulpy larva.

Marie fell out of bed and vomited on the floor. She was trembling so badly she couldn't stand up so she just rested on all fours on the puke-spattered rug. She moaned. Her stomach heaved and convulsed in shuddering waves. She tried to wipe her chin, but when she lifted her hand she fell forward on her elbow.

"M — Mommy!" Albert stood in the bedroom doorway pop-eyed in horror.

She snarled at him, "Help me!" Albert backed away from her. "Help me, you little bastard!" Sobbing, Albert ran to his room. She heard him slam his door. Marie steadied herself, then leaned her arms and head against the side of the bed as if she were saying her prayers. She rested like this for a minute before struggling to stand up. She tried to take a deep breath but the back of her throat was raw from vomiting. She wiped her face on her sweat-soaked nightgown before staggering to the bathroom.

After a scalding shower she felt a little better. She brushed her teeth twice and gargled with Listerine. Her legs were still rubbery as she walked out of the bathroom in Tommy's raspberry terry robe. Passing Albert's bedroom she remembered in a flush of rage his running away. She clenched her teeth and swung open the door so hard that the noise of the doorknob smashing against the wall sounded like a gunshot. Albert squealed and jumped to his feet. A furious cartoon battle was raging on television, with animals sailing across the screen and crashing somewhere out of sight.

"I — I I'm s — sorry," he sputtered, spraying spit, "M — Mommy." The sight of Marie standing in the doorway, chest heaving like a steaming Medusa, made him wet his pants. He stared with horror at the spreading stain, then at his mother with a mute, pleading look.

"AN-NI-MAAAL!" Marie shrieked, bounding across the bedroom to grab Albert's hair, pulling his head up so that he almost stood on tiptoe. Albert screamed and in a spasm of terror started pumping his legs up and down, running in place, Marie's fingers entwined like snakes in his hair.

Wildly, Albert looked around the room but dared not move for fear of Marie's tearing his hair out. His eyes became wet and he didn't know what to do with his arms. "M — Mommy, puh — please." Albert tried to stroke her cheek above his head but she snapped her head out of his reach and yanked his hair even harder. "I'm s — s — sorry, s — s — sorry," he gasped. Marie's face was quivering, her eyes nearly closed, her top lip disappeared into a thin white line of tension. She could feel his emaciation. The sight of his ribs sticking out even beneath his polo shirt chilled her with disgust. She wrenched him away from her, hurling him onto his bed, but he was up like a shot, flattening himself against a wall like a hunted animal. The cartoon on television exploded in star patterns, which cleared away to reveal a gunpowder-blackened coyote.

"Turn that goddamn thing off!" she screamed. With a wail Albert dove for the set, clicked it off and raced back to his spot. "Why do you hate me, *all* of us so much? I say, 'Albert, eat, Albert, eat, Albert, eat, please, Albert, eat, you're so skinny.' The doctor, no! No, you break everybody's heart, everybody who loves you, you break their heart. They look at you, and they wanna puke! Yeah! Yeah! Do you know last week your Aunt Phyllis was in *tears!* In *tears!* She said God forgive me, Marie, every time I see him so skinny like that I wanna vomit."

"No!" Albert screamed. The vision of his favorite aunt in tears over his selfish skinniness made him bray in anguish. He sank to the floor, rocking back and forth.

Marie's voice dropped to a whisper. "Why do you do this to us, Albert? What pleasure do you get out of torturing us? I beg you to eat. I cook for you anything. I walk and buy and I cook and pray to God please God let him like it, let him eat." Marie knelt on the floor, raising her clasped hands to the ceiling, threw her head back and bellowed, "God! God! What did I do, God? Why am I punished?"

"Mommy!" Albert ran in place again. His face was red and twisted with grief, his cheeks spattered with tears. "Mommy, I'll eat! I'll eat! Oh, Mommy, I swear to God I'll eat, I'll eat." He ran to the kitchen and ran back with a box of rice. "Look! Look!" He jammed a fistful of uncooked rice in his mouth. Marie ignored him, her eyes closed in prayer. Albert gagged and spit up rice and bile over the floor. Marie straightened in disgust. Albert grabbed for her legs.

"Don't touch me!" she screamed. She bared her teeth and pulled her hair. "I'm leaving! Forever! I can't stand you!" She left the room, slamming the door in his face.

"Mommy!" he screamed, opening the door, chasing his mother through the apartment and clutching the rice box. Marie ran into the foyer, grabbed a full-length fake fur coat and tan suitcase from the hall closet. "Mommy, look, I'm eating! I'm eating! Look! Look!" He blubbered and gagged, stuffing rice in his mouth, spitting out as much as he was swallowing. Albert grabbed her robe as she tried to pull on the coat. She shoved him onto the floor.

"I can't stand you!" she screamed at him. "I can't stand to *look* at you! You make me *sick!*" She put on the coat, grabbed the empty suitcase and before Albert could struggle to his feet was out of the apartment.

"Mommy!" He threw himself at the door, frantically pulling at the doorknob. "I'll be good, oh, Mommy, Mommy, I'll be good, I'll eat! I'll eat! I'm sorry, oh MommyMommyMommy Mommy!" The door wouldn't open. On the other side of the door, Marie, drenched with sweat, held onto the knob with bloodless hands. Nausea rose from her belly, but she held it down. She was dizzy. The heat rose in waves from the fur coat. She fought off fainting as she listened to Albert pleading and begging. Then she heard a door opening down the hall and quickly let herself back in. Albert was still screaming, but something was wrong. He didn't look at her. He stared at the door, still clutching the rice box. She threw off her coat and clasped a hand over his mouth. His eyes were wide and wet. When she took her hand away he screamed again. The doorbell rang, startling her. She covered Albert's mouth again and dragged him to the bathroom, locking him in. The doorbell rang again. Marie ran to the door. Mrs. Katz, the old cunt across the hall, stood in the doorway holding Marie's tan suitcase.

"Voss iss screaming?" Mrs. Katz cringed. Marie grabbed the suitcase from her and slammed the door in her face. She ran back to the bathroom. Albert was still screaming.

Marie unlocked the door and hugged Albert to her. "Ssh, baby, baby, Mommy's here, Mommy's here." But Albert wouldn't stop. He retched, gasped for breath, but he wouldn't stop screaming.

Ten minutes later Marie, white-faced and trembling, locked him in the bathroom again and while his shrieks shattered the air she picked up the pink receiver. "Oh my God, operator, give me Jacobi Hospital. Oh my God, oh my God."

~

Stony, Butler and Chili Mac sprawled on oversized throw pillows in Chili Mac's new living room. Along one wall stood three washing-machine-sized cardboard boxes stuffed with the Mac's clothes, books, kitchen stuff and miscellany. The walls were fresh white, the floor, newly polished parquet. Chili Mac had immediately set up his stereo, the speakers in opposite corners on either side of an enormous window. Nice place. The three of them sat there, sweating, drinking Coke from cans. Chili Mac had a plastic Baggie half filled with grass on his lap. He was busy rolling and licking joints. The Mac's real name was Matthew Mackell. Some people said he was called Chili Mac because he was a freak for Mexican food, but most agreed he got his name because he was just so goddamn cool.

"Chili, put on some J.B." Butler wiped his neck.

"Put it on yourself, man, I got my hands tied up." He popped a whole joint in his mouth, extracted it slowly and placed it on the floor.

Butler crawled over to a three-foot-high stack of albums, pulled out "James Brown — Live at the Apollo."

"Mac, what you payin' for this?" Stony looked around the room.

"A yard and a half." Now there were two joints.

"So now, ladies and gennelmen, it is *star* time. Are you ready for *star* time? Thank you and thank you kindly. It is *indeed* a great pleasure at this particular time to introduce the nationally and *in*ternationally known as the *haard*est-workin' man in show business . . ." The record had been played so many times, it had more crackles than a two-way radio system.

Mac lit up a third joint, took three staccato tokes and passed it on to Stony. Stony took a long drag and passed it to Butler.

"Mac, what they payin' you at the club?" Stony's voice sounded strained as he struggled to retain the smoke in his lungs.

"A yard for the weekend, but I got other income." He held up the Baggie, raising his eyebrows.

Stony felt jealous. "Shit." He exhaled.

Chili Mac wore a rayon leopard-skin tank top. On anybody else it would have looked ridiculous, but with the Mac's physique he looked like Black Power's answer to Tarzan.

"Hey, Butler," Stony sniffed, "when you gettin' your own crib?"

"Six months." Butler coughed, filling the air with smoke.

"Hey, man, you keep coughin' like that, I don't need to smoke. I'll just get a contact high off your bad lungs." Chili Mac laughed.

"Ladies an' gennelmen, the 'mazin, Mr. Please Please hisself, the star of the show, *James* Brown, and the Famous Flames!!"

"Six months, shit, I might be in Louisiana in six months," Stony bitched.

"You goin' in the army?" Chili Mac took the burning jay from Butler.

"Army! Shit. I might be goin' a college down there."

"Whyncha go to City?" Chili took a few more short drags. "It's open admissions."

"Yeah, I know." Stony rubbed his face. "That's the problem, they'll take anybody."

"Too many spades?" Mac held the joint delicately between thumb and index finger.

"It's not just that, there's also too many spics." Stony took the joint.

Butler snorted, then stifled himself. "Sorry."

"Butler, what *you* laughin' at?" Stony passed him the joint without taking any. "You so dumb you couldn't pass a blood test."

"Least I ain't dumb enough to go to Little Abner State."

Chili Mac snickered. "Stones, what's the school?" He took the joint from Butler.

Stony shrugged. "Purdy Free Normal or somethin'."

Chili Mac exploded in laughter. He fell off the pillow and rolled over on the floor holding his stomach. Butler and Stony glanced at each other. He sat up, supporting himself on one arm, tried to speak and fell flat on his back, kicking his legs. "You . . .

you . . . oh, man . . . you remind me a this cat I read about. This cat was freakin' out cause he was livin' in New York an' he was worried about an A-bomb attack, so he packed up his whole family an' moved to some Dakota or other. A month later they build a nuclear missile plant right in his backyard."

"What the fuck's that got to do with me?" Stony was getting nervous.

"Man, you goin' down to Louisiana cause a the bad el-e-ment up here, right? But you all goin' to Chocolate City!" Mac started laughing again.

"What?"

"Ain't you hip to Purdy, man? That school so black it makes Howard look like University of Vermont!"

Stony was speechless. Butler took a swig of soda, then started laughing so hard Coke spurted from both nostrils.

"Man, how you ever apply there?"

"My counselor was tryin' to think of a place I could get in." Stony looked like he just poured his Coke down the front of his pants.

"Hey lissen, man, I know Purdy, mah cousin went there. Hey, ain't . . . ain't you ever heard a . . . a Grambling or a Tuskeegee?"

"Yeah, but . . ."

"Then you heard a Purdy!" Chili Mac hooted with glee. "Ah hopes you get into a good fraternity, bawh!"

"Hey, Stony!" Stony turned mechanically to Butler. "I think we just got the results a your blood test."

As the day wore on and Stony got increasingly fucked up on the Mac's stash, his mood shifted from shock and embarrassment to near hysterical laughter. Fuck college anyway. When Stony left the crib he was too wasted to drive so he jumped a cab home.

~

"Where to, Rocco?" The cabdriver had a shaved head and a thick drooping mustache.

"Co-op City."

"Mind if I do it for myself?"

"Two bucks?" Stony bargained.

The cabdriver nodded in agreement. Stony noticed the driver's big shoulders and meaty face. With the mustache and the shaved head he looked like a heavy in a James Bond movie. After two minutes of kamikaze driving they stopped dead in heavy traffic. "Shit!" He flipped the car into neutral and leaned his back against the door, drumming his fingers on the top of the front seat. "Look a' this fuckin' traffic. This is no good." He shook his head disgustedly, picking at his mustache. "No fuckin' good for you an' no fuckin' good for me." In the rearview mirror he noticed a small green Triumph inching its way between lanes. "Look a' this cocksucker!" He put the cab in drive and moved it out of his lane, blocking the Triumph.

"Where you think you goin', shithead?" he bellowed, leaning out his window. The driver of the Triumph stopped and tried to appear nonchalant, casually looking out his window and tugging on the knot of his tie.

"Hey" — the cabby turned to Stony — "dig this clown." Stony twisted around to check the guy through the rear window. The driver's cheeks puckered and his lips pursed in what looked like a pantomime of whistling. Stony laughed. Traffic started moving. The cabby pulled back into his lane. The Triumph stayed put until the cars behind it started honking. The cabby cackled. "I could go two fuckin' miles an hour from here to Maine, that guy wouldn't dare pass me. Fuckin' college assholes. They all got the ol' man in Westchester throws 'em a TR-IV for their birthdays, right? You go to college?" He faced Stony.

"Me? Nah." Stony sat up straight. "I just got outta high school."

"Fuck college." He shifted lanes. "The only college worth two shits is the college of life. Am I right?"

"Yeah." Stony leaned back, extracted a cigarette from his shirt pocket.

"So whatta you doin' now, spongin' off yer old man?" The cabby winked in the mirror.

"My father's dead," Stony muttered.

The cabby sucked air through his teeth like he'd just slammed his finger with a hammer. "Hey lissen, I was only fuckin' aroun'. Look, don't mind me, I'm an asshole."

Stony chuckled.

"Where'd you go to school?"

"The Mount."

"Oh yeah, over on the border, right? I went to Evander. You know Evander?"

"Sure."

"I was on the football team there in sixty-two. I was a split end. Although as you can probably tell, I ain't got no split ends no more," he said, caressing his gleaming scalp. "The last fuckin' game a the season, we're playin' Clinton for the city-wides, we're down seventeen-thirteen. Tommy Algiers calls for a stop an' go long bomb, right? Ten seconds to go an' then it's all over. I pull a fuckin' fake on this Polack safety they had, I think the fuckin' guy is still lookin' for me. I'm out all alone on the two-yard line, nobody for *miles*. Algiers lets loose with this pass, *God himself* couldn't a thrown a more perfect spiral, I'm standin' there, 'Come to Poppa,' right? The fuckin' ball had *radar*. So what happens? The fuckin' ball slipped right outta my hands and we lost the championship. Meenga!" He put the fingertips of his right hand together and suddenly released them. "The guys on the fuckin' team were so fuckin' pissed they got me in the locker and shaved my fuckin' head, an' I wore it shaved ever since." He nodded sadly. "Now my friends call me Cleanhead."

"Jesus Christ!" Stony felt the pain.

"Hey, kid?" Cleanhead smiled mischievously in the mirror. "You believe that story?"

Stony frowned at the question, then remembered Evander didn't have a football team in the sixties because a girl had been knifed in a fight after a game with Clinton in fifty-eight. Cleanhead watched Stony's expression change from confusion to the old you-got-two-tens-for-a-five?

Cleanhead cackled again, pleased with himself. Stony debated telling him that they were even, that his old man wasn't dead, but he thought better of it.

"You know what I do? Every other time someone comes into

the cab, I try to make up a story on the spot about how come I got a shaved head. Some a those fuckin' stories are fuckin' gems too, an' I never use the same story twice." He burst out laughing. "Yesterday I tell this fuckin' guy my wife useta like me rubbin' my head in her pussy, then she got the clap and all my hair fell out, right? I turn aroun' to see if the guy's laughin' an' I see he's wearin' a priest's collar." Cleanhead hit the steering wheel with the flat of his palm. "Can you beat that? But dig this! You know, I say, 'Hey Jeez, Father, no offense.' I didn't know, but the fuckin' guy is laughin' so hard he didn't even hear me. For a second I thought I was on 'Candid Camera.'"

"We had some guys like that at the Mount," Stony said.

"Really? Boy, when I went to school the fuckin' priests, man, you look at them cross-eyed, you got clocked on the head. An' the goddamn nuns were worse. I got a sister that went to Catholic school in Brooklyn. She comes in one day with pierced earrings, some fuckin' nun pulls her outta line an' rips the fuckin' things right outta her ears, can you believe that?"

"So what else is new?" Stony had sixteen million horror stories of his own from those days.

"Them fuckin' fascist penguins is somethin' else, hah? So, anyways, kid, whatta you doin' now? You workin' anywhere?"

"Not yet. I got some bread stashed from when I was doin' summer jobs. I dunno what I'm gonna do yet."

"You got all the fuckin' time in the world, kid. You got some dough? If I was you I'd go to Europe for a couple a months. About ten years ago I had some money. I split for Europe, wound up in Amsterdam. The most incredible fuckin' city in the world. They got this red-light district they call The Wall. Two million hookers but young, nice, blondes like you never seen. Each one sits in a ground-level window with a red light over the door. They got beds right in the window. You go in, say how do you do, they pull the curtain an' you get laid right in the fuckin' street. The people in the city are nice too. Everybody speaks English."

As Cleanhead talked on, Stony studied the Bronx terrain. He never thought of traveling. The cab pulled into Co-op City.

"Where you goin', babe?"

"You know where the shoppin' center is? Drop me off there."
Stony threw him two-fifty and hopped out of the cab. "Hey,
kid." Cleanhead motioned Stony back to the cab. "Here." He
handed him a printed calling card and watched Stony's face as he
read it:

> They know me uptown, downtown, in the Bronx and
>   in Queens.
> When folks ride with me, I split their seams.
> Behind this wheel, in all my glory
> A day doesn't pass without a good story.
> I keep alert and on the beam,
> Because my head is shiny clean.
> So if you can't use a bus and want a cab instead,
> Here's my card — just dial CLEANHEAD.

He laughed, slapped Stony on the arm and roared off into the
sunset.

~

"For the life of me I can't figure out what happened," Tommy
fumed. He sat between Chubby and Stony in the back of the cab
they'd hailed at Jacobi.

"I never liked that fuckin' hospital," Chubby said. "How long's
he in for?"

"Stony, what'd that doctor say?" Tommy asked.

Stony didn't answer, he just stared straight ahead.

"I just cannot fuckin' understand it. Marie said she woke up
when she heard him screamin', ran into his room and he was just
like that," Tommy said.

"Maybe he had a nightmare." Chubby lit a cigarette. "Whatta
you think, Stones?"

Stony acted as if he didn't hear him.

"What's with him?" Chubby nodded at Stony.

"Poor fuckin' Marie, she's a nervous wreck."

"It's tough for a mother," Chubby said.

"He'll be O.K.," Tommy mused. "That doctor what's-his-
name, he looked like he knew his stuff."

"When a' they gonna take that tube out his arm? Those things always give me the creeps."

"I dunno, I didn't ask. When he wakes up I guess. Hey, the union covers for this kinda stuff, right?" Tommy asked.

"I don't see why not. Whyncha call Joe Ginsberg when we get upstairs?"

"It's a tough fuckin' life, Chub."

"Yah kid's in the hospital?" the cabdriver piped. "What's he got?"

Tommy and Chubby exchanged looks. "Tonsils," Tommy answered.

"No sweat." The cabdriver shrugged. "He'll be back in two days."

When the cab stopped in front of their building Stony strode ahead of his father and uncle into the lobby. He shouldered a kid who crossed his path. When Chubby and Tommy entered, Stony was already in the elevator. The door began to slide shut. Tommy stuck his arm in in time. Stony stood rigid in the corner of the car.

"Thanks for holdin' the goddamn door." Chubby was puffing from the short sprint.

"Leave him alone, Chub," Tommy said.

When the elevator opened Stony pushed open the apartment door and marched into the dinette. Marie sat at the dinette table in the approaching evening darkness. She was still wearing the raspberry bathrobe. Her eyes were circled in black and her hair was unkempt. Phyllis sat next to her, one arm protectively around her shoulders. Cups of coffee sat in front of them, but no steam rose from the cups. Stony stared at his mother.

"What'd you do to him?" His voice was flat.

Marie raised her eyes.

"What'd you do to him?" Stony repeated louder.

Marie sat up as if stung.

"What'd you do to him, ya fuckin' bitch!" Stony lunged over the table, snagged the collar of his mother's bathrobe with one hand and smashed her in the face. She fell backward, cracking her head on the rear wall, a whiplash of blood from her nose splattering the table.

Phyllis screamed as Stony leaped on top of his mother. He pummeled her blindly through his tears until Tommy and Chubby burst in and dragged him away. "What'd you do to my fucking brother, you fucking cunt bitch!" he screamed as they hauled him into the living room. Chubby sat on his chest, crushing his back into the burnt orange carpet, and his father pinned his flailing arms. The last thing he remembered before blacking out was his father's chalk white, horror-stricken face.

8

STONY LAY IN BED that night, hands behind his head, trying to make out the titles of books in the dark. Some he knew from their shape on the bookshelf, others were too uniform to identify. The row of books reminded him of the New York skyline. He could still feel Chubby's knees digging into his shoulders. The fat fuck. He got out of his bed and crawled into Albert's. The sheets smelled like his brother. After a few minutes he sat up, took his cigarettes from his shirt hanging over a chair and lit up. By the light of the match he identified some of the books he couldn't make out earlier. *Hamlet, Robinson Crusoe, Brave New World, David Copperfield, 1984, Animal Farm, Silas Marner* — all paperbacks, all required high school reading. All bullshit boring.

Stony ditched the cigarette and got dressed. He took down his suitcase barricaded on the top of the closet by the old games he or Albert hadn't touched in years — Video Village, Parcheesi, Stratego, a Gilbert microscope, two shoeboxes of baseball cards, Careers, a Nok-Hockey board and a big crumpled bag filled with the pieces of half a dozen never attempted jigsaw puzzles.

He threw in underwear, socks, a few pairs of dungarees and a couple of shirts. He slipped quietly into the bathroom, collected his toothbrush, his hot comb and his razor, dumped this stuff in and snapped the suitcase shut. Amsterdam. You pick them out of the windows, Cleanhead had said. Ten bucks a throw. Nice blondes. They'd go for him too. A guinea stud with New York soul. Cleanhead said everybody spoke English there, but even if they didn't all you had to do was throw in some ooks and icks every few words and you could make out O.K.

Stony took out his bankbook: 638 dollars and 41 cents.

Amster, Amster, doity woid
Amster, Amster, doity woid.

Two-thirty in the morning. Stony picked up the suitcase and
headed down the foyer.

"Stony . . ." Marie stood behind him like a ghost in the dark.
She turned on the hall light, blinding them both. She wore a white
nightgown. A bloody brown piece of cotton hung from one
nostril. A half-moon of dull red under her left eye. She grabbed
Stony's hand. "Stony, I just want you to know, that whatever you
do, I'll always love you." She pouted, ready to cry. "I'll always
forgive you."

Stony was dumbstruck. "Ma?" He tightened his grip on the
suitcase. "You're a fuckin' hoowah." He pulled the plug of
cotton from her nose. She winced, letting go of his hand, and he
was gone.

~

"I couldn't do it, Butler. Last night I got down to Kennedy, first
thing I realize, you can't pay for a plane ticket wit' a bankbook, so
I come all the way back up to the Bronx, hang around till the
bank opens an' take out all my money. I was gonna take a cab
back out to Kennedy, I think, at least lemme say goodby to
Albert, so I go to Jacobi instead. I walk into his room there an'
he's sleepin' like a baby. The doctor says he gonna be O.K., he
just needs to rest for a couple a days. The doctor wants to start
puttin' him on tranks, see a shrink for a while, *that* scares the
shit out of me. You know, seein' a shrink. The kid's eight years
old."

Butler and Stony aimlessly tossed around a basketball on a
concrete court. Stony took a one-handed jumper from twenty feet
out, missing the basket and backboard completely. The ball
clanked noisily into the chain link fence separating the court from
the sidewalk. The noon sun was hot. Made them slow.

"Anyways, so I just sit there in his room with my suitcase

watchin' him sleep. That kid never sleeps at home. Lays in bed late at night until two and he's up at dawn. I never really seen him sleep an' he's always having nightmares. He told me this dream once about Mrs. Halzer, his teacher, makin' him drink this big glass of milk that turns to blood when he's halfway finished."

Underhand Butler tossed the ball from the foul line, hitting the pole. "I remember this dream once *I* had. My old man is tryin' to screw me up the ass. What's with this fuckin' ball? Next mornin' I find out he had to go to Jacobi with a blocked prostate. Served 'im right, the bastard."

Stony tried to drop-kick the basketball into the hoop, almost booting it over the fence. "I was just sittin' there watchin' him sleep. I figure, shit, I'll leave next week when he comes home, make sure he's O.K., you know?"

"You got a passport?"

"A what?" Stony blinked. "Aw, for chrissakes!" He kicked the basketball into the fence again.

"So get one."

"Ah, fuck it." Stony blew down the front of his shirt to cool off, sitting on a low concrete ledge behind the pole. "Fuck it, fuck it, fuck it." Grimacing, scratching his head.

"Albert'll be O.K." Butler took a cigarette from his shirt pocket and sat down next to Stony.

"It ain't just that, it's, I dunno, you can't just . . . I dunno, I kept doing these weird numbers in my head all last night. I kept runnin' down all these . . . memories. I keep thinkin' about all these crazy things. Like this one time when I had ringworm on my scalp when I was a kid. My mother took me to a skin guy who was gonna use ultraviolet rays on my head, but he said if I moved a half inch or so my brains would turn to Cream of Wheat, so she said no dice, and I had to do this other treatment where they shaved my head. Can you imagine that? I was bald at six. And it was a real motherfucker too. I wore this stocking hat and all the kids called me Baldy. I would come home cryin' everyday. Fistfights, the whole shtick. But the real bitch was when the mothers found out I was bein' treated for ringworm and told their kids they couldn't play with me. I remember comin' upstairs after my best friend, Mitchell, told me his mother said I have a disease in my head and he couldn't go near me. I came home and I was laughing my ass off. I just bopped into the house and said, 'Mitchell's mother says I got a disease in my head'; laughin', laughin' and all of a sudden I just break into tears like I thought I was gonna choke.

"My mother got so damn mad she calls up this kid's mother an' that was the first time I ever heard an adult curse. She was screamin' and wavin' her arms. She called her a no-good lousy pig, told her to drop dead an' get fucked an' God knows what else. When my old man heard about it, he took me right down to this toy store an' he says, 'You don't *need* those other kids,' an' he bought me forty bucks' worth a cowboy stuff. I mean not just a goddamn gun an' holster either. I mean spurs, chaps, leather cuffs, a shirt with pearl buttons, goddamn bandi*lee*rs even."

"These foolish things, remind me uh-huh yooo," Butler crooned.

Stony laughed. "That ain't all. My father got me this big cowboy hat. It was a little too big so no one could tell I was bald. I used to wear it everywhere, even when my hair grew back, but about a week after he got me all the cowboy stuff, my family went out with Chubby and Phyllis to Nino's, this Italian restaurant in Monticello. I was all dressed up with all the stuff, the hat, the guns, the whole shtick. We're all sittin' there an' some mook puts 'High Noon' on the juke. You know, Frankie Laine? 'Do not forsake me, oh my dar-ling.' So all the grown-ups are talkin'. I start stalkin' aroun' the restaurant like Gary Cooper with my hands by my guns, right? Everybody in the whole place starts laughin'. I was so fuckin' cute. This waiter comes out with this tray an' when he sees me, he puts down the tray an' starts walkin' towards me like *he* got two guns an' we square off about twenny feet apart. Everybody's goin' berserk, Frankie Laine is singin' in the background and *I'm* serious as hell an' we're slowly gettin' closer an' closer. All of a sudden I pull out my two guns, they're loaded with caps, an' I shoot him. The fuckin' guy falls on the floor grabbin' his heart like he's dead. Everybody stands up and starts cheerin' and clappin'. I jus' blow the smoke from my guns,

put 'em back in my holster and go sit down. Chubby was laughin'
so hard he had to have two glasses a water to stop gaggin'. My
mother had tears on her face from laughin'. Later, Nino himself
came out and gave me an ice cream sundae for dessert. I didn't
see what was so funny. I thought everybody was laughin' because
they knew I was bald under my cowboy hat." Stony wiped the
sweat from the side of his face with his shoulder. "That's how I
got my nickname."

"Stony?"

"Yeah. When Nino came over to the table with the ice cream,
he slapped my father on the back an' said, 'Your kid got real
stones.' " Stony examined his nails, then squinted at the sun.
"You know somethin', Butler? I *knew* I wasn't goin' to Amsterdam las' night. I think I jus' went out there to see what it would
feel like."

"Like what would feel like?"

"Leavin' home."

9

ALBERT'S DOCTOR was Ralph Harris, né Hochman, a thirty-five-year-old heavy, bearded, pediatric resident who spent two of the first five years of his life in a concentration camp. He was saved from the gas chamber by a sympathetic guard who smuggled him out of the camp in a truck loaded with corpses. In 1955, at fifteen, Ralph Hochman migrated to America from Poland, where he had been living with relatives of the guard who saved him. The guard himself was executed in 1949 on atrocity charges. It had been his job to keep the children orderly on their way to the gas chambers. He had developed a whole repertoire of hand and shadow games to keep them amused and distracted while they waited for the chambers to be cleared of previous tenants.

In 1969 he graduated medical school. He also received his black belt in karate. He did two years' internship at Harlem Hospital, one year on the emergency ward and one year in the children's ward.

After graduation he had his tattoo removed by a plastic surgeon and changed his name to Harris. In 1971 he became a resident at Jacobi on the children's ward. His ultimate goal was to become a child psychiatrist. His special interest was the battered child syndrome. In all his years at Harlem Hospital and at Jacobi, he had seen maybe three or four kids more terrified than Albert De Coco.

On Thursday, when Doctor Harris looked in on Albert he was watching cartoons on a portable TV and sipping apricot juice through a straw. The inside of his elbow was blotched yellow-brown from the two days of intravenous feeding.

"Hiya, Albert." Albert smiled but didn't say anything. The doctor sat down on the bed. "How we feeling tonight?"

"O.K."

"You mind if I turn off the TV for a few minutes?" He reached over and shut it off. "I have some good news, kiddo, tomorrow you're going home!"

Albert's face tightened. A fleeting look of pure terror. "Can I take these comics?" he asked, motioning to a stack of *Superman*s a volunteer aide had given him.

"I don't see why not." Harris smiled. He felt troubled by Albert's reaction. "You still don't remember what happened Monday?"

Albert stared at him blankly, tucking his blanket closer around his body.

"Did you have any bad dreams last night?"

"Uh-uh." Albert looked over the doctor's shoulder. From Albert's dreams, Harris knew whatever had happened that day involved Marie. He didn't buy the bullshit about Albert waking up screaming. He watched Albert's response to his mother when she visited him. That cowering expression gave him the chills. He was sure that bitch did something and he was sure Albert was lying when he denied remembering what happened. He knew all the crap about the cyclical nature of brutality and you had to have been brutalized as a kid to be brutal as an adult and all that, but the buck had to stop somewhere and he also knew a stone psychopath when he saw one, and that was Marie. When he discussed Albert with her, he knew she was lying through her teeth, but he had to be nice, he couldn't scare her or corner her because that kid's only hope, short of leaving home, was analysis with a good child psychologist, and he knew from experience if parents felt too threatened by what the therapy might reveal, they would never grant permission. He didn't want to send Albert home, and he knew Albert didn't want to go, but there was no medical or legal excuse to keep him. He checked about keeping Albert for treatment of his anorexia, but it wasn't severe enough. Besides, how much longer could they keep him, even for that? Eventually, Albert would have to go home. So instead Harris had to smile, eat Marie's shit and hope she would give permission for Albert to sign in at the psychiatric clinic as an outpatient. The father was no help — it was clear he didn't give a shit either way. He would agree to whatever his wife decided. It was too bad that the older son had no say. That kid was the only thing keeping Albert alive.

Albert stared at the brown rubber of the doctor's stethoscope. Once Doctor Harris let him use it. He listened to his own heart, then the doctor put the metal piece on *his* chest and Albert listened to Doctor Harris' heart. It beat much slower and louder, and it scared him. He thought about going home. He liked the hospital except for the needles. He could watch TV all day and play sick. The nurses were pretty and nobody yelled at him to eat. He liked Doctor Harris except when Doctor Harris looked worried. He was afraid that meant Doctor Harris was getting angry because Albert didn't eat all his food. Doctor Harris had a beard. Stony had a beard once, but Daddy made him shave it off. Doctor Harris was fat too. Not as fat as Uncle Chubby, but fatter than Daddy. He didn't want to go home. He wanted to stay in bed here and watch cartoons and read *Superman* and have Stony visit him with presents every day and play checkers with the ladies in striped dresses.

Harris had been hung up on that dream Albert told him three days ago in which the kid's teacher made him drink a glass of milk which turned to blood. Albert had said the dream was recurrent. There was something in that, some connection to what must have happened on Monday, but he couldn't piece it together without more information. Albert couldn't remember any of the events on any of the days preceding any of the nightmares. Or so he said. Jerry Rosenberg was coming back from vacation next week. He would love to have Jerry talk to Albert. But Albert would be gone by then. Maybe Jerry could see him as a clinic patient.

Harris smiled at Albert, tousled his hair and said he'd be back later.

"Doctor Harris?" Harris wheeled around. "Could you please turn on the TV?"

~

"No. Uh-uh. No way, no day." Marie had been shaking her head in the negative since Doctor Harris started talking.

"Will you *please* explain to me why not?" Doctor Harris was trying to control himself, but he held his Bic pen like a dagger, shaking it in front of her face.

Marie regarded him through half-closed eyes. "O.K., O.K., you wanna know why not?" She puffed on a cigarette as she talked.

"Last year, when Albert was in second grade, his teacher thought he should see a psychiatrist, the school had one." She blew a cloud of smoke around them both in the hospital corridor. "She, Mrs. Becker" — she sneered — "called me in one day at lunchtime to tell me. She said Albert was too nervous, didn't get on with the other kids, was starting to stutter, the whole thing, whatever, she said that the shrink the school had maybe it would be a good idea to talk . . . you know. I said, 'Maybe, but ah, don't you think the other kids would tease Albert? You know how vicious kids can get.' " She looked to Harris for agreement. None was forthcoming. "Anyways, she said, 'Oh no, oh no, Mrs. De Coco. I promise you nobody will know about it but me, you, Doctor Huzinga and Albert' . . . Hu*zinga* yet. I had no reason to doubt her word, so I said O.K. I mean it wasn't like he was getting *shock* treatment." She raised her eyebrows at Doctor Harris as she took a long drag from her cigarette. "Two days later, he comes home from school laughing, laughing, laughing. 'O.K., what's so funny?' 'I went to the *nut* doctor today, Mommy.' " Marie glared at Harris. Harris frowned. "I said, '*What?*' He said Mrs. Becker told him, 'I was excused from math because Doctor Huzinga wanted to talk to me, and William Temple heard her and told everybody that I was gonna see the *nut* doctor and the whole class was saying I was gonna see the *nut* doctor, but that's O.K. because it's funny an' I don't care anyway,' an' then that poor kid bursts into tears. That baby was so humiliated. I felt my heart break into a million pieces."

Doctor Harris stood with his arms folded across his chest.

Marie dropped her cigarette on the floor and snuffed it with her heel. She looked at him, smoke still furling from her nostrils. She spoke through clenched teeth, her lips drawn back so Harris could see her gums and discolored teeth. "The next day I just marched into that class with Albert and dressed down that bitch *so* bad in front of her whole class that it's gonna be *years* before she even thinks of sending another kid to Doctor Who-*zing*-a."

"Mrs. De Coco." Harris sighed. "That was a regret — "

"Oh, cut the shit with me, Doctor Harris." Her voice was so loud people in the hall turned to look. "You wanna know what's re*gret*table? You wanna know what's *really* sick? An eight-year-old normal kid seein' a shrink." Marie stalked down the corridor, her clicking heels sounding like the opening of a long row of switchblades.

Tommy had taken Albert to the car while Marie stayed behind to talk to Doctor Harris. They sat silently in the front seat. About every six months Tommy would take a good long look at Albert, and it would hit him like a long-forgotten dream, jolting in its sudden remembrance, that this kid was his. Tommy studied Albert out of the corner of his eye. He had put on a couple of pounds while he was in the hospital, but he still looked like something from a UNICEF poster.

"How's it goin'?" Tommy ran his hand around the rim of the steering wheel and forced a smile. He wished Marie would hurry the fuck up. Of all the goddamn days for Stony to have a dentist appointment.

"What?" Albert smiled, tickled that Tommy said anything to him.

"I'm kinda tired, you wanna drive home?" Tommy affected a yawn.

"Daddy," Albert giggled. "I can't drive." His voice half-whine, half-delight.

"No sweat, c'mere." Tommy lifted Albert onto his lap. He was as light as a shopping bag filled with dry leaves. Tommy realized that Albert had never sat on his lap. For some reason this thought made him dizzy. He reached around Albert and started the engine. Albert squealed. Scared shit and beside himself with excitement. Keeping the car in park, Tommy placed Albert's hands on the wheel. "Move 'em out!"

Albert pulled back his hands as if the steering wheel were red hot. He twisted around in Tommy's lap, throwing his arms around his father's neck. "Daddy, I'm scared!"

Tommy strained slightly against the embrace. Didn't know what to do with his hands. Patted his kid halfheartedly. Albert held on for dear life. Giggling and tipsy with neediness. Finally, Tommy gently disengaged himself and lifted Albert back to the passenger's side. "Hey, how ya gonna be a truck driver if ya get scared so easy?"

Albert leaned toward Tommy like a sex-starved date. He couldn't think of anything to say. Just quivered in his seat like a 100-yard dasher at the starting block.

"Hey!" Tommy smiled. "Let's go get a hamburger!"

"Yeah!" Albert almost yelled. "But what about Mommy?"

Tommy winked conspiratorially. "This is for men only."

Albert clapped his hands. He felt himself starting to tear, but he didn't understand why. He was happy.

"Move 'em out!" Tommy chuckled as he briefly thought about spending more time with his younger son. Just as he was about to pull out of the space, he noticed Marie across the street impatiently waiting for traffic to clear. Albert saw her too. He stopped tearing, feeling cool water pouring inside, then in a last-ditch blurt, "Hurry!"

Tommy was startled. "Nah, we'll do it some other time." Albert started to whine, but his heart wasn't in it. As Marie made her way to the car, Albert moved closer to his father to give her room, then scrambled over the seat into the rear.

Marie cursed as she slid in and slammed the door. "Sonofabitch!" she fumed. "You know what that bastard doctor wanted to do?" She plunged her hand into her pocketbook for a cigarette. "You know what that sick freak wanted to do?" Tommy pulled out into traffic. "He wanted to put the kid in a psycho ward! Yeah! Howdya like that?" She tossed the match out the window, then twisted around to face her son. "Albert, how would you like to be in a nut house?"

"What nut house? What are you talkin' about?" Tommy demanded.

"Can Stony and Daddy come with me?"

She stared at Albert incredulously. "Maybe he's right. Maybe you *should* go!"

Albert had no idea what a nut house was, but if it was like Jacobi he might not mind. He played with a strip of torn vinyl on the upholstery.

"What he say, Marie?"

"Genius Jew doctor said Albert needs a shrink!"

"He said that?"

"Yeah, he said that!" Marie barked. The smell of Marie's perfume was putting Albert to sleep. For an instant he thought he saw big lipstick lips on the front window of the car. He blinked and they disappeared.

"He said Albert gotta go to a nut house?" Tommy honked up the rear of a beat-up Mustang. The driver gave him the finger. Tommy thrust his head out the window. "I'll shove that fuckin' finger up yer ass!" The driver calmly checked out Tommy in his rearview mirror and turned off the street. "What goddamn nut house?"

"How the hell do I know?" Marie yelled. "He said the kid needs a shrink. How the hell do I know what nut house?" She waved her cigarette hand around the car. Albert lay down in the back. He saw the lips again on the upholstered roof. Tommy cursed incoherently. Ran a red light.

"What he say to you, Marie, word for word!" He didn't know whom he was pissed at.

"I don't remember word for word. Whatta you drivin' *me* crazy for?" She tossed her cigarette out the window, glaring at her husband. "It don't make any difference anyhow. I'm not goin' back to that goddamn hospital. Buncha animals run that place." She rested her arm behind Tommy's head.

"Mommy?" Albert sat up.

Marie turned.

"Are you mad at me?" He ran his thin fingers over Marie's hand. Marie sighed, patted his hand.

"No, baby."

"Mommy, when I get home, I'm goin' to clean up my room. Stony's side too. And I'm not goin' to watch cartoons for forty-six days."

"Albert, when you were in bed, what did Doctor Harris talk to you about?"

"He gave me forty-nine comic books. All *Supermans* except for one Jimmy Olsen. I got them in my bag in the trunk." Albert picked on the edge of his seat. "Do you want to read some when we get home, Mommy?"

"Did he say anything to you? Did he ask you any questions?"

"He asked me to tell him about Superman."

"What?"

"I told him I got Superman pajamas at home, but I don't got a cape and I told him I had a dream that I was Jimmy Olsen and Superman saved me from a monster in the water, and then he asked me what the monster looked like, but I didn't remember."

Marie frowned. "Albert, I want to ask you something and I want you to answer me honestly. I promise I won't get mad. When you were in bed, did Doctor Harris ever play with your pee-pee?"

"What the hell kinda question is that?" Tommy yelled. Marie ignored him.

"Did he ever touch your pee-pee?"

Albert looked puzzled, then laughed in a high-pitched giggle, covering his mouth. "Ooh, Mommy, you said a bad word."

"Answer me, Albert." Marie fought down the impulse to slap him.

"No-o," Albert pshawed.

"Did he ever make you touch — "

"Hey, cut it out!" Tommy swung Marie around. "What the hell's a matter with you! What kinda — "

"*I* don't know what kinda doctor he is! What kinda doctor thinks an eight-year-old kid needs a shrink! What kinda doctor walks around with a beard like that!" Marie screamed into Tommy's ear. She started crying, her voice cracked and ugly through the sobs. Albert sank back into the rear seat. The three traveled in silence until they got home. As they waited for the elevator, Marie fished in her pocketbook for a plastic amber prescription bottle with Albert's name and dosage directions typed on the label. It was filled with 5 mg Valiums. She rattled them in front of Tommy's face. "I'm gonna give these to Schindler. I'm gonna have 'im analyze 'em. *I* don't know what the hell's in these and I don't trust that goddamn doctor!"

Annoyed, Tommy brushed her hand from his face. "Do what the hell you want."

10

AFTER A WEEKEND in which Albert was taken to a Mets game, the zoo, three movies and Adventurers' Inn for hot dogs and ketchup, the De Cocos settled down for a Monday night's TV. Marie and Tommy in the living room, Stony and Albert in their bedroom. The phone rang, and the two divisions played chicken to see who was going to pick it up. After four rings, Tommy cracked.

"Yo!"

"Is . . . ah . . . Stony there?"

Tommy frowned. A familiar voice, but he couldn't place it. "Uh . . . hold on . . . hey, Stones! Pick up."

Stony picked up the extension in his bedroom. "Yeah?"

"Stony? This is Doctor Harris."

"Hey, how ya doin'?"

"Good . . . how's Albert?"

Stony glanced at Albert sitting on the floor, mesmerized by the television. "He's pretty good."

"Is he taking the Valiums?"

"The what?"

"The pills I gave your mother."

"You gave her pills?"

"For Albert." Harris found himself getting into a rage.

"She never said nothin' about no pills." Stony raised his voice, turning with a frown to Albert.

"Listen . . . can you come in and see me tomorrow?"

"Me?"

"Yeah . . . I need to talk to you . . . it's very important."

"Sure . . . what time?"

"How about one, we can have some lunch."

"Sure thing."

"And listen, don't tell anybody you're coming in, O.K.?"

"Sure. What's goin' on?"

"Nothin', I just wanna talk to you about your brother. One o'clock, O.K.?"

"Right." Stony slowly replaced the receiver. Albert briefly looked up, then returned his gaze to the TV.

Tommy came into the bedroom. "Hey, Stones? Who was that?" His hand on the doorknob.

Stony sat down next to Albert, leaning back against the bed. "Who was that? A friend from the Mount." Stony tried to concentrate on the Flintstones.

~

"Doctor Harris?"

Harris smiled when he saw Stony standing in the doorway. "C'mon in." He rose and shook Stony's hand. "Grab a seat." Stony pulled up a chair to Harris' desk. "So how's it goin' at home?" Harris filled a pipe and crossed his legs.

"O.K., I guess, uh, what did you wanna talk about?"

"Albert. I still don't know what the hell happened to him, although I have my suspicions." He sucked at his unlit pipe, watching Stony's face for a reaction.

Stony snorted. "I know what you mean. I think my old lady did some kinda number, but I don't know what. You hear what happened that night?"

"What night?"

"The night when Albert was brought in. I flipped and I punched her out."

"Your mother?"

"Yeah." Stony looked down at his shoes. "I clocked her pretty bad. I thought they were gonna put me inna room next to Albert after that."

"Hmph." Harris reached for the matches on the desk. "What do you think she did?"

"Who knows. She gets into these tirades aroun' him not eating.

I seen him wig out once or twice. Coulda been something like that."

Harris lit his pipe, sending up cherry-scented smoke signals. "Well, let me give you a little advice." Harris held his pipe close to his mouth. "Any time she starts in on him, you clock her again."

Stony sat up as if he had received a small shock.

"You heard me." Harris nodded. "If a big kid was tormenting Albert, you wouldn't hesitate to cold-deck him, right?"

"Yeah, but it's my mother!" Stony laughed incredulously.

"Yeah, but it's your brother!" Harris countered. "Look, let me be more blunt than that, if I can. The only thing that keeps your brother alive is you. Your mother's out to get him and your father could give two shits. Now, Albert knows that, not in so many words, but we all have that instinct for survival. You're more than a brother to him — you're a lifeline. Do you know what anorexia's all about? Terror. Pure, simple shit-eating terror. There's not a goddamn thing wrong with that kid physically. But that mother of yours has got him hopping and jumping so bad he just can't eat. Now look, I wanted him in some kind of therapy. I don't know what your opinion of shrinks is, and frankly I don't give a damn, but it really doesn't make a difference now anyway. Your mother wouldn't grant permission, so there's nothing I can do about it" — Harris laid down his pipe — "except talk to you. Now you can't be Albert's shrink, but you can be his protector. Now, I'm telling you that your mother's out to do him in, and I'm telling you to slug her any time she starts in on him." He chuckled. "And you're looking at me as if to say, 'This bearded bastard's a doctor?' Well you're goddamn right. I'm a doctor and what's more I'm a goddamn *good* doctor, and I'll bet you a round-trip ticket to the ends of the universe that after your little outburst last week it'll be a long, long time before your mother tries any stuff on Albert with you around. All I'm saying is, we have to get her to feel that way, even when you're *not* around. Even if she thinks *you might hear about it*, you follow?"

"I dunno, Doctor Harris, you're talkin' some crazy stuff." Stony started to sweat.

"Stony, do you have a black suit?"

"No, what for?"

"Well, I suggest you get one, because you're gonna need it sometime in the next two years."

"What the hell for?"

"Albert's funeral."

Stony sank down in the chair. His eyes began to itch. "You just said there's nothin' wrong with him." His voice cracked.

"There will be." Harris relit his pipe. "I wonder what happened to those Valiums I gave your mother for Albert?" he asked innocently.

"They probably got ditched," Stony muttered.

"By your mother?" Harris asked with mock incredulity.

Stony glared at him. "O.K., O.K., I'll be King Kong, awright?"

Harris laughed. "Look, any time she starts in on him, if you can give her half the look you're giving me now, that'll put her on ice for six months."

"Oh yeah? How come *you* ain't scared?"

Harris sucked on his pipe. "Because I can wrap your ass three times around a doorknob before you could ever figure out where the door is, but I *would* be scared if I couldn't."

"You're crazy." Stony laughed nervously.

"Who isn't?" Harris stood up. "Let's get some lunch."

~

"Nice day." Harris munched on a hot dog as he scanned the park. Stony sat next to him on a graffiti-scarred bench. "You jog?"

"Nah. I used to run when I was playin' ball." Stony yawned. "That was somethin' else. The whole team used to run together, forty guys in cleats around the reservoir. We sounded like a goddamn army," he snickered, "we scared the hell out of everybody."

"You don't play ball anymore?" Harris rolled his napkin in a ball and tossed it into a trash can.

"Nah, those days are over."

"Are you going to college?"

"I got in someplace in Louisiana, but I ain't goin'. You ever been down south?"

Harris smiled. "Once or twice."

"You go to school down there?"

Harris flash-imaged sit-ins, dogs, black faces, jail, sunglasses like mirrors. "In a manner of speaking." He picked a shred of sauerkraut that was dangling from his beard. "So if you're not going to college, what are you going to do?"

Stony shrugged. "I guess be an electrician with my old man."

"You don't sound too excited."

"Well, you know, the bread's good. What can I tell you?"

"You ever think of doing something else?"

"To be honest with you, I never given it much thought, except . . ." Stony leaned forward, elbows on knees. "I useta have this fantasy a workin' with kids. I dig kids. I get along with them. About four years ago I was a camp counselor. I really dug that. I had fifteen third-graders, yeah. I really had some heavy times. I'm a dynamite storyteller, you know?"

"So why don't you work with kids?"

"I dunno. You can't just work with kids all your life."

"Why not? I do."

"Yeah, but you're a doctor."

"If I wasn't a doctor I'd still want to work with kids, why not you?"

"I dunno, I can't do that. It's . . . I dunno."

"Do you want to be an electrician?"

"Well, I dunno." Stony grimaced. "Not really, I mean, I guess I could get into it." A gray-haired man in bermuda shorts and an orange beret zoomed by on a bicycle. "I mean, it's responsible work. I dunno what I'm talkin' about." Stony laughed apologetically. "Like I said, I never really thought about it either way. It's a living."

"How old are you, Stony?"

"Eighteen."

"You sound like you're forty-five."

"Is that good?"

"It's pathetic. If you feel like this now, how do you think you're going to feel twenty years from now, coming home for dinner, watching TV, going to sleep, going back to the construction site in the morning?"

Stony felt himself getting angry. "Hey, look, I stick with it twenny years I ain't gonna be runnin' around in a damn T-shirt. I'll be a goddamn foreman pullin' down forty-thou."

"I asked you how do you think you'll feel coming home, eating dinner, watching TV, going to sleep and starting all over the next day. How much juice do you think you'll be getting out of your life?"

"How the hell do I know?"

"I can make a phone call and get you a job as a recreation assistant at Cresthaven Hospital in the children's ward starting Monday."

"Hold it, hold it." Stony held his forehead. "Slow down."

"No. Give me a yes or a no." Harris draped his arms on the back of the bench.

"How much does it pay?"

"Peanuts. Yes or no?"

Stony laughed. Mad. Cornered. This guy was nuts. "Why not?"

Harris stood up. "Good. I'll make a call this afternoon." He smiled. "You have a good heart, Stony. That beats out forty thou, all the union benefits you can eat and a full house, aces high, but you have to play your hand."

Stony felt like he'd just done something bad, that he was going to get his ass kicked by somebody, that he just broke his mother's favorite lamp, but somewhere in the back of his head there was a nagging, irritating, terrifying, undeniable sense of excitement the likes of which he hadn't felt since the first time he got laid. "I'll give it a crack."

~

After work Tommy bopped into Banion's laughing his ass off. He spotted Chubby at a small table. Tommy waved to Banion and pulled up a chair. "Hey, Stony sent a letter to that school down south." He cracked his knuckles.

"He's goin'?"

Tommy laughed. "He found out the school is ninety-five percent nigger."

Chubby belly-laughed. "Tell Banion."

"I'll tell 'im later. Anyways, it's all set. I spoke to Frankie Finnegan. Stony can work with me over in Riverdale this summer an' in the fall he'll start apprentice classes out in Queens."

"Last I spoke to Stony he still wasn't too crazy about comin' in."

Tommy leaned back in his chair, hissing through his teeth. He stared at Chubby. "What else is he gonna do?"

"Look, I'm not arguing with you. I think he should go in too, but it would be nice if *he* thought he should go in, don't you think?"

"Ach . . ." Tommy stared off in disgust, then got up. "You want anything?"

"Scotch."

Tommy went over to the bar, joked around with some guys and returned with a drink in each hand.

"Some day he'll thank me." Tommy solemnly nodded and winked.

"I hope so," Chubby said.

"Oh lissen, I almost forgot." Tommy leaned over the table and whispered, "You got fifteen bucks?"

"You short?" Chubby reached for his wallet.

"Nah, nah, we found out tomorrow's Banion's birthday. A couple a guys are gonna go down and pick up a new wheelchair for him. We'll close the place tomorrow night and throw him a surprise party. You wanna chip in?"

Chubby thought for a moment. "Tom, I think I wanna get Banion my own present."

"It's on you." Tommy rose from the table. "I'm gonna go home, get some dinner. Come in tomorrow night about ten, O.K.?"

Chubby winked. After Tommy split, Chubby got up, yawned and sat at the bar. He studied Banion moving around, making drinks. "You know, Banion, I was thinkin', since las' week

when you was tellin' me about what happened with your kid,
I was thinkin' that maybe you should give him a call or somethin'."

Banion sipped a milk on the rocks, nervously drummed his
fingers on the armrest of his wheelchair.

"The reason I think that, Mikey, is because I think you really
love him, you know? I dunno, somethin' just tells me you do."
Banion finished the milk, shaking some ice from the glass into
his mouth.

"You know, I never met a parent who somewhere deep down
inside, in spite of all the crap and thunder, deep down inside who
wouldn't die for their kid." Chubby took out a pack of cigarettes,
offered one to Banion. Banion shook his head no. "It's like
cuttin' off your nose to spite your face what you're doin', and I'll
bet dollars to doughnuts he really wants to see you . . . you're his
goddamn father." Chubby lit his cigarette.

"I don't wanna talk about it," Banion said.

"Aw c'mon," Chubby persisted, "you mean to tell me you don't
care if you never see him again?" Banion wheeled away from
Chubby, served up some drinks at the other end of the bar.
"Banion, get the fuck back here."

"Hey look," Banion snapped across the room, "if you know
anything about anything you'll lay off me about that."

"I only meant — "

"I said you'll lay off."

"Hey c'mon, Mikey."

"You'll lay off."

Chubby opened his mouth to speak, but his words subsided in a
sigh. "O.K."

Banion wheeled back to Chubby's end of the bar. "Chubby,
how come you never had kids?"

"I dunno." Chubby shrugged. "I guess I was afraid they'd all
be fat and ugly like me."

"Cut the crap, Chubby, I'm asking you serious." Banion
poured himself another milk.

"I'll tell you something, I never felt like I needed a kid. I got
Stony, Tommy's boy. He's the best goddamn kid in the world. A

goddamn kid-and-a-half." Chubby popped his knuckles. "You know, when we talk, me an' Stony, when we talk we're just like two guys, like two buddies. None of this Uncle Chubby garbage. An' I'll tell you somethin' else, that goddamn kid loves my ass. Jus' between you and me, I think the kid digs me even more than he does Tommy, but don't ever tell Tommy that." Chubby laughed.

"How about your old lady? Is Stony like a son to her too?"

Chubby looked pained. "Sometimes."

"Whatta you mean sometimes?"

"I dunno, sometimes yeah, sometimes no, what the hell's the difference?"

"Whatta you gettin' so mad about, Chubby? I just wanna know how come you don't have kids."

"I *told* you goddamnit, Stony's — "

"But he *ain't* yours."

"Hey, look, what the fuck you want from me? You want me to say I can't have kids? You want me to say Phyllis can't have kids? Well I won't cause I can! Phyllis can! She gave me a goddamn *son*, the most beautiful fat baby boy in the whole fucking world . . ." Chubby stared at his drink, his face burning, his hands clasped in a bloodless knot of fingers. Banion started to say something, but Chubby cut him short. "He's dead and buried so goddamn long it seems like he was never here, like the whole thing was a dream."

Banion stared at Chubby's hands.

"Louis De Coco, Jr." Chubby smiled as he looked up at Banion. "He weighed in at thirteen pounds, four ounces. *Thirteen pounds and four ounces,* can you imagine that? The goddamn doctor said Louie was the biggest friggin' baby he ever delivered." Chubby laughed. "Everybody came over the house, you know, when Louie and Phyllis came back from the hospital. I used to love to watch their eyes pop when they got their first look-see." Chubby bulged his eyes and shook his head in reverie. "That seems like a million years ago. A goddamn different world. I weighed seventy-five pounds less, and Phyll weighed thirty pounds more."

"What happened, Chubby?" Banion asked softly.

"What happened," Chubby repeated. He rubbed his eyes. "Two weeks after they came home from the hospital I'm working for Delta Electric on this housing project that was going up at that time; I'm puttin' in navigation lights on some buildings, you know, just pullin' cable all fuckin' day. We were livin' over by Yankee Stadium then. I come home that day, I remember it was a really crazy cold day for April. First thing I notice I don't smell no dinner or nothin'. I figure, well, maybe she's busy with Louie so I call out, 'Phyll? Hey, Phyll?' No answer, nothin', an' I figure now that's weird . . . I know she don't go out and leave the kid or anything. So I walk into the bedroom." Chubby ran his finger around the rim of his glass. "I walk into the bedroom, and it's almost dark. Phyllis sitting up in bed with Louie in her arms, neither of them is movin'. I can't see so good so I go to turn on the lamp, and Phyllis says, *'Don't!'* . . . She don't even look at me, she just says, *'Don't!'* like really sharp. I felt scared shit when she said that. I don't know why I did it but I reach over and touch Louie's face. His face is cold, really cold . . . an' the room is hot. The steam's hissing from the radiator, and the pipes are clanking like crazy. An' his face . . . I could almost feel the color blue through my fingers when I touched his face. After that I felt like I was sleepwalking. I never turned the lights on. I fished around the room until I found a newspaper. I took Louie out of Phyll's arms, an' I wrapped him head to toe in that paper. I walked right out of the apartment with him in my arms, down the stairs, into the street, got into my car, laid him next to me on the seat, drove over to Ciccio Funeral Home, walked into the director's office, laid him down on the guy's desk, emptied out my wallet — thirty-two dollars — dumped *that* on his desk and said, 'Bury him.' Then I got into my car, drove home, got undressed, got in bed with Phyllis and cried my heart out."

Chubby sighed. "I dunno. That night the cops came, doctors came, relatives came, it was like a fucking nightmare. It was unreal, like I was underwater or something, an' poor Phyllis. What had happened was that she was laying in bed with Louie, fell asleep and rolled over on him. He suffocated. When she woke

up he was dead. That happens from time to time. I dunno, I
don't blame her, she feels punished enough, you know?"

Banion poured him a Scotch.

"Ach, it ain't worth moanin' about." He accepted the drink
from Banion with a nod. "That night was the last time I ever
cried. I felt like that kid just sucked up all the hurt and heartache
I was ever gonna let myself feel. The doctor said we should have
another baby right away. I just said no day, no way. No more
hurt. The next year Stony was born. I said to myself, 'I'll love my
brother's kid, I'll treat him like I would've Louie, I'll play with
him, I'll be the best goddamn uncle a nephew could have.' Uncle,
not father, nephew, not son. And that's the way I want it. I got
no room for nothin' else." Then Chubby added as a postscript,
"You know, one thing I remember from that night just like it was
yesterday, an' I don't know why this should stick in my head of all
the fuckin' shit from that night, but I remember the sports
headlines on one of the papers that I wrapped Louie in. 'Mays
Grand-Slams Spahn, 4–3,' New York *Mirror*, April tenth, nineteen
fifty-six." Chubby hunched over the bar, cradling his drink in
both hands. "You know, I always was a Giants fan, even when
they moved to San Francisco, but I never *did* like that black
bastard."

~

"Albert, eat your string beans." Marie glared at him.

Albert hastily jammed two forkfuls in his mouth.

Stony lunged across the table in Marie's direction. Marie
gasped, almost tipping her chair backward. Stony grabbed the
salt by her plate and fell back into his seat, lightly salting his roast
beef.

The blood drained from Marie's face. Stony busied himself
with his food.

Tommy frowned. "What the hell's goin' on here?"

"Whatta you mean?" Stony looked at his father, fighting down
a slight smile forming at the corners of his mouth.

~

"Hey, Stones?" Tommy popped his head into Stony's bedroom after dinner. Stony was doing James Brown splits in front of the closet door mirror. He jumped when he heard his father's voice.

"Yeah?" He quickly picked up a comb and, blushing, started doing his hair. Tommy sat on Stony's bed, squinting, a cigarette hanging from the corner of his mouth.

"I got some good news, babe, I swung it so you can work up in Riverdale with me."

Stony sighed, pocketed his comb and swung the closet door closed.

"Hey, don't go droolin' all over me with gratitude. A simple thanks is enough, you know?" Tommy leaned his elbows on his knees.

Stony balanced against his desk, arms folded across his chest. He stared at his father's shoes. "Hey, Pop? I thought we went through this deal awready. I don' wanna do construction this summer."

"So whattaya gonna do, drive around Harlem in a Good Humor truck again?" Tommy walked over to the window and flicked the butt into a spin fifteen stories to the street.

"It was Carvel," Stony said.

"Oh, excuse me." Tommy returned to the bed, lying back on the pillow.

"Hey look, I jus' don' wanna do construction, O.K.?" Stony twiddled a pencil between his fingers in a seesaw motion.

Father and son glared at each other across the room. Tommy suddenly bolted from the bed and headed for Stony. Scared, Stony sidestepped to the closet. Tommy charged past him to the desk and began pulling out drawers and rifling through the crap until he found a blank piece of loose-leaf paper. With his other hand he picked up a chair and banged it down in front of the desk. *"Siddown,"* he barked at Stony.

Stony hesitated for a second, then cautiously sat, Tommy towering over him. Tommy slapped the sheet of paper. "Gimme that pencil." Tommy grabbed it from Stony's fingers, leaned over the desk and numbered the paper. "Here." He jammed the pencil into Stony's hand and closed Stony's fingers around it. "Now, I want you to write me three things you wanna be."

Stony held the pencil upside down and stared puzzled at Tommy.

"G'head. Write!"

"What?"

"Write down three things you wanna do witcha life."

Stony bent slowly over the paper, frowning like he was doing a surprise quiz.

"You got two minutes." Tommy stood over him, arms folded across his chest like a proctor.

Stony turned and twisted his head, looking up at Tommy. "You wanna get outta my light?"

Tommy walked out of the bedroom. "You got two minutes." Stony heard the bathroom door lock and a second later a glissando of piss. He stood up and gave the bedroom door crossed forearms before plopping back down to his task. He stared out the window and chewed his pencil. He held his head in his hands. He drew a big prick and labeled it, "Thomas De Coco, Sr." He bit off half the eraser and spit it out the window. He wrote down, "Work with kids." He picked his nose with his pinky, examined it and wiped his finger on the underside of the desk.

"You got one minute," Tommy warned from the doorway, lighting another cigarette.

Stony jumped up and saluted, "Sieg Heil!"

"Faggot fascist hard hat" was number two. He eliminated the prick and Tommy's name with what was left of the eraser. He stared at the paper, the number three, noticed an old James Brown album, "Mister Dynamite," lying under the TV, chuckled and wrote, "Mister Dynamite."

Tommy grabbed the paper from Stony's hands. "Whadda you, a smart-ass or somethin'?"

Stony smiled meekly, a fuck you in his eyes.

"You wanna be a nursery school teacher and you're callin' *me* a faggot?"

"Who wants to be a nursery school teacher?"

Tommy picked up the paper and read out loud: "Work with kids." He dropped the paper. It floated into Stony's lap.

"So?" Stony tossed the paper on the desk.

"So what's that mean? Kindergarten? 'Romper Room'? Milk and cookies? Whatta they gonna call you, Miss De Coco?"

"No! I can get a gig in a hospital workin' with kids. A friend a mine got me a deal if I want at Cresthaven."

"A hospital! Ugh! That's the pits! What'll they pay ya? A hundred?"

"I dunno, what's the difference!" Stony glared.

"The difference is, you come with me you be makin' more bread in two weeks than you'll make candy stripin' for two months."

"I ain't *candy* stripin'. I'll be a goddamn recreational assistant."

"What makes you think you can handle hospital work? I seen you go green at a nosebleed." Tommy lit another cigarette.

"I ain't doin' brain surgery, I'm just playin' with the kids."

"Ah, grow up, Stony. That's woman's work."

"Oh yeah, right, sorry, you're right. I should be runnin' aroun' in my T-shirt with a screwdriver and a red hat on. Yeah, then I'd be a real man. Right, sure!"

"Hey look!" Tommy pointed a finger an inch from Stony's nose. "I can still kick your ass all over this fuckin' room!"

Stony's face was composed. "I don't suggest you try it." His legs were trembling, but he wouldn't crack.

Tommy stood motionless, red-faced, his finger like a gun in Stony's face. Stony tried not to even blink. Tommy flung his cigarette toward the open window and stalked out of the room. The cigarette hit the window in a splash of embers and lay smoking on the windowsill. Stony flicked the cigarette out the window. "Candy-ass," he muttered, not too loud, and collapsed in his seat. He sat there, not moving, until Tommy came back into the room.

"Hey lissen." He tentatively laid a hand on Stony's shoulder. "I'm sorry. You do what you want this summer. You wanna be a candy striper or whatever, it's on you. It's none a my business." No reaction from Stony. "But if you want my opinion, you're a jerk if you don't go into the union."

Stony sighed, shaking his head sadly.

"O.K., look." Tommy sat on the desk. "I'll make a deal with you. You wanna do hospital work? Fine! Do two weeks hospital, then do two weeks with me, you know, like a test." Stony started to protest, but Tommy cut him short with a raised hand. "You do those two weeks with me, after that you can clean sewers for all I care." Stony walked around the room, his hands in his pockets.

"Stony, God as my witness." Tommy stood, one hand on his heart, one hand raised palm toward Stony like a saint. "God as my witness, Stones, gimme those two weeks and I won't say another word about nothin' until I'm dead. I swear."

"Awright, awright." Stony threw in the towel.

Tommy put an arm around Stony's ribs. "Stony, I'm your *father*. I don't want *nothin'* but the *best* for you." On every other word he squeezed Stony's side like an accordion. Stony felt relieved that Tommy had backed down from kicking his ass. "Do the hospital first so you can compare, but just do yourself a favor and lissen to yer old man."

Stony nodded. Fair enough.

"Oh, an lissen" — Tommy threw over his shoulder on his way out — "forget the Mister Dynamite number. Demolition's good bucks but someday you'll wind up wit' your ass blown halfway to China."

11

CHUBBY TOOK OFF from work at noon the next day. He told the contractor he felt sick, but instead of going home he headed for midtown Manhattan. He had special shopping to do. Chubby stood on the periphery of a gaggle of smartly dressed women surrounding a young man demonstrating a juicerator in the kitchenwares section of Bloomingdale's. The man made juice from celery, carrots, radishes and spinach. For the entire twenty-minute show, Chubby never took his eyes from the demonstrator's face. The man passed out small, clear plastic cups of the exotic juices among his audience. Amid the oohs, ahs, hmms and sounds of disgust, Chubby was silent, tasting none of the samples. And after the man quoted the price of the juicerator, Chubby stood alone in front of the demonstration table. He took out his wallet and laid down five twenties. "Can you gift-wrap that thing?"

"Yes, sir. Ah, you pay the cashier." He wore an immaculate white three-piece suit, a purple shirt and a white tie.

He even dresses like a faggot Chubby thought. "I'm buyin' this for a friend a mine," Chubby said. "His birthday's today." He watched the man's face for any reaction. "A very good friend of mine named Mikey."

The man flinched, stared at Chubby. "I'll bring it over to the cashier for you." He bent down under the counter for a boxed juicerator.

"Mikey Banion."

Slowly, the man stood up. The color drained from his face. "Who the hell are you?" He was three inches taller than Chubby and leaned forward, his palms flat on the table. Chubby resisted an impulse to grab him by the knot of his tie and yank him over the counter.

"I'm a good friend a yah father's, Paulie."

Paulie stared open-mouthed. "He send you here?"

"Uh-uh, he don't know nothin' about it. Today's his birthday, Paulie. You know what would make a nice present for him? You."

Paulie blew air out of his mouth, his head cocked to the side, a dazed expression in his eyes. "Lissen, Jack, I don't know who the fuck you are, what's the story with you an' my father, or how the hell you found me, but just buy your goddamn juicerator and get the hell outta here, O.K.?" The color came back to his face in mottled splashes. "Jim, you want to take care of this gentleman?" He started to turn away.

Chubby grabbed his tie. "Lissen a me, ya little snot, I don't give a flyin' fuck about you or ya fuckin' job. I'll fuckin' drag you outta here an' throw you at your goddamn father's feet you turn away from me while I'm talkin' to you. You got that?"

Both men were shaking.

"You don't let go of me right now I'll have your ass bounced outta here in two seconds flat," he whispered.

"An' you'll be on disability in three."

They stared at each other, neither blinking for a long moment. Chubby relaxed his grip. Paulie stood up, twisted his neck and straightened his tie. Chubby smoothed down his shirt. "Lissen, kid, I'm sorry. I'm excitable sometimes. I apologize." Chubby raised his hands in submission, then extended one. "My name is Chubby."

Paulie greeted the extended hand with a boxed juicerator. "Please pay the cashier."

"Paulie . . ." Chubby reached into his back pocket and pulled out a birthday card. "Look, forget comin' home." He placed the card on the demonstration counter. "Just sign this card."

Paulie glanced down.

> As you get older, year by year
> My love for you grows, father dear

And on this day that your life had begun
Accept this gift of love from me, your son.

"Get out of here!" His eyes bulged, his voice a strangled whisper.

Chubby whipped out his wallet and slid two twenties under Paulie's hand. "Just sign it. I swear to Christ you'll never see me again!" Chubby felt like his guts were being kneaded by brutal hands.

Paulie stepped out of Chubby's reach. The unsigned card and the two twenties lay like a cryptic still life on the counter. "Jim, you want to take care of this gentleman?"

Chubby left slowly, feeling every ounce of his three hundred pounds weighing him down.

"Hey, Chubby," Paulie drawled. Chubby turned. "You see my old man, you tell him he's a grandfather."

~

"Hey! Hey! Whatta you doin'?" Banion shouted, craning his neck over the bar as one of the regulars hung the "closed" sign and locked the door.

"HAP-PY BUR-THDAYY TOO YOOO," twenty-five guys started singing. Someone hit the lights and Tommy and Ray Buckley emerged from the back room carrying an enormous birthday cake lit with forty-seven candles. Banion sat speechless in the flickering shadows. They placed the cake on the counter and everybody crowded around the bar.

"Blow 'em out!"

It took Banion four long puffs to get all the candles. Shouts and cheers. Somebody turned the lights back on. Somebody opened the john door and Big Dave Stern came whirring out in a brand-new, fully motorized, thickly upholstered, snakeskin wheelchair. He whirred right up the platform and parked next to Banion, whose eyes were popping out of his head. Dave got out of the wheelchair and with Chubby's help lifted Banion into his birthday present. Banion was in shock. All he could do was sit there stroking the material on the seat and armrests.

"Hey, Banion! Banion! Feel under the seat! Hey, Banion!"
Banion finally looked up. His face was smeared with tears.

"Feel under the seat!"

Banion poked around under the seat and found a snub-nosed
.38 with "THE BOUNCER" neatly printed in white on the barrel.
Everybody cheered again. Banion let the gun lay on the flat of his
palm.

"Hey, watch it. It's loaded!"

"There's a holster sewn on down there."

"Yeah. Don't fart. You'll get shot in the ass!"

Everybody laughed.

Banion felt for the holster and replaced the gun. He sat with his
elbows on the armrests, his hands covering his face.

"Banion, ah, you think we might get a drink on the house?"

"You fuckin' guys." He wiped away his tears as Tommy and
Chubby moved behind the bar and started serving drinks. He
shook his head and laughed. "You fuckin' guys."

12

AFTER A DRAG-ASS WEEK and weekend made even more drag-ass by Stony's hunger to get started at the hospital, Monday came as a total shock. His first day at work was like nothing he expected, and by the end of the day he was completely blown out the back door. Devastated. That night it took all his strength to drag himself downstairs into Butler's waiting car.

"You wanna do D'Artagnan's?"

"Nah." Stony picked his teeth with his thumbnail, occasionally examining whatever stuck between flesh and nail.

"Camelot?" Butler moved out on the street, leisurely following the curving road dwarfed by the gigantic high rises of Co-op City.

"Nah, you wanna do some clams?"

"City Island?" Butler suggested.

"Yeah."

Butler floored the accelerator and tore ass onto the Hutchinson River Parkway. "How'd it go today?"

"The pits, Butler. Fuckin' blue Monday the likes of which I never seen. They got no jobs in the children's ward, so they gave me a gig in geriatrics."

"What the fuck is that?"

"Old people, *very* old people. The fuckin' joint is like the Greyhound terminal for death. An' all these scuzzies is waitin' with their bags packed."

"Whyncha quit? You can do construction work witcher ol' man."

Stony sighed. "I'll stick it out. There might be an openin' in the children's ward next week. If I split now I can't get nothin'."

"So whadya do there?" Butler readjusted his rearview mirror.

"I'm a lifter. I lift people outta beds, into wheelchairs, outta wheelchairs, onta toilets, outta toilets, into whirlpool baths, outta whirlpool baths, back into wheelchairs, outta wheelchairs an' into beds."

"Hey, that sounds all right." Butler turned off the Parkway and drove across the bay bridge onto the mile-long strip of seafood joints and marinas of City Island. "Lobster Box?"

Stony nodded in agreement. They drove slowly along City Island Avenue. The streets were packed with Puerto Ricans. "Geriatrics, hey?" Butler parked the car in front of a bayview restaurant.

"I tell you somethin' though, Butler, the worst thing about that fuckin' place is all the help, all the nurses an' aides an' orderlies. They're all West Indians, man, an' you know I ain't a prejudiced dude, but I hate the fuckin' Bimis with a passion." They sat at a small red-and-white-checked table overlooking Long Island Sound and a parking lot. Butler lit his cigarette from the flame of the candle on their table.

"Whatta you havin', boys?" A white-uniformed, middle-aged waitress in harlequin glasses stood over them, order pad in hand.

"Dozen cherrystones and a Seven-up."

"We got Sprite, orange and root beer."

"A Sprite."

She nodded to Stony.

"Ah, gimme some steamers and a Coke."

"Sprite, orange or root beer."

"Some water with a lot of ice." Stony watched her walk away. "You know what I mean about West Indians? They're the fuckin' angriest, meanest, snottiest people goin'."

"How 'bout Reggie Powell?" Butler leaned back in his chair, tilting it on two legs.

"He's all right." Stony thanked the waitress as she brought over the water. "So they all suck except Reggie."

"Chili Mac's West Indian."

"Get the fuck outta here!" Stony looked shocked.

"I met his old man once. He sounds like Harry Belafonte."

"You're kiddin'!" Stony frowned and gulped down half his

glass of water. The waitress brought the clams and steamers. They dug in. "I'll tell you what it is with them. Jamaica's a very heavy-duty place, very poor, especially Kingston. There's a lotta rough numbers goin' down there, some very bad scenes. Everybody's poor as a nigger, that whole colonial riff. They got these dudes, Rudies they call them; bad-ass lots, farm boys that came down to the big city, got stiffed and just hang around rippin' everybody off, an' they got these other dudes called the Rastafaries — you ever see them with those big rug heads? They walk aroun' with machetes tellin' everybody that Haile Selassie's God. They got a lot of these bad boys out in Brooklyn, that whole reggae number. I'll tell you something, the only good thing comin' out of Jamaica's grass." Stony methodically dunked the snout-shaped steamers in a bowl of clam broth and popped them in his mouth.

Butler sat silent except for the slurping noises he made sucking his clams from their shells.

"You know, and they come up here, an' some of them get into a bougie trip, X-ray technicians, registered nurses, white-collar office jobs, go uptown and see Rev Ike every Sunday. You know, money is honey and all that, and they *hate* niggers, New York niggers, street people. They're into this whole high yellow attitude, you know? An' they're closer to Africans than any cat you'll see on Lenox Avenue, but maybe it's that thing of comin' from an English colony. They think they're Limeys. An' when they got jobs in hospitals, uh! Fo-geet a-baht it! *Brutal* motherfuckers, not physically, at least not what I seen, but mentally, they got no respect for human dignity. They talk to these old people like they're six years old. Throw 'em around like sacks a rice. You know, an eighty-year-old dude who's paralyzed takes a dump in bed the fuckin' nurse comes in. 'Oh, Meestah Cohen, you a bod boy, now I got to clean you op.' But like really loud, you know?" Stony winced. "An' I look into this guy's eyes, right? The guy has a Ph.D., spent fifty years teachin' in some college somewhere. He wrote three books." Stony pushed his empty plate away, crossed his legs and lit a cigarette. "It's tragic, Butler. No sense of dignity, ach!" He bit his lower lip. "I gotta get the fuck outta there. You know what this fuckin' guy says to me? The guy's *forty-six* years old. He got Parkinson's disease, paralyzed from his eyebrows down. A goddamn courtroom *lawyer,* Butler. I come into his room, ask him if he needs to go, he mumbles, 'No,' so I says, 'Is there anything I can get for you?' Forty-six-years-old, Butler, a *vegetable,* but I can see his brain is cookin', right? He mumbles somethin'. I can't heàr, so I says, 'What?' An' he mumbles it again, still can't hear him, so I put my ear to his mouth. You know what he says? He says, 'Can you get me justice?' "

"Oh shit." Butler motioned for the waitress. "You got cheese-cake?" He turned to Stony. "You want cheesecake?" Stony motioned no. "One piece. You want coffee? Two coffees."

"An' I only worked a half day today. They gave us a four-hour training session this morning that was like somethin' out of "The Twilight Zone." We had to sit in this little classroom that had a dummy in a hospital bed instead of a desk. This nurse came in and showed us how to lift the dummy out of bed, how to put it in a wheelchair. Oh yeah, there was this toilet bowl in the corner of the room an' she showed us how to put the dummy on the pot. It was in-fuckin'-credible. The dummy's name was Mister Ruben-stein, an' she was talkin' to the dummy in this Bimi singsong like, 'Now, Mees-tah Roo-bon-steen, eet ees time to go to de bath-room.' I swear she wasn't playin' with a full deck, you know? An' everybody was so fuckin' serious, except this spade cat sittin' next to me, MacDonald." Stony paused as the waitress brought the coffees and cheesecake. "This spade MacDonald, he was laughin' his ass off an' this nurse kept stoppin' an' sayin', 'Thees ees see-re-os beez-noss, Mees-tah Mac-Do-nold,' an' he would straighten out for a minute but when she showed us how to wipe the dummy's ass MacDonald totally fell apart. He lets out with a 'Shee-it, I ain't wipin' *no*body's ass.' We all fell on the fuckin' floor." Stony pinched his face and put his hands on his hips. " 'Mees-tah Mac-Do-nold, pre-haps you weel dee-mon-strate to os all every-ting I been sayin.' MacDonald's sprawlin' all over his seat like this." Stony slouched in his chair, slowly turning his head from side to side, his eyes half-closed and a lazy half grin on his face. "And this cat's wearin' dark blue shades and he's bald, right? The Isaac Hayes number, O.K.? He looks more like a dude that would put people *in* the hospital than help 'em out. MacDonald looks aroun' at everybody an' then he gets up. This fuckin' cat musta been eight feet tall, an' the nurse puts the dummy back in the bed an' she says, 'Mees-tah Mac-Do-nold, take Mees-tah Roo-ben-steen to de bathroom.' MacDonald bops over to the bed and throws back the covers and she yells out, 'Gently! an' tok to heem!' MacDonald does one of these numbers." Stony turns his head to show a hard smirk. "He stares at her for about thirty seconds, an' he turns back to the dummy in the bed an' he says, 'Hey! Mah man Rubenstein! You-all gotta take a dump?' An' this dummy's all dressed up in pajamas, right? He grabs the front of the dummy's pajama top wit' one hand an' he just drops him in the wheelchair. I'll bet he's the only cat who can do the Memphis Glide while pushin' a wheelchair." Stony jumped up and pretended he was pushing a wheelchair, walking with a dip and bop shuffle around the small table. "The nurse is havin' a shit fit, man, she is beyond words. MacDonald takes the fuckin' dummy wit' two hands, raises it over his head an' *throws* the dummy down on the pot. The head falls off, one of the arms falls off. I almost had a heart attack from laughin'. The nurse is screamin' her ass off, an' MacDonald just looks at her an' says, 'Aww, stuff it, bitch! Ah quit!' An' he bops outta the room like he just finished shootin' hoops. The fuckin' room, everybody's dyin'. The hip people are on the floor. The straight an' narrows are havin' the horrors like *they* need the wheelchair. The nurse, Mrs. Churchill, *that* was her name, Mrs. Churchill, she's chasin' after the dummy's head which was rollin' all over the room. The rest of the dummy fell on the floor. Excedrin headache number two-o-two, you know?"

Stony finished his coffee. "Just remember, Butler, no matter whatever else you forget in your life, always remember that when you're wipin' an old guy's ass, always do it *gently* and make sure the strokes are all upwards towards the spine. You got that?"

Butler belched into his napkin.

"This afternoon, they assigned us one-on-one to lifters who've been there a while, so they could show us the ropes, right? I got assigned to this guy Reynard, a very hip spic about twenny, twenny-one. The cat's goin' to hairdresser school on the sly. I tell him what happened in the classroom. He cracked up. He says to me, 'Churchill's the meanest fuck in the whole place.' He takes me down to the locker room. There's nobody around. He opens his locker and whips some bad shit on me, we split a big jay sittin' on this bench. He says, 'This'll make it easier,' then he takes me up to geriatrics. I got a mean buzz on. We're walkin' through the halls in baggy whites, all these people in wheelchairs or staggerin' aroun' in their bathrobes. I realize right away gettin' stoned was a big mistake. I'm comin' down with a bad case of the horrors. I start trippin' out on death, an' what's it all mean, an' I'm gonna do myself in before I get on this stage, an' I'm really fuckin' scared, Butler. See, Reynard, he's been there two years, so like he's immune, you know? He can function like he's at an office somewheres an' I don't wanna tell him what I'm feelin', right? Anyways, he takes me into this long room with maybe twenty beds. All I hear is moans and gags an' screamin'. There probably ain't one guy in this room who got six months to live, all old, old." Stony rubbed his nose with the heel of his palm. "An' I'm blitzed outta my skull, right? I don't wanna look right or left, up or down, I just look straight ahead at the far wall, an' all these guys are yellin' out, 'Hiya, Reynard, hiya, Reynard,' but like babies, you know? So I'm just walkin' with my eyes straight ahead, an' all of a sudden I trip over somethin' an' almost break my ass. I look down, an' I swear, Butler, I scream like a cunt. There's this fuckin' *leg* layin' in the middle of the floor. Reynard laughs an' he picks it up. It's an artificial leg. He puts it next to this guy's nightstand an' he says, 'Be cool, baby.' I just flipped. I said, 'Reynard, I gotta get outta here.' He says, 'Don't sweat it. You'll get used to it,' and then he tells me the first day he was workin' there he got so sick he puked all over this old guy's head. Then he asks me if I want more grass."

Stony raised his eyebrows. The waitress dropped a bill face up on the table. "More grass I need like a third nut, you know? So Reynard takes me into these private rooms down another wing, the rich vegetables' ward. He introduces me to all these guys, runs down their schedules with the john, the showers, physical therapy, occupational therapy, the whole shtick. Half these guys looked like they needed gardeners instead of doctors. He's tellin' me some of the life stories of these cats when we're outside the rooms. One guy was the head of the psychology department at Yeshiva University, that guy I was tellin' you about before with the sixty-two Ph.D.s. Another guy played baseball with the New York Highlanders, that was the Yankees before they was the Yankees. This guy, forget about it. He looked like a scrotum. He was all wrinkled and scrunched up." Stony screwed up his face as he talked. "He had these old team pictures all over the room, baseball players with handlebar 'staches an' striped beanies. I swear, Butler, I don't know what I'd do if that was me. If I was a fuckin' professional athlete reduced to that. I didn't wanna ask which one a those guys in the pictures was him because I didn't think I could take it. Another guy's that lawyer I was tellin' you about — 'Gimme justice' — you know, I'm lookin' at these guys an' I can see how you really gotta keep it in your head that there's a *mind* workin' in all that busted machinery there, you know? I really can understand how somebody workin' in a hospital for a few years can blank on that, but you look into those eyes, the whole fuckin' story's in those eyes, man. They are real fuckin' people, man, an' they are in fuckin' *agony*, an' those fuckin' spics and Bimis come there, man, an' they're treatin' 'em like potted plants or like infants with brains like BBs, an' those eyes are screamin', man, they're screamin' *I AM*. I'm a doctor. I'm a lawyer. I'm a fucker. I'm a baseball player. I'm a *goddamn human being*, an' all they get is 'Oh Mees-tah Roo-bon-steen, you make in you bed a-gain, you bod, bod boy.' It makes you wanna vomit, Butler, it makes you wanna vomit."

"That's the way it goes." Butler eased himself away from the table.

"Butler, if I ever got like that, and I asked you to check me out, would you do me the solid?"

"If I had the strength, I'd probably be suckin' wind myself by then."

13

TUESDAY, 8:00 A.M. Stony sat on the narrow locker bench scraping crud from the corners of his eyes. He had half changed into his hospital whites. The other orderlies were dressing, drinking from hip flasks of Old Mr. Boston apricot brandy and bullshitting around in general.

"Hey." Reynard discarded his wet-look vinyl jacket and opened his locker next to Stony's. "We late, man, we only got time fo' some quick tokes." He removed a white Baggie from his locker.

"Uh. No way." Stony shielded himself from the dope. "I almost jumped out the window yesterday."

Reynard lit a joint, took three long wet sucks, ground out the burning end and put the roach back in the Baggie. "You on you own today, baby." Reynard struggled out of his street clothes. "But you need some help, give me a yell."

They punched their time cards under the gridded wall clock and walked through the beige, glazed-tile corridor past a vast stainless steel kitchen and scattered stainless steel food carts toward the elevator. Reynard slapped five to every other guy they passed, shouting and laughing, taking his ease. Stony knew Reynard would never become a hairdresser.

"Mr. Plotkin?" Stony braced himself as he walked into the pale green room.

A small, hairless, toothless, blind man sat on the bed, smiled beatifically as if touched by the voice of God. "Yas?"

Stony could see his eyeballs moving under his shut lids, his wide gum-grin stretched from ear to ear. His white gown was too big for him and hung off one skeletal shoulder in a parody of a 1945 movie goddess. Stony clenched his teeth. "Enjoy your breakfast?"

"Yas I did. Who iss dis I yam talkink to?" As if he was on the phone. He kept smiling nervously, jerking his head in the direction of Stony's voice.

"I'm the new lifter."

"Vere is Rey*nard?*"

"He's around, I'm helpin' him out." Stony moved the wheelchair into position, locking it with his foot. "I'm gonna take you to the john now."

"O.K." In a singsong.

Stony cringed for a moment before slipping his arms under Mr. Plotkin's armpits. He was surprisingly light. When Stony lifted him high enough and the blanket slipped away, he saw why. Plotkin was legless. Stony gasped. Plotkin laughed. Stony held him at arm's length, afraid of the smooth stumps. He deposited him in the wheelchair, replaced the blanket, unlocked the catch and wheeled him down to the huge white tile and stainless steel bathroom. He dumped him on the pot and stood there while Plotkin grunted, plopped and farted for ten minutes, smiling all the while. Stony unwound a wad of toilet paper consuming half the roll, lifted Plotkin with one hand across his chest and wiped his ass, his head behind Plotkin's back, almost in the bowl. Stony held his breath the whole time. His eyes were screwed shut. But somehow he still managed to get a lungful and an eyeful in the scant ten seconds the whole operation took.

"Misteh leefteh, you ah colid boy?"

"Nope. I'm Italian." Stony wiped the cold sweat from his face. He was chilled with disgust.

"You are vhite boy? Vhat you do dis for?" Then he whispered, "Dis a chob for der niggers."

~

"Come in here, please." The black nurse beckoned to Stony in the hallway. Stony's heart sank. It was ten-thirty. Hour and a half until lunch. Ten ass-wipes to go. "Meestah Beckahmon vomited all over heself," she said, ushering him into the room. "Please clean him op. I have to go get sheets and a gown. I be back in five minutes."

Stony stared at a cadaver rigid in his bed. An oatmeal-textured catastrophe lay on his chin, chest and blanket. His eyes burned into Stony like a black fire. "Hey look, that's an orderly's job. I'm a lifter." Stony pointed to the name-and-job tag on his breast pocket.

"Meestah De Coco, ah don care what you are. You work in de hospital, you got to do all jobs."

"Oh yeah? When do I get to hire an' fire nurses?"

She glared at him for a second, then marched out of the room. Behind him in the room came a high-pitched cackle. Stony wheeled around.

"Das sweet!" A short, thirtyish Puerto Rican in a gray custodian's outfit was mopping the floor, a galvanized steel bucket with a wringer attachment at his feet. "Dat bitch sometin' else!" He slapped the mop around, making semicircles on the already immaculate floor.

Stony grimaced as he approached Mr. Beckerman. A stainless steel bowl half filled with an antiseptic-smelling green bubbly solution lay on the radiator. A small yellow sponge floated on top like a dead fish. Stony took the bowl over to the bed, squeezed out the sponge and took two half swipes at Mr. Beckerman's face. He avoided looking into his eyes. The stench made him tear. He dropped the sponge into the bowl, splashing the bed. "Shit!"

"Aw, fuck dat chump!" The custodian winked.

"I can't swing it, Jack." Stony slapped his thighs in exasperation. Mr. Beckerman blinked.

"Hey!" The custodian tapped Stony on the shoulder. "Look." He placed the bowl on the floor next to his bucket. "Take off his shirt, man." As Stony gingerly removed Beckerman's pajama top, the custodian wrung out his mop, splashed it in the steel bowl and then proceeded to swab down Beckerman's face and chest. He wrung out the mop, dunked it into the remainder of the soapy solution and gave him a second coat. Beckerman's eyes were blazing with outrage. Stony was caught halfway between laughing and crying. "Das all dere is to it, man." He wrung out his mop again, flung it over his shoulder, stooped, picked up his bucket and left the room. Stony grabbed a towel off the radiator, patted Beckerman's dripping face and chest. He wouldn't look into Beckerman's eyes on a bet. When he finished he tore ass out of the room.

~

"Lifter!" Resisting the temptation to duck into the john, Stony walked into the room. A young nurse leaned over another stiff, naked this time, who looked like Beckerman's twin. "Lifter, I need some help here. Mr. Garro had a little accident. Can you just lift him a sec so I can pull the sheets out?" As Stony headed to the bed someone behind him clawed his sleeve. Stony jumped. The old woman was about four-foot-six. Her hospital gown hung down, revealing withered breasts the size and shape of Santa Clara prunes — Stony looked. Her face had more cracks and crevasses than the Grand Canyon. She was almost bald — the scattered wisps of white hair on her scalp reminded Stony of an empty cotton candy machine before it's cleaned. She squeezed his arm with an anguished urgency. "Be careful."

"Mrs. Garro!" The nurse charged around the bed. "I *told* you not to hinder the help!" She gently pushed the doddering old lady into a second bed. "Just lift him real quick." She hustled over to Mr. Garro. As Stony lifted him from behind he noticed the old guy had gigantic balls. The nurse pulled out the sheet like a magician yanking a tablecloth without disturbing the dishes. There was a four-by-four shiny black oilcloth underneath. "O.K., drop him." Stony did and stepped back. This was a his and hers private room. Between the twin beds on a night table stood an eight-by-ten gilt-framed photo of Mr. and Mrs. Garro sitting in a restaurant. They were both laughing, he had his arm around her shoulder. They wore leis around their necks, his over a loud pineapple shirt, hers over an aqua blue sleeveless dress. The inscription read "Tommy and Marie — Oahu Hilton 3/2/62."

Stony backed out of the room as Mrs. Garro struggled out of bed and fluttered around her naked husband like a bird with buckshot in its wing.

~

Stony wheeled an old guy named Valentine Valentino to the john. As he lifted him out of the chair, he slipped through Stony's fingers, bounced off the toilet seat and fell on his side, his pajamas wrapped around his ankles, his flaccid skin pressed against the cold tile. Stony gasped, grasping him under the arms to lift him onto the seat, hoping nothing broke.

Reynard wheeled a patient wearing a Yankees cap into the john. Stony and Valentine were holding each other face to face, knee to knee, in a semierect crouch.

"He's peein' on ya! He's peein' on ya! Get 'im onna toilet! Get 'im onna toilet!" the old fuck in the baseball cap yelled like a wheelchair general.

Stony looked down. The legs of his baggy whites were slowly turning yellow. "Shit!" Stony almost dropped him again, as he twisted and turned, trying to get out of the line of fire.

Reynard ran behind Valentine, slipped his forearms under the hairless armpits and dragged him backward to the toilet. Straddling the bowl, his spine against the upright toilet lid, he deposited Valentine on the seat, swinging his leg over the old guy's head to free himself. Stony furiously wiped the piss from his dripping pants with a fistful of toilet paper. Reynard's charge wheeled himself over to Valentine on the pot and shouted in his ear, "Yer awright, Valentine? Yer awright, Valentine?"

Valentine sat hunched over, gloomily staring at his white kneecaps, his lips moving, the expression on his face a cross between Buster Keaton and a basset hound.

"Where's your head, Jim?" Reynard rubbed his hands together as if just finishing a grimy job. Stony didn't answer, still wiping his pants. "Don'choo know how to lift someone? You coulda *killed* the dude!"

"If that's a dude, I'm James Brown."

Reynard turned to his charge in the wheelchair, jerked him up and swiftly deposited him on the toilet seat next to Valentine. He turned back to Stony. "You better get your act together, bro'."

The piss trickled into Stony's shoe.

"Hey, Reynard! Hey, Reynard! I'm finished! I'm finished!"

Glaring at Stony, Reynard roughly jerked his patient off the toilet, wiped his ass and almost threw him back in the wheelchair. He started out of the bathroom, then turned. "Valentine's finished."

Stony tossed the ball of toilet paper on the floor, lifted Valentine off the pot, pulled up his pajama bottoms and tried to maneuver him into his wheelchair. He forgot to lock the wheels and as he began Valentine's descent the wheelchair rolled away from him. Reynard pushed the chair back and braced it as Stony sat Valentine down.

"You forgot to wipe his ass," Reynard reproached.

"He didn't shit."

After depositing Valentine back in his room, Stony stomped through the corridor, eyes straight ahead.

"Lifter!"

Stony ignored the nurse and ran down six flights of stairs to Personnel.

~

"Miss Guardino, I can't hack it." Stony shook his head as he leaned forward hunched over in his seat. "It's too depresso up there. I'm up to my elbows in shit, I got piss on my pants, and I got death up my nose. Excuse my language."

Miss Guardino regarded him with a half smile, played with a pencil on her desk. "Well, this is a hospital."

Despite his misery Stony noticed she had some fine bosoms on her. "Yeah, I know, but this isn't what I was promised. What's the story on the children's ward? Because I'll tell you honestly, if nothing's gonna happen, I'm gonna hafta quit."

She picked up the phone, dialed once.

"Three-four-three, please." She winked at Stony. "Yes, Mrs. Pitt, please. Thank you. Florence? Rae Guardino. Hi. Listen, I have a boy in my office now who's been working on six and he was promised last week that he would be working with you. Uh-uh. Uh-uh. Yeah. Thomas De Coco Junior. D–E–C–O–C–O. Uh-uh." She lightly scratched her nose with a chipped pinkynail as she talked. "Well, he's been having a rough time on six and . . . Yeah, O.K. O.K. Thanks. Bye."

"Go up to the fourth floor, Room Four-o-one, and see Mrs. Pitt. She'll try to switch you over today." She winked again.

"Fantastic." Stony got up. "I was really gettin' the horrors up there."

"Geriatrics isn't for everybody."

"You can say that again. Thanks a million." As Stony left the office Miss Guardino studied his ass, whipped out a brown paper bag and a thermos from her desk drawer and had lunch.

~

"Have you ever worked with children before, Mr. De Coco?" Mrs. Pitt was a short, heavyset woman in her sixties who wore her gray hair in bangs. Stony could tell by her patient smile that she had worked with kids for two hundred years.

"Nah, not really, unless you wanna count my kid brother. He's eight. I take care a him pretty good. He's anorexic." Stony scratched his jaw and glanced at a photo cube on her desk, stuffed with Instamatic shots of a family around a Christmas tree.

Mrs. Pitt followed his gaze. "That's my son's family, they live in Hawaii."

"Oh yeah?"

"He's a sergeant in the air force at Pearl Harbor."

"Pearl Harbor? Far out," he said, still scratching his jaw.

She picked up the cube and rotated it, revealing a photo of a six-month-old infant wrapped in a blue blanket. "That's the newest addition, Tracey."

"Wild." Stony tried to appear impressed.

"Tell me about your brother." She tossed the cube on her desk.

"Albert?" Stony straightened up in his chair. "He's all right. I mean, there's nothin' wrong with him except that anorexic thing. He's really skinny. He's pretty nervous too. I just sort of look out for him, you know? See, my mother . . . she's not exactly what you would call a portrait a mental health. I mean, she yells a lot and I don't know how to put it exactly. It's like there's two kinds of people in the world. Her and the enemy, right? An' she takes it out a lot on Albert. I just try to cover for him from time to time. Hey, look, she's my mother, right? An' I love her as such, you know?" Stony leaned forward, lightly touching his fingertips. "But just between you, me 'n' the apple tree, she's a stone whacko sometimes."

Mrs. Pitt leaned her cheek on her hand, still smiling. "Do you like kids?"

"Hell, yeah!" Stony sat back. "I dig 'em a lot, more'n I dig adults."

Mrs. Pitt laughed briefly.

"I mean, no offense." Stony felt like he had just tripped on his dick. "I dig adults too."

"O.K." She brushed his apology aside, righted the photo cube so that Tracey was visible. "It's twelve now, why don't you take the afternoon off. What's tomorrow, Wednesday? Come in at eight and we'll see what we can do for you."

"Fantastic." Stony stood up. "Lissen, after geriatrics you can throw me in a dress an' call me a candy striper. I'd get into it."

"I don't think we'll have to do that." Her chair, on casters, squealed as she pushed away from her desk.

Stony hesitated at the stairway, debated whether to pop up to six one last time to tell Reynard that he had swung the switch. Fuck him. He was a full-time chump if Stony ever saw one.

14

IN THE DAY ROOM on the children's ward at Cresthaven, early morning sunlight filtered through soiled beige curtains in a crossfire from three huge windows. The white linoleum floor was littered with the remains of Lincoln logs, Tinkertoys, playing cards, assorted multicolored balls, crayons and scraps of brightly colored construction paper. The pale green walls were decorated with drawings of houses, stick people, boats and animals done in crayon on manila paper. Against the only windowless wall forty metal folding chairs leaned against each other like a collapsing chorus line. Four high-wattage unshaded overhead bulbs were always on so that despite the clutter the room had a merciless and barren air.

As Stony walked down to the day room, his baggy white pants and oversized short-sleeve white shirt made him feel filthy and helpless as if he hadn't had his diaper changed all day. When he heard voices from the day room, his first impulse was to backtrack down the corridor, but he sucked in, put his hands in his pockets and casually sauntered into the room. Two black kids about Albert's age sat in wheelchairs by one of the windows. They wore the regulation St. Joseph's aspirin orange bathrobes over loose, pale yellow pajamas. They were arguing with each other, but when Stony walked in the conversation stopped.

At first Stony ignored them and made a big deal of examining a drawing of a boy sitting on an ocean liner taped to the wall. The liner docked on the lawn of a house. When the silence persisted he became intensely preoccupied with the texture of the curtains.

"Hey, man, you new here?"

Stony wheeled around a little too fast for his liking. "Yeah, I just started today." Stony felt terrified of the wheelchairs; they were too big for the kids, making them look like they were sitting in government issue thrones, with numbers stenciled on the sides. He tried to keep his eyes at shoulder or head level. They sized him up again. Stony was just about to split when one kid said to the other, "Let's as' him."

"Aw, man, he don't know."

"You just afraid he gonna say you *wrong*, sucker."

"What's the problem?" Stony forced a smile.

"Who you think is badder, Shaft or Bruce Lee?" demanded the fat kid.

Stony made a what-kind-of-question-is-that face. "Bruce Lee."

The fat kid laughed loud and flat. "This dumb motherfucker think *Shaft* is badder." He laughed again, teasing the other kid, a small big-eyed boy with a pointy head.

"All *ah* know is, that kung fu sucker come at *me*, I fuckin' drill him through, bawh, just like mah man Shaf'." The small kid glared at his friend and Stony.

"Yeah, an' Bruce Lee go *choo!*" The fat boy karate-chopped an imaginary bullet speeding toward him. He looked up at Stony. "You know kung fu?"

"Nah, I know somethin' better."

"What?" they both said.

"Garlic." Stony was thinking a mile a minute.

The fat boy frowned.

"Yeah, if some guy is comin' at you, you eat some garlic real fast an' when he shouts 'Kung fu' you just stick your face in his and say 'Wwhhoo cares!' "

Nobody laughed. Stony was trembling even though he tried to chuckle at his own joke.

"Man, you better get back to bed before they find out you missin'." The fat kid rolled his eyes. The other boy laughed as they slapped palms.

"Yeah, you better get back to bed." He looked at his friend again, then made circles with his finger at his temple. He was absolutely tickled at his own wit.

Stony flushed even though he kept smiling. His hands were soaked with perspiration. He hadn't taken them out of his pants pockets since he walked into the day room. "Little nigger bastard. I'll throw you right out the fuckin' window," Stony thought to himself.

As if reading his mind, they both stopped laughing. Suddenly the air stank with fear. Stony looked at his two antagonizers. They were studying their laps, faces brittle. He didn't understand what had just happened. All he knew was that he felt deep shame, and his anger U-turned onto himself. He plunked down a folding chair in front of them.

"What's your names anyways?" He addressed them both.

"Tyrone," the fat one answered sulkily.

"Derek," the small one pouted.

"Yeah, well, my name is Bruce Shaft," he said.

Tyrone smirked.

"No, it ain't," said Derek. He began rolling himself back and forth in place, his hands on the rims of the large spoked wheels. "O.K., you want to know what my real name is?"

"I know your name." Tyrone squinted as he read the tag on Stony's chest pocket. "T. De–Co–Co." He screwed up his face with the strangeness of the sound.

"Hey" — Stony raised a finger — "you know what that means in Italian? T. De Coco in Italian means 'Enter The Dragon.' " He nodded his head seriously.

"Aw, man," Derek dismissed Stony with a wave of his hand.

"You don't believe me?" Stony challenged. "You know what my brother's name is?"

"My brother's name is Martell," Tyrone said. "He's in the marines."

"Oh yeah?" Stony was impressed.

"Yeah, he could kick your ass."

Stony ignored the last comment. "Derek, you got a brother?"

"Got a *sister*, she's twenny . . . two I think."

"Yeah, an' she got nice titties," Tyrone giggled.

Derek leaned over and punched Tyrone on the arm. "You shut yo' *face,* motherfucker, or I shut it for you." Derek pointed a finger at Tyrone, staring at him with all the menace he could muster.

Tyrone sucked air through his teeth as he rubbed his arm. "He hit *hard* for a little *mouse*," he complained to Stony.

Derek let loose with another shot in the same spot.

"Cut it *out!*" Tyrone bawled. Stony was up and between the wheelchairs in an instant. He didn't know what to do. The feel of the cold metal of the armrests made him dizzy.

"Hey, you guys, whynchoo be cool?"

"Then you tell *Fat Albert* not to call me a *mouse!*"

"See? See?" Tyrone whined in protest.

"Well, you *are,* you fat motherfucker." Derek raised his eyebrows and leaned around Stony to see Tyrone.

"Hey look . . . look." Stony raised his hands like a referee. "You guys wanna hear a story?"

Tyrone winced, rubbing his arm.

"I don' wanna hear no fuckin' story." Derek propped his elbow on the arm of the wheelchair and rested his chin on the heel of his palm, staring away from Stony and Tyrone.

"C'mon, you guys, it's a really good story."

"Is it 'bout kung fu?" Tyrone asked.

"Nah, it's about Indians."

Suddenly Derek whipped around furiously in his chair. "An' you tell that motherfucker to lay off mah *sister!*" There were tears on his cheeks. He bit his lip in an effort to stop his chin from quivering. Tyrone got frightened by Derek's teary display. So did Stony. Stony sighed. "O.K., Tyrone, whynchoo apologize to him."

Derek roughly wiped at the tears on his face, waiting for Tyrone's apology.

"I'm sorry," Tyrone said down low.

Derek pretended he didn't hear as he busily wiped his tears, but Stony could sense the small boy's rage subsiding.

"O.K., look, you guys wanna hear a story or no?"

"*I* do," Tyrone said. He shot a quick glance at Derek as he spoke. Stony didn't bother to ask Derek for the go-ahead but got right into it.

"Thousands a years ago, there was this desert tribe a Indians in the desert."

"What was they called?" Tyrone asked. Stony couldn't remember the name that the scoutmaster used when he told the story in Boy Scout camp. "Ah, the Hondos. Anyway, this tribe lived in the desert an' you know there ain't much food or water in the desert, so it was really important that everybody eat an' drink only a little at a time an' share what they got with everybody else. But this tribe was cool. They been at it a long time an' they pretty much had their act together."

Stony took out a cigarette and lit it, drawing deeply with pleasure. "Except for this one Indian in the tribe who was really fat and greedy."

"Was his name Tyrone?" Derek snickered.

Tyrone started to protest.

"As a matter of fact, his name was Derek."

Tyrone laughed.

"No it wasn't." Derek suppressed a smile.

"Well, really his name was De Coco."

"That's your name," they both said.

"Yeah, well, he was my ancestor."

"You an Indian?" They stared at him popeyed.

"On my mother's side," he said.

"You *really* an Indian?"

"Hey, c'mon, you gonna let me tell the story?"

They both stared at him with awe.

"Anyway, De Coco was a fat an' greedy Indian, an' his family was always starvin' because he would eat everybody's food. His squaw got really mad an' went to the counsel o' chiefs an' said, 'Chiefs, my man De Coco is one greedy sucker. Me an' my babies ain't had no grub for three days. He just eats everybody's share. Why I got to count my babies every night just to make sure he ain't eaten one of *them*.' So the chiefs call De Coco to stand trial, an' he comes into the tent, all fat an' greasy like he just swallowed a bass drum, an' the chiefs take one look at that gut he got an' they know his squaw is tellin' the truth, so they say, 'De Coco, we heard you was more pig than man an' we can't afford to have greedy braves in this tribe. You like to eat us *all* out of house and home, so you got two choices: either we knock you down an' let you roll until you starve to death, or we give you some rations and banish you from the tribe an' let you wander around the desert. What's it gonna be?' Well, De Coco felt like there wasn't much of a choice so the next day they booted him out of the tribe into the desert. They gave him three days' supply of food and drink, you know, some beef, some cheese, two salamis and a six-pack o' Doctor Pepper, and off he goes. Well, he traveled maybe two hundred feet when he starts feeling hungry an' before you know it, he plunks himself down in the sand an' in ten minutes he ate the whole three days' worth o' food. So now he got no grub and he's wanderin' aroun' the desert an' he starts to get hungry again. An' he says to himself: 'Gah-*damn*, I'm hungry!' But he knows if he go back to the camp they'll kill 'im so he just trudge on ahead for miles an' miles, an' it's hot in the desert an' he's sweatin' an' puffin'. Finally after walkin' ten miles he come to a little water hole. He just lay himself down on his belly an' he's gulpin' it up like a camel. Well, after he got enough, he's sittin' there under that burnin' sun an' he says, 'Ooh-wee! It's hot. I gots to find me some shade!' an' he puts his hand up to his eyes an' he's searchin' the lay of the land."

Stony imitated the action, searching the day room. "An' way off in the distance, he sees some hills."

Stony peered over their bodies. Tyrone looked behind him to see what Stony found.

"So he gets his rear in gear an' starts trekkin' off to the hills an' he walks ten more miles before he gets there an' he finds himself a nice cool cave an' that boy just plain passed out for two days he was so tired."

Derek exhaled wearily.

"Anyways, he wakes up two days later an' he's hungry an' he's thirsty, but he still don't got no food or water an' he got so damn angry he just started kickin' and screamin' an' yellin' just like a baby."

Tyrone laughed.

"But that don't get him no food. An' then he remembers that

water hole ten miles out into the desert. Well, he tries kickin' and screamin' for a couple a more hours, then he realizes he better save up his energy for that ten-mile hike he gotta make an' off he goes, ten miles to the water hole an' ten miles back to his cave. He does this for a couple of days an' realizes he's ain't eaten. A man gotta have more than water. Well, he knows he seen some desert rabbits hoppin' aroun' but how can he catch them?"

"With a bow an' arrow," Derek said.

"He don't got no bow an' arrow," Tyrone said.

"Shut up," Derek said in annoyance.

"Nah, Tyrone's right, but you know what he does? He tears off some material from his buckskin shirt an' he takes the lace out of one a his moccasins and he makes himself a sling. An' he takes some rocks out a the cave an' he goes off into the desert huntin' rabbits just like David and Goliath."

"My aunt told me that story," Derek said. "It's in the Bible."

"Yeah, well, he goes, an' he's flingin' them rocks right and left but he ain't hittin' no rabbits because they are *fast* little mothers, an' they ain't just gonna sit there waitin' to be bonked, an' he's goin' at it for days until finally he beans one right on the noggin', an' De Coco's so damn hungry he wolfs it down raw fur an' all."

They both made faces of disgust.

"Man, you get hungry enough you don't care," Stony impressed upon them. "Anyways, so now he's truckin' out twenny miles a day for water an' he's runnin' aroun' the desert with his sling beanin' rabbits an' he's gettin' pretty damn good at that too now, an' this goes on for two years until one day he's at the water hole an' he looks at his reflection in the water."

Stony peered at the floor. Derek and Tyrone stared between Stony's feet. "You know what he saw?"

"He got skinny!" Tyrone shouted.

"Skinny! That boy made Bruce Lee look like Humpty Dumpty. He was all muscle an' rawhide! He was lean an' tough! He made Shaft look like Fat Albert!"

Derek and Tyrone smiled with satisfaction.

"I mean that man was like *whipcord!* Then one day he wakes up in his cave an' he hears voices. At first he thinks he's goin' crazy, but then he crawls out to the lip of the cave an' there they are, a hundred Indians on horses an' they all got war paint on, and he can tell by their language that they're Shalako Indians, the sworn enemies of the Hondos, an' he overhears that they're on their way to the Hondo camp to pull off a surprise attack. Well, he just ran out the back entrance of the cave, an' he takes off like the wind. He's gonna warn the Hondos of this attack an' he's *flyin'*! He runs thirty miles to the camp an' he bursts in an' runs up to the chief's tent an' he says, 'Get your braves ready, the Shalakos are on the warpath!' an' the chief looks at him an' says, 'Who the hell are you?' an' De Coco says, 'I'm De Coco,' an' the chief laughs an' says, 'You're not De Coco, De Coco's fat and greasy, you're lean an' strong' an' De Coco's feelin' frustrated but he's got no time for 'To Tell the Truth' an' he says, 'Where are your braves?' an' the old chief says, 'They're all out hunting. There's nobody here but women, children and old men like me.' "

"Oh no!" Tyrone slapped his forehead.

"*Stupid* motherfucker!" Derek cursed.

"An' now De Coco's flippin' out. He don't know what to do. He can't fight all the Shalakos so he says to the chief, 'Get all the people together an' I'll lead them to safety in the desert but *hurry* because the Shalakos are almost here an' you *know* De Coco knows all the hidin' places in the desert pretty good after all these years.' The chief looks out his tent an' sees a cloud of dust way off in the distance an' he knows that it's the Shalako war party comin' down hard an' De Coco's tellin' the truth. Well, in ten minutes he gets everybody ready to go an' De Coco's leading all the women, children an' old men through the desert. An' he's takin' them up and down these tricky paths an' windin' ways, an' behind them now they can see two clouds, one is the Shalako war party and the other is the smoke comin' from their burning village."

"The Shalakos burned it down?"

"Yup, an' now they're hot on their trail. An' every time they turn aroun' that cloud is gettin' closer an' closer 'cause all them Shalakos is on horseback. Well, finally De Coco leads the Hondos into this hidden valley between these two mountains. One end of the valley is wide, but the other end is really narrow, too narrow for a horse but wide enough for a person to crawl through. An' if he can get the Hondos out the other end of the valley, they'll be safe. Well, he runs everybody through the valley an' they get to that narrow passage, but there's about a six-foot-high smooth ledge of rock that everybody's gotta climb to get to that passage, an' it's smooth, too smooth for anybody to climb, you know, they're all children and women an' ol' men. So they're all standing there trapped between two mountains an' suddenly they see the Shalakos at the other end of the valley an' they're a whoopin' an' screamin' about two miles off. Suddenly De Coco gets an idea. He stands like this."

Stony stood up and bent his arms into right angles. "An' De Coco's standin' there an' all the women an' children start climbin' over him and through the passage to safety and the Shalakos are gettin' closer and closer an' every once in a while an arrow lands near them an' the Hondos are tearin' ass to get outta there an' De Coco's standin' up there like the friggin' Rock a Gibralta. All those people climbin' over him an' the arrows are landin' closer an' closer an' the Shalakos are about a hundred yards away an' there's two people left and De Coco's knees are givin' way an he's sweatin' an' bleedin'.'"

"Hurry!" Tyrone shouted.

Stony maintained that strange crucifix position, spit flying as he talked. "An' just as the last Hondo child scrambles over De Coco's shoulders to safety, the Shalakos get there an' see how De Coco cheated them out of their massacre. An' there's nobody facing the Shalakos now but De Coco, an' he's too damn tired to escape an' just stays in that position against the ledge."

Stony collapsed against the wall, exhausted, but holding his arms in that position.

"Well, the Shalakos are so damn angry, all one hundred of them take out their bow 'n' arrows an' shoot De Coco right where he stands. An' all those arrows pin him to that ledge in that position, an' he got a hundred arrows stickin' in his body, but he dies with a smile on his face because he knows he saved his whole tribe."

"Why didn't he escape?" Derek's eyes were glistening.

" 'Cause he was tired, right?" Tyrone said.

"But the Indian gods were watching an' they thought that De Coco's dyin' was the bravest thing they ever saw, and even though he was dead, they were going to make him immortal . . . an' the next morning when the sun came up in the desert, there were thousands of plants, a new kind of plant that stood straight up and had two arms that were stretched out just like De Coco's arms an' that plant was covered with a hundred long needles just like the arrows in De Coco's body an' do you know what plant that was?"

They stared at him blankly.

"The cactus," he answered himself. "And now all over the world anybody wandering the desert can get food from the cactus and he can get water, or maybe some tequila if he's lucky."

"Man, if I was De Coco I woulda just . . . choo!" Derek made a motion of flying. "I woulda just . . . *jumped* away up that rock, man." He fidgeted anxiously in his wheelchair. He looked up at Stony and asked with a strange softness, "Can you tell us more stories?"

"Gimme a break." Stony fought back a smile.

"What's a cactus?" Derek asked.

"They got needles in 'em, right?" Tyrone offered.

"You never seen a cactus?" Stony was taken aback.

"I seen pictures, but I never seen one before," Tyrone said.

"Come to think of it, I never seen one live either."

"They're in Texas, right?" Tyrone picked his nose.

"They really got needles in 'em?"

"Well, you know, stickers, like a rose but bigger ones," Stony said.

"Ugh! I hate needles." Derek made a bitter face. "Las' night I dream I run aroun' the hospital an' break all the needles and when Mrs. Le Pietro come in the mornin' to give me a needle, it all broke an' I jus' laugh."

Tyrone jerked his head back and looked at Derek with scorn. "You crazy nigger! You do that an' lotta people gonna get *sick!* If ah don' get a needle in the mornin' ah *die!*"

"What?" Stony sat down and stared horrified at Tyrone.

"He got diabeanies." Derek nodded gravely.

"Tha's right! An' I got to getta needle every mornin' or ah *die!*

But it don't hurt no more. They even teachin' me to do it mahself," Tyrone said cheerfully.

"My mamma stick me once." Derek held up his left hand and pointed to the center of his palm. "Wit' a sewin' needle right here." He stabbed the spot repeatedly.

"She did *what?*" Stony felt barraged.

"Yeah, 'cause I was bad. I was a little kid, like six." Derek squinted at the ceiling. "Yeah, I was six."

"What you do?" Stony and Tyrone asked simultaneously.

"I was playin' with matches."

"Did you cry?" Tyrone was hypnotized, eyes big as saucers.

"Shit yeah! I was a baby, man! That sucker *hurt!* She jus' put mah hand out on the dinin' table and went wham!" Derek jabbed his palm again.

Tyrone twisted away in his wheelchair. "Stop!"

Derek laughed. "Tyrone, you *still* a baby!"

"Wait a second, wait a second." Stony put out his hands. "You mean to tell me she took a friggin' sewin' needle and put out your hand onna table or somethin' an' . . ."

"Right through, look." He held up his hand, revealing a small star-shaped white scar dead center in the palm. "Hey. Tyrone! Look!" Tyrone kept his face buried in the crook of his arm. "Tyrone, look!"

"No!" A muffled cry.

"Tyrone, you a *faggot*," Derek taunted.

"I don't fuckin' believe it," Stony said to no one.

"You think I'm lyin', man, you can ask my mother. She jus' upstairs."

"She's visitin'?"

Derek laughed. "No, man! She's in the psycho ward. She bus' up mah legs wit' boilin' water. Tha's why I'm inna wheelchair. She try an' come down everyday, but ah jus' hide under the covers. When ah get out I'm gonna live onna farm wit' my granma in South Carolina."

"Hold it, hold it." Stony was getting dizzy. "Your mother's upstairs onna eighth floor?"

"Right! An' they gonna keep her there too! Look!" Derek raised his pajama legs, revealing blistered skin. The worst of the burned tissue was smeared with a yellow salve. Stony fought back the impulse to vomit. "This lady come an' she say to me, ah don' have to see mah mother anymore if ah don' want to. They gonna sen' me down to my granma when mah legs get better."

Stony got up and walked around the room. Behind him, Derek tried to make Tyrone look at his ravaged legs. Stony leaned against the window overlooking Bronx Park and tried to space out, counting the number of people walking or biking along the curved pathways.

"Hey! Hey! De Coco!" Stony turned around and leaned against the sill. "You ever been on a farm?" Derek wheeled himself in a circle.

Stony returned to the folding chair. "Nah."

"I'm gonna milk the cows, and feed the chickens, man." Derek stopped wheeling.

Tyrone sat holding his stomach, looking like he'd just drunk cod-liver oil.

"Wait, hold on. Your mother comes down an' *visits* you!"

"Only once. She ain't supposed to, but she slip down las' week. I was sleepin' an' I wake up one mornin' and she jus' standin' over mah bed, man, she jus' standin' there. Ah jus' start screamin' an' Mrs. Le Pietro runs in an' drags my mama out there. I screamin' for *hours,* man. Mrs. Le Pietro gotta gimme a needle, man, an' I ain't got no diabeanies, I jus' go back to sleep an' I wakes up again an' everything cool."

Stony exhaled through his mouth and shook his head. "I remember once when I was five my mother made me touch a hot iron because I broke a window kickin' a football in my room."

Derek laughed.

"You lose the football?" Tyrone asked.

"That thing hurt like a bitch." Stony shook his hand as if to cool off the burn.

Derek asked, "You play football, man?"

"Well, yeah. I played for three years in high school."

"You ever on TV?" Tyrone asked.

"One time, when we was playin' Christ the King for the championship. We lost."

"You ever on 'Get Christy Love'?"

"Who?"

"She a cop, she fox-yy." Derek rolled his eyes.

Tyrone snickered.

"Tyrone! What *you* laughin' at? Man, Christy Love come in here an' take her clos' off you run the other way!"

Tyrone giggled, "Shut up!"

"I dream once, man, Christy Love come inna my room, man, an' take me in a convertible. An' we drivin' down to my granma's farm in South Carolina."

"My granma live in Newark," Tyrone said. "You know where that at?"

"New Jersey." Stony was still trying to place the name Christy Love.

"But she come in every Sunday for Reverend Ike, you know him?"

"Sort of."

"He a ba-ad preacher, man. My granma come in wit' all her frens an' they all dress up and go to see him. One time she took me. I wore this nice suit, man, it light blue except the pockets. They dark blue." Tyrone ran his hands down his sides as he talked. "We all sit in this big gold movie house and all these ol' ladies what look like my granma they all start yellin' an' jumpin' aroun' when Ike come out." Tyrone laughed. "You know what he tell them? He say, 'Give yo'se'ves a big *bear* hug,' an' my granma and all her frens they hug theyse'ves an' go, 'Mmm.' I start laughin' an' my granma smack me."

"My mama say Rev Ike fo' fools!" Derek sneered.

"Yo *mama* a fool," Tyrone countered.

Derek reared back to punch Tyrone. Tyrone wheeled backward fast. Stony held the rear of Derek's wheelchair to keep him from chasing Tyrone all over the room. "You know I got a brother that's eight."

"He a Indian too?" Tyrone asked.

"Nah, he's black." Stony smiled.

"You liah." Derek squinted skeptically.

"It can be! It can be! Ah knows this white boy in mah class las' year, Robert Parker? He black an' he got a white sister!" Tyrone wheeled himself in front of Derek. "Right?" he asked Stony.

Stony shrugged, stuck on his joke.

"Is yo' brother in the hospital?"

"Nah, he's home."

"What's his name?"

"Albert."

"Fat Albert!" Derek and Tyrone exclaimed together.

Stony snorted. "Yeah, Fat Albert."

"Hey, De Coco, you got a car?" Tyrone asked.

"Yeah."

"I can drive," said Derek. "My granma got a tractor an' she gonna show me how to drive it."

"What kinda car you got, a LD?"

"A what?"

"A LD! A Catalac."

"LD, LD." Stony frowned. "Oh, an Eldorado! No way, try a Mustang."

Tyrone and Derek smirked. "Tha's weak! Tha's a honky-mobile!"

Stony shrugged.

"Man, ah wouldn't be caught dead in nothin' but a LD," Tyrone said.

"That's too bad, I was gonna offer you guys a ride when you got better."

"Where you gonna take us?"

"What's the difference? All's I got is a honky-mobile."

Derek punched Tyrone. "Stupid!"

"You ever drive down to South Carolina?"

"I drove all the way to Florida once."

"That's near California, right?"

A nurse came in, hands in the pockets of her white dress. She wore a white crown cap and rimless glasses. "O.K., boys, time to go back." She grabbed the rear handles on Derek's wheelchair. They groaned in protest. "Could you take Tyrone?" she asked Stony. Stony jumped up. "They just go down the hall."

Stony wheeled Tyrone down the corridor into a long room lined with beds. Stony stopped in front of Tyrone's bed and locked the wheelchair. He slipped his hands under Tyrone's armpits and lifted him up onto the sheets. The nurse did the same with Derek at the next bed.

"Hey, De Coco! You comin' back tomorrow?"

"Sure!"

"You gonna tell us more stories?"

"Hell yeah! See you guys tomorrow!"

"Mrs. Pitt wants to see you," the nurse said as they walked down the corridor.

~

"So how'd it go today?" Mrs. Pitt leaned back and her chair squeaked and snittered with every move.

"Whew!" Stony shook his head. "Heavy, very heavy. I just hung around with two kids in the day room, Derek and Tyrone?"

Mrs. Pitt nodded.

"God! Derek showed me his legs. I couldn't believe it."

Mrs. Pitt sighed. "I've known Derek Walcott since he was an infant. He was first brought in here with malnutrition in nineteen sixty-six. Then he was back two years later with severe cuts and bruises. We had a neighbor testify and got his mother put away for six months. We sent him up to live with an aunt in Brooklyn, but after two years his mother sued to get him back, successfully. After this, what you saw, I think we can finally separate them for good. When his legs heal we're moving him into a city home for boys on Staten Island with the possibility of foster parents taking him in the next year or two."

Stony was puzzled. "He told me he's gonna live with his grandmother in South Carolina."

"He doesn't have a grandmother in South Carolina."

Stony sat silent for a moment, glanced again at the pictures of Mrs. Pitt's family secure in their photo cube.

"Somethin' else. His mother's *really* upstairs on eight?"

"In psychiatric?" Mrs. Pitt laughed. "Soon as he got into the hospital Mrs. Walcott took off for California. If we ever find her, we'll put her away all right, but not in a hospital, I can promise you that."

~

When Stony got home from work he made a gigantic bee for the phone. "Doctor Harris?"

"Yeah?"

"Hey, howya doin'? This is Stony De Coco."

"Hey, Stony. How's it goin'?"

"It's wild. I did two days' geriatrics, then they switched me to kids."

"Geriatrics? Sorry about that."

"No sweat. The kids is what's happenin' now."

"Good, good."

"Lissen, I wanna thank you, man. It's like I was walkin' aroun' thinkin' the world was flat, you know? There's no way I'm gonna ever do the construction number now."

"Well, that's great, Stony, but — "

"But what?"

"I hope you're strong enough."

"Strong enough for what?" Please don't piss on my fuckin' parade.

"You know what they say, blood's thicker than water."

"Whadya mean?"

"Well, Stony, this whole thing might start some machinery going in your life that, ah, that you might not be ready to handle."

"Like *what?*"

"Like you might feel you need to leave home."

All of a sudden Stony felt shanghaied. Hustled. "Who's leavin' home?" he shouted.

"I'll tell you, leaving home is the hardest thing in the world."

Stony got the chilling feeling that Harris was enjoying himself. Cat and mouse. "I asked" — Stony tried to control himself — "who's leaving home?"

"You, maybe."

"Whatta you talkin' about?"·

"You'll find out soon enough. Hey look, I'm going about this the wrong way. I just want you to know I think it's terrific that things are working out and I have every faith in you following through."

"Lissen, Doctor Harris, maybe this is a bad connection or something, but . . ."

"Stony, you got a pencil or a pen?"

"Yeah."

"Write down this number . . . OL 4–3827. Got that?"

"Yeah."

"O.K. That's my home number. If you ever have any trouble, or if you just want to talk, give me a call."

"What kinda trouble?"

"Maybe none, who knows. How's Albert?"

"He's fine, he's startin' to eat."

"Great. O.K., I got to go. Put that number someplace, O.K.?"

"Yeah, sure." Crazy bastard. Stony slipped the paper with Harris' number under his desk blotter and called Butler.

"Bobby B!"

"Hey, how's the mummies?"

"Fuck that. Dig this! They switched me to kids. It's fuckin' incredible, man, all's I do is tell stories. I *dig* it, man. I was with two spade kids all afternoon. I was like really relatin' to them. I *love* it. I mean it's freaky, they're in wheelchairs an' shit, but it's a whole different scene. Butler, I'm *poppin'!*" Stony tucked the phone under his chin and lit a cigarette.

"Whatta you wanna do tonight?" Butler asked.

"I'm up for anything."

"Oh, hey listen, I got a job."

"What?"

"I'm gonna work in my uncle's hosiery store."

"What's he payin'?"

"A yard a week. How much you gettin'?"

"One forty less taxes. Where's his store at?"

"Up on two seventeenth, White Plains Road."

"That's schvug country, ain't it?"

"Half schvug, half guinea."

"When you start?"

"Tomorrow. I'm workin' behind the counter. I sell panties, bras and stockings. How much you wanna bet I get laid before August in there?"

"Who you gonna bang, some sixty-year-old black lady comin' in for corrective underwear?"

"No, man, they got some nice chicks around there. I went to junior high in that neighborhood."

"You think your uncle gets any?"

"Nah, see, it's a funny thing up there. Everybody's in a very heavy neighborhood head, what goes around comes around, you know what I mean? But I'll bet he gets a lotta offers."

"Ooh! Bite my Supp-hose!"

"Listen, another thing, my Uncle Frank's like sixty-two an' he wants to sell in a few years. If I dig it, an' I stick with it, I might be into buyin' the place, you know? I got ideas how to do a really nice number in there. Get in some better stock, ex*pand* and shit. 'Cause he don't know nothin', he's old, been there thirty years. I can really do it up nice."

"Yeah, except by the time *you* take over, that neighborhood'll be black as a coal miner's asshole at midnight."

"That's cool, listen, I'll throw in a line a wigs, hire some foxy soul sisters to run the place and get a heavy-duty alarm system. I'll just come by on Fridays to pick up the cash. Maybe I'll even hire a security guard. Shit, anybody even *thinks* a jumpin' bad he'll get eighty-sixed so fast he ain't gonna even *know* about it until it's in the papers."

Stony heard the apartment door open. "Listen, I gotta go."

"Shit, man, I'll show those cats what bad-ass means, fuck with the bull an' you get the *horns!*"

"Butler, call me later."

"Hello!" Tommy wandered through the house.

"Yo!" Stony shouted back. Tommy came into the bedroom.

"This lady gets raped so she calls the cops. The cops round up suspects and get 'em into a line-up, right? The lady's in the front row. As soon as they throw on the spotlights this big Polish guy in the middle of the line-up jumps out and points at her. 'There she is!' "

Stony thought about it for a second, then laughed.

"Hey, an' you hear about this college down south finally gave an athletic scholarship to a nigger? He's a javelin catcher."

"That's old." Stony smirked.

"Ain't as old as those people you workin' with."

"I got switched today . . . I'm workin' with kids now."

"Whatta they doin', playin' musical chairs witcher time card?" Tommy picked at his mustache.

"No, man, that's what I wanted to do all along."

"So how's it goin'?"

"I love it, man, I really dig workin' with kids."

"They give you a raise?"

"Nah, I'm workin' there three days, whadya you want?"

"Just remember, Stones, in two weeks you're comin' in with me. You promised."

"Don't remind me."

"Don't *make* me remind you."

~

Frank's Hosiery House was a small, cramped store with an ancient ornate pressed-tin ceiling. One wall was completely covered with white pegboard on which hung cheap two-dollar earrings and three-dollar necklaces. Under the pegboard were cardboard boxes filled with cellophane-wrapped red and blue slippers, two pair for three dollars. Toward the back was a seven-foot-high rotating fan; next to it a black curtain separated a small storeroom from the front. The other wall supported two five-foot-long glass counters filled with more jewelry, evening purses, long pink tubes containing girdles, garters and assorted corrective underwear. At the edge of one of the counters sat an old-fashioned gilt cash register. Next to the register was a box of rayon panties, three for a dollar. Two snapshots were taped to the register — one of Frank smiling behind the counter and one of Frank's daughter, Cissy, holding two of her kids in her lap in front of a Christmas tree. Also taped to the cash register was an index card with the slogans "If you believe in credit, lend me five dollars" and "In God we trust; others pay cash." Two foot-high cards leaned on the other counter. Brown and red key holders, a dollar each, were advertised on one card. The other had dime and quarter slots, a picture of Joe Namath along the top and the legend "Fight Muscular Dystrophy." Three quarters and five dimes were Scotch-taped in the slots. Behind the counter, flush against the entire length of the wall, were six-foot-high shelves stocked with thousands of boxes of stockings and pantyhose.

Butler stood behind the counter reading the *Post*.

"This is a stickup."

"Hey! How's it goin'?"

"Awright." Stony walked behind the counter.

"It's like creepin' Jesus in here today, man." Butler exhaled wearily.

"Where's your uncle?" Stony pulled up a chair by the cash register. He felt a strange giddiness about being behind the counter.

A six-foot-tall woman with an expression like she just chugged lemon juice entered the store.

"You wanna take this one?" Butler side-mouthed to Stony. She threw a small wrinkled brown bag on the counter. "Mrs. Di Angelis." Butler smiled.

"I bought these yesterday. I specifically asked for thirty-eight-inch opera length. I put them on last night, they came up to here." She pulled up her dress above her knee. Both Stony and Butler leaned over the counter to look. She had legs like a road map. Butler removed the stockings from the bag and stretched them thigh to heel against a tape measure thumbtacked along the inside of the counter.

"They're thirty-eights, Mrs. Di Angelis." Butler's smile was wearing thin.

"Impossible."

"Here, look for yourself."

She walked behind the counter. "Well, you're stretching them!"

"They stretch on your legs, Mrs. Di Angelis."

"Well, I don't understand it. I've been coming in here for ten years, your uncle always gives me thirty-eight opera length and they always fit."

"Maybe you got taller," Stony offered cheerfully.

Butler struggled to keep a straight face. "Look, if you want I can give you forties or forty-twos."

She sniffed. "Or you can give me the thirty-eights that your uncle's been giving me."

"Look, dear, they all come out of the same box."

"Well, give me forty-twos."

Butler carefully folded the stockings. "Taupetone?"

"Taupetone."

Sucking his teeth Butler ran his thumb up and down the piled boxes behind him.

"All we have in a forty-two opera length is lollipop and peter pan. I got off-black in a forty."

"Off-black," she grimaced. "That's for tramps."

Stony laughed. She narrowed her eyes at him.

"How 'bout a peachpuff in forty-two?"

"Let me see."

Butler pulled out the box, dropped it on the counter, folded back the tissue, slipped his hand inside one stocking to show her the color against flesh.

"I dunno. Yeah, I'll take it." She shrugged.

Butler folded the new pair in its tissue and slid it into the wrinkled brown bag.

"Do you think you might be able to spare a new bag?" She smirked, drumming long nails on glass. Butler took out the stockings, crumpled the bag and tossed it behind him. He put the stockings in a new bag. She gave each of them one last hard stare before leaving the store. Butler ran in front of the counter, spread his legs, grabbed his crotch and shook his basket at her back.

"That fuckin' lady's been breakin' my uncle's balls for years."

"*Peach*puff?" Stony gawked.

Butler returned the other stockings to their box. "I'd like to give her douchepuff."

"She had nice fuckin' legs, Butler. I bet you get laid in here before the end of July."

"I shoulda banged her on the Fourth. You see those legs? Very patriotic." Butler slapped the box into place. "Red, white an' blue."

"Hey, meanwhile, speakin' a Old Glory, guess who I racked with last night?"

"Martha Raye?"

"Close, Three-Finger Annette."

"Really?" Butler grinned, pulled up a chair facing Stony. The el train roared overhead, deafening everything within two miles. Stony waited for the train to pass.

"Yeah . . . I was watchin' *Mary Tyler Moore* last night an' I got horny. I always get horny watchin' her . . . anyways, I was a cunt hair away from callin' Cheri."

"Bad news."

"So I figured. Anyway, I'm going berserk and I don't know what to do. Suddenly the goddamn phone rings. It was the seventh cavalry." Stony pretended he held a phone to his head, his pinky in front of his mouth, his thumb in his ear.

" 'Hello, Stony? This is Annette Palladino.' 'Hey, Annette, howya doin'?' 'I got my own place last week, Stony, an' I was wonderin' if you wanna come over.' " Stony clasped his hands together and smiled beatifically at the ceiling. "Thank you, *God!* Butler, I was over there before she hung up. She got a nice crib on Dyer Avenue, one room, but nice. Anyways, I got over there and she lays this dynamite boo on me, I mean *super* shit. One jay between us an' we're flyin'. I just took her fuckin' face in my hands" — Stony closed his eyes, his hands in front of him — "an' I started kissin' her. This sounds nuts, Butler, but we were just kissin'. Her lips felt so fuckin' good, like warm and firm, an' I was goin' bananas. We weren't even tonguin', Butler." Stony puckered his lips and kissed the space between his hands. "It was fantastic. I felt really warm, you know?"

"That all you did?" Butler bit his thumbnail.

"Hell, no! We got in the bed. I just laid there an' she took all my clothes off. It was like heaven. You ever have your nipples sucked? It's the most incredible feelin', Butler. It stings but nice. Anyway, she just peeled me down. I was comin' before she even got to my pants. She unlaced my boots, everything. She goes into the bathroom, comes out, she's wearin' only these panties. I almost had a heart attack. They were this deep blue, silky, with tiny straps by the hips. My fuckin' dong was blowin' itself . . . an' she comes out with this coconut oil . . . you ever see that smile she got? She's the fuckin' sexiest bitch I ever racked with. I swear to you. Anyway, she's rubbin' this coconut oil over me . . . oh!" Stony shuddered. "My fuckin' armpits, my toes, in *between* my toes, my cock, my fuckin' cock was *screamin'*. She started jackin' me off with the fuckin' coconut oil an' both hands twistin' in different directions up an' down." Stony slowly jerked off an invisible cock with both hands, a pained expression on his face, his shoulders heaving with every stroke. "*Jee*-zuz! . . . an' just as I was gonna come . . . glomph!" Stony spread his lips over the top fist. "Sucked the juice right up from my balls. An' later when I was eatin' her out, her fuckin' pussy tasted like honey. I was goin' down on her an' lookin' through the pubes up at her face. She was doin' one a these numbers." Stony arched his back, extended his arms from his sides like limp wings and slowly did a grind on his seat, his face a cross between ecstasy and agony. "I swear, Butler, I almost got off again. An' then she starts licking her own tits." Stony imitated the action, a cupped hand under each nipple. "An' she starts *screamin'*, pullin' my hair, pullin' *her* hair. An' when we were ballin', Butler, it felt like I didn't know where my cock ended and her cunt started. It was like we had a Siamese crotch an' she kept comin', an' comin', an' comin' . . . *rivers,* Butler; the goddamn bed was like a *swamp* . . . oh! An' she would grab my ass an' wrap her legs aroun' my ribs an' she would be like climbin' up me with her legs, an' that coconut oil smelled *ree*-lly nice through the whole fuckin' thing." Stony lit a cigarette.

"Don't stop now, I'm gettin' off!" Butler had been holding his crotch through the whole story.

"But the best, Butler, the best thing, the fuckin' coup de grace a the whole night" — Stony grinned triumphantly — "we did it up the chute." He smiled like a winner.

"You banged her in the ass! You fuckin' bastard! You fucked her up the ass!" Butler was jumping around like a hopped-up rooster. "I can't fuckin' believe it! You fucking cock . . . sucker! You really did it up the ass!" Butler hit the cash register, pulled out a dollar and shoved it into Stony's chest pocket. "Buy that man a cigar! I *love* ass fucking!" Butler fell back into his chair.

"Oh, Butler, it was incredible, with the fuckin' pillows under her belly, the fuckin' K-Y jelly, mmmmuh! All the way in."

"She took it all the way, huh?"

"All the fuckin' way in, man, she didn't even flinch. It was so tight an' nice an' that fuckin' jelly. I don't know who invented that K-Y but the guy should get the Nobel Prize. It's greaseless, it's stainless, painless, you name it."

"Did she dig it?" Butler was spread-legged in his chair, eyes going in different directions.

"She came!"

"She came?" Butler slid off his chair and fell on the floor.

"An' in the mornin' I wake up and she made me breakfast in bed. Like a *sultan*, Butler, *or*ange juice, toast, a mushroom omelet, hot coffee."

"Mushroom omelet!" Butler groaned, covering his face with his hands.

A girl came in, long black hair, dangling earrings, lean face, make-up. Butler scrambled up from the floor. "Yes."

"Two pairs, thirty-four, honeytone."

"Thirty-four, honeytone." Butler gawked at her. He turned to Stony, "Thirty-four honeytone!" He turned to the shelves. "Thirty-four honeytone!" Stony saw Butler had a hard-on a mile long. He pulled out a box, flipped it open on the counter, extracted two pairs, draped one across the inside of his forearm, caressed the material while staring at the girl. "This is honeytone."

"Yeah, I know." She looked at him suspiciously, opened her pocketbook and fished around for money.

"Anything else? Pantyhose? Bras? Panties?" he asked hopefully.

"No."

Butler handed her the package. She put a dollar-eight on the counter. Butler took her hand and placed it over the money. "On the house, dear." He looked like he was in pain. Stony held a hand over his eyebrows as if shielding his eyes from the sun. He tried not to crack up. She slid the money off the counter back into her pocketbook. "Thanks." She stared at him queerly.

"Come back soon." Butler waved at her retreating back, then squeezed Stony's knees. "Honeytone!" He got down on his knees. "I found my calling." He collapsed on his back.

Butler's Uncle Frank came into the store, a short bald guy with gray sideburns, gold-rimmed aviator glasses, a silky brown body shirt over a pot belly, gold and brown hound's-tooth double-knit slacks. He was startled to see Stony behind the counter. "Where's Bobby?"

"He's on the floor."

Butler got up, dusted off his pants.

"What the hell you doin' on the floor?"

"I lost a contact."

Frank leaned over the counter, looked down. "I thought maybe there'd be somebody down there with you."

Butler smirked at Stony. "Wise guy here."

Frank grinned, revealing perfectly even gleaming white false teeth. He grabbed Butler around the neck and pinched his cheek while grinning at Stony. "I love this fuckin' kid, he'd like to bang everything that walks inta this place, wants to get some nice granma in trouble." Butler's face turned red. He rolled his eyes and stuck his tongue out in mock strangulation.

"Least I don't go after the delivery men." Butler straightened his collar, the red draining from his face.

"I'll fuck *you* under the table any day a the week." Frank laughed.

"You believe this old cocker?" Butler said to Stony.

Frank faked a punch. Butler ducked. "Bobby, I'm goin' home." He came behind the counter, flipped open a long rectangular covering over the keys on the cash register where the total receipts were registered. "Eighty-one fifty?" he squawked. "Whatta you *doin'* in here?"

Butler shrugged. "It's a slow day, Frank."

"Yesterday you had over two hundred!"

"So that was yesterday! Yóu wamme to pull 'em in off the streets?"

Frank glared at his nephew, faked another punch. "I'll *kill* 'em someday. I'll *kill* 'em." He walked out from behind the counter. "I'll see you tomorrow, lock up nice." He left the store.

"Lock up nice, what the fuck does that mean?" Butler laughed to Stony. "He's on his way out, Stones, he doesn't have that many good years left. About two weeks I'd say offhand."

"I dig him." Stony chuckled.

"Yeah, he's O.K." Butler tilted his head back and massaged his throat with his fingertips. "So anyways, Annette's the one now, hey?"

Stony shrugged. "She ain't gonna be my main squeeze, if that's what you mean."

"Where's Cheri in your head?"

"Cheri who?"

"Three-Finger Annette," Butler announced, "da woman dat makes you fo'git da *other* woman."

"Hey, Butler." Stony winced. "Don't call her Three-Finger no more, O.K.?"

~

At the age of ten, Annette Palladino had developed full woman's breasts that, coupled with the fact that she started smoking cigarettes at eleven, sealed her fate at Saint Anne's School for Girls as a hoowah in the eyes of students and nuns alike. Other girls smoked too, but they didn't have tits as big as Annette's. When she lost two fingers to a paper-sorting machine on a class trip to a newspaper plant, the sisters smugly attributed it to God's evening the score. Also at eleven, the powers that be advertised Annette's calling by putting scarlet letters all over her face, in the form of severe acne. She had no friends among her classmates

— the contempt was mutual. She ran with an older crowd, girls among whom she didn't stick out, so to speak. The only problem was that her body was about five years ahead of her mind and the track she ran on was a little too fast for a twelve-year-old. At fifteen she got knocked up by a twenty-year-old ex-con smack freak who told her she couldn't get pregnant if they did it standing up. Her mother sent her to a Catholic retreat for wayward girls to have the baby. It was a boy. She couldn't see it, name it or touch it. He was given away immediately to a couple in Florida with six kids. Their identities and address were verboten information. She returned home and stayed in her curtain-drawn room for eight months, eating canned ravioli, watching TV and lying in bed. When she finally emerged, she had gained sixty pounds — her complexion had gone from ruddy to death white and she had developed severe astigmatism. She hitched to Haight and Ashbury streets, was informed she missed the party by about five years, got locked up on vagrancy and conspiracy to commit prostitution charges and celebrated her sweet sixteen in a detaining cell in a women's prison in Oakland. The court released her on the stipulation that she be sent home to her father in the Bronx. Her father shipped her off to a convent in the Hudson Valley to become a nun. She ran away from the convent after three days, fell in love with a bartender in Rhinebeck, New York, and lived with him in a farmhouse for a year. During that year, her skin cleared up, she lost seventy pounds, went back to school, got a high school diploma, discovered she had a mind and worked part-time with kids in a day-care center. But a year away from the city was about all she could take, so at seventeen she split from her boyfriend and returned to the Bronx, supporting herself by cocktail waitressing and every so often turning a few tricks. Even though she was the same age as Stony and his friends, she felt miles and years ahead of them and naturally gravitated to the bar owners, bartenders and older bouncers in the clubs where everybody hung out. She developed a crush on Stony because he reminded her of a younger version of Fred, her ex-boyfriend bartender, in Rhinebeck. The only problem was that Stony and his crowd related to her in a way reminiscent of the eleven-year-olds at Saint Anne's.

Stony was a little different. When none of his friends were around he smiled at her in a particular way, something in his expression conveying to her that he knew there was something else out there beyond his teen-age friends and chump-change family. And that, whatever it was, he wanted some. She knew that when he was back with his pals, he got into the "ol' Three-Finger Annette" number, but that didn't really bother her. Small thrills for small minds. She had watched him and his cocktease girlfriend who looked like that big-titted blonde in "All in the Family." She had *her* number from the git-go. The Jewish princess with the Crown Jewels between her legs. One of the true hookers of the world. When the grapevine had it that they split up, she waited two weeks until she figured Stony was climbing the walls with horniness, then called him up. He was over to her crib in ten minutes flat. Just to blow him out of his socks she gave him the Royal Harem treatment that night. She knew, by the expression of his face after twenty minutes in bed, that Cheri was nothing but a childhood memory. Annette had a nice time racking with him that night. He was a little too fast and sloppy and he had to learn a little about lying back, relaxing and appreciating things done to him instead of running through all the male performance numbers, but basically he had it in him to develop into a class A fuck.

As nice as the sex was, what really stuck in her head was the conversation. After fucking, they sat up in bed all night talking. She felt on her guard, so she didn't tell him anything of the scenes she had been into since ten, but he poured his heart out. He talked about his family, his brother, his uncle, the doctor that got him the gig in the hospital, what it felt like working with kids, how his own brother reminded him of the black kids he cared for every day, the new thoughts and connections he was making in his head about kids and parents. All these new ideas of his were things she could have told him when she was twelve. As she listened, she had the feeling he was telling her all this to get a specific reaction from her. He wanted to hear something. Finally, she said that he might as well slash his wrists if he quit the hospital and worked with his father and uncle. He was crazy even to consider becoming an electrician, and that the further he removed himself from that family the more of a human being he would become. That if he went into construction and became a full-blooded De Coco, whatever heart and feeling he had would shrivel up inside him faster than a hard-on in a room full of nuns. Stony freaked out and started running around the apartment, shouting at her that she was a dumb cunt and didn't know shit from Shinola about anything and basically saying that she just didn't understand. Annette just shrugged and felt O.K., I'm wrong, no sweat. But later that night, when she sat up because Stony was tossing and turning, moaning in his sleep, she knew she had hit it dead on the nose.

15

STONY HELD COURT in the day room facing a semicircle of six
wheelchairs. Besides Derek and Tyrone his fan club had ex-
panded in the course of the day to a red-headed nine-year-old
anemic named Felix; a horribly scarred ten-year-old, Freddy, who
had fallen on a third rail while hitching a ride on the back of a
subway and had been in Cresthaven for a year undergoing skin
grafts; a long-haired, thin, eight-year-old girl, Esperanza, who had
an undiagnosed blood disease; and an eleven-year-old girl named
April, who had a wired jaw.

"Anyway, folks, this next story is true. It's about something
that happened right outside this hospital."

"Man, you lyin' awready." Derek laughed.

"Hey look, I'm an Indian, you forget?" Stony leaned forward
in his folding chair. "Indians don't lie."

"You really an Indian?" Felix asked.

"Ask Derek and Tyrone. My grandfather's name was Cochise.
You ever hear of him?"

Six negatives. "Well, how 'bout my father, Creamchise?"

Freddy laughed, the others still indicated no. Stony winked at
Freddy.

"Well, see, my tribe, the De Cocos, useta live on a reservation
hundreds a years ago right outside on Fordham Road, which was
pretty good because we could get out of our tepees in the mornin'
an' go shoppin' in Alexander's, right?"

Finally everybody laughed, except April, who couldn't move
her jaw.

"Well, actually, there was nothin' to Fordham Road in those

days, just a couple of hamburger places, a beauty parlor and the
Loew's Paradise. Matter of fact, Fordham Road used to be such a
drag that the Indians called it Boredom Road. There was really
nothin' there but Indians, millions a Indians an' they were all De
Cocos, just one big fat tribe."

"Was there buffaloes?" Esperanza giggled, covering her mouth
after the question.

"Buffaloes! Man, there was buffaloes, antelopes, lions, ele-
phants, turkeys, there's *still* a lotta them, there was tigers, gorillas.
Hey, look, down by this water hole there was so many different
animals, that they just threw a fence up and called it the Bronx
Zoo."

April smirked as best she could. Stony gave her Groucho eyes,
tapping an imaginary cigar.

"Was there snakes?" Tyrone asked with a look of disgust on his
face.

"No, no snakes."

"Good!"

"The snakes in the zoo came up on the subway from Manhattan." Freddy flinched. Stony cursed himself.

"Anyway, gettin' back to my story, hundreds a years ago
Fordham Road was nothin' but Indians. An' these were tough
Indians, man, they were so tough they useta eat steak with a
spoon."

"I hate steak," said Tyrone.

"Shut up, stupid!" Derek sneered.

"The De Cocos had a ritual you had to go through to be a
full-blooded Indian. See, when you got old enough they gave you
a test to see how tough you were. There useta be this big cave
right outside this hospital. This was way before Cresthaven was
built, and what they would do was they would line up all the
young men and blindfold 'em, give 'em an ax each, an' one by one
they would take them way, way back into the cave, where there
was spiders an' bats" — Stony curled his face in disgust — "but
no snakes. Now this cat was blindfolded, remember? And they
would leave him there, just one scared, blindfolded young brave,
and the test was he had to get out of the cave without takin' off the

blindfold an' the way he had to do that was by takin' the ax and tappin' the walls like this." Stony rapped his knuckles slowly and at paced intervals, like heartbeats, on the seat of his chair. "Y'see? An' as he moved along the cave an' got closer to the opening, the sound of the tapping would get lighter because the walls would be gettin' hollower, you got that? An' in this way, he would find the opening where all the braves would be waitin' for him. When all the braves passed this test, they would have this big party to welcome them into manhood."

"Would they do war dances?"

"*War* dances! This was a *party*, man! They would throw on some heavy jams, some Curtis, some James Brown, Tower of Power, you name it! These cats would put 'Soul Train' right outta business. They had this dynamite dance called the Funky Buffalo, lemme see if I remember it." Stony got up, thinking fast. "Now gimme a sec, it's an old ancestral dance. I gotta remember how to do it." Stony finally decided to get down on all fours, made grunting noises and kicked his legs back while moving in a circle.

"Tha's weak!"

"I woun't dance wit' *choo*, man!"

All the kids laughed, slapping their knees and imitating Stony's buffalo grunts.

Stony got up, his face flushed, laughing along with them. "Well, y'see they *had* to dance like that, you know, on all fours, 'cause the women in the tribe were only nine inches tall, man, an' if you do one a these numbers" — Stony did a high-stepping rain dance — "you dance like that, you likely to wipe out the whole ladies' club if you ain't careful. But I'm gettin' away from the story here. One day for the initiation they send this young brave way back in the cave, and they're all on the outside waitin' an' they hear" — Stony tapped on the chair seat — "from inside 'cause he's tappin' the ax, right? Then all of a sudden they hear this 'rrrrrr.' " Stony made a rumbling noise in the back of his throat. "An' all of a sudden everything went *Boom!* It was a *cave*-in! Rocks started flyin', the earth shook, clouds a dust came bloomin' outta the cave, oh, it was terrible!" Stony held his head.

"What happened to the Indian?"

Stony started tapping on the seat. "Well, they heard him tappin' inside, so they tried to dig him out soon as the earth settled, an' the rocks stopped flyin' an' the dust cleared. But the cave was blocked to the sky with gigantic boulders and they couldn't get in more than two inches an' they tried, boy, they tried, they pulled, an' yanked and tugged, but they couldn't move one boulder. I mean they tried for *hours* while they could still hear that tappin' and all the women were weepin' an' wailin' and the men were gruntin' an sweatin' but *nothin'* from *nothin'*, man."

Stony kept tapping as he told the story. "There wasn't one Indian who wasn't knocked out to the bone. They just couldn't go on anymore. Even the women and children were exhausted. Then all of a sudden the tapping stopped."

Stony stopped tapping the chair.

"He was dead?" In a whisper.

"Instead of havin' a celebration they wound up havin' a funeral." Stony sadly shook his head. "They never tried another cave initiation again. They just put flowers in fronna the blocked cave for the dead young brave's spirit and called it a day. That woulda been that, except that the next year on the first anniversary of the cave-in, in the middle of the night" — Stony started tapping his chair and said in a hoarse whisper — "the tapping started again!"

Derek looked worried, everybody was frowning. "An' every year after that, on the same midnight that tapping was heard, and all the De Cocos shook in fear and prayed to their gods and made sacrifices; they sacrificed crops, they sacrificed white birds, they sacrificed lambs. One year they even sacrificed a great buffalo whose burned bones spelled 'murder,' but the tapping wouldn't stop and slowly, year by year, the De Cocos started leaving, wandering all over the world until there was nobody left to hear that midnight concert but the wind." Stony continued to tap, the sound filling the room. "Then, many years later, white men came to build a town and they saw that cave, and it was in the way, so they blew it up with dynamite and started building houses and banks and train stations and a big town was in full swing, but every year on this one particular midnight they heard strange tappings from the spot where the old cave useta be — it echoed through the town like the ticking of a giant clock and nobody knew what it was or where it was coming from. This old, crazy lady said she saw a blindfolded Indian wandering the dark streets one night with an ax in his hand, but when she went to touch him to take off the blindfold, he vanished right in front of her face. Nobody would believe her because she was out of her tree, but she knew she really saw him and every year when that tapping sound was heard she would go out into the street, see him stumbling around and she would try to help him, but he always vanished before she touched him. Then one year on that special midnight, she heard the tapping, got dressed and went out looking for him. Before she could find him, two robbers tried to hold her up. When she wouldn't give them her money, they stabbed her. When the mornin' came, they found the old lady dead in the street, clutchin' an old piece of cloth, what looked like it coulda been used as a blindfold. And about a hundred yards up the road they found two more bodies — the robbers." Stony started tapping again. "Their heads was split open with an ax."

"It was the Indian?"

"Right after that, the tapping stopped, for *years* nobody heard nothin' ever again. Except last year when I was walkin' around the hospital outside I heard somethin' like tappin'."

"Was it him?"

"I didn't hang around to find out, I'll tell you that much . . . but I wouldn't worry about it; it was probably a woodpecker or somethin'."

"Ah bet it was him!"

"He only go after bad guys, right?"

"Hey listen, you know somethin' I just realized? Tonight's the night! This is the day a the year he got killed in the cave-in!"

"Is he comin' here?"

"Ah'll kung-*fu* that motha!"

"Look, I got a confession to make. That Indian was my great-great-great-great-great-great-grandfather, so if he comes around I know I'm safe because I'm his blood, but what can I do to protect you guys?" Stony screwed up his face in concentration. "I know! I'll make you all spit brothers!"

"What's that?"

"It's like bloodbrothers, but it don't hurt. O.K., everybody take your thumb and spit on it like this." Stony pressed his thumb to his lips and made a blow-dart sound. All six of them followed suit. "O.K. Now hold up your thumbs." Stony pressed his wet thumb against theirs.

"Naka-Maga-Walla." He solemnly passed from one recipient to the next. "Naka-Maga-Walla." When they had all received communion, Stony stepped back. "We are now all spit brothers, safe from any danger. The Indian ghost is on our side. Whenever you're in trouble just hold up your thumb an' say, 'Naka-Maga-Walla!' and the ghost Indian will help you out. An' in case he's busy an' can't make it, since you're all spit brothers, you gotta help each other out, so any time you hear anybody say, 'Naka-Maga-Walla,' you come runnin', O.K.?"

They nodded seriously.

"And the next time you see any a your friends or any a the nurses or the doctors you make 'em spit brothers a yours 'cause the more spit brothers you got, the better off you are. So just spit on your thumb, hold it up to theirs an' say — "

"Naka-Maga-Walla!" they finished, more or less in unison.

Stony looked at his watch. "Jeez, it's four-thirty, I gotta go, kiddos, see you tomorrow." As Stony left the day room, two nurses coming in to take the kids back to their rooms for dinner were assaulted by thumbs and Indian chants. Stony watched as the two confused and amused nurses were initiated in a solemn ceremony, expanding the Naka-Maga-Walla spit brotherhood to nine.

Stony whistled as he soft-shoed into the locker room. Weekend coming up. He and Annette were going to Bear Mountain tomorrow and could have a nice time if she'd just shut her yap about his family. He got a half ounce of Ciba-Ciba from Chili Mac, and they was going to do some communing with nature. "Ah said le's hear it for da com-*mu*-nin' wit' *na*-ture!" Stony clapped his hands and did a James Brown slide over to his locker in the deserted room. Three aisles over, out of Stony's sight, sat a totally stoned orderly grooving on his combination lock which he couldn't remember the combination to. "Naka-Maga-*Walla!*" Stony cackled. "De Coco da *Indian!*" He slipped out of his whites. "*Cave*-dwellin' Indian!" The orderly gave up on his lock and decided to blow some more hash. He took out a corncob pipe from his shirt pocket and sluggishly tried to scrape out the ash with his finger. "Ah said watch out for da *cave*-dwellin' Indian!" The orderly rapped the pipe on the long bench to clear out some crud. The slow, hollow tapping echoed through the locker room. Stony was in the middle of lacing his boots when the sound froze him in mid-crouch.

"Motha*fuck!*" The orderly weaved on the bench like a cobra coming out of a basket as he caught the blur of Stony running half-dressed and wild-eyed through the exit. He squinted at his chunk of hash and nodded. " 'S' good shit."

16

CHUBBY SLEPT LATE Saturday, got up at noon. He ambled to the john, pissed and studied his face in the mirror. Good day for a haircut.

~

"Hey! Bobby B!" Chubby came grinning into the hosiery store.

"Hey, Chubby! Long time no see." Butler extended his hand over the counter. Chubby gave it a squeeze, a shake and a light slap. A cigarette hung between his lips and he squinted through the smoke.

"What can I do for yah?" Butler winced from Chubby's grip.

"Nothin'. I just came down to try out that barber across the street, the guy up at Co-op cuts hair like he got some kinda palsy."

"You gonna go to Domenick?"

"Whatever his name is," Chubby said. "Is he good?"

"You're askin' me?" Butler hadn't had his hair cut in more than a year.

Chubby laughed. "So how's the store?"

"It's slow, you know, the summer."

Chubby walked around, fished a cellophane-wrapped pair of red slippers with pink pompons from the cardboard box. "How much a' these?"

"They wouldn't fit yah."

"Wise guy." Chubby chuckled and tossed them on the counter. "I'll get somethin' for the old lady." He winked. "Keep it quiet on the western front, you know what I mean?" He pulled out his wallet.

"On the house." Butler laid a hand over the wallet while stooping for a paper bag.

Chubby grinned and pinched Butler's cheek. "Hey, Bobby, how's Stony doin'? I haven't seen 'im around."

"He's doin' O.K." Butler put the slippers in a bag and folded the top: "He broke up with Cheri, you hear that?"

"What!" Chubby grimaced and shook his head. "Is that kid a sap or what?"

Butler shrugged. "I think they're both better off."

"Ah hor'shit. She was a real sweetheart. He jus' din' know how to handle her. All you fuckin' kids, you slip 'em the schvance an' you think that's all there is to it."

Butler smiled uneasily.

Chubby leaned straight-arm on the counter. "He got somethin' goin' for him now?"

"Well . . ." Butler started arranging boxes on the shelves. "He's seein' this chick, Annette, Annette Palladino."

Chubby's eyes fluttered at half-mast as if someone had just shoved smelling salts under his nose. He looked down at his shoes and shook his head.

"Hey, you know her?" Butler turned from the shelves.

Chubby nodded without looking up. "She gives the best underage blowjob this side a Harlem."

"How do you know?" Something defensive and angry rose in Butler.

Chubby looked up, gave him a brief, hard stare, then returned his gaze to his shoes. "I'll see you, Bobby."

"Yeah."

Chubby walked out of the store without raising his head. He left the slippers. Butler didn't call after him.

17

TOMMY AND MARIE planned a small cousins' club meeting for the Sunday family day activity. The house was spotless. Marie broke out the teakwood lazy Susans, filled them with potato chips, pretzels, Brazil nuts, silver-foiled chocolate kisses, Snowcaps, assorted miniature Hershey bars (nuts, no nuts, crunch and semisweet). She laid out the special cocktail napkins with the dirty jokes and big-titted women on them and even took the vinyl slipcover off the couch. Tommy displayed the liquor, bottles of Seagram's, Canadian, Wilson's, Cherry Heering and Early Times. He lined up the bottles beside an army of glasses on a white cloth he draped over the dining room table. He filled three silver ice buckets to the brim and loaded a tall, smoked glass with a fistful of wooden swizzle sticks carved in the shape of big-breasted Ubangi women. An old-fashioned glass held lemon slices and another maraschino cherries. The glasses had a woody smell, because they had spent the last year inside the huge liquor cabinet since the last cousins' club gathering hosted by the De Cocos. As a final touch, Tommy replaced the toilet paper in the john with a roll he had bought in a novelty store. It had dollar bills printed on it with oval portraits of a cross-eyed George Washington. Under each dollar was the legend "It's only money." When the cousins started arriving Tommy greeted them at the door wearing a gorilla mask he picked up with the toilet paper. Among assorted shrieks, giggles, gasps and "Hiya, Tommys" an eighty-year-old great-aunt in a wheelchair fainted when Tommy bent to kiss her at the door. They revived her with a shot of Cherry Heering. Tommy, Albert and Stony wore identical sky blue Banlon shirts — a shopping coup of Marie's. Stony bitched and moaned about the party, but as always, when relatives started arriving, he felt a strange thrill in his guts. He loved all the big mouths, morons, assholes and scuzzy aunts, no matter how much he poor-mouthed them to his friends — this was his blood. He especially got off on his aunts and uncles marveling at his good looks, how much he looked like his old man.

After the ordeal of hugging, kissing and handshaking was just about over, Chubby cornered him by the bar. "Oh, yah so cute! Don' he juza looka lika he faddah!"

Stony laughed.

"C'mere." Chubby grabbed his arm. "Inta the bedroom, I gotta talk to you."

Chubby ushered him through the crowds. They had to joke, laugh and kiss half a dozen women before they made it to the bedroom. Chubby closed the door, partially sealing off the noise. "Whew! I gotta hand it to yer folks, I never would have all these animals up at my place."

"Just wait, you're next. What's up?"

"Nothin', I just wanted to shoot the shit for a while. So, ah, how's your love life?"

"Whatta you, an Ultra-Brite commercial?"

"No, I just heard you broke up with Cheri." Chubby picked up a copy of *Jaws* from Stony's desk. "This any good?"

"It's awright, where'd you hear that?"

Chubby flipped the pages absently, tossed the book back on the desk. "I heard, I heard around."

"Yeah, I was just thinkin', things were gettin' too much. I felt more like a goddamn watchdog than a boyfriend. Jealousy's a humiliatin' emotion. I felt like shit. So, like ah, so like I rehearsed." Stony started pacing the room. "I rehearsed for hours, for *days* what I was gonna say to her, things like 'Ah, Cheri, I think it's time we went our separate ways'; 'Ah, I know we love each other but I think we have two different ideas in our heads what that means' . . . ah, who knows, it was all a buncha shit anyhow. If I had balls I woulda said, 'Cheri, you fuckin' tramp, if you wanna run with me you stay locked in your room whenever

I'm not around. You spend all your time thinkin' about me, you hereby get the hots just at the mention a my name.' "

Chubby leaned his ass on the corner of the desk, his arms folded in front of him. "So what happened?"

"So I call her, right? And I got this whole jive speech worked up about why we should split and I say, 'Cheri, I think the time has come when we should go our separate ways,' and then she says 'O.K.' just like that. That was the whole thing. An' I was sittin' there, you know, like waitin' for the bomb to drop, the pain, the remorse, the whatever. Nothin', nothin' at all. I'm sittin' there thirty minutes just waitin'. Finally, I realize, what the fuck am I doin', if you don't get slammed, just go with the flow, so I go. Jump into some nice threads, run down to D'Artagnan's an' I party all night. After closin', I go out with Chili Mac, you know, that spade cat I run with sometimes? We go down to the Village, bop aroun'. I din't get home till seven in the mornin'. I guess I got sick a runnin' around like a mope allatime." Stony sat on his bed and lit a cigarette.

Chubby frowned. "So how's Annette?"

"Where'd you hear about Annette?" Stony felt something rising inside.

"Around."

"Around, around, around, what the hell is this, a village? Who'd you hear about Annette from?" He stood up, ditched his cigarette.

"What's the difference?"

"I wanna know, Chubby. Who the hell is goin' aroun' reportin' my business to the papers?"

Chubby shrugged. "I ran into your friend Bobby."

"Butler?" Stony stamped around the room. Chubby hooked his arm. "Hey, don't get your balls in a uproar, it just came out in conversation. It's no big deal. I just wanna know, how serious are you with her?"

"Whadya mean serious? We just racked a couple a times, I have a nice time with her." Stony was shouting.

"Easy, easy. There's people out there."

"Whatta you drivin' at, Chubby?"

"Look, I just been around a little longer than you, and I been through a lotta different things, an' there's women you get involved with, an' women you don't. Now, I hear things about this Annette, I don't hafta go into details, you know what I mean."

"What, she's a village pump?"

"Now . . . O.K. You wanna call a spade a spade, yeah, that's what I heard. Now, you wanna have a good time, she's a good lay, whatever. Enjoy yourself, but *don't . . . fuckin' . . . get . . . involved*. The minute you split she probably takes on the janitor for the month's rent. A chick like that doesn't even need carfare. You remember once you said to me Cheri uses her cunt like spare change? Now that was a exaggeration, you know it too. O.K., maybe she played around with a guy or two, maybe not even that, but a girl like Annette, she *really* uses her cunt like a fuckin' Master Charge an' I seen guys get hung up on tramps like that too. It's heartbreaking to see these guys, an' I just don't want you to be one a them. Like I said, have all the fun you want, but if you think you had heartache with Cheri, God have mercy on your soul if you fall in love with this one."

All through Chubby's talk Stony was getting sick to his stomach; now the nausea was creeping into his face.

"Whassamatter?"

"Huh? Nothin'."

"You O.K.?"

"Yeah, yeah!" Stony forced a laugh. "You know, Chubby, you're talkin' like I'm plannin' to marry her."

"Not even in a joke, Stony."

"Yeah." Stony shrugged. "No sweat."

Chubby gripped Stony's wrist. "Stony, you know I love you like a son, I'd cut off my balls for you. I just don't want to see you hurt, do you dig what I'm tryin' to say to you?"

Stony felt something click off inside him. "Yeah, sure. She *is* a village pump, *I* know that."

Chubby slowly began to smile. As he stood up he placed his hand on the back of Stony's neck. "C'mon, let's go join that fast crowd out there, I don't want anybody thinkin' we're goin' queer on each other in here."

18

AFTER WORK on Monday as Stony approached Frank's Hosiery House he noticed three police cars converging on the corner at abrupt angles, lights flashing, doors flying open. Stony double-parked across the street, sprinted under the el, waded through the empty cop cars, radio squawk blaring from under the dashboards and raced inside. A half-dozen cops were milling around Butler's Uncle Frank, who sat in a torn vinyl chair in the middle of the store gasping for breath. Without his aviator glasses his face looked blanched and popeyed and old. The front of his red silk sport shirt was ripped and he held a bloody piece of gauze to the side of his neck. He looked scared. "Thirty years," he wheezed, "I been here thirty fuckin' years . . . never . . ."

Butler emerged from behind the curtain separating the store-room from the front. He was wild-eyed and livid. "*I'll* get those motherfuckers!" he screamed at the cops. "*Fuck* you guys! *I'll* get them. I *know* those nigger bastards!" Two cops tried to calm him down. Two others jotted notes from Frank; one examined the knocked-over cash register and one spoke over a walkie-talkie.

When Butler saw Stony he grabbed him. "*We'll* get those motherfuckers! Me, you, Chili Mac, we'll tear down that whole fuckin' school."

A cop nudged Stony. "Who're you?"

"I'm his friend. What happened?"

"I'll kill every fuckin' nigger on this block!" Butler screamed. Four of the cops were black, tried to ignore him. Stony seized Butler in an embrace and pushed him back a step. "Ssh, ssh, easy, baby, easy," he whispered in his ear. Butler windmilled his arms around Stony, but Stony wouldn't let up. He patted Butler's back, caressed his neck, whispering all the time until Butler calmed down. Cautiously Stony let him go, but not completely, holding him around the waist. Frank twisted in his chair to look at his nephew. Stony winked.

Butler tried to catch his breath. "Three niggers from the high school," he exhaled, "come in here, right? Frank's behind the counter . . . Pull a fuckin' shiv long as my dick . . . I'm in the back. I come runnin' out . . . they go . . ." Butler grabbed Stony's hair, yanking his head back, laid his thumb against Stony's neck. " 'We'll *kill* him, honky.' I'm fuckin' *standin'* there like a fuckin' statue. They go through the register, drag him to the door and run like the yellow cunts they are."

"You say you know these guys?" asked a cop.

"I seen 'em around, yeah."

"Can you describe them?"

"No . . . no." Butler swung his head emphatically. "You guys take care a Frank, I'll take care a them. Me, him an' some friends." He nodded to Stony.

"Look, is it O.K. I talk to him private?" Stony asked the two cops. Putting his arm around Butler's neck he ushered him behind the curtain. Stony busied himself adjusting the curtain for a second, then abruptly swung around, punching Butler in the gut as hard as he could. Butler gasped, slid down the wall onto the floor, a pained why in his eyes. Stony lifted him under the armpits and slammed his shoulders into the wall. He held Butler's jaw in a vicelike grip. "Now you lissen to *me,* you stupid bastard! *I* ain't runnin' down no vigilante shit. Chili *Mac's* not runnin' down no vigilante shit, an' *you,* you dumb cunt, ain't runnin' down no vigilante shit, you got that?" He shook Butler's jaw, Butler held his stomach. "I don't wanna find your ass inna cardboard box behind some *soul* palace — you got that? Your fuckin' uncle's out there, halfway to a heart attack, an' you're jumpin' around like a fuckin' wild man. So just *cool out,* you dig? And another thing, *stupid!* You're runnin' aroun' jumpin' bad about killin' the niggers an' you got four coons out there wit' thirty-eights. If they don't put a fuckin' bullet in your small brain right now, I

guaran*tee* you . . . I guaran*tee* you, the next time you need a
fuckin' cop in here your ass is cream cheese. Can you understand
that? Hah? Hah?" Stony viciously rattled Butler's head until
Butler nodded. "Good, now first thing, you go out there an' you
apologize to them for being such an asshole, then you fuckin'
cooperate. You know these guys? Fine, then they'll get 'em then,
O.K.?" Stony released Butler's jaw. Butler slumped over, trying
to catch his breath. Stony kneaded his shoulders. "I'm sorry I hit
you, babe, I just had to get your attention." Stony hugged him,
then kissed him on the side of the head. "You know I love you, I
just don't wanna go to your funeral yet, you dig?"

~

That night Stony picked up Annette for dinner. He was moody
and silent. Chubby's little talk yesterday was like a pebble in his
shoe.

Stony humped away, but his heart wasn't into it. Finally, he
began to lose his hard-on. Annette stared up at him, nervous
beneath his automatic-pilot thrusting. Stony pulled out, rolled on
his back shielding his eyes with his arm. Annette lay next to him
wondering what the hell happened, where he went to.

"You didn't come?" She leaned on her side, facing him.

"Yeah, I came."

"Don't bullshit me, you did not." Annette had a broad,
freckled face. Her eyes were the slightest bit crossed, that and the
fact that she had the disarming habit of licking her lips whenever
she talked to a guy she liked gave the impression that she was
always dizzy with lust.

"How do *you* know?" Stony raised his arm from his face.

"When somebody comes in you, you know it."

"You know, Annette, when you talk like that, you got no class."
Stony absently played with her long red hair, then dropped his
hand to his side.

"Oh! Excuse me, Mister Firstnighter! I din't notice any cuffs
on *your* underwear."

"Now you talkin' stupid. I just meant, ah, forget it." Stony sat
up and reached for his cigarette pack wedged between the bed and

the wall. Annette sat up and took one from the pack. "Hey, Annette, how many guys you ever slept with?" She leaned away from the offered light. Stony mistook the blush of anger in her face for guilt.

"I don't know," she answered coldly.

"More than ten?"

"You mean this week? Or just the weekend?"

"See that shit? There you go again!" Stony stared at the smooth stumps of two fingers on her left hand.

"I don't like questions like that, Stony." She started dressing.

"What the hell you gettin' so defensive about! I just ast you a simple question. Whadya got, a guilt complex or somethin'?"

"A guilt . . ." Annette froze, half-dressed. She was beside herself with rage. Bewildered and furious at the sudden change in Stony, she looked at herself, then at him. "What the hell am *I* gettin' dressed for! I *live* here! *You* get dressed!" She pointed a finger at Stony. "An' get the hell outta here, you goddamn nowhere asshole!" Stony casually ditched his cigarette, slipped into his jeans and shirt. "I ain't nowhere." Stony tucked in his shirt. "I'm just somewhere you ain't." Inside, his guts were falling apart. He felt like a little kid slugging his best friend in the back of the head just to see what would happen. As he sauntered to the door, he threw one out: "Give my regards to the janitor."

"The *who?*" Annette stood in her panties and unhooked bra staring incredulously at Stony.

Stony tried to look flip and cool but felt the bile shooting up. He left quickly, quietly closing the door behind him.

Dazed and in pain, Annette looked around her for a clue to what had just happened.

19

TUESDAY AFTERNOON Stony heard his name paged over the hospital PA system. He felt like Ben Casey as he trotted down the hall in his hospital whites to the phone at the nurses' station.

"Stony."

"Butler! What's happenin'? They catch those guys yet?"

"It's mine."

"What's yours?"

"The store. Frank wants out. He says he'll sign it over to me for free. He's movin' down to Florida."

"Whoa! Hold on."

"It's mine. Butler's Hosiery Palace."

"Wait up. What the fuck do you know about that shit? You don't know how to run a business."

"I'll learn, man, my own goddamn place."

"Hey, last week you were talkin' summer job, now you're talkin' life career."

"I can really make it though."

"Hey, c'mon, Bobby, be right! You wanna spend the next thirty years there in that little hole?"

"I'll expand."

"Expand what? Your uncle's dyin' in there; whatta you gonna do, sell panties until you're sixty? An' how many times you think what happened yesterday is gonna happen again? Some lady comes in to buy stockin's in the A.M., her kid holds you up in the P.M., right?"

"I'll take care a that."

"What with? You gonna sell girdles with a Saturday Night Special under the counter? What's witcha head, Butler?"

"I already ordered the sign."

"What sign?"

"Butler's Hosiery Palace."

"Fantastic. You awready ordered the fuckin' sign so that's it for the next thirty years, you ordered the sign."

"Stony . . . I'm fuckin' scared."

"Don't do it, Bobby."

"I want it."

"How much juice you think you're gonna get outta your life runnin' a fuckin' hosiery store?"

"What?"

"You heard me."

"I want that fuckin' store."

Stony massaged his temples. "Lissen, Butler, my fuckin' head is splittin'. I feel like really bent outta shape about somethin'. I really don't know what to tell you now, you know? Maybe I'm not the greatest person to check this out with."

"I ain't checkin' it out, Stony, I'm tellin' you what's goin' down. You wanna come down to the store tomorrow, help me out?"

"I don't know, Butler. I really can't think straight."

"Hey, Stones, lemme explain somethin'. I really dig where you're comin' from, you know? I'm hip to what's been goin' down in your head with yer old man an' shit. See, like maybe you're too on top of everything right now to not take the store personal, you know? Like, the trick with a lifetime gig isn't to run away from home. The trick's finding somethin' you want so fuckin' bad you can taste it, family business or whatever. You with me? Now your idea of a heavy-duty trip might be somethin' entirely different from what I'm into. I mean, you might think it's just a little pissant store, but I see it as a stake, baby. It's *mine*. I don't take orders, I don't pick up a paycheck. I don't kiss ass. If a nice piece a tail comes in an' I wanna slip her a free pair a pantyhose I don't gotta worry about the boss findin' out. *I'm* the fuckin' boss. I sink or swim on my own power, man. And that's as legitimate

and honorable a trip as gettin' off on kids, O.K.? I told you I'm
shittin' bricks now, I mean, I really got the shakes, but it ain't
because I'm goin' in there with my head up my ass. I'm scared
because I'm so goddamn close to I-T, *it,* my dream. Now how
many guys our age can say that? And another thing, I really
fuckin' respect what you want, you know? And I would really,
really dig gettin' some of that respect bounced back my way,
O.K.?"

"R–E–S–P–E–C–T — found out what it means to me."

"Hey, I'm not fuckin' witchoo, Stony."

"Butler, what you want from me? You know how I feel about
the fuckin' store. I'm not gonna jerk you off. It seems your idea
of movin' in life is goin' from the bedroom to the bathroom."

"Don't be such a fuckin' big shot, De Coco. You still playin'
summer job musical chairs?"

"Uh-uh, baby, this one's for keeps."

"Yeah, right, an' next week you gonna be runnin' with your
daddy."

"Hey, Butler, what the fuck you call me for?"

"Right now I couldn't tell you, but whatever it was you ain't got
it." Butler slammed down the phone.

"Cunt!" Stony stormed down to the day room.

"Hey, De Coco!" Tyrone threw a checker at Stony as he
walked into the room. It bounced off his arm.

"Hey, grow up! Hah?" Stony snapped. Tyrone's face dropped.

"You fuckin' kids." Stony stomped around the room collecting
garbage. "Look a' this goddamn place!" The six kids in the room
shrank from his presence. "Whatta my supposed to be in here, the
goddamn maid?"

"You sound like my mama," Derek said sullenly.

"Baby, this afternoon, I'm *every*body's mama!"

~

When Stony got home he slammed the bedroom door and sulked
until the next morning when he had to go back to work. That was
it for Butler. At the hospital he tried to get his act together, but he
was going through hell doing it.

"You ever see a tiger?" Derek snarled, curling his fingers into claws at Stony.

"At the zoo." Stony was busy picking up assorted debris from the day room floor. That morning Mrs. Pitt had told him there was a chance he could be in charge of the day room in a few weeks' time. Stony disappointed her by not jumping at it. He didn't, because he was still in a shit-ass mood about Butler and because he hadn't yet told her he had to split for two weeks come next week. But there was also another reason, something else going down that Stony didn't understand. A nagging fear like he had signed a contract without reading all the small print. Not that he thought that anybody was out to fuck him over. Something about consequences. Something about his last phone conversation with Doctor Harris and leaving home.

"You ever see a lion?" Derek asked.

"Yeah, at the zoo." Stony was distracted.

"Where you at today, De Coco?" Tyrone peered at him.

"Huh?" Stony stood up, his arms filled with junk.

"You sure ain't here."

Stony did a double take, then smiled.

"I'll tell you, you talk about bad animals." Stony dumped the stuff in a white plastic garbage bag. "You know what the meanest animal in the world is?"

"A lion?"

"A snake?"

"Nope, it's a two-headed Italian kabooni."

"He's lyin' again." Derek raised his eyes to the ceiling.

"No, really, man. The kabooni got two heads, one on each end."

"Then how do he shit?" Tyrone challenged.

"He can't, man, that's why he's the meanest animal in the world."

Neither of them laughed. Tyrone whispered to Derek, hand over his mouth, his eyes darting at Stony. "Oooh," Derek howled, slapping his knee. "You know what he said, De Coco?"

"Don't tell him, man!" Tyrone giggled.

"He say your *mama* a two-headed Italian kabooni."

Stony shrugged. "I didn't even know you'd met her."

They broke up, rocking back and forth in their wheelchairs like hinged rocking toys.

"I'll tell you really though." Stony sat down. "You know who's *really* a two-headed kabooni in my family? My brother!"

That broke them up even more.

"You think I'm kiddin'? I'll bring him in."

"When?"

Stony thought for a second. Albert was the same age as these kids. "Now! You just stay there." He sprinted down the hall to the pay phone. It felt crazy, but the idea of bringing Albert to the hospital had been nibbling at his mind for a week now. One of the many thoughts he'd been having in the last week without understanding what put them in his head.

"Ma? Is Albert there? Lissen, do me a favor . . . put him in a cab and send him down here . . . yeah . . . yeah . . . so take a minute out . . . *I'll* pay for the cab, O.K? . . . just put him in a cab. No, no. Just do it, O.K.? Thanks." Stony ran back to the day room. "One two-headed Italian kabooni comin' up!"

Stony met the cab at the hospital entrance. He threw the driver two bills and hustled Albert into the hospital. "C'mon, kiddo, I wancha to meet some guys."

"Doctor Harris?" Albert was bewildered at being back in a hospital, but he dug taking the cab ride by himself. He walked down the corridors like his head was on a revolving turret. He held onto Stony's hand and wasn't afraid. Stony was frightened enough for both of them. Albert had a way of saying things to people.

Derek and Tyrone looked up when Stony entered the day room with his brother in tow. The three eight-year-olds stared at each other in silence, their mood a mixture of embarrassment and curiosity. Stony wanted to say something witty about kaboonies but it didn't seem appropriate. Disengaging himself from Stony Albert sat down on a folding chair facing Derek and Tyrone.

"You De Coco's brother?" Tyrone asked.

"How come you so skinny?" Derek asked.

Albert smiled at Stony. He looked back at Derek and shrugged, his feet dangling below the seat. His eyes wandered to the stacks of games strewn over the floors and tables.

"What's your name?"

"Albert."

"Are you an Indian?"

Albert looked at Stony.

"Yeah, he's an Indian! He's my brother, right?"

"How come he don't talk?"

"Albert, talk."

"I dunno what to say." He hunched his shoulders and curled back into his chair.

"He dunno what to say."

"Do you play all these games?" Albert asked them.

"Nah, they broke," said Tyrone. "What grade you in?"

"Third."

"I'm in fourth," Derek said.

Albert walked over to a stack of games on a Formica table. "I got this one at home," he said, pulling out a Chinese checkers box. "Do you know how to play?"

Stony watched in amazement as Albert laid out the board on the floor, set up the marbles and started explaining the game to Derek and Tyrone. The three boys played for over an hour. Stony straddled a folding chair, his chin on the backrest, and watched Albert through that hour. His brain was on fire. This was the first time he ever saw Albert play with kids away from the house. He was loose. Relaxed. Yelled a lot. Laughed a lot. Derek and Tyrone dug him. He had balls. Real stones. Out of the house he came alive. He could take care of himself. Himself. Maybe Albert didn't need him around all the time after all. Stony felt confused. The expression "ace in the hole" popped into his head.

"Hello!" Stony snapped out of his thoughts as Mrs. Le Pietro approached Albert.

"Hello." Albert smiled up at her.

"Who're you?" She checked a list of names on her clipboard.

"Albert!"

"Albert, huh?" She rechecked her names.

"Uh, he's my brother." Stony walked over.

"Oh! He's not a patient? I'm sorry, he'll have to leave immediately. Hospital rules. No children under fourteen as visitors."

"Oh, man!"

"Aw!" Derek and Tyrone protested.

"Sorry, boys, when you get well you can play all you want." She shook her head.

"Ten more minutes?" Albert whined.

"Sorry."

Albert struggled to his feet, brushed the knees of his dungarees. "You wanna come to my house?" he offered.

"They'll come as soon as they're better." She gently ushered Albert from the room.

"See you." Albert waved.

Derek and Tyrone waved back.

"Let's go, chief," Stony said. They walked down the corridor toward the entrance. At the door another nurse stopped them. She knelt in front of Albert and smiled. "We going home today?"

Confused, Albert looked up at Stony.

"He's not a patient," Stony said.

"He's not?" She straightened up. "Well, what's he doing here?"

Stony sighed. "He's my brother. I brought him in to play with the kids in the day room. I didn't know it was against the rules. I'm *sorry*. I'm takin' him home."

"Can I see his discharge slip?"

"His what?" Stony squawked.

The nurse peered at Stony's name tag. "Mr. De Coco, you can't expect me to believe this child is not a patient."

Stony glared at her. "*Yeah,* I expect you to believe he's not a goddamn patient. He's my goddamn brother. You don't believe me, go check it out with Mrs. Le Pietro. She just kicked him out!"

The nurse stared at Albert, her thumb and index finger caressing her chin. "I'll do that. Please wait here."

"What the fuck?" Stony muttered as the nurse vanished in the shuffling crowd.

"Can you believe that?" he complained to Albert. Albert was busy picking his nose. As they waited for the nurse to return, Stony took some good hard looks at his brother. It hit him that Albert didn't look any different than any kid he'd seen in that day room. He even looked worse than some. If Stony and that nurse were to switch roles, Stony would have acted the same way. In a strange way, although it made him ashamed of himself, Stony found the thought comforting.

~

As much as Stony dreaded working the construction job, he equally dreaded springing the news on Mrs. Pitt that after two weeks in the hospital he had to take a two-week vacation. Every day he found a different excuse for not telling her, but now he had no more days to put it off.

"Mrs. Pitt." Stony sighed. "I got this hassle I gotta work out. Before I took this job, I promised my old man I'd work with him in construction for two weeks this summer. He was breakin' my chops about me wantin' to do hospital work when I could be makin' triple the bread with the electricians." He shrugged. "So like I promised him I would do two weeks here, two weeks with him, and then I could decide what I was gonna do, you follow?" Stony sat sprawled hand over mouth.

Mrs. Pitt frowned. "I follow, Stony, but I also feel like you're exploiting me. I hire you in good faith on a long-term basis. Then you come in here and tell me you want to do something else for two weeks and *maybe* you'll come back. That's pretty damn unfair, don't you think?"

Stony's guts started spinning. His hand moved from his mouth to his forehead. "Lissen." He leaned forward in his seat. "You don' understand my family. It's like . . . like . . ." Stony fretted and fumed, searching for the right words. "Shit. Look, there's this very heavy number goin' down with my father and uncle. They're both electricians, right? An' ever since I was a kid, see, you don' . . . oh shit." He rubbed his face, eyes darting around the room. "You don't know what I had to go through to get this hospital gig, like, uh, you know, that Jewish thing, my son the doctor?" Stony slapped himself on the chest. "My son the electrician. An' they got me boxed in, Mrs. Pitt. I'm tellin' you, the whole thing with the job, the union, the men, the House a De Coco, it's like puttin' on a goddamn hard hat, it's like puttin' on the crown a England, you know? An' I'm next in line. My grandfather was in there bustin' heads, settin' up the union in the thirties, the whole thing." Stony studied his hands. "I tell you, sometimes I think it woulda been a lot easier if I was a girl. God forbid. I mean, no offense. I had to run a gamut to do this job like you wouldn't *believe*. I wouldn't be here if I didn't promise my old man I'd do two weeks with him." Stony lowered his voice. "I don' wanna be a goddamn electrician, those guys are nowhere! They get twenty grand a year for luggin' pipes up an' down buildings. I don' care about money, I'll make it some way. I ain't no sap. I get more outta jivin' aroun' with these kids for one hour than I would in *ten years* doin' construction." He bobbed his head in emphasis. "It's my *life* we're talkin' about! I don't wanna be one of those lames that lives for the weekend, you know? I wanna live seven days a week. I wanna go home everyday feelin' like I accomplished somethin'. Look, I was gonna go down to this ditso school in Louisiana in the fall, then I figure, screw that, I come outta there a veterinarian's assistant with a concentration in turkey mange, you know? School doesn't *mean* anything to me, just to go so you can say you went, right?" Stony glanced around the room. "But *now* I'm thinkin', lemme do this for a year see? Then, maybe this time next year I'll apply to some college, study social work, recreation, physical therapy, who knows? Somethin' so I can keep workin' an' get some kinda degree in somethin' that *means* somethin', you know? But look, I gotta pay the devil his due. I gotta give my old man his two weeks, then I got him off my back, he can't say nothin'." Stony signaled finito with his hands. "I fulfilled my end an' that's that, I'm free as a bird." He sat back in the chair, his hands clasped in his lap, a whatta-you-say look in his eyes.

Mrs. Pitt looked out the window to her left for a long moment as she rocked slightly in her swivel chair. "What would you do if I said, 'No, if you don't come back Monday, don't come back at all'?"

Stony felt his guts deflate. "Then I would be out of a job I really dug." He fought back the impulse to cry, staring into his lap, feeling the muscles in his face start to buckle.

"Normally I wouldn't do this" — Mrs. Pitt picked up the photo cube, idly rolling it around in her hands — "but I think I understand the situation better than you think I do. My father wanted me married and pregnant as soon as I graduated high school. I had to run away from home to get on with my life. Never went back." She returned the cube to the desk. "The kids like you very much, Stony, and I sense you like them." She smiled and nodded resolutely. "Two weeks you need, two weeks you got."

A rush of relief like a wave knocked him flat against the chair. He jumped up. "Hey, I can't tell you . . ." He started choking up again.

"Just be back here in my office three Mondays from now and tell me then."

~

On Friday Stony came into work in the lightheaded mood of a kid on the last day of school. In the morning, he made up three more stories, got into two heavy games of Stratego and taught the kids how to play charades. After lunch he conducted a joke-telling contest in which Derek was disqualified for poor sportsmanship (What's the difference between Tyrone and a elephant? About five pounds) and Tyrone was disqualified for obscenity (Why is Derek's sister like the Alaska pipeline? 'Cause she got laid by six hundred men across the state). Felix got disqualified for grossness (What's burnt, shriveled and hangs from the ceiling? A Polish electrician). Stony declared himself winner by default (Why can't you starve in the desert? Because of all the sand-which-is there). By the time Stony was debating the feasibility of a wheelchair race, the nurses came by to round up the kids.

"Four-thirty already?" He looked at his watch.

"Hey, De Coco, see you Monday."

"Stay cool over the weekend."

"Yeah, don't kiss any girls."

"See you guys." Stony waved. When the day room was empty, Stony remembered that he wasn't coming back Monday. He walked down the long children's ward, entered the twenty-bed room. The nurses were serving dinner. He sat on Derek's bed and spoke to him and Tyrone. "Hey, lissen, I forgot to tell you guys, I ain't comin' back for two weeks."

They stopped eating. "Where you goin'?" Tyrone frowned.

"Oh, I gotta do something with my family."

"How come?"

Stony shrugged. "You guys behave yourselves, don't fight."

They didn't answer. Stony got up, grabbed Tyrone by the ears and kissed him with a loud smack on the top of his head. The kids in the room screamed with laughter. Tyrone, giggling and embarrassed, buried his head under his pillow. Stony turned to Derek. Derek screeched and hid under the covers, waiting for Stony's attack. The kids shouted encouragement. Stony waited silently until Derek got impatient enough to pop his head out of the sheets. Stony kissed him right on the head to Derek's mortified delight. Then he strode from the room, waving to everybody as he left. "See ya in two weeks!"

As Stony changed at his locker, despite feeling sad about leaving, fearful of the next two weeks, the strongest, most disturbing emotion he sensed in himself was an undeniable sense of relief.

20

BUTLER LIKED THE STORE best on Saturday when it got crowded and the ring of the register was music in his ears and coins in his pocket. He still couldn't believe the store was his, and every morning as he drove down and unlocked the door, he felt like a kid going to Candyland.

"Hey, howya doin'?" Butler smiled as Annette walked into the store wearing hot pants, a striped halter and rectangular red-tinted shades.

"Hiya." She cracked gum. "Stony around?"

"Stony? Nah. Anything wrong?"

She raised her eyebrows and shut her eyes. "You tell me." She dropped her bag on the counter.

"Whadya mean?" Butler felt wary. He leaned back on his stool, shaking a cigarette from his pack.

"I dunno, we had a couple a dates, right? Next thing I know he comes over one night insultin' the shit outta me, fuck you, fuck me, fuck us, wham bam out the door, bye-bye, Stony." She shrugged helplessly, slapping her sides on the downstroke.

"That don't sound like him." Butler studied her face, picked his teeth with his thumbnail.

"Well, look, he's your friend. I'm sure you know him better'n me, but, ah, if you want my opinion I think that kid's in trouble."

"Stony?"

"Who else we talkin' about?"

"What kinda trouble?" Butler crushed his cigarette after two puffs.

"Well, I was thinkin' about what happened, you know, like he really did me shit, I mean, he just got . . . *nasty* all of a sudden. I

mean, he just about came out and called me a dirty tramp, and I
showed 'im the door. At first I was just pissed, then I felt hurt, but
I started thinkin'. I mean I really did some heavy-duty thinkin',
and I started puttin' two an' two together. I remember the first
night we had this long talk about him and that whole mess about
two weeks here, two weeks there, the deals, the this, the that. I
mean like he really opened up, right? I told him that he should
fuck the deals an' just do what he wants, an' I knew what he
wanted was to work with those kids, but he started freakin' out on
me. I think he got scared. I guess nobody ever told him straight
before. I mean I was workin' mainly onna hunch, but he really
wigged, you know? So, what was I supposed to do, take back
what I said? But ever since then he acted funny with me, like he
was scared a me or somethin', until that night when he made me
boot him out, an' he *made* me boot him out, *that* was as plain as
the nose on my face. After I figured that out, I didn't feel mad or
hurt anymore. I just felt concerned, so like I tried to call him up,
but every time he hears my voice he hangs up." She took one of
Butler's cigarettes, after folding her gum in a tissue. "Look" —
she struck a match — "he don't wanna see me, fine, but somebody
better get to that kid before he does himself in."

"Whadya mean 'does himself in'? So he jerks his old man's bird
for a few weeks, then he does what he wants."

Annette smiled, her tongue slightly protruding between her
teeth, and slowly shook her head.

"What, no." Butler sounded petulant, but he was starting to get
worried.

"He's too scared," she whispered. "He'd never go against his
old man."

"Don't sound like that to me." Butler felt shaky.

Annette smiled. "You don't think so, hah?"

Butler didn't answer.

"Well" — she grabbed her bag and hitched it over her shoulder
— "I gotta go. Tell 'im I'm lookin' for 'im, although I really don't
think he's gonna wanna talk to me, but, ah, you're his friend, why
don't you check him out?"

"He ain't talkin' to me either."

21

MONDAY MORNING Stony dressed in new, stiff dungarees and a tight white T-shirt. Tommy peeked in as Stony laced his boots. "You look more like a 'lectrician than me." He had oily chinos and a T-shirt rolled and wrapped in a tool belt under his arm.

When they got into Tommy's car, Tommy reached under his seat for a box. "Here's a present from me an' Chubby."

Stony opened the box. Inside was a white canvas tool belt, pliers, a screwdriver and a pair of channel locks. "Thanks."

Tommy winked and started the car. "That's all you'll prob'ly need today. I was gonna get you some wire clippers but I forgot. How you feel?"

"O.K.," Stony lied. He felt as if he were going to vomit. He couldn't sleep all night, and he had a headache. The tools in his lap weighed a ton. He was afraid of doing something stupid on the job. He was afraid that the guys would think he was a skinny faggot. He was afraid the guys were going to razz him about being Tommy's son. He hadn't felt this nervous since his first game for the Mount three years ago.

Tommy was exploding inside with pride and excitement. He had waited for this day since Stony was a little kid. He was proud of Stony's physique and strength. All the guys knew Stony had been a halfback for the Mount because Tommy had reminded them everyday for the last six months. He was a little worried about the teasing Stony would get the first day on the job, but everybody had to go through that. Last night Tommy lay awake in bed playing out that one moment when he would walk into the electricians' shanty with his arm around Stony and say, "This is my son."

When they arrived at the site, a high-rise luxury apartment going up in Riverdale, they sat in the parked car.

Tommy looked at his watch. "We got a few minutes. How you doin'?"

Stony looked through the link fence across the street. The thirty-story skeleton of the high rise towered over everything. He noticed the rows of wooden shanties and men in hard hats walking about. The parched dirt around the site was littered with wooden planks bridging potholes.

"How you doin', babe?" Tommy asked again.

"I think I'm gonna puke." Stony had a pained look on his face.

Tommy laughed and got out of the car. Stony followed him. He couldn't figure out how to strap on the belt so Tommy helped him. "You'll be O.K." Tommy put his arm around Stony, escorting him across the street, through the link fence and up the steps of a trailer converted into an office. A huge fat man in a gray business suit and a red hard hat stood over a white-haired guy sitting at a desk. They were examining blueprints. The fat man looked up when Tommy and Stony walked in.

"Artie." Tommy put his arm around Stony again. "This is my kid." The white-haired guy ignored them. Artie nodded, said something else about the blueprint to the white-haired guy, then extended his hand to Stony. "Hiya. You gotta fill these out." He handed Stony two work forms. "You got a pen?" Stony said no. He was fucking up already. Artie handed him a Bic pen from his shirt pocket. "Where it says employer write 'Empire Electric.'"

Stony leaned over a desk and wrote neatly.

"Stay with it, Stones, an' in ten years you'll be richer'n this fat fuck." Tommy laughed and winked at Artie. Artie scowled at him. Stony couldn't remember his social security number and had to take out his card.

"You play ball for the Mount?" Artie regarded Stony.

"Yeah." Stony wrote down the number.

"All-City Honorable Mention CHSAA," Tommy interjected. Artie ignored him. "What was your record?"

"Six, three and one." Stony handed him the forms.

Artie nodded his head in mild approval. "I useta play for Cardinal Spellman."

"Oh yeah?"

"O.K., your father'll show you what to do. Just remember to be careful an' wear this all the time." He tapped the hard hat.

"Artie's the contractor," Tommy said as they walked down the trailer steps. "He started out just like you. The guy pulls down forty grand a year, got a house in Pound Ridge, a gold Caddy and two racehorses. An' he's a nice bastard too."

Stony ducked down to enter the long, dark wooden electricians' shanty. Ten men in various stages of dressing for work sat or stood balancing on one leg, pulling on greasy chinos, lacing orange boots, folding sport shirts and strapping on utility belts. Tommy had his hand on the back of Stony's neck. "Here he is!" They looked up and checked Stony out. He felt embarrassed.

"This is Eddie, Vinny, Malfie, Blackie, Jimmy O'Day, Jackie, Augie and Carlos." Stony shook hands with some, nodded to others. Most were younger than Tommy, but Blackie and Jimmy O'Day looked close to Tommy's age. Tommy laughed and chattered as he changed into his work clothes, every fifth word out of his mouth "My kid." A splintered bench ran the length of the shanty. Above it, overhead, ran a long ledge with assorted hard hats ranging from shiny new red ones to battered paint-peeled old ones. On the short far wall under a window covered by chicken wire hung a calendar with a split beaver blonde laying on a chaise longue. Two dim light bulbs on the ceiling gave everyone a sickly subterranean tinge. When a shrill whistle blasted, the men filed out. Artie La Russo stood outside the shanty next to a pyramid of cable reels. Each man as he passed Artie bent down, grunted and hoisted a reel on his shoulder.

"Stony, you work on twenty-two today with Malfie. Vinny, you got the deck with Jimmy."

Stony stooped down and lifted a cable. Artie stopped him with a hand on his shoulder. "Sonny, you lift like that you gonna look down an' see your balls on the floor. Never stoop, always bend."

Stony climbed the temporary wooden stairs up twenty-two flights. There were no banisters and some of the landings were only a broad beam of wood lying diagonally over a five-by-five space that covered a drop of anywhere from one hundred to two hundred feet, depending on the floor. The cable weighed seventy-five pounds and after five flights Stony's shoulder was on fire, but he couldn't rest because he was in the middle of a caravan of men, all carrying the same burden. At fifteen, Tommy and Blackie dropped off to work that floor, at eighteen, two more, at twenty, two more; he and Malfie got off at twenty-two, and Vinny and Jimmy O'Day kept going until they hit the highest level of the building, the deck. Once off the stairs, Stony dropped the spool of cable on its end and used the other round end as a seat. He sat there, head between his knees, trying to catch his breath. When he looked up he could see for miles across the Bronx from this height, a chunky sea of TV antennas, high-rise buildings and housing projects. Stony was awed by the ugliness of it all. Malfie passed Stony, dropped his load about fifty feet away, sat down on the spool and lit a cigarette. As Stony was getting up to roll his cable toward Malfie, Tommy's head appeared. "Hey, kiddo! Howya doin'?"

Stony groaned. "My back is killin' me."

"Nothin', you'll get used to it. Hey, lissen, you're the gofer today. You got a pencil and paper?"

"No."

"Here." Tommy handed him a scrap of brown paper and a chewed pencil. "Go get all the guys' coffee orders an' go over to the Greek's, that luncheonette where I parked the car, O.K.? An' don't forget the guys on the deck."

"Right now?" Stony was exhausted.

"Right now, an' come back fast so the coffee don't get cold. You can put me down for a black no sugar and a cheese Danish, O.K.? An' don't forget nobody — get Artie too down in the trailer." Tommy winked and ran downstairs.

Stony started with the deck, stopping at all the floors where the electricians worked. Eager to please, he tore ass out of the building to get Artie's order in the trailer. Artie stood on the steps.

"Whoa! Whoa! You run like that, you'll knock out an eye. Take it easy, take it easy." Stony made himself slow down.

"I'm goin' for coffee, you want anything?"

Artie dug into his pocket and gave Stony a dollar. "Yeah. Get me a black coffee and an English muffin." He ducked his head into the trailer. "Hal, you want anything? The kid's goin' out. Make that two blacks, an' don't run!"

As Stony raced to the luncheonette, all the electricians except Malfie congregated on the twentieth floor to drink the coffee they had bought and sneaked upstairs before Stony took their orders.

Stony walked carefully out of the luncheonette. He held a rectangular gray cardboard box bottom containing twelve Styrofoam cups of three blacks no sugar, three blacks with saccharin, two regulars, one cream no sugar, two teas with lemon and a Pepsi. In addition, he had three cheese Danish, one English muffin, one ham and egg on white, one Drake's cake, and a salami and egg on an onion roll. The cups were capped with plastic tops that spurt liquid from the center. Code letters were penciled on top. After dropping off the trailer orders, Stony cautiously climbed the stairs. Coffee and tea dripped from the slightly soggy bottom of the box, soaking his chinos, but he was proud of himself. He got back in ten minutes flat. He was sure it was a new land speed record for gofers. His first stop was fifteen, but Tommy and Blackie weren't there. Eighteen was devoid of electricians too. Nervously he hit twenty where he found all of them.

"Where the fuck you go, Queens?"

"The fuckin' kid prob'ly stopped for breakfast."

"He's holdin' up the whole goddamn show."

"Stony, this ain't the way to start off here," Tommy said.

Stony's armpits started to sweat. He was mortified.

"Whatta you talkin' about! I ran!"

"He ran. My dead gran'mother woulda had it up here faster."

"I don' wanna talk about it."

Griping and bitching they picked out their orders. Stony stepped back, close to tears. He looked pleadingly at Tommy, who only shook his head sadly.

"This fuckin' coffee's cold!" Augie dashed his cup to the ground.

"I ast for no sugar, you cocksucker! I got fuckin' diabetes! You wanna see me go into a coma?"

"I ast for Seven-up, this prick got me Pepsi." One by one they threw their cups to the ground.

"This fuckin' kid gotta go!"

Stony spluttered, three notions away from suicide.

"Hey, kid." Vinny, a fat, gap-toothed thirtyish guy, squinted at him. "When you left the Greek's, you feel a tap on the back a your head?"

"Huh?"

"That was your change."

Stony, open-mouthed, had no idea what the fuck he was talking about. Then Augie cracked up. Tommy stifled a laugh. In seconds, they were all howling. Stony stood there like a schmuck with earflaps, rivers of tea, coffee and soda at his feet.

"I don't get it."

This comment redoubled the laughter. Jimmy O'Day fell to the floor, curled up on his side, tears of laughter threatening him with a coronary.

Stony sensed the worst was over. Tommy grabbed him and kissed him on the side of his head.

"I don't get it."

One by one, the electricians shook his hand, welcoming him into the clique. Stony smiled uneasily, still trying to put two and two together. As they filed back to work, laughing and eating their Danishes or sandwiches, Stony felt like a jerk for not seeing what the hell was so goddamn funny.

At eleven o'clock the guys sent Stony back to the Greek's with lunch orders. At eleven forty-five, Tommy, Jimmy O'Day, Eddie and Vinny came down, picked up their lunches from Stony, collected their thermos bottles from the shanty, walked off the site and sat on the grass island dividing traffic on the Henry Hudson Parkway.

"Aw Christ!" Vinny stared in disgust at his open thermos.

"Look at this." He pulled out two chunks of glass that had been floating on top of the coffee. "Bastad!" He flung the broken thermos behind him. It rolled off the grass and into traffic.

"Hey, shithead!" Tommy watched the thermos roll slowly across the band of highway. They all shifted to see if the red plaid cylinder would make it. A white Ford zoomed right over it — the tires missing by six inches. "Hey!" they all shouted, ducking and shielding their faces with their arms. When the Ford passed they all laughed. A burgundy VW tore past, just missing the thermos. Again they ducked. A wood-paneled station wagon, trailing the VW, hit the thermos dead center. There was a loud pop and a crunch. The force of the crush spurt the coffee out of its container like a gigantic brown gob of spit, spraying them all. Vinny jumped up and threw his apple at the flying station wagon. Everybody was laughing and taking swipes at the coffee on their shirts and in their hair.

"Vinny, you're a real jibone, you know that?" Jimmy O'Day brushed coffee off the knees of his khaki chinos.

Eddie got up, waited for a lull in the traffic and sprinted to pick up the mangled thermos. "Look at that." He dropped it on the grass. It was crushed flat as cardboard. Jimmy O'Day picked it up with two fingers. Tiny grains of glass trickled out of what was left of the mouth.

"Hey, Vinny, that should be your head, you know that? We coulda gotten a piece a glass in our eyes." Jimmy O'Day sprayed egg salad as he talked.

"I dropped it this mornin' down a stairs. I thought maybe if I don't open it an' forget about it it won't be broken at lunchtime."

"It should be your head."

"I got enough problems." Vinny scarfed down half a salami and prosciutto sandwich. He reached for Jimmy O'Day's thermos. Jimmy O'Day snatched the thermos protectively.

"Drink piss, ya bastad!"

Vinny smiled, nodding in Jimmy O'Day's direction. "You believe this green nigger?"

Jimmy O'Day didn't respond, licking the traces of egg salad from his fingertips.

"Here." Tommy tossed a half-pint orange wax carton into Vinny's lap.

"Thanks." Vinny shook it up, peeled back the lip and chugged half the contents. "Feh!" He spit in the grass.

"Whassamattah!" Tommy sat up indignantly.

Vinny grimaced, closed the mouth of the container and tossed it back to Tommy.

"What the fuck's with you. That's good orange juice." Tommy was insulted.

"That's orange *drink*," Vinny said wearily.

"Bull*shit!*"

"Tommy, can you read?"

"Yeah, I can read."

"Well, read the fuckin' label then."

"Sunkist orange . . . drink. So big fuckin' deal. What's the goddamn difference? It taste orange, don't it?"

"Tommy, you know how they make orange drink? They take some boonie after he works all day at Nedick's and they make him take a bath. When he gets out they put the water into them little orange things an' they sell it to assholes like you."

"Hor'shit! It tastes better than that Tropicana garbage."

"Hey!" Vinny raised a finger as case in point. "Now, Tropicana, that's *real* orange juice. That's the best. If you don't like Tropicana then you don't like real orange juice."

"Bullshit, I don't like real orange juice! Who the fuck are you to tell me I don't like real orange juice!" Tommy turned to Stony sitting cross-legged, quietly eating. "You just gonna sit there an' let this fuckface insult your father?"

Everybody laughed. Stony wondered what the fuck he was doing sitting in the grass in the middle of a highway with a half a dozen grown men in T-shirts, earning a hundred grand a year among them. He shrugged, wiped a dab of egg salad from his mouth. "Hey, Vinny, don't tell my father he don't like real orange juice."

～

"So?" Tommy moved the car out onto the Henry Hudson Parkway.

"So what?" Stony rolled down the window.

"So how'd it go today? Roll up the window." Tommy flipped on the air conditioner. The car filled with a mildly musty smell.

"It was all right."

"You pissed about this morning?"

"Nah." Stony put his foot up against the glove compartment.

"You looked like you were gonna have a heart attack." Tommy laughed, slapping Stony's leg off the dash.

Stony sighed. "I'll tell you, it wasn't as bad as I thought."

"Good!" Tommy said with a slightly mocking tone.

"Hey, you know when they sent me out in the truck for beer? I was about a mile away from the building. I look up, I can see all you guys playin' cards on the deck. What would happen if Artie caught you?"

"Never happen," Tommy shook his head, "never happen."

"Why not?"

"Could you see Artie La Russo climbin' twenny-four flights a stairs? That guy hasn't made it to the deck of a buildin' in ten years."

"You guys, you send me out for breakfast, you *wait* until I get back, you eat, then you don't work for half an hour after."

"We gotta digest."

"You send me out for lunch, same thing, you send me out for beer, same thing. I can't figure out how anything gets done."

"The work gets done," Tommy answered calmly.

"I saw Jimmy O'Day got a chaise longue up there on the deck." Stony laughed.

"I'm gonna bring me one up there next week too." Tommy turned off the highway onto Mosholu Parkway. "Stony, how much kickback you get from the Greek's today?"

Stony dug into his pocket, took out some bills and change. "Six and a half."

"You tell that greaseball if he don't give you ten tomorrow you'll start goin' to the supermarket instead. He gave you free lunch at least?"

"Yeah, I got a veal Parmigian to go."

"You tell him tomorrow, ten bucks or you go to Daitch."

"You really bringin' in a chaise longue?"

"Look." Tommy sighed and turned to Stony. "Lemme explain somethin' to you. Every one of those guys there are trained, experienced journeyman electricians. Me, Jimmy O'Day and Eddie are *master* electricians. We're the best there is in this whole goddamn field and Artie and everybody else knows it. O.K., we screw off a little, we screw off a little. We ain't foolin' anybody. You don't think Artie knows we play cards? You know why he don't bitch? You know why *his* boss don't bitch? 'Cause they know we're the best an' when we work, we *work,* an' they know they can count on us. We don't make mistakes that's gonna cost them a lotta time an' money. So, if we wanna jerk off an extra hour?" Tommy shrugged. "See, you may think those guys are clowns, and you may think those guys get too much money for what they do, but let me tell you somethin', no matter how those guys come off like *gavons* at lunchtime, they are professional, skilled electricians." Tommy winked at Stony. "This field's been good to me. There's never been nothin' you, your mother or your brother ever needed or wanted that I couldn't give like that." Tommy snapped his fingers. "You been eatin' meat every night a your life. You went to a private school, you got your own car."

"I paid for the car," Stony interrupted.

"Who pays the insurance? Look, all I'm tryin' to say to you, Stony, is that it's a good field, it's always done all right by me, it keeps me and my own from ever knowin' what hungry means. And it could do the same for you, Stony, it could do the same for you."

22

ON TUESDAY, Tommy got transferred downtown to another site for the day. After work he drove to Banion's.

"I heard the weirdest thing today." Tommy leaned over the bar talking to Banion. "I'm workin' down on Orchard Street today on that new public school, you know. I'm walkin' on Second Avenue goin' over to Katz's Deli for some lunch, an' I see this kid comin' towards me. Couldn't a been more'n seven, a Puerto Rican kid, really little. Anyways, he's walkin' by himself an' he got a slice a pizza in his hands. He comes up to me an' he's *frownin'*, you know. He looks up and he says, 'This pizza taste like *puh*-sy,' just like that, an' he keeps walkin'."

Banion chuckled and shook his head.

"I swear I almost dropped dead laughin'. Hey, Chubby!"

Chubby sat down next to Tommy, nodding hello to Banion. "Tom, len' me twenny?"

"For what?" Tommy chewed on an ice cube and flicked his mustache with a pinky.

"For what?" Chubby mimicked.

"It's six o'clock! Whatta you, a animal?"

"My cock don't wear a watch. See ya later." He took the twenty, pinched Tommy's cheek and left the bar.

"What a lover." Tommy fiddled with his mustache.

"I wouldn't want him on top a me," said Banion.

"Don't let his size fool you, the man knows what he's doin'. I bet you he could outbang this whole bar."

"I still wouldn't want him on top a me."

"Well, then you don't know what you're missing. The dude's a top stickman. Do you know why he's so good? I been in on a lotta three- an' four-way deals with Chub, so I know what I'm talkin' about. He's good 'cause he loves to fuck. He don't get hung up on that whole 'Was it good for you? Didja come?' number. He just goes right in there. I never seen a guy so much in love with pussy as Chubby. You gotta see him in action to believe it. I mean he loves the way it smells, the way it tastes, the way it feels. He's the only guy I know who can sing and scarf pussy at the same time."

"Hmpf, you'd never know it." Banion was fuming. Sex was such a major production for him because of his crippled legs. His wife had to get on top of him and do all the work or it was no go. The agony of his helplessness was such that at forty-six he had just about lost interest in screwing altogether.

"Oh, an' if you think Chubby's somethin' *now,* you shoulda seen him thirty years ago. Jesus Christ, he was built like a brick shithouse, like a fuckin' *rock.* He got an offer to play pro ball when he was eighteen . . . he ever tell you about that?"

"Really?" Banion started fidgeting.

"Oh yeah. Nineteen forty-four Chubby was the triple crown champ at James Monroe, hits, homers an' RBIs. You know who he looked like? You remember that guy used to play for the Reds, Ted Kluszewski? You know, that guy with arms like tree trunks? He useta play with his sleeves cut off to his shoulders."

"Yeah. Yeah, I remember."

"Chubby looked just like him. In-fuckin'-credible. He was the most popular guy at Monroe. I remember I was a sophomore when he was a senior. I used to get laid by sayin' to girls, 'If you put out for me I'll put in a good word for you with my brother.' " Tommy laughed.

"What happened with the pros?" Banion didn't want to know but felt compelled to ask.

"That was the funniest thing. I don't mean funny ha-ha; it was more tragic than that . . . Chubby got an offer to try out with the Browns, that's when they had guys like One-Arm Pete Grey an' such. With the war goin' on they were really hard up for talent. So Chubby's supposed to go out to St. Louis on a Sunday. That

Saturday night we had a party, Banion, the likes a which I never been to since. The *whole* team, all twenty guys, we went down to Union Square and rented out an entire whorehouse for two hundred bucks, the pussy, the booze, the this, the that, in-fucking-credible. Fifteen guys lost their cherries that night, guys runnin' aroun' 14th Street in the nude, puking, coming, screaming. It was the most memorable night a my life, Banion."

"So what happened with . . ."

"So what happened, so what happened is Chubby got drunk and he's trying to bang this chick while standing at the head of this long flight a stairs an' he loses his balance. She got a concussion an' he busted his fuckin' leg. Spent the next three weeks in the hospital."

"Couldn't he a tried out after his leg healed?"

"You know, that's one thing I could never figure out. I remember the Browns scout Buzzy Baker visitin' Chubby in the hospital an' tellin' him to call when his leg healed. Chubby never did. Always said, 'I'll call 'im tomorrah.' Then one day about six months later he joined the merchant marine an' shipped out to Surinam an' that was that. He came back a few years later an' started workin' with our old man as an electrician. To this day, I don't know what the fuck went on in his head." Tommy sighed. "Whatever, it's ancient history, right?"

Banion wanted to tell Tommy about playing forward for the All-Hallows High School basketball team. That his three-year career point total was the highest in All-Hallows history. That it took fifteen years and a six-eight nigger who later went pro to break his record. But it all seemed so distant and dim, it made him feel so angry to think about it.

"Yeah, ancient history." Banion whirred down the line. Tommy noticed somebody had stenciled "Ironsides" on the back of Banion's new wheelchair.

Tommy sat there thinking about Chubby. He had always felt that he knew Chubby inside and out, but every once in a while something would come up, like Chubby not going to St. Louis, like Chubby not having another kid, that would throw Tommy for a loop and a half.

~

Chubby cruised Eighth Avenue in the Forties, strolling down the block, occasionally stopping in porn book shops as a warm-up. It seemed to him most of the hookers were black, about six-foot-two, skinny, dressed in dirty hot pants and Afro wigs. Bad news. The street was steaming. He felt covered with a thin film of sludge and a slight wheeze crept into his lungs. He walked down from 48th Street to 40th by the Greyhound terminal, crossed the street and walked back up to 50th Street. Pimples and platform shoes. He was about to leave and check out the Carnegie Hall area when he saw her, coming out of a Blimpie's. Chinese. Bangs. Nineteen.

As they climbed the narrow stairs, Chubby's wheeze got worse. She was half a flight ahead of him. Aloof. Swinging her ass like a censer. She looked so much like Sooky Chubby had the shakes.

"Hot! Hot! Hot!" She minced over to the window across the small room, her hand waving in front of her tits like a fan. Chubby sat heavily on the corner of the narrow bed, trying to catch his breath. As she pushed up the window, her short white backless fishnet dress hitched halfway up her ass. Chubby smiled. "That's better!" She turned to Chubby, reached behind her neck to untie the strap holding up her dress and in an instant she was nude. Her dark brown nipples stood out like pencil erasers.

She patted the bed. "Come on. Lay down!" Cheery and efficient as a nurse.

Chubby stood up and undressed, sitting back down to pull off his pants. "What's your name, darlin'?"

"Tiny."

"Tiny, hah? You from Hong Kong?"

"California."

"California, hah? It's nice out there."

"Come on, big boy, lay down."

Chubby crawled across the bed and collapsed on his back. She sat by his side and took a foil-wrapped condom from her pocketbook. Then she stroked his fat, semihard cock gently but mechanically. Chubby lay with one hand behind his head and reached out to touch her nipples. He was having a tough time

getting a hard-on. The pain in his lungs, the work he had to do to
keep breathing, distracted him to the point of mortal fear. He
didn't want sex. He wanted an iron lung. Tiny frowned at him.
"What's the story?"

Chubby winked. Never say die. Finally he was hard enough
for her to slip on the rubber.

"You want me to wear this?" She held up her hand displaying a
wedding ring.

Chubby shrugged. "I'll tell you what, though, you into playin'
make-believe? For the next twenny minutes your name's Sooky."

She nodded. "Sooky it is."

Chubby moved to get on top of her, but she stopped him. "I'll
be on top, you're a pretty big guy."

Chubby laid her down on the clammy sheets and arched his
body over her. "Never heard no complaints before."

She brought up her knees under his chest and guided him in. A
band of pain encircled his chest and the room filled with the
sound of his labored breath. She scratched her nose and looked
off to the side. Chubby stopped moving and tried to gulp in air.
He lost his hard-on.

"C'mon, baby, I don't got all day," she bitched.

Chubby fell off her and clutched his chest. "Can't breathe!"

She sat up in alarm. "You gettin' a heart attack? Don't get no
heart attack on me!"

Chubby didn't answer, stroking his chest, rolling his head in
pain.

"Shit!" She jumped up and quickly pulled on her dress. "Don't
get no heart attack on me! I get all the fuckin' basket cases!" She
ran from the room, slamming the door.

Chubby struggled to a sitting position on the edge of the bed,
the rubber pinching the skin on his shriveled dick. He was too
weak and dizzy to stand up.

The door exploded inward and two tall spades — one dressed in
a yellow three-piece suit with a matching gangster lean, the other
in a red and black two-piece with alligator platforms — ran in
followed by Tiny.

"Oh *shit*! He a *big* mothafucka!"

The taller of the two men glared at Tiny, who cowered behind
the door. "He pay you?"

She nodded yes. They hoisted Chubby by the armpits.

"Pull on his fuckin' pants!"

The one in the red and black suit grunted from the strain of
Chubby's weight. Tiny slipped Chubby's pants over his con-
domed dick and buckled his belt. They let him drop on the bed.

"Hey, whadya . . . whadya doin'?" Chubby gasped weakly.

"Like I don't get enough motha*fuck*in' trouble," the one in
yellow bitched. "Put on his fuckin' shoes!"

Tiny hastily obliged. They pulled Chubby up on his feet again
and dragged him out of the room, Chubby's head rolling back, his
tongue hanging out of his head. They cursed as they slowly
carried him down the steep flight of stairs into the street, propping
him up on the hood of a car, his head almost hanging to his knees.
The spade in red threw Chubby's lime green sport shirt at him.
Then they all split, the pimp in yellow screaming at Tiny. Blindly
Chubby slapped the back of his pants for his wallet. It was still
there. Staggering to his feet he clutched his shirt and made it to
the traffic side of the car to hail a cab like a drunk. A police car
stopped, two cops jumped out.

"S — Sooky?"

"What?" The cops supported him.

"Asthma," Chubby panted.

They helped him into the back seat and the car screamed
uptown to Roosevelt Hospital.

~

An hour later, the phone in the back of the bar rang.

"Hey, Tom!"

"Yo!" He leaned back to see who was calling him.

"It's for you." Ray Buckley stood half out of the booth.

"Who is it, Ray?"

"Don' recognize the voice, some guy." He extended the
mouthpiece as Tommy walked over.

"Hello."

"Tom."

"Who's this?"

"It's me."

It was Chubby. He was wheezing so badly it sounded like braying.

"Whassamatter?" Tommy's face darkened.

"I'm inna fuckin' hospital."

"Asthma?" He could hear only gasps and wheezes on the other end of the line. "What hospital?"

"Roosevelt."

"I'll be right down."

Tommy sat with Chubby on a wooden bench in a deserted room at Roosevelt Hospital. Between them stood two Styrofoam cups of cold coffee. Hunched over, Chubby stared glassy-eyed at the wall. The doctor had given him four shots of epinephrine to cut his asthmatic wheezing. He wanted Chubby to stay overnight, but Chubby refused. The doctor respected his wish but asked a nurse to hang around just in case.

"I can't even fuck no more, Tom. I got on top a her, an' I start gaspin' like I needed a oxygen mask." Chubby's hands were trembling from the speedy effects of the shots. He rubbed his forehead and yawned nervously.

"It's just an attack, babe, you had 'em before."

"No, no, it's gettin' bad, Tom. Soon I'll be like Jimmy O'Day. Can't fuck unless I got a nitro pill under my tongue."

"C'mon, Chubby, be right." Tommy opened a crumpled brown paper bag. "Here, Banion sent this for you."

Chubby accepted the pint of Haig & Haig with a grunt, setting it on the bench. "She was *bored*, Tom. I was just an old bag of shit to her." He shuddered and yawned again.

"Hey, c'mon, Chubby, she's just a Times Square pump."

"*I know, yah fuck!*" Chubby shouted.

The nurse popped her head in the door. "Is ev . . ."

Tommy waved her out of the room.

"Oh shit!" Chubby collapsed against the bench, eyes wildly searching the ceiling.

"Tommy, I feel so lost, what am I gonna do? What the fuck am I gonna do?" He blinked back tears, shaking his head from side to side.

Tommy squeezed Chubby's knee, patted his leg.

"I'm so lonely sometimes, Tom . . ." he gasped and his face wrinkled in an effort not to cry. "I feel so god . . . damn lonely sometimes. I sit, an' eat, and I watch TV. I wake up sometimes an' . . ." Chubby doubled over in slow motion as if he had just been kicked in the gut. Tommy put both arms around his brother, leaning his cheek on Chubby's shoulder. Chubby rocked back and forth. Tommy's tears ran down his nose. Chubby rocked them both. Tommy squeezed Chubby until his arms trembled. The nurse peered through the window confused, not sure she should be looking.

"I feel so old, Tom," Chubby whispered hoarsely. "I'm gonna die soon, I can smell it. I'm too fat. I ain't gonna last. I got a wheeze what makes me feel like I live in a box. . . . I was thinkin' a Pop the other day." .

Tommy wiped the tears from his nose and held on tight.

"You remember that night? He just sat up an' said, 'I ain't sorry for *nothin'!*' That was it. I didn't cry 'cause I thought he woulda gotten up again just to punch me out." They almost laughed, rocking. "It's so scary, babe, it's so hard to get outta bed some days. I'm gonna be fifty come April." Chubby coughed and blubbered. Wrenching free from Tommy he stood up and shouted, "I was just eighteen!" He punched the wall. "What the fuck is goin' on!" Tommy grabbed him. Chubby didn't resist. He just looked into his brother's face. "I read this *Reader's Digest* once, you know, in a couple a years I'm gonna start gettin' pee dribble in my drawers in the mornin'." He tried to laugh. Tommy broke the seal on the Scotch. He handed the bottle to Chubby.

"Here, you can get a head start now."

Chubby snorted and took a long swig. Tommy took a longer one. Chubby laughed, took another. Tommy took another. Tommy laughed. Chubby took a long belt and gargled, half of it running down his lime green shirt. Tommy licked the Scotch from Chubby's chest, laughing.

The nurse, totally confused, was afraid now to walk in. Tommy
and Chubby noticed her face in the window. They looked at each
other and roared. Simultaneously they ran to the door, whooping
and hollering, and chased her down the corridor.

~

Chubby and Tommy faced each other in the warm night air in
front of the hospital.

"C'mon, babe, I'll drive you home." Tommy started walking
toward his car. Chubby held back.

"C'mon."

"Nah, you go ahead, Tom, I wanna walk a while. I'll be home
later."

"You sure?"

"Yeah. I jus' wanna do some thinking, you know." Chubby
was pulling back again. Tommy was worried. "You O.K.?"

"Yeah, I jus' wanna walk a while."

"You want me to walk with you?"

"Nah, I wanna be alone for a while. I'll go home soon."

Tommy hesitated. "Call me when you get home, yeah?"
Chubby hugged his brother. "Go home, Tom."

"You call me."

"Yeah, I'll call you. Thanks for comin' down, babe."

Tommy walked to his car, looking over his shoulder at Chubby.
Chubby stood there with his hands in his pockets until Tommy
drove away, then started walking down Eighth Avenue. He
thought of trying some pussy again, but he was too scared. The
Scotch was starting to make him spin a little. He kept thinking of
his father, gaunt and wasted. He thought of pee stains in his
underwear, helpless. The wheeze crept back into his lungs. He
leaned against a parked car. He needed to sit. He went into a
topless bar and sat staring at his drink for half an hour, oblivious
to the fishnet and pasties dancing above his head. Sooky was a
woman. The only real woman he'd ever known.

"I ain't sorry for *nothin!*" Chubby declared to the barmaid.

"O.K., then," she said unimpressed, taking his money and
ringing it up.

He started weaving in his seat. "She was a *real* woman. *You* ain't *shit!*" She gave a little nod to a big Puerto Rican in a double-knit suit who came up behind Chubby. "You jus' a whore." He gestured at the dancers. "You *all* jus' fuckin' whores. You —" Chubby felt himself lifted off his seat and shoved out onto the street before he could finish his sentence.

He stood bewildered in the middle of Eighth Avenue looking around for his drink.

~

Summer night Forty-second Street was luminous black and slick wet. Strange and dangerous. Chubby walked past the gaudy neon, weaving through multicolored crowds, his lime green shirt open to the waist. Cardboard blowups of tits and fists wrapped around his head like a red band. In Chubby's rageful dream state he could only see blurred colors. Voices came from far away like he was dozing at the beach. The subway — go home.

"Blood, you got twenny-fi' cent?"

Chubby turned from the head of the subway stairs. A tall, young spade in a bright plaid shirt stood behind him, hands in pockets.

Chubby scowled.

"What you lookin' at, sucker?" Chubby turned to go down the steps. "Fat mothafucker."

Chubby stopped, took a deep breath. Mumbled something to himself. Turned again. He kept his head low, chest-level. The young spade's shirt was box plaid. Big boxes. Yellow-red-orange-green. Chubby hesitated until the kid's hands came out of his pockets empty. Then he zeroed in on a red square over the heart. Two quick strides, fingers closed around a chicken neck. Chubby slammed him twice in the same spot, lifting him off the ground both times. The kid grunted, dazed, finding himself on the pavement. Shouts. A crowd forming. Chubby swung around to face the crowd, they stepped back in unison. Chubby laughed. Taxis flew by in the street. Yellow blurs. Bruce Lee devastated a cardboard enemy across the way. Chubby lifted the kid with one hand, thumb digging into the soft flesh under the chin. The kid's eyes wild, teeth bared clenched, hissing in pain. Chubby carried him three steps to a parked Cadillac, sat him down on the hood, the crowd closing in. Laughing. Chubby held out a nickel.

"I don't have a quarter, *blood,* all I got's five cents." With his thumb he jammed the nickel into the kid's mouth. Pinching the back of the kid's neck, shoving it GAG ACK down his throat. Two hands slapped down on Chubby's shoulders, yanking him away. Chubby wheeled around, ducked, came up swinging from the ground. A 300-pound fist smacked into open crotch. Chubby backed off, lowered his head and charged, ramming the crippled cop into a woman into a newsstand in a splash of girlie magazines and newspapers. Laughing, the crowd danced around Chubby as if he were a Pamplona bull. Chubby turned to the kid doubled over and gagging between parked cars. Chubby drop-kicked him into a double somersault. Screeching tires. Screams. The neon bubbled furiously around the marquees. Chubby looked up at the stars. The woman buried under hundreds of *Daily News*es screamed for blood. Chubby saw the word "SURCHARGE" in all the headlines. The cop was unconscious. The news dealer stood there in thick glasses and a white apron. Chubby sniffed, buttoned his shirt and pushed through the crowd down into the subway station. Sirens. Some of the crowd followed him from a safe distance, but he got on the train alone.

Chubby sat on the rocketing train, swaying back and forth like a moron. He saw everything as if he were wearing tinted glasses. White skin had the pastiness of death, black skin looked sickly green. He had his fat man's wheeze again, sitting hunched over, hands dangling below his knees. There was blood on his shirt. He sniffed it. The nigger kid's.

"He begged me, heh, heh." Chubby grinned and his eyes lit up as he talked to the white poles in front of him. " 'Please, mister, please, mister,' " Chubby whined. "I said, I said, heh, heh," he cackled. " 'Please, mister,' he said to me, whining, 'Unh!' " Chubby leaped out of his seat, lunging with an invisible sword at the groaning doors as they opened at 72nd Street. "Heh, heh." Collapsing back into the gray molded seat.

A middle-aged dumpy black lady in a brown coat and

horn-rimmed glasses made a face as if she smelled shit, and moved away from Chubby. Chubby laughed and thrust his sword at her. She walked faster, banging into a pole.

"He said, 'Please, mister, I'm sorry.' " Chubby rolled his eyes and licked his lips. "Oh yeah, oh yeah, oh yeah." Resting his head on the subway map, shutting his eyes, rubbing his palms over his face. His belly peeked out under his lime green shirt.

"Sooo-ky!" he moaned loudly. From the back of his throat came that eerie whine like a demented croon.

The sharp rap of a nightstick on the metal seat made him jump. "Hey, whatchoo doin', man?"

Chubby looked up into the bland face of a big black T.A. cop. He smiled like a little boy with his hand caught in a cookie jar and shrugged. "You be cool now, hear?"

Chubby winked and got off at the next stop.

The South Bronx. Fort Apache. The pits. Chubby wandered the humid streets like the last survivor of World War Three. Human shadows shifted along brick walls like rats. Building entrances like one-way tickets. Latin music sifted through the air high above his head. Chubby laughed, kicking a can into the gutter. A man in a flowered beige shirt and a denim beach hat passed him on the street. He called out something in Spanish and three more men strolled out of a candy store. The four of them followed Chubby for two blocks, until Chubby turned around, thrust his sword at them, laughing, and ran like hell for the safety of a bar.

"Tommy."

"Hey, Chub."

"Come an' get me."

"What?"

"Come an' get me. I'm in a bar in a very bad neighborhood."

"Whatta you talkin' about?" Tommy stood up and shut off the TV. "Chubby, where the fuck *are* you?"

"Sweetheart" — Chubby leaned out of the phone booth and smiled at a heavily mascaraed woman in a blond wig at the end of the bar — "sweetheart, where am I?"

She said something in Spanish to three people sitting next to her. They leaned back from their barstools and stared at him.

"Hey, where am I?" Chubby repeated.

"You lost." They all laughed. Chubby looked out over the sky-blue-painted pocked plaster walls of the room.

"They won't tell me, Tom." Chubby laughed. "Oh shit," he sighed.

"*Who* won't tell you?" Tommy passed the living room, the white cord of the phone trailing him like a tail.

"I dunno." Chubby picked his nose. "I'm somewhere aroun' a Hunnert Thirty-fifth Street, I think."

"Just *stay* there!" Tommy shouted. "Don't *move!*" Chubby froze like a statue, then burst out laughing again.

Tommy hung up, ran into the kitchen, grabbed a long steak knife, slipped into his pants and ran from the apartment in his bare feet.

Chubby sat down at the red and white Formica bar and lit a cigarette. Everybody at the bar stared at him. A loud pachanga played on the juke box. Chubby got up, one hand flat on his gut, the other raised at a right angle in the air, and cha-cha'ed into the street. He cha-cha'ed for two blocks down 172nd Street to Vyse Avenue before a forearm whipped around his throat, arching him backward. A mustached face came out of the darkness in front of him. The black barrel of a Saturday Night Special was shoved into his mouth.

"Ssh!" The man with the gun put a finger to his lips. "Just suck on it, like a tit." Chubby's lips formed a pink, fleshy O around the gun. He wasn't scared, just curious. Three men led him into a small hallway.

"Lay down." The gun was held in his mouth as he slowly lay back on a rolling wave of cracked, warped mosaic tile. As the three of them quickly searched his pockets, as he calmly sucked on the gun, as he stared up at the ornate brown plaster ceiling with its dim yellowish solitary light bulb, he thought for the first time in forty years of the time he had his tonsils taken out; sitting on his mother's lap, the doctor working without an anesthetic, cutting and yanking like a dentist, not able to scream, the sharp burning singeing pain like a starving rat in his throat, his mother's hands

wrapped around his body, the doctor yelling at her to stop shaking
her leg, the blood like a bib on his chest . . .

Chubby was crying as he lay spread-eagle on the broken floor.
He was alone. Latin music drifted over the rooftops.

~

Chubby let himself into his dark apartment and felt his way to the
bathroom. He sat on the fur-covered toilet lid in the blackness
and smoked a cigarette in painful slow motion, flicking the ashes
after each puff into the sink. His arms and legs felt stiff and
heavy. His head felt huge — too big to be supported by his neck,
and he let it droop onto his chest. When he eventually stood up to
lift the lid and drop the butt into the toilet, his whole body ached
as if all his joints and tendons were inflamed. Sitting on the edge
of the tub, he ran his thick fingers through his hair, then slowly
began to unlace his shoes. He took off his socks, flexed his toes
and lit another cigarette. This one he ditched in the sink. Every
once in a while he thought of Sooky and his body would twitch as
if he'd just received a small electric shock. If a clear image or a
vivid moment flashed across his brain, he flinched it away in a
muddy blur. The cigarettes helped. He chain-smoked, ignoring
his strangled lungs, his raw ripped throat. A smoky haze drifted
through the small room. He followed a slow snaky wave of smoke
until it wandered ghostlike into the hallway.

Chubby refused to collect his thoughts. He concentrated on
each puff, listening to the soft crackle of tobacco and paper. He
tried to say her name, but all that came out of his mouth was a
stuttering hiss. Leaning over the tub, he peered through the
partially open tiny frosted window at a vast field of buildings and
a scattered grid of lit windows. Elbows on the window ledge, he
watched as the constellation of lights randomly diminished by
ones and twos. He was reminded of the logo for "Million Dollar
Movie," the shot of the clapboard superimposed over the night-
time New York skyline, the theme from *Gone With the Wind*
playing in the background. Jackie Gleason came to mind. Many
years ago, some of his friends called him Ralph because he looked

like Ralph Kramden. He absently hummed "Melancholy Serenade," the theme song from "The Honeymooners." "To the
moon, Alice!" he muttered, then chuckled. His back started
aching. He pushed himself erect, away from the window, slowly
rubbed his hand across his expansive belly, and ran tap water to
wash the ashes down the drain. He squeezed an inch of
toothpaste into his mouth and ran his tongue across his teeth,
spitting the toothpaste out under the thin stream. He sucked air
through his tingling mouth, spat again and turned off the water.
Chubby felt his way down the foyer to the bedroom, running his
palm against the cool wallpaper, making a smooth sliding sound
until he got to the doorway. As he sat on his side of the bed,
Phyllis moved under the blankets.

"Whachoo makin? harden oranges sit down," she mumbled,
then turned on her side and was silent again. Through the wide
window over the bed he saw a grid of fluorescently lit parkways
with occasional speeding headlights. Far in the distance he could
see an elliptical string of lights, the curved contours of the cables
of the George Washington Bridge. He reached for another
cigarette in his chest pocket, decided against it, achingly slipped
his shirt from his shoulders, stood up to drop his pants, quietly slid
under the warm covers and fell into a mercifully dreamless sleep.

~

"Chub!"

Chubby bolted upright in bed.

"Chub, it's nine o'clock. You're late."

Phyllis' warm hand lay on his naked shoulder. Chubby
swallowed. His throat felt like sandpaper. He rubbed his fingers
briefly and fell back down on his pillow.

"I'm not goin' in today, hon. Do me a favor an' call for me."

"Whassamatter?" She frowned. Her scent drifted over to him
as she rearranged her bathrobe. A familiar smell.

"My back hurts."

"Ya back?"

"Yeah, I pulled somethin'."

"Tommy called last night."

"What for?" Chubby reached for his cigarettes in the pile of clothing on the floor.

"He didn't say, he just wanted to know if you were home. He sounded nuts."

Suddenly Chubby remembered last night. He moaned, throwing an arm across his face.

"Whassamatter!" Phyllis got scared and leaned across him. "Ya back?" She reached out gingerly, afraid to touch him, tentatively bringing her fingers to her lips. "Ya back?"

With his forearm across his eyes, Chubby exhaled from his mouth long and low.

"Phyll? Do you love me?"

"Is it ya back?"

"Do you love me, Phyll?"

"A course I love you, what hurts, Chubby?"

"Get under the covers." His face still hidden, he pulled back the covers on Phyllis' side of the bed.

"Chubby, stop foolin' aroun'. I got a lotta things to do today. Tell me what hurts."

"*Everything* hurts. Will you get under the goddamn covers?"

Confused, Phyllis crawled into bed, pulling the blankets around her. Chubby hugged her to him. She folded her arms in front of her, her hands between her chest and Chubby's.

"You're my wife, Phyllis, and I love you." Phyllis blinked nervously. Her hands were curled toward her.

"Chub, does anything hurt?"

"Nothin', nothin' hurts."

23

TOMMY STAYED home to comfort his brother, so Friday Stony
went in alone. At lunch, instead of sitting on the traffic island, the
guys decided to do lunch in Tooky's Tavern and have a few.
Stony sat at the bar with Eddie, Vinny and Jimmy O'Day in a
crowd of construction workers and businessmen.

"I heard that creep got another kid over in Parkchester."
Jimmy O'Day tapped his cigarette on his wrist before hanging it
from the corner of his mouth.

"I can't understand somebody like that," Vinny said, tapping
his money on the bar to catch Tooky's eye. "A guy like that . . . a
guy like that ain't human."

"He's a fuckin' animal," offered Eddie. Tooky brought another
bourbon and water to Vinny and picked up the dollar. "I tell you
somethin', that guy should have his dick cut off an' then they
should make him walk down the street an' give all the mothers
guns and knives."

"That's what I figure they shoulda done to Eichmann, just let
'im walk down the street in Israel."

"Screw the Jews. Eichmann didn't fuck no six-year-old kids up
the ass," said Vinny.

"I don't understand how he could get it up there." Jimmy
O'Day finally lit his cigarette.

"I'll tell you somethin' else," said Tooky. "I told Patrick if he
ever leaves the house without me or his mother I'll beat his ass
black and blue."

"I tol' my kid the same," said Eddie. "I don't care if he sits there watchin' TV for the rest of his life, long as that bastard's on the loose he ain't goin' nowhere without me or Ginny."

"Fuck that. Ain't lettin' my kid out even *with* my wife. Anybody'd do that to a kid, God knows what he'd do to a full-grown woman," said Vinny.

"No offense, Vinny, but I don't think your wife got nothing to worry about," said Jimmy O'Day.

Eddie and Tooky laughed.

"Lissen, douchebag . . ." Vinny pointed a finger at Jimmy O'Day.

"I'm only kiddin'." Jimmy O'Day laughed, laying a hand on Vinny's arm. "Tooky, giv'im another." Jimmy O'Day took a dollar from his own pile and dropped it a few inches toward the inside edge of the bar.

Tooky poured two fingers of Wild Turkey into Vinny's glass and rung up Jimmy O'Day's dollar.

"I think they should string that guy up by the thumbs and give sticks with nails and razors to all the kids," said Eddie.

"You're fuckin' sicker than him," said Vinny. "Hey, Tooky, bring over that picture." Tooky took a police pencil sketch off the window and laid it down on the bar.

"Hey, Jimmy, it looks like you," Vinny said.

"It looks like your mother," said Jimmy O'Day.

"It does a little at that."

"Not even on a joke," admonished Tooky.

"Lissen here." Eddie squinted at the sketch. "Has bad acne scars. That's it, the guy's had a rotten childhood, he had acne."

"Big fuckin' deal," said Tooky. "When I was a kid I had a face like a pizza pie. I don't go around molestin' little kids."

Eddie didn't pursue it.

"All you guys live in Parkchester?" They turned to Stony.

"Aroun' there." Jimmy O'Day smiled.

"You hear about this guy?" Eddie said.

"The Parkchester Pervert?" Stony used the name coined in the *Daily News.*

They laughed. "Looka' this fuckin' kid," Vinny said. "He looks like he's been here ten years."

Stony's skintight T-shirt was smeared with lubricating oil. His biceps glistened dully in the bar light. He took a cigarette from Eddie's pack on the bar. Feelin' good.

"How they treatin' ya, Stony?" Jimmy O'Day offered him a light.

"Can't complain." He nodded graciously.

"You like workin' here?"

"Can't complain."

"Whada *you* think a this creep?"

Stony took a plunge. "Who ya mean, Vinny?" They all laughed except Vinny.

"The other creep."

"He's a sick man." Stony tensed his muscles. Strike one. A chorus of groans.

"So was Hitler," Tooky said.

"So was Nixon," Stony replied. Strike two.

"Aw Christ, another one a these college liberals." Vinny smirked.

"Nah, I mean . . ."

"Hey look, Stony, I don' wanna give you no lectures." Eddie grabbed his wrist. "Forget that crack about college liberals, I'm talkin' to you man to man. Now I'm not sayin' you ain't smart or anything. Look, for all I know you're smarter than all a us here put together, but one thing that you don't got is — "

"Experience," Stony finished for Eddie.

Eddie bobbed his head in confirmation.

"Now you talkin'." Vinny winked.

"You see, Stony" — Eddie shook Stony's wrist every few words for emphasis — "when we talk about this degenerate that's goin' around, we're talkin' as fathers, as husbands, you know what I mean?"

They nodded in unison. Stony nodded too.

"You know? An' when you go equatin' Nixon and Hitler . . ." He shook his head sadly. "Look, Nixon mighta been a prick, I dunno, but . . . O.K., look at it this way. You always read about the hard hats did this an' the hard hats did that, beatin' up war protestors an' that shit, but how many a those kids ever put their lives on the line for their country? I was at the invasion a Sicily. Those fuckin' Germans had that whole goddamn beach cross-coordinated, you know what that means? That means any time those fuckin' Krauts saw a cluster of men on the beach all they had to do was fix the coordinates on their guns and wham! Six a your best friends crawling up the beach, ten yards to your right, vanished — not even a goddamn corpse . . . But we kept comin' an' we took that motherfuckin' beach."

Vinny interjected. "You know Artie? Fat Artie? Artie saw his own brother jump on a grenade in Korea, so four other guys wouldn't get killed." Eddie grabbed Stony's wrist again. "Now what's a guy like Artie, or me, or any of us, whatta we supposed to think, whatta we supposed to do when we see some long-haired eighteen-year-old prick come marchin' down the street with a North Vietnamese flag? I'm askin' you serious, what a' we supposed to do?"

Stony felt moved but confused. He didn't give two shits about Vietnam either way, and he didn't understand what that had to do with the Parkchester Pervert. But the story about Artie La Russo's brother made him want to cry. He imagined himself jumping on a live grenade to save Albert. Then he pictured Albert molested by some forty-year-old sex maniac in the stairway outside the apartment. His mother's face. Albert crying. Derek and Tyrone in their wheelchairs terrified of him. Albert with tears on his face. Derek and Tyrone. Marie. Albert. Derek. Tyrone. Stony. Him. Thomas De Coco Jr. Junior.

". . . I'm askin' you, Stony, whatta we supposed to do when some kid comes marchin' down the street with a Vietnamese flag?"

Stony looked at Eddie, at Vinny, at Tooky and Jimmy O'Day.

"Well, it's plain as the nose on your face. You take the goddamn flag, break it in two, then you shove one part down his throat and the other part up his ass. Right? I mean, really, whatta you gonna do, salute? Teach him a fuckin' lesson he'll never forget. I guarantee you, someday he'll be grateful, right? You know how kids are, right?"

Stony smiled. He disengaged his wrist from Eddie's fingers and dug into his pockets for money. "Sure" — he started walking out of the bar — "makes sense to me, right?"

~

Chubby bucked and heaved on top of his wife like a rutting sea lion. The words came from somewhere else. "You comin'? You comin'?" Like a third frantic presence in the steaming room. Chubby pumped for his life, Phyllis' legs twitching under his bulk. The bed gasped for air beneath his panic. Phyllis held on for dear life, grasping his hair like a lifeline. "Yes!" She screamed, half pleading, half tribute. Chubby slammed her bones, rattled her teeth. As if he could bring her back. Bring her back. Coming, coming, coming. He arched his back in a last thrust, ramming her into the headboard. Her legs trembled. Phyllis was so scared by the changes in her body she started laughing. But she didn't come. Chubby bucked once more.

Chubby lay on top, gasping, hurting. "Oh . . . Phyllis." He'd almost said Sooky as Phyllis wrapped her shaking arms around his fat neck. "Oh, baby," he cried. "Do you love me?"

"Yes!"

"Do you love me?" gripping the nape of her neck.

"Yeah! Oh you know I do!"

"Then say it!"

"Yes. I love you! I love you!"

Chubby was grateful for a clear-lunged fuck. Fifty. That was a pretty good hump for fifty. Phyllis was his wife. No more hookers. No more booze. Play it close to the vest. She was his wife. Fifty.

~

For the next few days he followed her around the house. He brought flowers home. They went for walks in the park, rides in the country. Her bedtime was his bedtime. They laughed at Johnny Carson together. He stopped hanging out at Banion's. He took her for Chinks every night. They even got back into fucking. Phyllis was scared shit.

"Marie, I'm worried about Chubby." She picked at the crusty corners of her well-done hamburger with long nails.

"Whadya mean?" Marie wriggled on the revolving stool at the crowded Woolworth's lunch counter.

"All of a sudden he's gettin' romantic with me. I think maybe he's sick or somethin'." Phyllis pushed away the thick white plate.

"You don't want that?" Marie gathered the discarded hamburger with a sweeping motion of her hand. "It's a sin to waste food. Whadya mean, romantic?" She lifted the hamburger to her mouth with both hands.

"I dunno, he follows me around the house like a big dog all the time. He didn't go inta work this week because a his back an' all he does is be nice to me, takes me out every day, brings me presents. I mean, I'm not complainin'." She quickly frowned. "Yes I am . . . there's somethin' wrong. He's actin' crazy."

Marie raised an eyebrow. "I wish Tommy was so crazy."

"Look, I'm not a hard person to please, Marie." A tall, thin pimply girl in a pantsuit slipped a check under Marie's plate. "You know that" — they both looked at the tab — "I just like a little attention now and then."

"Miss." Marie caught the waitress' eye with a fluttering hand. "Miss, what was one sixty-four?"

The girl blinked vacantly. "Hamburger."

"Hamburger's a dollar-fifty." Marie pointed to the cardboard hamburger poster hanging over the coffee machine.

"Tax." The girl fidgeted.

"Then you should have a dollar sixty-four up there. What if I only came in here with a dollar-fifty?"

The girl looked away. "I'm very busy, ma'am, you want to talk to the manager?"

"Forget it." Marie dismissed her, turning to Phyllis. "Snotty bitch, I'm not comin' in *here* anymore."

"You know, we had sex five times since Wednesday?" Phyllis whispered.

"You braggin' or complainin'?" Marie dug into her purse.

"Something feels really weird about it. After we're finished, he keeps askin' me if I came, if I came, if I came. He's always askin' me if I love him."

Marie looked up but didn't say anything.

24

STONY WAS in a good mood. Wednesday. Two days to go. Monday, back to Cresthaven.

"You know, you got a really good voice." Stony smiled curiously at Malfie, who was busy feeding cable into the mouth of a pipe. Malfie made like he didn't hear Stony and kept singing in a high, yet throaty tremolo.

Stony bent down and continued pulling cable from a similar pipe. Malfie was the best-looking guy Stony had ever seen. He had a tight and smooth profile that seemed almost manicured with high cheekbones, a small, slightly upturned nose, thin, perfectly defined lips and glittering blue eyes. He combed his dirty blond hair high and straight back. When he was finished feeding cable he stood up. Tall and thin. A real killer.

"You ever hear a the Convoys?" he asked Stony. Stony stopped working and turned to Malfie.

"Yeah, they did what . . . 'Rock 'n' Roll Serenade.' "

Malfie nodded slightly. "Yeah, I used to sing with them."

Stony stopped working. "You shittin' me?"

Malfie casually threw out a couple of powerful ooh-wahs that echoed throughout the cavernous level where he, Stony and about ten other electricians were circuiting wire through a field of pipes.

"Goddamn! Whatta you doin' here?"

"I quit two years ago." He moved to another pipe five feet away, knelt down and started shoving the braided multicolored strands down its mouth. "It's comin' out up there." Malfie tilted his head at a short pipe protruding from the poured concrete ceiling. The head of the cable peeked out where Malfie indicated, and he waited for Stony to climb a stepladder and pull out the wires before he continued feeding his end of the pipe.

"Wha'd you quit for?" Stony grunted. The wires were snagged somewhere in the invisible network of conduit. He teased and tugged the cable until it came loose.

"Lucy," Malfie sang something in husky Spanish.

"You know Spanish?"

"*Si, por supuesto.*"

"You're fuckin' amazin'." Stony stopped for a second to adjust his work gloves, flexing his fingers for a tighter fit.

"My father knew seven tongues." Kneeling, Malfie bounced lightly on the balls of his feet to keep his circulation going. He tied the end of the cable with a few deft movements.

"French, Italian, Spanish, German, Dutch, Portuguese and English. He met my mother in Cuba."

"Your mother Spanish?" The wire pulled taut on Stony's end and Malfie tied it off for him.

"From Havana, we lived there until Castro came in." For the first time Stony noticed a slight staccato clip in Malfie's speech. "Had maids an' everything. My father was head croupier in one a the biggest casinos down there. El Gato Negro." Malfie finished tying the wires, stepped back and extracted a pack of unfiltered Kools from the chest pocket of his beige workshirt. Stony declined the offered pack, taking out one of his own Marlboros. Malfie held out a red see-through butane lighter under Stony's cigarette. None of the brickwork had yet been started on the exterior walls, even though the small octagonal concrete foundations for the terraces jutted out over the edge of the building. They stood twenty stories high between two layers of concrete overlooking the Hudson. The vast floor was a maze of chalk lines and markings noting the outlines of walls and apartment partitions yet to be installed. Every thirty feet or so sat a bathtub and a toilet bowl — which wouldn't fit through the narrow doorways once the walls were built. It was a gray day and the somber light lent the place the mood of a deserted underground garage. Augie ambled over to one of the protruding borderless terraces, stood spread-legged, whipped out his dick and pissed into the Hudson.

Malfie sneered. "Animal."

Stony looked over the field of toilets and shrugged.

"My father knew Batista." Malfie spat neatly. "We had everything, man. I even had my own fuckin' horse, until that scumbag with the beard came in." He picked his front teeth.

Stony leaned against the ladder enjoying his smoke.

"You know, my father was French." Malfie delicately scratched a raised eyebrow. "So I got French blood. That's why I'm light and that's why I'm tall." Then he added almost as an afterthought, "It's good to be tall, because in a fight you can't get to my face. Look, I don't give a flying fuck what a guy does or says to me but nobody touches my face. He makes one move to hit my face, I'll kill him. The only time I hit Lucy was once she went to slap me. I don't take that from nobody, even her. The only person I let hit me like that was my mother, and she only did it once." Malfie spoke calmly and earnestly. Stony made a mental note never to bash in Malfie's face.

"I hit your face and take the back a your head off." Augie walked over to the ladder, rested a boot on the second rung, his elbow on his knee. He looked like Fred Flintstone — big, lumpy and hairy.

"Then I come after you with a gun." Malfie didn't blink. Augie laughed, winking at Stony. "I ain't kiddin'. I'll blow you apart." Malfie's voice kept rising. He took a step toward Augie.

"Relax, hah?" Augie examined a chunk of snot on his pinky.

"I ain't fuckin' around wit' you, you guinea prick." Malfie lightly touched his high cheekbones. His face was getting red. He took another step toward Augie. "You *touch* me, I'll tear your heart out."

Augie affected a yawn. He knew he could break Malfie in two, but he was an easygoing guy who enjoyed razzing excitable people. Malfie was crazy and had no sense of humor. "See ya, Malfie." Augie flicked the snot off his finger and strolled away.

"I'll *kill* that motherfucker." Malfie's eyes were buzzing with rage as he pointed a quivering finger at Stony.

Malfie had Stony pulling wire at a furious pace the rest of the morning. There was no more conversation. Malfie stormed around the pipes muttering incoherently, occasionally barking orders at Stony.

At noon, the electricians returned to the shanty to pick up their lunches. Stony got ready to go to the traffic island with his father and some of the other guys.

"Malfie, you comin'?" he forced a friendly tone.

Malfie ignored him, roughly shouldering his way through a half-dozen electricians loitering around the shanty door. He walked rapidly to a beat-up old pink Cadillac parked by the entrance to the site. A young Puerto Rican girl sat in the passenger seat. Malfie got in on the driver's side, slammed the door and screeched onto the Parkway.

"That's the last we'll see a *him* today," Artie La Russo bitched, watching the Cadillac disappear. "That fucker bastard pulls that on me one more time I'll have him on unemployment so fast." The electricians knew Artie was talking out of his ass. He was afraid of Malfie and said that every time Malfie took off in the middle of the day.

"That fuckin' kid's ready for the couch," Tommy said.

"Let's eat!" said Augie.

25

"Tomorrow's *it,* baby, I put in my time." Stony tore off his greasy T-shirt and unlaced his boots. "I'm a free man."

Tommy hovered over him, ballooning with desperation. "You're really goin' back there?"

"Look, you said two weeks, and two weeks you got." Stony pulled off one boot with a grunt.

"You're really walkin' out on me, huh?"

"Aw, Pop!" Stony tossed the boot under the bed. "Gimme a break, hah? We had a deal." He got to work on the second boot.

"You know, Stones, you really fuckin' disappoint me."

"Well, don't make the feeling mutual."

Tommy lunged at Stony, cracked him across the mouth. Stony flew back on the bed, his hand to his bleeding mouth. Tommy towered over him, his huge hands shaking with rage. When the stinging jolt subsided, Stony felt cool. Twenty-twenty vision. "Thanks a lot, Pop." He licked the blood from the corner of his mouth. "You just made everything a lot easier."

~

"I'm quittin', Chub." Stony had developed the habit in the last few hours of gingerly touching the bloody crust on his mouth. "I just don't wanna do it."

Chubby clasped his hands in front of him on the dinette table. "It's on you, Stones, it's your life."

"Don't I know it."

"I'll tell you though, I think you're bein' hasty. Whynchoo give it a few more weeks?"

Stony flushed with panic. "No way! Come Monday morning you can catch my act at *Crest*haven!"

Chubby sighed, shifted his weight on the high Formica-backed dinette chair. "You know, you may not be able to get in the union ever again."

"I'll live."

"Yeah, you'll live, but — "

"Hey look, my quittin' ain't no reflection on you an' Pop. It's just — "

"But it *is*, Stony, don't you see that? What's it gonna look like when your old man shows up for work without you Monday morning?"

"It's gonna look like I quit."

"You're killin' your dad, Stony," Chubby said sadly.

Fear hit Stony inside like a strobe light. He stared at his thumbnails pressed side by side in front of him. "Chubby," he whispered huskily, "lemme breathe."

~

On Friday, the last day, Stony and Tommy drove into work boycotting each other, Tommy staring straight ahead, Stony, his head at right angles with his body, staring out the side window.

After Stony changed into his gear in the shanty, he started taking coffee orders, but Jimmy O'Day stopped him.

"Let Phillip do it today."

"Who?" Stony, poised with paper and pencil, followed Jimmy's stare to a far corner of the shanty where a red-headed kid about Stony's age struggled with his utility belt. Stony glared at Jimmy, but Jimmy just winked.

"Hey, kid." Blackie smiled. "We're gonna start you off easy. You know what a gofer is?"

"Huh?" Phillip looked up, embarrassed at the difficulty he was having with the buckle.

"Hey, take that off," Blackie said. "Stony, give 'im the list. Just take everybody's coffee order an' go over to the Greek's. You know the Greek's?"

"The luncheonette?"

"Hey, this kid's on the ball!"

Phillip smiled, pleased he was off to a good start.

"Lemme go with him," Stony said.

"He can handle it himself." Eddie took the paper from Stony and handed it to Phillip.

Phillip wrote down every word of the orders, abbreviating nothing. Stony and Malfie didn't want anything.

"Make sure you get Artie's order in the trailer," Tommy added, bending down to lace his boots.

Phillip ran from the shed wearing his hard hat, the money in one hand, the order slip and pencil in the other. After he'd scampered across the street, Eddie dragged out an open gray cardboard box with rows of coffee in Styrofoam cups and stacks of cellophaned Danish.

"You fuckin' guys." Stony scratched his head. Everyone grabbed a coffee and a Danish and filed out to the building.

Stony and Malfie sat on upended cable reels smoking and staring over the smog-shrouded rooftops.

"Hey, Stony!" Vinny's head appeared in the stairwell. "C'mon, he's comin' back!" Vinny's fat face looked twice as wide with that gap-tooth grin. Sighing, Stony crushed his cigarette with his boot. "Malfie, you comin'?"

Malfie indicated no with the slightest motion, not taking his eyes from the antennaed skyline.

"I guess I'll go, make sure the kid doesn't have a breakdown." Head down, Stony broke into a light trot across the littered concrete floor.

The men had congregated on the twenty-first level, sitting on upended cables or on a hip-high green metal trash bin.

Stony leaned against the bin, his back to them. Phillip trudged up the stairs, his milky face blotched with red. The legs of his chinos were matted to his skin with spilled coffee.

"Where was you guys?" Phillip puffed and panted. "I thought you . . ."

"Vinny, what time is it?" Eddie scowled. Vinny looked at his watch, cursed and showed the time to the men. Stony chuckled in spite of his contempt.

"You know how much money you just cost the contractor, kid?" Tommy folded his arms across his chest.

"What!" Phillip looked like he was going to cry. Just like Stony had the first day.

"You know how much money and time you just wasted?"

"Don't even fuckin' bother." Blackie waved in disgust. "The fuckin' kid's a jerk-off, I knew it the minute I saw him with that fuckin' belt."

"Yeah," Stony added almost inaudibly. He had walked around the bin and was standing next to his father.

"I ran!" Phillip's Adam's apple was going like a bubble in boiling water. He stooped to set down the box, splashing out half the coffee.

"Now the little prick's washin' the floor with our breakfast!" Vinny slapped his leg in exasperation.

"Wait! Artie didn't complain! I ran!" Phillip scratched his face nervously.

"Artie didn't complain!" Tommy mimicked nastily. "The fuckin' kid's an ass-kisser, sure! Artie's the boss. I can see it now, this kid's gonna be another Carlos."

"You think so?" Blackie squinted.

"Sure! Two days from now we'll find the kid behind the trailer with his pants down his ankles playin' drop the keys with Artie."

"Yeah! How you think he got the job to begin with?" Jimmy O'Day pouted.

"My father got me the job!" Phillip's voice was starting to crack.

"Uh-uh."

"Right."

"Sure."

They each picked up a coffee cup and in fifteen seconds all the cups had been dashed to the ground, the men cursing and bitching. Stony found himself pouring out a cup on the floor.

"This kid's got to go." Vinny smirked.

"I got fuckin' hunger cramps," Augie whined.

"Christ," Stony complained.

"Where's my fuckin' wrench?" Tommy glared at Phillip, clenching his teeth.

Phillip looked desperate. After ten seconds of painful silence, Stony stepped forward, his heart pounding. "Hey, kid?"

Sensing all eyes on him, he put a hand on Phillip's sweaty shoulder. A charge of power and excitement ran through him like alcohol. Phillip looked at him for help. Another kid. "When you left the Greek's, you feel a tap on the back a your head?"

~

"Those fuckin' guys." Stony was giddy as he returned to Malfie, confused yet turned on. Malfie snorted. They began pulling cable. For an hour and a half Stony worked in silence, chewing over what had happened. He had felt a sense of brotherhood that morning. It was mean, yeah, but . . . He didn't know if he felt like a jerk or a man. But he knew he felt good. One of the guys. Tommy pounded down the stairs. Stony's back was to him, and he watched the sweat shimmering on Stony's straining muscles. He watched his son work. Finally, Stony turned around and saw Tommy staring at him. They looked at each other blankly, then simultaneously grinned.

~

"Hey, Malfie?" Stony hunched over the cable, chewing a mouthful of tuna and rye. "You remember when I asked you how come you quit the Convoys an' you said 'Lucy' "? Malfie sat against a concrete pillar, eating a sandwich. He removed a faint trace of mayonnaise from his lower lip. "Who's Lucy?"

"My woman." Malfie cleared his throat, his fist lightly pressed against his mouth, returning his gaze to the buildings in the distance.

Stony brushed crumbs from his pants. "You married?"

Malfie shook his head in the negative.

"You ever miss the Convoys?" He crumpled the silver foil in his lap into a ball.

Malfie wrinkled his nose. "Made a lotta money, man, a *lotta* money." He bobbed his head, a distant expression on his face. "But ah spent it. Women, liquor, drugs. Got tired. I was blowin' away my life. Had a good woman, a lovin' mother just waitin' for me, an' I was runnin' like a fool. We was in L.A. I just walked off the stage and took the next plane home. You can't run away from love. You can't run away from love, so I came home. Had seventeen thousand dollars left. Bought mah mother a house with it. Me, Lucy and mah mother live in it now. Someday, someday we're all goin' back to Cuba, live on the beach" — he winked — "get me another horse."

They sat in silence.

"Hey, Malfie? Do you dig this?"

" 'Lectricians?" He shrugged, a hand over his mouth. "Yeah, yeah, I got peace here. Good money and peace. I can think a lot when ahm workin'."

Stony tilted his head. "Whadya think about?"

"Lucy."

"Hmph . . . You get along with the guys?" Knowing that he didn't.

Malfie frowned. "I'm a lone wolf, ah don't need anybody here. I got Lucy, mah mother and mah Cadillac an' someday I take 'em all to Cuba."

"Did you dig bein' away from home?" Stony started unfolding the silver foil. Malfie touched his cheekbones, wrinkled his nose.

"Nah, it was bad."

"Was it fun?"

"Fun?" Malfie shrugged as he lit a cigarette.

"This is my last day here," Stony said.

Malfie looked at him, the faintest glimmer of curiosity in his eyes. "What're you gonna do?"

"I'm workin' inna hospital. Cresthaven?"

"You gonna be a doctor? That's good money."

"Nah, I'm just workin' with kids." Stony smoothed the silver foil against his thigh.

"I dig kids." Malfie bent down and picked up a small strand of cable wire under his boot.

"You think I should stay here?" Stony concentrated on the silver foil, eyes directed toward his lap.

"I don't give a fuck what you do," Malfie answered without malice.

~

At two-thirty in the afternoon a carpenter was killed when a brickie on the twenty-fourth floor couldn't fit a forty-pound 4 by 4 wooden pallet in the covered garbage chute, so he just tossed it over the side.

When the whistles down below started shrieking like crazy, Stony and 240 construction workers ran to the lip of their concrete floors and peered over the side of the building. Twenty-four layers of men, their faces reflecting every response from amusement to horror. From Stony's viewpoint on the twentieth floor the body in the dirt looked like a swastika.

"An' people bitch 'cause we make so much fuckin' money," Tommy muttered, staring down from the twenty-second floor.

"Hey, I just sat on the bus with that guy yesterday," Vinny said, his mouth open in amazement.

On the sixteenth floor, Eddie crossed himself.

"Ah, the poor fuckin' guy was wearing a galvanized steel hat too," Jimmy O'Day said to Augie on the top deck.

"Great!" Augie laughed. "So his fuckin' brains woulda looked like chopped liver instead a soup."

~

At three-thirty, after the whistle, men lingered in the various shanties discussing the death.

"Them fuckin' guineas," Augie said, pacing the dimly lit floor. He was naked from the waist down and pulled his dick as he talked. "Them fuckin' wops, they're animals. Who took my fuckin' shorts?"

None of the Italian electricians took offense. Augie was talking about real guineas. Real just-off-the-boat mustache-and-baggy-pants paisans.

"It shoulda been two a them," said Vinny.

"You think they'll ever catch the guy?" Stony was the most shaken of anybody in the shanty. His face was chalky.

"Yeah, right away." Tommy's cigarette dangled from his mouth as he hitched up a pair of dress pants with both hands. "C'mon, kid, let's go." Tommy ushered Stony from the shanty, an arm around his shoulder.

"You had a good time this morning, hah?" Tommy asked. They picked their way through the assorted debris and rubble of the site to the car.

"You don't think they'll catch the guy?"

"Nah, them guinzos is thick as thieves. Have a good time today?"

"It was all right." Stony repressed a smile.

"Still doin' the hospital Monday?" Tommy tried to control himself.

Stony sighed and expelled air from puffed cheeks. "Pop, get off my back." Flat and tired.

"You know you're killin' me, Stony?" Tommy's voice cracked as if he were going to cry.

Stony felt terrified. He wrenched his shoulders free from Tommy's arm, jammed his hands into his pockets and walked rapidly back toward the site. For the second time that day Tommy stared at his son's back.

Stony veered clear of the electricians' shanty as he walked to the far side of the building. He sat down on a square chunk of concrete, stared at nothing. He remembered what Malfie had said, "You can't run away from love." He didn't know which word stuck in his craw more, "can't" or "love." Maybe both together. Mrs. Pitt had said she had to leave home to get on with her life. Never went back. Never went back. Scary shit. He remembered trying to get to Amsterdam with a bankbook and no passport. Harris said leaving home is the hardest thing. The hardest. With no passport. No money. A fucking bankbook. He thought of Derek, Tyrone and the other little niggers in wheel-chairs. Who the fuck were they? Who were they to him? What the fuck was he going to do? Sit there and tell stories to cripples all his life? Candy striper. You can't run away from love. You can't. Run away. From love. You can't. Love. Can't love. They loved him. Chubby. Tommy. Albert. Oh Jesus Christ. Albert. Are you man enough? Understand enough? When you left the Greek's you feel a tap on the back of your head? That was your change.

Stony got up and pitched small stones into a slime- and oil-filled pothole. He tried to think of Albert. Save Albert. Got to. But somehow the thought felt like a sexual fantasy he couldn't really get into. Couldn't get a good hard-on about. Something rang false. He thought about himself on his own. Sometimes, I feel, like a mo-tha-less child. Breaking up is haard to-o, ha-ard to do-o. The *Night* Train! The green green grass of ho-me. My da-ad. He is-n't much, in the eyes of the world. Hit the ro-oad Jack, and don'choo come back no more, no more no more no more. Wi-ild hor-orsess, couldn't drag me away-yay.

But why would working at Cresthaven have to mean leaving home? Who said anything about leaving home?

Stony stopped tossing rocks, rubbed his eyes and staggered aimlessly around the building, his hands back in his pockets. Just a fuckin' job. He wandered over to the spot where the carpenter had died. Nothing, you couldn't see nothing. Just dirt. Earth. Garbage. And the shattered wooden pallet that did the job. He looked up twenty-four stories, imagined it screaming down at him. Picking up speed, slightly turning in the air. Bigger and bigger. Crunch! Stony shuddered. Tough job. Man's job. Stony flexed his muscles. Ahm a Mayn! Ah spell EM! AY! EN! NO BEE! OH! WHY! Runaway chil' runnin' wil'. Play hooky from school can't go out to pla-ay. For the res' a the week, in yah room you go to sta-ay. Eighteen was pretty young for leaving home. Twenty-one's a good time. Besides, who said anything about leaving home?

Suddenly he thought of Butler. He hadn't seen or talked to him since he started working construction.

～

Tommy waited ten minutes for Stony. When Stony didn't return, Tommy got in his car and roared off for Yonkers to drown his sorrow in pussy.

~

Stony took a cab home. His mother and Phyllis were in the kitchen whispering like assassins. He quickly changed, took some money from his desk and left the house.

26

"I CAN'T STAND it no more. That's it, that is *it*." Marie's eyes were like red stars.

Phyllis frowned as she examined the contents of the folded invoice Marie had handed her. It was a bill addressed to Tommy from the Saw Mill River Motel.

"Now, honey, you don't know for sure." Phyllis' voice sounded weak.

Marie propped her elbows on the kitchen table, her mouth resting against the back of her hand. Balefully she stared at Phyllis.

"It could, could be business. You don't . . ."

Marie shut her eyes as if to acknowledge a headache. "Just stop. I'm not a kid an' neither are you. At least he could have the goddamn decency not to have the goddamn bill mailed here." She hunched her shoulders and shivered. "Stupid. I don't even know why I'm getting so goddamn upset. I knew all along."

Something snakelike slithered rapidly through Phyllis. An awful tingle. "Whadya mean?"

Marie exhaled through her nose and pushed back strands of hair from her forehead. She felt like she had a fever.

"Go do your wash," she dismissed her sister-in-law with contempt.

"Whadya mean you knew?" Phyllis pulled out a cigarette, forgetting the unlit one between her lips. Marie took the cigarette from her hand and lit it, dropping the lighter in front of Phyllis. Her forehead wrinkled as she exhaled.

"For years an' years an' years . . ." Her voice trailed off. "I dunno what I'm makin' such a goddamn federal production for, I really don't. We shoulda been divorced after a year, before I even got pregnant with Stony. It was good when we dated, it was good for a couple a months after that, then . . . I dunno. The cheating isn't even it. It's somethin' that happens before that." She stared at her cold coffee. "There's this one moment, this one moment when you realize that after all those I love you's you say to each other for hours, days, months, *years* even, after all those I love you's you realize that somebody's lyin'. It's like at some point your heart goes on automatic pilot, an' no matter how you hold onto each other, an' no matter how it feels in bed, you know the whole damn thing's a crock. An' you feel lonely, you feel hurt, you feel angry, but I'll tell you the truth, what you really feel is empty, like a big wind tunnel. And, honey, that's the most godawful feeling of all. Because then, you just died."

Phyllis wanted to shake her head violently, scream at Marie to shut up, but she felt that if she moved, if she so much as lifted a finger, something inside would shatter.

"After that you just get wrapped up in the bullshit. It feels like all that matters anymore is who's right, who gets the credit, who wins today. I mean when you're forty-five, who . . . the . . hell cares? Who the hell is keepin' score? Even a lousy nigger pushin' a *broom* for twenny-five years gets a goddamn gold watch. Whadda *you* get?"

She stabbed out her cigarette.

"They all cheat, they're all the same. They're like a goddamn army marchin' off to . . . I dunno. Maybe I should take one a those motel management courses, I'd make a mint."

"Not Chubby." Phyllis stared at Marie, shaking her head slowly, afraid to take her eyes from Marie's face. "Not Chubby."

Marie said nothing, a bitter half smile forming.

Phyllis felt like she had never really seen Marie before. Fat, ugly, horrible bitch. "No day, no way, not Chubby."

After Phyllis left, Marie threw out the invoice and started doing the dishes. She felt a little better now, she even felt a little sympathetic to Tommy. After all, they hadn't screwed in six months — can't expect a man like Tommy not to get restless. It hadn't always been like that, especially in the beginning. That first time in Tommy's parents' house — bled like a gusher. Tommy cried when he came, in the beginning he always cried when he came. The white sheets — when they'd finished Tommy saw the bloodstains and said, "Hey! It's a Jap flag!" He scrubbed like crazy at the stain, throwing out the sheets, throwing out the mattress, throwing out the box spring, scrubbing the floor. We had a fire, Dad. I think Louie dropped a live butt on the bed. I took care of it. Chubby got grounded for two weeks, wouldn't talk to Tommy for a month. Until the wedding. Gave us rubber sheets and a fireman's hat for a present. Elsie gave us a toaster. Mama gave us a thousand dollars and great-grandma's dinner linens. Lefty and Sy and Frankie Finnegan chipped in for a movie projector. Gabby and Blossom got us that phonograph. Chubby talking about this skinny Jewish girl he met named Phyllis. Tommy's father kissing Tommy. Chubby crying. Tommy's father dancing with Mama. Tommy's mother puking on the dais. Theresa Finnelli had a crush. Caught the flowers. Married a lawyer. Bought a house on Pelham Parkway and changed her name to Inez. Niagara Falls. From the rear. Too scared. Never again. First anniversary. Too drunk. Too dry. No Vaseline. Tommy wanted to use toothpaste. This way I can eat you out and brush my teeth at the same time. Slap. He slapped back, walking out. A terrific cry. Lonely. Called Mama. So sad. Mama said . . . what did she say? Tommy came back two hours later with flowers. Corny. Put toothpaste in his eggs. His balls so big they would spill out of my palm. Like to hold them when he . . .

Marie realized that she was washing dishes she had just washed a minute before, taking them out of the drainboard and then putting them back.

~

Stony ambled into Butler's store, his hands behind his back. Behind the counter Butler looked up, then returned his attention to an order form from a hosiery jobber. Stony watched him in silence. Butler couldn't concentrate, but he refused to look at

Stony. Stony produced a champagne bottle from behind his back and smacked it down on the order form.

"Here, yah dumb fuck. If you're gonna bury yourself in here, at least do it in style."

Butler glanced at the bottle, smirked, then reached over the counter and hugged Stony. "Asshole." Butler lightly patted his back.

Stony disengaged himself. "You got glasses?"

"I got some paper cups in back." Butler moved to the rear.

"Class, real class. I bring in champagne an' he comes up with the sanitary Lilys."

"Whatta you bitchin' about? That's a three-dollar bottle a Cold Duck."

"Three ninety-five." Stony popped the cork, hitting the fan. He poured two shots. Butler picked up his drink. "Hold it. You gotta do it like this." Stony raised his cup, then carefully linked elbows with Butler. "Continental style."

"Faggot."

"L'chaiym."

They downed their drinks in one gulp.

"Nineteen seventy-four, an excellent year." Butler smacked his lips and belched.

"Yeah, for Tab. What time you close up?"

Butler looked at his watch. "Any time now."

"Well, lock the door and let's finish off this bad boy."

Butler hung the "closed" sign on the inside of the glass door and locked up nice. Stony refilled the cups. Butler made himself comfortable on a padded stool while he delicately sipped his drink. Stony caught his hand. "No, no, don't sip. The true flavor of Cold Duck can only be appreciated when chugged." Stony threw back his head and emptied the cup. "See, that way it tickles your nose."

"Hey, where'd you learn all this stuff?"

"I'm a charter member of the Frank De Nardo Memorial Drinking Society."

"Bad taste." Butler shook his head sadly. "Bad taste."

Frankie De Nardo, a friend of theirs, had died at fourteen by downing a quart of straight gin for a ten-dollar bet.

"Shut up and drink." Stony poured off two more. "Hey, speaking of Frank, your uncle really flew the coop, hah?"

"Yeah, he really got shook. You know, times change. The poor guy thought he was still livin' in a Jewish-Italian neighborhood."

"Yeah, an' Roosevelt's still the Prez."

"Teddy Roosevelt." Butler poured himself another.

"So you're really gonna do it, huh?" Stony smirked.

"Yeah, I'm really gonna do it."

"Butler's Hosiery Palace."

"Butler's Hosiery Palace."

They smiled at each other, then cracked up.

"To the Palace!" Stony raised his cup. Butler tried to link elbows, but Stony pushed him off. "Whatta you goin' queer on me here?"

"No man! That's continental style!"

"It's Greek to me." Stony poured another. Butler sipped. "Get it?"

"Get what?"

"It's Greek to me."

"So?"

"Greek, you know, up the ass? Queer?" Stony grinned expectantly. He was beginning to have a hard time focusing his eyes.

"Looka this fuckin' guy!" Butler tilted his chin in Stony's direction. "The world's only eighteen-year-old sot."

"Butler, you got no sense a humor. That's the first sign a someone goin' insane, they lose their sense a humor." Stony poured himself another, splashing the counter. Butler produced a roll of paper towels, started sopping up the mess.

"Extra absorbency, hah? Looka this fuckin' guy." Stony cautiously filled his cup, then moved the bottle to Butler's cup.

"So, Stones, what's happenin' with you? How's that construction thing goin'?" Butler poured himself two fingers.

Stony sighed, elbows on the counter, and rolled his forehead on his folded wrists. "I dunno . . . I dunno what to tell you." He looked up and covered his mouth, rubbing it absently with his fingers. He seemed to sober up. "Lotta pressure, Butler, lotta pressure."

"What, the construction work?"

"Nah, the job's a gut, no sweat. It's jerk-off work. I'm talkin' about somethin' else."

"What?"

"I dunno." Stony pushed away from the counter, shoved his hands into his back pockets and paced the floor. "I finished up today, so now I can go back to the hospital, right? And I can do it too, you know? It's completely on me."

"So what's the problem?" Butler set the bottle under the counter.

Stony reached over and retrieved it. "I was thinkin' about you this week, takin' over the store, what you said to me on the phone, you know, if I work with my family, like, so what? You know? I mean, shit, Butler, they're such a heavy number on my head, you know, like I *love* them, I don't wanna hurt them, or anything, ah, I dunno what the fuck to do. I don't wanna be a fuckin' construction worker but then I think, what's the dif? A job's a job, right? I mean, it's only what you do for bucks, right? What the fuck do I know about hospitals? I mean, who the fuck do I think I am, Albert Schweitzer? I go to the hospital to help people an' I kill my family."

"You ain't killin' anybody, an' gimme the fuckin' bottle. I don't wanna hold your head over the bowl all night."

Stony didn't resist. "I talked to that cat Harris, remember him? He knows . . . he knows what's goin' down. I was all gung-ho with the hospital, the this, the that. You know what he said to me? Here I think the cat's gonna be all hurrahs and back slaps, he says to me, 'I hope you're strong enough.' I figure, 'Fuck him, what's that, code?' Strong enough for what? An' now I know, I really know. He said to me leaving home is the hardest thing in the world. I said, 'Who's leavin' home?' The fuckin' construction site's farther away than the goddamn hospital." Stony rubbed his mouth and nodded solemnly. "He's right though, Butler, he's

right. I do that hospital gig an' I'm on my way out. Gettin' that
gig is like gettin' a divorce from them, you know? Really, it's like
a split wit' that whole head set. There's no way they could ever
understand or dig what I'm into. We'd have too many fuckin'
fights. I'd have to get my own crib, you know?"

"So?"

"So first I get my own crib. I go over for dinner a few times a
week, and we'd fight at dinner, 'cause all the daily fights I would
be havin' if I was still livin' there would all get stored up for the
times I would visit, so then I'd start comin' over less an' less, an'
the fights would get more concentrated, you follow? Finally, I'd
stop goin' over there all together."

"How do you know?"

"I know, I know."

"So, you're not gonna do the hospital, right?"

"No, no. I'm gonna do it, these are just the things runnin'
through my head."

"Uh-huh, what else is runnin' through yah head?"

"Then I started thinkin' about Albert. That kid's in bad fuckin'
shape, man. He needs me around. They'll eat him alive if I ain't
there. I tell you, if I ever split, he'll be the first casualty. Scumbag
Harris was the one who told me that. The fuckin' guy pulls my
coat about Albert, then he sets me up to split."

"You on the horns a the dilemma."

"I is on the hone a the scone." Stony chuckled. "But it ain't
funny. None a this shit is funny. I'm in a lotta fuckin' pain,
Butler. I feel like I'm jugglin' fifty-two oranges. It's not just me
I'm thinkin' about, it's my parents, Chubby, Albert, the kids in the
hospital, it's all them people. They're like flies aroun' my head,
an' I jus' can't think straight."

"What kicked *this* off?" Butler looked around him in bewilder-
ment. "Last I heard you were flyin' so high I thought you was
gonna be the next Ben Casey."

"You know what turned me around? I'll tell you honest. I
brought Albert into the hospital to meet the kids I was workin'
with, right? He's playin' with 'em, everything's cool, then some
nurse asks me who he is. I say he's my brother, she says he's gotta

split, no kids allowed for visits. I was disappointed but I figure
rules is rules so I go to take him home and get to the front door,
some nurse says where you takin' that kid? I said I'm takin' him
home. You know what she says? She says lemme see his
discharge slip. Can you fuckin' believe that? I says he's my
goddamn brother, he ain't no patient. She wouldn't let him leave
until she checked it out with the children's ward! At first I was so
fuckin' pissed I was spittin' blood, but then I took a good look at
him, and I'll tell you something, if I was that nurse, I would have
done the same fuckin' thing. That kid not only looked like a
patient, but he didn't look in any way ready for a discharge
either." Stony nodded emphatically. "*That* shook me up. He
didn't look no different than the little niggers in wheelchairs, you
know? He's a little nigger inna wheelchair too. Then I started
thinkin', my whole family is just a bunch a little niggers in
wheelchairs. They're all fuckin' cripples comin' an' goin'. Even
my old lady. I usually just write her off as a dinosaur, a real
whacko with a mean streak as long as my leg, but like, she don't
know any better. I mean the way she acts aroun' Albert. My
grandmother, my ol lady's mother, man, you wanna hear horror
stories, you gotta hear what my mother had to go through as a kid
with this cunt. You know when my old lady was six, her mother
broke her nose because she wouldn't go to the store? Right? So
what's somebody who had to go through that gonna be like as a
mother? An' then my old man and Chubby, two fuckin'
fifty-year-old pussy chasers. Whatta they tryin' a prove? Old men
playin' stink-finger. Do you get what I'm tryin' to say? I mean,
my whole family's like a private ward. There's enough goddamn
pain in that house to knock a whole city block on its ass. An' I
love them Butler, and they love me. If I was really serious about
helpin' little niggers in wheelchairs I don't hafta work in no
hospital."

"Yeah, yeah. O.K. I hear what you're sayin', Stones, but dig,
the whole fuckin' world's like that, man. I mean check out the
sickos who come in here, the six-foot-eight jobs wit' the peachpuff
this an' the peter pan that, I mean, everybody's out to lunch, you
know? The whole fuckin' Bronx is like a combination open-air

loony bin an' Red Cross disaster tent, right? Your family ain't so special. It sounds to me like you're scared a doin' what you want, an' I *know* what *you* want, baby, you want that hospital, an' I agree wit' everything you're sayin' except the conclusion, an' you can jerk off this one, an' jerk off that one, an' you can jerk off *me*, but don't fuckin' jerk off yourself, sweetheart, 'cause twenty years from now you're gonna wind up just like yer old man with your fuckin' putz in your hand hanging outside some bar in Yonkers, married to some bitch with a heart like a piece a coal, and a kid for a punching bag, O.K.? You *see* that now, man, an' if I was you I'd fuckin' run the other way, but you're talkin' about divin' in an' savin' everybody. You ain't savin' shit, there's sharks in them waters an' you're gonna get eaten. Don't worry about Albert, he'll sink or swim on his own. You're just usin' him as an excuse, you don't have to sit on his head to look out for him. If you wanna split, you split. You just worry about your *own* ass. 'Cause I see it, baby, they're starting to nibble you to death right now. You talk about love. Your fuckin' Uncle Chubby loves you so much, he loved you right outta what coulda been something very tight with a very heavy person."

"Who?"

"Annette."

"Annette! She's a fuckin' pump!"

"Oh yeah? You didn't sound like that three weeks ago. I talked to her last week; she came in here askin' about you. She told me all about the things you was talkin' about with her, an' how you douched her almost right away after that night, an' I *know* Chubby had a hand in it, 'cause I *told* him you was runnin' with her, an' I saw that look on his face, and I *knew* that cocksucker was gonna pull a number on you to fuck things up, and I swear to you, Stones, I could just hear him. 'You know I love you like my own kid, Stony,' am I right? An' you let him jerk you off, an' you blew a fine, together lady. I didn't *know* how together she was 'cause I never talked to her until she came in here and *I'm* an asshole for *believin'* all the trash that goes down about her, but you *knew* better, you bastard, an' you fuckin' blew it right out your ass 'cause a your goddamn family. An' I'll tell you somethin' else.

It's more than Chubby, you dumped her 'cause she was talkin' straight to you just like I am now and you didn't want to hear that 'cause it scared the shit out of you." Butler slammed his fist down on the counter and shook his finger in Stony's face. "You goddamn phony, you're talkin' about love and takin' care a people, an' you stepped all over her 'cause she cared about you enough to talk straight life. Well, sucker, I'll tell you somethin' else, I ain't waitin' to get stepped on just 'cause I care about you. You don't do that hospital number, an' it's all over between us — an' that's the God's honest truth. 'Cause I don't *dig* little niggers in wheelchairs, an' I don't want 'em for friends, an' I ain't sittin' by an' watchin' you turn into one. 'Cause that's what you were that night when you eighty-sixed Annette. You were nothin' but a little nigger in a wheelchair, an' the more you hang aroun' that family a yours the more you gonna be like that. See, Stony, I know you goof on the store, an' maybe I don't have that much in the brains department, but at least I got the fuckin' heart to go and get what I want outta life. An' I don't wanna be around people who can't cut it. You hear me? An' that includes you! An' I don't wanna hear any a this shit about all the goddamn pain in your family an' blah blah blah. You just worry about your own goddamn pain." Butler was red-faced. He pulled up the bottle and took a slug.

"Hey lissen, you hard-on, don't gimme no ulti*ma*tums. I *told* you these are just the fuckin' *thoughts* in my head. I *said* I was gonna do the hospital." Stony waved his arms around his head as he yelled, but there was a trace of hesitation in his voice. "I don't understand you, Butler. I come in here as a friend, I bring champagne. Whatta you, some kinda hot shit now you got a pissant store?" Stony grabbed the Cold Duck and slapped the cork into the bottle. "I'll fuckin' know better next time before I pour out *my* heart to any friends!" Holding the bottle by the neck he strode to the door and pulled on the doorknob.

Twirling the key ring around his finger, Butler slowly came from behind the counter. "Hey, Stony? If you're not in the hospital Monday, don't come by here Monday night." Butler unlocked the door.

"No sweat, fucko." Stony stormed out into the street, trashing the Cold Duck in the nearest garbage can.

~

Stony drove out to Orchard Beach. He didn't know where else to go. He sat on the deserted boardwalk chain-smoking cigarettes and watching the waves. The beach was like a city dump with sand. A few old guys wandered around with headphones and long metal detectors combing the sand for lost change and cheap jewelry. A soft twilight wind made Stony shiver. Ever since Butler got that fucking store he sure was going through some changes. All bad. Uppity bastard. He didn't understand shit. Just like Annette. They probably started balling the minute she walked in the store. Albert'll sink or swim on his own. In a pig's ass. Stony thought of that day Albert came to the hospital. He didn't even know Albert could play Chinese checkers. Worry about your own goddamn pain . . . Butler and his fucking ultimatums.

Stony got up, yawned and walked over to a concrete pillbox hot dog stand. Two Puerto Ricans in baggy white shirts were wiping down a grease-caked grill. "Gimme a frank."

"We're closed, man," one of them said, his back to Stony.

"You look open to me." Stony didn't give a shit.

"Register's closed."

Stony walked off, hands in his pockets, and ambled down the boardwalk. You know, you're killing me. Stony . . . You know you're killing your father . . . what a fucking crock. Chubby and Tommy probably got together and rehearsed. He remembered Chubby dueling those guys in the hallway. Albert did a better job in the rec room than himself. I think you're scared, Stony.

Stony imagined he was in a movie walking alone on the beach into the sun, a sad soundtrack playing in the background.

A lumpy, gray-haired lady trudged up the beach toward the boardwalk. She wore a dripping one-piece black swimsuit and a white rubber swimming cap — the turned-up flaps jutting out over her ears like airplane wings. She placed a thumb against one nostril and blew out a gob of snot. Stony shuddered, leaning over the rail. He covered his face with his hands and peeked at the sea through his fingers.

~

Tommy came home at two-thirty in the morning. He was shit-faced, beat and sated. Earlier in the evening he'd run into that chick who took on him and Chubby last month, grabbed her and a bottle of Canadian and rented a room for a few hours at the Saw Mill River Motel where he was a regular. She came four times, twice when he went down on her and twice when they fucked. He came in her mouth and he came in her box. Everybody went home happy.

Tommy sneaked past the kitchen where Marie sat chain-smoking and waiting. Three steps past the kitchen Tommy stopped and backtracked.

"Whatta you doin' up?" he challenged.

"Where were you?" she asked flatly.

"Out."

"Where?"

"Out."

"Where?"

"Hey look, I was out, that's all you gotta know."

"Out at that motel?" As she stubbed out her cigarette she knocked the ashtray to the floor. Tommy's eyes narrowed. Then he noticed the half-empty fifth of Heaven Hill bourbon.

"You're drunk."

She rose shakily. "You think I'm stupid, don'cha?"

"I'm goinna sleep." Tommy started toward the bedroom, his mellow head burning away into an early hangover.

"I'm gonna cheat on *you!* Ya bastad!"

"Do whatcha want."

"Does she give you a good blowjob?" she shouted after him.

There was dead silence for about thirty seconds before Tommy reappeared in the doorway. "She gobbles it down like it was from the goddamn fountain of youth."

Marie felt as if she'd been hit full force with a breaker. The red rage drained from her face. She heard the bedroom door slam. She reached for the bourbon, but her hands were shaking so badly that the bottle slipped from her fingers and fell on its side. She watched it roll slowly to the edge of the table, disappear over the edge and crash on the linoleum.

"Cheat on *you!* Ya bastad," she mumbled as she cradled her head on her forearms and was swallowed up by a terrifying loneliness.

27

MARIE WOKE UP at four-thirty in the morning with a burning headache. She lit a cigarette, took one drag and felt like she was going to vomit. She rose unsteadily, dropped the cigarette in the sink and started down the hallway to the bedroom. She pushed against the walls for support. When she heard Tommy snoring, she clenched her teeth, not knowing what to do. Finally, she wheeled around, staggered back down the hallway, past the kitchen into the living room, and fell face-down on the couch and passed out. She awoke momentarily at seven to the sound of clashing pots and Tommy and Stony arguing in the kitchen. The next time she opened her eyes it was ten-thirty in the morning, the living room was blasted with sunlight. She stumbled to the bathroom and sat on the toilet for half an hour, her head in her hands. Then she took two Excedrin and crawled into bed. She lay there on the rumpled sheets swathed in the odor of Tommy's body. The whole room reeked of his presence, and her rage kept her awake. She ran last night's dialogue over and over in her head.

"Cheat on you!" she heard herself say out loud to the empty room. She thought she was going crazy. She picked up the phone and dialed her mother's number. A male Spanish voice answered. In horror she slammed down the phone. Her mother had been dead almost a year. The rage subsided, replaced by terror. She started to cry, her hands over her face, giving the sobs a muffled echo. She fell into a fretful sleep. Every time she closed her eyes she had a nightmare, although when she awoke she couldn't remember what it was about. Soon she was in a panic, drenched in sweat, battling to stay awake, but even staying awake felt like part of a nightmare. She couldn't tell if she was awake or sleeping. Then the paralysis set in again, her brain was screaming, her body immobile, her lungs collapsed. She struggled to open her eyes, wiggle her toes. Suddenly she lurched from the bed and found herself standing in a fog of panic. A thick cream of nausea rose inside her, and she made a motion to crawl back into bed. Stopping herself, she backed away, violently shaking her head from side to side in an effort to wake up. In the bathroom she ran cold water over her face. Gradually, as the nightmare dissolved and the panic subsided, the rage began to swell again. Tommy came back into focus. Tommy made her go through this hell. Tommy — arrogant cheating bastard. Tommy. Her rage felt like a heavy rain.

~

In the afternoon Marie pushed a shopping cart with two pillowcases filled with clothes down to the laundry room in the basement. As she wheeled the cart through the cinder-block maze of the basement, she heard the distant drone of the dryers. The minute she had stepped out of the elevator she could tell by the volume of the noise exactly how many of the five big dryers were in use.

The laundry room was deserted except for a twelve-year-old boy reading *The Red Badge of Courage* and thirty-year-old Jack Cutler, who sat with his legs crossed and hands in his lap staring across the room at the large salmon pink dryers. He sat on one of a connected row of twenty hard plastic sky blue chairs. In the center of the room stood a rectangle of twenty white enamel washing machines. The walls were beige-painted cinder block covered with taped index cards and fliers advertising everything from baby sitters to a starting karate class for women in the community center. The laundry room always gave Marie the blues.

She emptied the pillowcases into a machine, threw in two Salvos and fished around in her pocketbook for quarters. All she found were three dimes and a five-dollar bill. She looked around the room angrily, then approached Jack Cutler. "Honey, do you have change of five?"

Jack jumped up, searched his wallet and his pockets. He had two singles and a fistful of change.

Marie smiled, shrugged and was about to approach the twelve-year-old.

"Wait, here, you need quarters?"

Jack offered her two quarters from his change.

"But I don't have — "

"No . . . no . . . it's O.K., I insist." He pressed the money into her hand.

She regarded him curiously. He seemed a little feverish.

"Thanks," she said haltingly. "I'll catch you next time."

"My pleasure." He smiled, almost bowing to her.

Marie used the laundry room on Saturdays and nine times out of ten Jack would be there. At first she thought he was a security guard or a washing machine mechanic, then she figured he was a faggot. Then she decided that he didn't look like a faggot and probably was just some nut who liked to watch women do their laundry, then go upstairs and play with himself or something. Eventually she lost interest in trying to figure out what his game was and regarded him as another washing machine.

With the wash going, Marie listlessly thumbed through a magazine. She heard the squeaking of a shopping cart approaching the laundry room. A woman Marie knew only by sight came into the room. They nodded vaguely at each other. The other woman was six feet tall with water-bag tits and an ass like the rear of a wagon train. Her angular yet fleshy face was topped with short, stiff black lacquered bangs. Marie watched her unload her laundry. She wore a sleeveless, faded floral print blouse and tight dark orange clam diggers. Marie saw the outline of her panties right through the clam diggers. Marie was disgusted. A woman built like that should wear a chemise. Then Marie looked down at her own clothes. She knew her own dark red slacks showed the outline of her underwear, that her slacks were an advertisement for her own fat ass. Her bra was visible through the armholes of her own sleeveless blouse. Her own hair was as falsely shellacked black. Marie felt like she couldn't stand up. She felt intense embarrassment about herself. Tommy was tall, lean, with a flat cowboy belly, deep chest, long, muscular arms. She pressed her fingers into her flabby paunch and felt nauseated. The other woman walked past her to the dryers. She was chewing something, reminded Marie of a cow. She imagined that woman having sex, grunting and squealing like a pig. A cow. A pig. She thought of that woman having sex with Tommy, moaning and slobbering. Tommy's small ass bouncing and rolling like a pile driver, that woman, gasping and groaning, spreading her treelike legs as far apart as they would go, digging her nails into his broad, smooth back, pulling his hair, grabbing his ass, making him drive into her deeper and deeper, trembling and gushing come.

Marie stood on shaky legs and in a dazed state headed toward Jack Cutler.

~

Jack Cutler was in heaven, his two favorite women were in the laundry room. First Marie, with her nice fat ass and roly-poly tits, then Helen, his goddess, who had the biggest tits in the whole world and an enormous ass that couldn't help but quiver every time she took a step. His dream fantasy was to have Helen come into the laundry, take off all her clothes, throw them in the machine, then walk around the room naked until they were done. Now that Marie *and* Helen were down here together he imagined *both* of them dumping their clothes into machines and *both* of them walking around naked. First he imagined them walking around the machines in opposite directions, then he imagined them walking around the machines arm in arm, four joggling titties, two jiggling tushies. Just as Jack was about to fall off his chair in a swoon he noticed Marie walking toward him. He looked around him to see if maybe she'd left her cart or her coat nearby. There was nothing around him but him. Maybe she needed another quarter. Her face was flushed, her steps a little unsteady. Maybe she was drunk or had that virus that was going around. He didn't want her to come near, she was disrupting the fantasy.

"What's your name?" Her voice was husky. He could smell her.

"Jack Cutler." He gripped the plastic edges of his chair.

"Do you know what apartment I live in?"

"Yes." He felt like he was ten years old.

"Come up in a half-hour." She left the laundry room on unsteady legs.

Jack felt as if his head were filled with bees. A numb buzz ran through his body. He sat motionless and blank for five minutes, then wandered around the cinder-block labyrinth of the basement checking his wristwatch every thirty seconds, a periodic whimper catching in his throat.

~

Marie's hands were shaking so badly she couldn't separate the door key from the other keys on the ring. Once inside, she bumped around the apartment. Her heart was beating so fast her ears hurt. She ran to the vestibule, locked, chained and bolted the front door. What did she ask him up for? Maybe he was *crazy*. Dangerous. A lunatic. He hung around laundries all day. She had never slept with another man but Tommy. What if he butchered her? She ran into the kitchen, grabbed up all the knives in the drawer, clutching them to her, and threw them under the living room couch. She roamed around the living room in a daze, then bolted into the kitchen, grabbed up all the forks and dumped them under the couch. Then with a squawk of alarm she kneeled down on all fours, swept all the knives and forks from under the couch and ran with them into Albert and Stony's room and piled them in the closet. Then she raced into her room, tore off her clothes and searched her drawers and closet for a nightgown or a negligee. Nothing. She ran into the bathroom and dumped out the few remaining clothes still in the hamper until she found a wrinkled acetate tangerine shorty nightgown. Slipping it on, she dashed into her bedroom and slapped on some perfume, spritzed her armpits with scented deodorant and ran a slash of lipstick across her lower lip. When the doorbell rang she screamed, collected all the knives and forks and threw them out the window.

~

After fifteen minutes of waiting around the basement, Jack had the panicky thought that his mother was home. He sped up to his apartment. She wasn't there. But maybe she was on the way home. Maybe she got that virus that was going around and was coming home early. To make sure he called the dress factory where she worked just to make sure.

" 'Lo, Pollyanna Dresswear."

"Is Mrs. Cutler there?"

"Yes, one minute."

"Never mind. I just wanted to know if she was there." He hung up.

No. Shit. That was stupid. What if that woman told her mother a man called for her and then hung up? She might get scared and come home. Or call home. And he wouldn't be there.

" 'Lo, Pollyanna Dresswear."

"Is Mrs. Cutler there? I'm her son, I called a minute ago. Can I speak to her?" Jack was sweating.

"Jack?"

"Hi, Mom, how you doing?"

"What's wrong?"

"Nothing, Mom, I just wanted to say hello."

"So hello. You sure nothing's wrong?"

"Yeah, I just wanted to say hello."

"I don't believe you, you don't sound good. Are you sick?" Jack was in a panic. "I'm great, Mom, really."

"So why are you calling me?"

"What do you want for dinner? I'm gonna go shopping now."

"Jackie, what's wrong?"

"Nothing." His voice was cracking. "Can't I call you up to say hello?"

"Jackie, something's wrong, I'm coming home."

"No! I'm fine. I'm fine. Don't come home."

"You sure?"

"Yeah, Mom, really. I love you."

There was silence on both ends.

"I'm going shopping now, Mom. I'll be gone about an hour."

"Get some fish."

"Sure, Mom, see you at five." He hung up. Goddamn motherfucking bastard. She was coming home. He knew it. Maybe not. He shouldn't go up to Marie's apartment. She'd know. After five minutes of sitting on the couch he jumped up again, fumbled with all the locks, flung open the door and ran up the stairs to Marie's apartment. Maybe just a quick one.

~

Jack rang the front doorbell a second time.

"Who is it!" Marie saw Jack through the peephole.

"Jack Cutler," he whispered into the peephole.

Marie unlocked the door but kept the chain on, opening it a few inches. "What do you want!"

"You told me to come up here!" Jack was starting to get hysterical.

Marie closed the door, took off the chain and let him in. He stared at her figure in the nightgown.

"I asked you up here to give you back your two quarters."

Jack didn't hear her. He could see her nipples standing out against the acetate. Her legs were veined and potholed but real woman's legs. Marie got scared. He wasn't listening.

"I have my period, so just take your money and leave," she said.

He grasped her arm and immediately let go.

She gasped, stepping back. Suddenly she imagined Tommy looking in on this scene and laughing his ass off. Pathetic. She was a grown woman of forty-five years. Mother of two children. A nonvirgin of twenty years.

"I'm sorry." Jack cringed.

"In the bedroom." She nodded in that direction, leading the way.

Jack started to undress tentatively.

Marie sat on the edge of the bed, some of her momentary bravado fading. He had a decent body. Paunchy a little, not very muscular, certainly not like Tommy's, but he was O.K. He hesitated at his underwear, embarrassed to go on. She tried a flirtatious smile to encourage him. She pulled her nightgown over her head. Instantly he got a hard-on, its tip peeping up through the elastic of his briefs. Marie started getting excited. She walked over to him, her breasts gently swaying back and forth, and tugged down his underwear. He had a bigger dick than Tommy. She touched it. Jack caught her, throwing her back on the bed. She started kicking and screaming, he was panting like he was brain-damaged. With his dick in his hand he fumbled for a hole. Any hole. Unwittingly he started giving it to Marie up the ass. Marie reached between his legs for his balls, squeezing for all she was worth. He yelled and jumped up, red-faced, gasping for breath.

"Hold it! Hold it! Ya goddamn animal! Ya goddamn degenerate!" Jack had doubled over, both hands between his legs. Marie wasn't scared anymore. She was boiling. The guy was a slob. An asshole. "Now look, first thing, you bring condoms?"

"What?" His face was screwed up in pain.

"Condoms, rubbers, scumbags!"

"No. Oh, God, ah . . . ah . . ."

Again Marie thought of Tommy looking in, laughing. "Maybe my husband has some." Nice touch. Tommy'll get the horns with his own bags. Marie opened Tommy's bottom dresser drawer. He kept a twelve-pack of Trojans in a brown bag under his sweaters. She lifted the sweaters. The rubbers were gone. She tossed the sweaters around the room. "Shit!" She turned angrily to Jack. "Shit," she said louder.

"I can go down and get some," he said a little easier. The pain was subsiding. He started getting dressed.

"No, wait!" Marie stopped him in his tracks. "Lay down on the bed."

He obediently lay on his back, watching her. She crouched next to him, perpendicular to his crotch. He reached over to touch her dangling breast, but she pushed his hand away. He lay there spread-eagled and motionless.

She had never given Tommy a blowjob because she thought it was vile, disgusting and sinful. He had always wanted one. Twenty years of head pushing. Twenty years of "C'mon, just lick it once." She had never given in. But now her hunger for revenge overcame her loathing and fear. This would be the supreme galling fuck you she could throw in his face. She hesitated for a moment, then held his dick. He started to sit up, she pushed him back.

"If you come in my mouth I'll brain you." Her voice was trembling. Holding it in her hand she gave it a tentative lick. It had no taste. It was just hot. He gasped. She gave it another lick. He gasped again. She felt dizzy. She could smell his crotch. She put half the head of his dick in her mouth and held it there. He started moaning. With the tip in her mouth she began jerking him off with her fist. She rolled her tongue around its head. He started pulling his hair and flailing his arms. She jerked him off faster, moving her mouth up and down over the tip. She felt herself getting wet. She let out an involuntary moan and with her other hand cupped his balls.

"Teeth," he moaned. "Ah . . . no teeth." She didn't hear him. She kept licking and pumping, squeezing his balls, pressing her thighs together so tight her knees shook. With a shriek he came in her mouth. She pulled away gagging and spluttering, come dripping from her hair and chin. She retched, furiously wiping her face. "Oh, thank you, thank you," he droned, drunk with pleasure.

She spit come in his face and, snarling, slashed him across the cheek with her fingernails. "You filthy disgusting pig! I'll kill you!" She gasped for air, her chest heaving.

The streaks of white on Jack's cheek turned pink, then dark, then crimson. Jack leapt out of bed, stumbled into his pants, threw on his shirt and barefoot ran out of the apartment, slamming the door behind him. Marie retched some more, then, wiping her chin, collapsed on the bed.

~

Running down the stairs Jack heard sirens in his head. What had happened, he was sure, was just this side of murder. He was crying when he opened his door and almost ran smack into his mother in the vestibule.

She grabbed his arms. "What happened!"

"Nothing, Mom!" He struggled to get past her, but she wouldn't let go.

"Don't tell me nothing!" she screamed. "You're crying, you're bleeding! Don't tell me nothing!"

Jack broke loose and ran to his room, his mother hot on his trail. He couldn't close the door on her. He sat on the corner of his bed, his head in his hands, trying to collect himself.

"Where are your shoes?" she screamed.

"Oh . . . Gaw-wd!" He let out an anguished cry, jumping up and hugging his mother, shaking and crying. She felt confused, angry and frightened. She sat him back down on his bed, trying to control herself.

"Jackie, what happened, where are your shoes?"

He gingerly touched his cheek. His fingers came away bloody. With a cool damp cloth she wiped away the blood.

"Who did this?" she asked.

Jack told her the whole story in graphic detail. She sat there ashen, horrified, hand over her mouth. When Jack got to the part about Marie blowing him, his mother stood up and in a wrathful and terrible voice said, "What is this woman's name!"

Jack didn't want to say, but he couldn't fight his mother. "Marie."

"Marie what?" she demanded.

"Marie De Coco."

"De Coco." She nodded with terrible knowledge. "De Coco."

She left the room and picked up the phone in the kitchen. "Information, give me a listing for a De Coco in Co-op City, please?"

"One moment. I have a *Louis* De Coco on — "

"That's it . . ."

~

Chubby lounged on the couch watching an old Robert Mitchum movie. Phyllis was out. Said she would be back around five.

Four forty-two. Chubby constantly kept checking the time, his guts jumping. Whenever Phyllis was out Chubby now counted the minutes, the seconds, for her return, like a housebroken dog who hadn't been walked all day.

The phone rang.

" 'Lo."

"I would like to speak to Mr. De Coco, please."

"You got 'im." Chubby ate a tuna sandwich as he talked.

"Mr. De Coco,. I won't give you my name. I'm a neighbor of yours. I'm calling you about your wife."

Chubby frowned. "What about 'er?"

"I think you should know that she's in the habit of seducing young men in the laundry room and bringing them up to your apartment and — "

"Who the fuck is this!" Chubby dropped his sandwich. His face was burning. Mrs. Cutler started to quiver with emotion.

"She brings them to your apartment and makes them do — "

"Who the fuck is this!" Chubby shouted.

"I'm a mother!" Mrs. Cutler bawled back, slamming down the phone.

"Makes them do what!" Chubby screamed at the dial tone.

~

"If he's any kind of man at all, she'll be taken care of," Mrs. Cutler said as she applied first aid cream to Jack's face.

~

Chubby slammed down the phone. "Phyllis!" he bawled in rage. He kicked open the bedroom door. Phyllis wasn't home. "Phyllis!" He stormed through the house. He grabbed his jacket. "Fuckin' hoowah!" He slammed the door.

28

THE SKY was a nightmare of luminous grays. Chubby steamed across the street as the first drops hit the ground in ugly slaps. As he reached his car, the clouds ruptured into a furious jungle-thick sheet of rain. The car door slammed.

Banion's was deserted when Chubby tramped in trailing water like a dog climbing out of a lake. He collapsed onto a barstool, slammed his forearms on the counter and violently shook his head, spattering the area with rainwater.

"Banion, gimme a towel." Chubby furiously rubbed his hair dry. He shivered as the wetness of his shirt seeped under his skin. His teeth chattered. Banion sat behind the bar watching him. "Banion, you got a extra shirt?"

Banion wheeled down the bar, pulled out a heavily starched white busboy shirt from under the counter. He hadn't seen Chubby since he was in the hospital. Banion was nervous. Chubby seemed totally bent out of shape.

Chubby sat nude from the waist up, drying his back and his armpits. He took the shirt from Banion.

"It's freezin' in here!" Chubby's teeth sounded like castanets. "Don't you got no heat?" He pulled on the shirt. It was so small that it pinched the hair in his armpits, the front of the shirt not even making it around his ribs. He leaned over the bar for a tall glass and a bottle of Scotch.

"Hey . . . Chub. How you been feelin' since las' week?" Chubby ignored him, poured the glass three-quarters full, drank it down like Coke. "I gave Tommy some Haig to bring to you." Chubby poured five fingers, took a fistful of ice, dropped it in his drink and slugged it down. Banion automatically reached under the seat of his wheelchair and felt the police .38 held there. "I was gonna call you, but I kept gettin' hung up."

Chubby rubbed his mouth, frowning at something invisible to Banion's left. "Banion, what does seduced mean? Fucked, right?"

Banion brought his hand up from under the seat, empty.

"What?" He was sweating, fanned himself with a rolled-up crossword puzzle magazine.

"Se*duced*, se*duced*. He se*duced* her, means he *fucked* her, right?"

"Who did?"

Chubby sighed, rubbed his eyes, his arm flapped down on the bar, palm up. "Banion, take the fuckin' cotton outta your ears. Se*duced* means fuck, right?"

"Yeah." Banion pouted. "Sure."

"Yeah, yeah. I thought so." Chubby shook his head in affirmation. He slapped both palms down on the bar again and grimly stared at the row of spout-capped liquor bottles along the mirror. "FUCK!" He hurled his empty glass at the bottles. Banion ducked, loosened the .38 in one motion, but when he brought it up and pointed it with two shaking hands, the bar was deserted except for the wet mound of Chubby's discarded shirt.

Chubby drove at ninety miles an hour on the rain-blind highway. From the back of his throat emerged a whiny high-pitched singsong note, which he repeated over and over as the car swerved and skidded. He was calm, but his eyes were glassy, his foot frozen on the accelerator.

He didn't slow down until he hit the Bronx. He ran stop signs and red lights on the empty streets, pulled the car to a screaming rocking stop half up on the sidewalk in front of his building. He sprinted to the entrance, the busboy shirt pulling away in the back like water wings, his naked gut bouncing and rolling with every step. He hit the elevator button, cursed, punched the door and ran up the stairs. On the fifth floor he collapsed, panting and wheezing, resting his head on the banister. He staggered into the elevator and rode up to eleven.

~

Phyllis paced the empty house, muttering, shaking her hands and pointing her finger in emphatic gestures. As she did this, her face took on a rapid range of expressions, like a street schizo.

"Now, Chubby" — she pointed at Allen Funt, chortling on television — "I want you to tell me straight and don't *bull*shit me." She glared at the screen. "Who is she?" The elevator door creaked open, and she scooted into the kitchen, heart pounding in her ears, frantically pulling out pots and pans without rhyme or reason. She dropped a griddle, the clatter making her flinch. She crouched to pick it up. Chubby stood wheezing and steaming, dripping wet in the kitchen doorway. His eyes were wide-open crazy and his teeth were clenched. His asthma-stuffed chest, naked and slick, labored with every breath. From her crouch Chubby's head looked like it almost touched the ceiling.

"Chub . . ."

"Hoowah!" His backhand slap knocked her rolling, sprayed the white glossy enamel of the stove with a riddle of blood from her split lip. She sat up on the floor, staring at him in wild-eyed disbelief, lightly touching her wounded mouth.

Chubby aimed a kick at her face, but Phyllis deflected the tip of his shoe with her arms. A sickening crack. She screamed in pain, staring at the limp hand hanging from her broken wrist. The kick threw Chubby off balance, and he flopped backward on his ass with a grunt.

"Chubby! Oh God!" Phyllis tried to drag herself to the corner of the kitchen. Chubby was all business. He crawled after her and dragged her to him by the ankle. On his knees now he held her by the front of her blouse, reared back and punched her square in the nose. A flash of pain like lightning branched out over her face. The linoleum was splattered with rain and blood. The momentum of the punch toppled Chubby over her as if they were in the kitchen for a quickie. From the back of his throat rose that high-pitched whining singsong again. She tried to scream, but the pressure from her broken nose sent shock waves across her face. Chubby heard laughing. He struggled to his knees again, straddling her chest.

"Laughin', hah? Funny?" He lifted her slightly off the ground by the hair, caught her with a murderous slap along the jaw. Her head bounced hard against the floor. Chubby still heard the laughing. Pulled her unconscious to her feet, her head bobbing backward as if her neck were a broken hinge. Laughing. Chubby bellowed as he punched her in the chest. She sank to the floor, knocking over a dinette chair. Chubby lunged after her but his feet got tangled in the legs of the upended chair. He sailed into the living room wall, smacking his head. He sat up in front of the TV like a six-year-old, watched Lassie for thirty seconds, holding his forehead and rocking in a circular motion. Far away he heard fists pounding on the door. Squinting, his eyes focused on Phyllis' impossibly twisted body. He reached forward to straighten her out, decided to turn off the television first and dropped on his face out cold.

~

Early Sunday morning Tommy and Marie sat in Cresthaven Hospital staring in shock at the centerfold of the *Sunday Daily News*.

VIOLENCE IN CO-OP CITY

Louis V. De Coco (49) (c) is being led handcuffed from 100–12 Kennedy Place, Co-op City by Ptl. Lucius Packard (r) and Ptl. Frank McConnachie (i) after severely beating his wife Phyllis De Coco (45).

De Coco sees wife on stretcher emerging from building entrance, begins to break loose from Packard and McConnachie.

De Coco on knees, crying in front of stretcher as Packard and McConnachie take him back into custody.

Responding to complaints of screams from apartment 11A, Patrolmen McConnachie and Packard broke into the De Coco residence at 9:15 P.M. yesterday evening, found the apartment in shambles. Both Louis and Phyllis De Coco were unconscious on the living room floor. Phyllis De Coco is in fair condition at Cresthaven Hospital suffering from a broken nose, a broken jaw, a fractured wrist, a cracked sternum and numerous contusions and lacerations. Louis De Coco suffered a mild concussion, was treated, booked and is being held for psychiatric observation at Jacobi Hospital. The cause of the fight is unknown.

Tommy and Marie sat pale and numb like battered refugees on a long wooden bench in the waiting area outside of surgery.

"Mr. De Coco?" A black cop knelt in front of them, supporting his weight on the balls of his feet. "I'm Officer Packard." He glanced down at the newspaper. "Do you have any idea what that whole thing was all about?" He produced a thick, black, paper-stuffed worn leather notebook from his rear pocket.

"You tell me." Tommy was impassive.

"Mrs. De Coco?"

Marie nodded dumbly.

"Has your brother ever had any history of any kind of . . . ah, disorder? Has he ever been hospitalized?"

Tommy thought of last week at Roosevelt Hospital. "No way."

"How's Phyllis?" Marie asked.

"She's pretty busted up. But she'll be O.K. She's not pressing charges."

"What's that mean?"

"That means we can't hold him. He's over at Jacobi. He'll probably be out in a day or two. They got him out on sedatives. He had a concussion."

"Yeah, I read it in the papers." Tommy smirked.

"Why don't you people go home?"

"Can we see Phyllis?"

Packard turned to Marie. "No visitors tonight. Maybe tomorrow or Tuesday."

"Well, what's the story with my brother?" Tommy asked.

"I don't think so." Packard shook his head. "He'll be home soon."

The double doors in the hallway swung open. Stony strode in in a T-shirt and wrinkled chinos, a copy of the newspaper rolled in his fist. His eyes were red, and his hair flew in six directions. When he saw his parents he started crying. Packard glanced down, noticing Stony was barefoot. Tommy grabbed Stony's hand and sat him down. "This is my kid." Stony leaned against his father's chest, rubbing his eyes.

"You have any idea what happened?" Packard asked Stony.

"He don't know nothin'. Hey, you sure it wasn't burglary?"

Packard nodded. "No way." He stood up, hissing, as he stretched his legs. "You folks want anything? Some coffee?"

Three mute no's.

"Well, look, if anything comes up, call me at this number." He tore a piece of paper from his notebook and handed it to Tommy. He smiled briefly, walked away, then turned around. "Mr. De Coco?" He nodded for Tommy to come to him. They walked down the corridor out of earshot. "Lissen . . . ah . . . did your brother have anything goin' on the side?"

"No." Flat and formal.

"How about her?"

"Phyllis? You gotta be kiddin'."

"Hmph." Packard placed his hands on his hips. "You got the key to his place?"

"Yeah." Tommy dug into his pocket. Packard stopped him. "Look, I seen a dozen of these things before. Guys flippin' out like that, tearin' up the place, beatin' on their wives. You been up there yet?"

"Whadya mean?"

"The apartment."

"No." Tommy shrugged, confused.

"That place is a mess, lotta blood and busted-up furniture. Now, your brother will probably be home Monday. If I were you I would go up there sometime today and clean it up. Your brother comes home, sees it like he left it, he might go nuts again, you know what I mean?"

~

That afternoon it poured worse than Saturday. The four De Cocos walked around the house like zombies. Nobody talked, turned on the TV or the lights. When the phone rang, everybody jumped out of their skins.

"Tommy?"

"Chub!" Tommy's stomach flipped. "Howya doin'? What happened? Where are ya?"

"I'm fuckin' sick to my heart, Tom. I'm so goddamn ashamed. I'm still in Jacobi. I can't ever look her in the face again."

"Hey, the doctor says she'll be O.K."

"I know."

"What the fuck happened?"

"I can't talk about it. How the fuck am I gonna make it up, Tom? How many fuckin' flowers do I gotta buy? Oh God, I just wanna fuckin' crawl into a hole somewheres an' die. When I heard she didn't press charges I broke down an' cried like a baby. How's Stony takin' it?"

"Stony? He's O.K. He's a little blown out. So am I. Were you drunk?"

"A little. Tom, look, I can't talk. I want you to do me a solid. I'm comin' home tomorrow. Please, you an' Stony, go up there tonight and clean the place, O.K.?"

"You wanna live with us until Phyllis gets out? Stony'll sleep on the couch."

"No . . . no, just clean it up."

"It's no hassle, if you wanna . . ."

"No, no, babe, just clean up my place."

"Sure. You want me to get you anything?"

"No thanks. Look, I'll be home tomorrow morning. I'll talk to you then, O.K.?"

"Sure, babe."

"Tom? I love you."

"I love you too, Chub."

~

Stony lay on his bed in the rainy darkness. The shades were drawn. He lay with his hands behind his head staring at the skyline of books. Thinking about Monday. Back to the hospital. Derek. Tyrone. Spit brothers. Construction work. Doctor Harris. Butler's Hosiery Palace. Anything but Chubby.

A knock on the door. "Yeah."

"Can I come in?" Tommy sounded almost apologetic.

"Yeah."

Tommy sat on the bed next to Stony's legs, putting a hand on his stomach. "We got a job, kiddo."

As father and son approached the door to Chubby's apartment, Stony was shaking. He had walked to this door a million times before, but now it seemed unfamiliar — sinister. Murderous. Tommy carried a mop and a red plastic bucket filled with sponges, dustcloths and Comet. Stony also held a mop. They were silent as Tommy dug into his pocket for the keys. He fumbled at the lock. Cursed. Dropped the keys. Dropped the bucket. The Comet rolled down the hallway. Stony chased after it. When he stooped to pick it up he felt dizzy and almost keeled over.

"Pop?"

Tommy didn't answer. He kept fouling up opening the double locks. Locked one, unlocked the other. Unlocked one, locked the other. Finally the door swung open. Tommy and Stony stepped back then. Tommy strode in; Stony hesitated, then followed. The apartment was like a haunted house. Cautiously they walked down the long foyer, holding their mops like carbines. Everything was immaculate but it felt like someone might jump out any second and dismember them both. They heard laughter from the living room. Music. The television was still on. Stony was relieved that everything was in order. They walked into the kitchen. Stony gasped. Cold enamel blazing white under the fluorescent overhead light splashed with brown blood. Splattered linoleum. A smashed blender on the floor. A bloody handprint blurred on the washing machine. Tommy whistled long and low. The light chain swung lazily over their heads like a noose. Stony felt nauseated, dropped his mop. Bent down to pick it up and fell backward on his ass. Automatically he reached for a cigarette.

"Oh, my God," Tommy groaned. Stony followed his stare into the dinette. A smashed chair lay like the carcass of a rotting animal. A broad stroke of blood was smeared on the dinette wall, as if it had been laid on with a paintbrush. Stony crawled through the dinette into the living room. Ran his hand lightly over the

stained rug. The stiff fibers were caked with blood. Stony scraped
a tiny ball of crust off the rug with his nails. Sat there rolling it
between his fingers like snot.

"We'll never get this out." Tommy stood near Stony.

Stony looked up at him. "Turn off the TV," he mumbled. As
Tommy moved to the set, Stony stretched out like a cat on all
fours, arched his belly downward, heaved a few times and finally
vomited, the vicious contractions of his stomach making him cry
in pain.

~

Stony sat powwow style in the kitchen, a sponge pungent with
Comet in his lap. Tommy was rigorously scrubbing the rug with
something foamy laying like sediment on top of the stains. "It's a
good thing Phyllis uses them plastic slipcovers," he yelled into the
kitchen. "Saved the fuckin' couch. She shoulda had one on the
damn rug," he grunted as he scrubbed.

Stony stared at a small bloodstain in front of his face on the
cabinet door below the sink. It looked like the profile of a witch
on a broomstick. She was flying into a strong wind that swept
back her hair and her long brown skirt. Her nose was hooked like
a claw. She was old.

"What the fuck you doin' in here?" Tommy fumed. Stony
didn't move. Tommy knelt down, grabbed the sponge from
Stony's lap, curled Stony's fingers around it and moved his son's
hand up and down the side of the washing machine.

"Snap out of it, Stones." He moved Stony's limp arm up and
down like a puppeteer. "Act like a man."

Stony continued to stare straight ahead, oblivious to the
movement of his arm. He screamed. The witch had moved.

~

Stony lay in bed, the covers up to his chin. The room was pitch
black. Tommy opened the door, a slice of light like a deep cut in
the darkness. Television noise trickled into the room. Tommy sat
on the bed. Stony stared over his shoulder.

"You cold?" Stony didn't answer. Tommy lit a cigarette, the

small explosion of light illuminating his face like a Halloween pumpkin. He exhaled into the darkness. "Stony, there are some things a man has to do." He ran his thumb down his mustache. "Ah, fuck it. Look, it's over. Tomorrow you go back to the hospital. I ain't gonna hassle you no more." He smoked in silence for a long moment. "When I was a kid I useta belong to this gang, The Fox Street Gougers, tough kids. The initiation was you had to jump on the back of a subway train, you know, hang on to the rail on the last car and ride it three stops. Me an' this kid Pete Maddarasso was doin' a double initiation. We jumped on the train at a Hundred and Forty-ninth Street and the Concourse. The whole gang was on the platform watchin'. I was scared shit but I wanted to be in that gang so bad. Anyways, we both jump on, ride down to a Hundred and Thirty-eighth Street. Everything's cool. All of a sudden the subway makes this sharp turn 'n' Pete loses his grip. I tried to catch him, but it happened too fast. The poor fuckin' kid fell on the third rail — burned to death. You know what I did? I stayed on the back of the train for the next two stops so I could pass the initiation." Tommy took another drag. "There's a fuckin' initiation for everybody." He stood up, sighing. "Baby, tonight was yours." He leaned down and kissed Stony on the lips.

29

AN HOUR LATER Stony was walking naked through the sleeping apartment. His fingers still smelled of Comet. To him it smelled like cunt, but he knew what it was and why it was on his skin. Leaving the light off, he washed his hands in the bathroom, rubbed some after shave on his palms. He shuffled into the living room, sat down on the overstuffed couch and listened to the distant grinding of the electric wall clock in the kitchen. The brocade material of the couch felt scratchy on his ass. He got up, squatted next to a tall stack of records. In the darkness he pulled out a James Brown album, slipped it onto the turntable, adjusted the volume to the lowest audible level and sat cross-legged on the rug. Before the arm hit the record the phone rang with a shrill heart-freezing suddenness.

Stony leapt to his feet, ran into the kitchen and grabbed the receiver before the second ring. The clock read two-fifteen.

"Hello?" he whispered.

"Stony?" Chubby's voice sounded childlike and alien. Stony covered his crotch with a dishtowel.

"Chubby?"

"Yeah, it's me. Stony, did your dad go up to my place tonight?"

"Yeah, we cleaned it all up."

"You went too? Oh, Stony, it was a mess, hah?"

Stony shrugged but didn't answer.

"Stony, I'm so ashamed. I can't tell you," Chubby whined. The tone of his voice made Stony want to cry.

"It's O.K. now, Chub, it's clean, you wouldn't even know that . . ." Stony cut himself short.

"Stony, you're a good boy. You look after your own people like a man. You help me, Stony. I need you."

For the first time in his life, Stony felt like he was bigger than Chubby and that frightened him.

"I need you, Stony." Chubby sounded like a midnight lover. A woman. "I'm gonna be home tomorrow."

"I'll come up tomorrow night, keep you company." Stony wanted to be a little kid again.

"Maybe we can watch TV or go to the movies, hah?"

"Sure." Stony pinched the flesh between his eyes, fought back tears. "I gotta go, Chubby."

"You come up tomorrow night."

"Sure. I gotta go, Chubby."

"I can lean on you, Stony."

"You can lean on me."

"You're a man, Stony."

"I'm a man."

"You're one of us."

"I'll come up tomorrow."

Stony listened to the dial tone for a long time before hanging up the receiver. He walked back to the living room. James Brown screamed with insect tinniness on the barely audible stereo. He sat down in the middle of "King Heroin." "You're *hooked* . . . your . . . foot . . . is . . . in . . . the stir-*rup!* So *mount* the steed . . . and ride . . . him . . . *well* . . ." Stony got up, padded back into his bedroom, sat down at the desk, lifted the blotter and slipped out the piece of paper with Doctor Harris' phone number, lifted it into the moonlight and dialed in the darkness. Albert mumbled something in his sleep. One ring, two, three, four . . . Stony slammed down the receiver. Albert jumped upright in bed and whimpered in a half-sleep.

Stony sat next to him on the bed. He touched Albert's chest with an outspread palm. Albert gasped, focused his eyes on his brother.

"Ssh." Stony eased Albert back down on his pillow. Albert fretted and whimpered but fell back to sleep almost immediately, his hand closing around Stony's arm. Stony stared at his brother, then gently ran a hand over his face, his chest, his crotch, his legs. Albert's face had a petulant frown as if he were in the middle of a nightmare. Stony freed his wrist from Albert's grip.

He returned to the living room.

"Ah was talkin' . . . ah was talkin' to a cat th' other naht, he say what ev-bahdy lookin' for today is *escap*-ism." The record clicked off and Stony was alone with his thoughts. He collapsed on the couch, one arm flung across his eyes. Take care of his own. One of us. You don't do the hospital Monday, don't come by Monday night. Butler. Bastard. Stony crossed his arms in front of his chest, stared at his biceps. "I'm a *man!* Mah father's a *man!* Mah uncle's a *man!* You, you're a fuckin' *pan*tyhose salesman an' you're tryna *fuck me up!* Stony ran back into the bedroom and dialed Butler's number. After two rings he quietly replaced the receiver. "Ah, bullshit," he muttered. Fresh air. Need some fresh air. He fumbled for his dungarees and stumbled out of the apartment.

~

Efram Concepción was the security guard on the midnight to 8:00 A.M. shift for the Roosevelt Loop section of Co-op City. For $140 a week he hung around jerking off his nightstick five nights a week while the three high rises and six town houses on his beat slept. Usually he was an easygoing lay-back guy, but tonight he was in a mean and twisted head. Five hours earlier his wife had discovered a diaphragm in his sixteen-year-old daughter's bottom dresser drawer and all hell broke loose. For the first time in his life he struck his daughter — knocked her right out of her platform shoes. *Puta!* She ran from the house cursing as his wife cried and fluttered around like a bird out of its cage. He took the diaphragm, holding it with delicate disgust as if it were a huge dead roach and dropped it down the incinerator. When he left for work at eleven, his daughter was still out. Now at three-thirty he was sitting on a bench in Roosevelt Loop, his face rigid, his back straight as a ramrod, steadily slapping his nightstick into his open palm, his brain filled with images of low income housing, all-nigger gang bangs, cocksuckings, ass fuckings. Those goddamn platform shoes . . . He got up and paced his beat like a caged animal. He gripped his nightstick so tightly his knuckles were almost translucent with tension.

He wheeled around at the noise. Thirty yards away a half-naked teen-ager stood in the doorway of one of the high rises. He stepped forward, stopped, then headed for the garage. "Hey! Yo!" Concepción strode toward the lurching form. At the barking command, Stony stopped dead in his tracks. He inhaled, hitched up his pants and slowly turned. Shit. Sergeant García.

"Where you runnin' to?" Concepción laid his nightstick across Stony's naked chest. Stony looked down at the stick, then back up at his interrogator. Fucking spic Mickey Mouse cop.

"You take that stick outta my *face*, Cap'n *Bubba*, and I *might* just tell you!"

Concepción pressed the stick harder into Stony's chest. "I'll lay your fuckin' brains out all over the ground." Despite the calm tone of his voice, Stony felt Concepción trembling through the wood across his chest. "Fuck off," Stony sneered and pushed the nightstick away. Concepción smiled, allowing Stony to turn. Out of the corner of his eye Stony saw the stick coming down, lunged to the left and felt a stinging pain in his shoulder. Struggling to keep his balance and wheeling around he charged head down at Concepción's gut. Concepción fell over backward with Stony on top. Stony grappled for the nightstick, flung it into the grass and brought his fist down across Concepción's cheek. Stony went berserk. Tried to pound Concepción's face into jelly. "Where you *run*nin'! Where you *run*nin'! Where you *run*nin'!" in rhythm with the blows. Concepción was out cold. Blood trickled from his nose and the corner of his mouth. Stony got to his feet with a delicious exhaustion. He tasted blood in his mouth. He was high as a kite. With his bare foot he kicked Concepción in the ribs. Concepción grunted but hardly moved. Stony stumbled to a bench near the back of the building, sat down and tried to stop shaking.

He took some deep breaths through his nostrils. The faint familiar stench of the bay was soothing. He shut down all his other senses and concentrated on that smell. Stony felt calm. His

mind was clear. Blank. Peaceful. He rose and headed upstairs.
One ring, two, six, ten . . .

"Yeah?" Doctor Harris' voice was thick with sleep.

"Harris? You stay the *fuck* away from me . . ." Stony jabbed
the air with his finger as he hissed in the phone. "You stay the
fuck away from Albert. You stay the *fuck* away from *all* of us,
unnerstand?"

"Who the hell is this?" Harris growled.

"Take a goddamn guess." Stony almost spat the words, then
hung up.

He started to remove his dungarees, stopped, zippered them up
again, took the white canvas utility belt that was hanging on the
bedpost and buckled it on. He sat cross-legged, hunched over,
staring at the weak gray light filtering through the curtains. The
pliers in his belt stuck him under his ribs but he didn't move.

"No wait, hold it, hold on, hold on." He couldn't tell if he spoke
out loud or if he just thought the words. He couldn't tell if he was
crying or not.

He was.

An Interview with
Richard Price

Talk about how you came to write Bloodbrothers *and the place that inspired this story.*

I came from an outer-borough housing-project culture, and I don't think I've ever written a book in which a housing project wasn't a character unto itself. This goes right up to *Lush Life*. I don't do it by design, thinking "I've got to have a housing project." You live many places in life, but you're always only from one place, and for me it's the *Bloodbrothers* environment: working class, housing project, Bronx.

    Bloodbrothers was based on the two summers I spent as a construction worker in college, where I worked on Co-op City, a highrise in Riverdale, and the Albert Einstein Medical Center. It was sort of a cushy job for the college sons of members of the union. My father was not an electrician, but I did meet Harry Van Arsdale, who was a major labor figure in New York from the 1950s into the 1970s. He offered me one of the summer jobs that the union had set aside exclusively for their own sons. Your job basically was to walk up twenty flights of stairs with a heavy spool of wire on your shoulder and a hard hat, get everybody's coffee break and lunch orders, and for that you were paid at the fourth-year apprentice rate, even though you're basically unskilled. It was a sweet deal for the college boys; went a long way in paying the next year's tuition.

    When I wrote *Bloodbrothers* I was in my early twenties, and it was a time when I was looking back as opposed to looking forward. I was never going to live in the Bronx again, and the past only exists as long as you can remember it. Out of that realization came a great urge to re-create those times and that place so they wouldn't disappear on me.

Bloodbrothers was also about the question of how one separates from one's parents, how do you leave home without destroying home, how do you get away without burning it all down?

Did you know Stony when you were young?

Basically everybody I knew growing up was a variation on Stony. In the housing projects in the fifties and the sixties whoever didn't go directly to college ended up in the police academy or with a good trade-union job. It was a very different time. Stony is a stand-in for an entire crew of kids that were born around 1949 into families that were basically blue-collar. There's a lot of me in him, but not all of me.

The family in this book is volatile, and there are many complex exchanges of anger, affection, fear, and frustration among them. Talk about how, as a writer, you bring a family like this to life on the page.

It's almost like an acting exercise: Bring five people to the table and do an improv, and if you're really aware of who each person is and how their brain works you know exactly what their response is going to be to someone else's comment. The characters reveal who they are by what they say, and both the family and the scene wind up creating themselves right there on the page. Sometimes I knew what I wanted to happen, had it all laid out like a carpet, but mostly I would just unleash everything to see where it would go.

And yet the family in Bloodbrothers *is very different from your own, ethnically and otherwise.*

Yes, but all fiction is autobiographical; I don't care if it's science fiction or a crossword puzzle, your autobiography gets into everything. My family was not at all as violent as the one in *Bloodbrothers,* but they had some of the same dynamics. Sometimes you work better when you pick avatars that are at a remove from your own personal experience, and I think I needed the beard of a more operatic family than mine. I just gave people different costumes and vocal registers. It's all coded.

And why Italian?

I don't know why in my first couple of books the characters were primarily Italian. Maybe I thought of my Italian friends' families as more externally dramatic than my own.

You were twenty-four when you wrote Bloodbrothers, *and it was your second book. What was it like to publish so young?*

It was both good and bad. Once you're published the only struggle then is to write another good book. You're not struggling to become an author anymore, you *are* an author (before you're an author you're just a writer). The bad thing is that once you're an author there's the danger of becoming too self-conscious about your writing; you have a track record from the previous book, and if you're a certain type of person, you develop a habit of constantly looking over your shoulder to see who's chasing you, when basically who's chasing you is yourself. When I wrote *The Wanderers,* my first book, it was a piece of cake, there was no pressure, I was just writing for writing class, but after that I became an author, and writing was never quite as much fun and easy.

You said that everything is autobiographical on some level, but in your later books, research played an important part, particularly research about police work. Talk about the art of turning nonfiction into fiction, and seeing things as an artist versus seeing them as a cop.

While writing *Clockers, Samaritan,* and *Lush Life,* whenever I would go with the cops into a housing project, I would be radioactively alert to every small detail because every apartment hallway and elevator were so familiar yet alien to me; and my brain turned into a camera. The cops, on the other hand, had been going in and out of these places since the day they came on the job, and after a few years they just didn't see them anymore. So when we come out and I say "Did you notice this, this, this, and this," they're always like "Huh?" Somebody once said that the only way to write about Africa is to either go there for ten days or for ten years. With the ten-day approach, your eyes are as big as dishes. If you can communicate the shock and awe of seeing something that way in your fiction, preserve that visceral sense of discovery, then I'd say you're pretty much good to go.

These days my novels pretty much embrace the current moment, but *Bloodbrothers* was most definitely written via my rearview mirror.

Screenplays, teleplays, books: How is the approach different from one medium to the next?

It's different in the sense that when you're writing a book it's all yours; you're in charge, you're in control, and your only requirement is for it to be a good read. If you want two people to sit on a bench and talk for ten pages, the only mandate is to make it an absorbing conversation. Scriptwriting, on the other hand, serves a two-dimensional medium; there's no authorial voice in a screenplay, no style, no narration, no God. There's just description of action and words coming out of peoples' mouths. It's like a one-hundred-twenty page memo to the actors and directors. Novels are four-dimensional, because you have the interior life of the character and God the narrator. You have actual writing. So if you're a novelist by trade and you're writing screenplays, you have to be very aware that you've got to move it, move it, move it; less-is-more, less-is-more. You can't ever have enough "less"; it's more "less." It's like playing speed chess.

TV writing is a different critter altogether, because you're usually part of a team. On a series like *The Wire,* for example, which is the only TV writing I have experience with, no matter how good or bad the finished product—and *The Wire* is as good as it gets—you're basically part of an assembly line and you cannot come in and surprise people with these brilliant little quirky inspirations you've had, because it screws it up. Basically you have to know exactly what the guy writing behind you is setting you up for, and then you've got to set up the guy coming after you. I put up with that kind of straightjacketed writing because I liked and respected all the other people on the assembly line, and because it was *The Wire*. But I don't think I could do that on another show: I don't think I'd enjoy it.

Who are your influences as a writer?

Hubert Selby, Jr., Richard Wright, James Baldwin, Henry Miller, John Rechy. And Lenny Bruce, who just slayed me. When I was a teenager I read a paperback of his monologues, just straight-up transcripts, and I responded to everything: his speech patterns, his rhythms, his free-firing cultural non sequiturs. But most important, I recognized the voice of my future self. We always read to locate our selves, and that guy was my soul mirror.

Talk about your day-to-day process as a writer.

At the time of *Bloodbrothers* it was simply wake up, have breakfast, sit down, open that vein, and write via the rearview mirror: Pieces of cake. That all changed in 1990 with *Clockers*. For the last fifteen years I find that I spend as much time hanging out with the people and in the environment that I want to write about as I do sitting down and putting it all on paper. With *Bloodbrothers* and the other novels I wrote back in the seventies, the world was all in my head. It was pretty much a matter of parking myself and writing. That well ran dry after about four books.

I agonized very little over *Bloodbrothers*. Back then, unlike now, I was a great fan of myself. It's a young person's book, and there's a young person's sensibility behind it. There wasn't a terrible amount of self-reflection or nuanced thinking involved, which is not a good thing, but neither was there a lot of angsty second-guessing myself, which was great—a state of mind I'd kill to recapture these days.

Bloodbrothers *is about young people,* Lush Life *is about young people. What is it like to write about young people then and now?*

It was easy to write about young people back then because I was one of them. I was the same age as the waiters or the uniformed cops in *Lush Life*. Now when I write about young people I'm looking at it from the other side. When I wrote *Bloodbrothers,* I was writing about my generation; now I'm writing about their generation, and there's nothing worse than an aging *enfant terrible.*

But I think we've overblown the notion that what it's like to be young now is different from what it ever was. A lot of the proper nouns and a lot of the venues change, but it's the same dynamic. When I was writing *Bloodbrothers* I was at an age when I thought I'd never die, and I had all the time in the world to write a trillion books, and I knew everything in the world. It's amazing what I knew at twenty-five that I don't know now at fifty-eight.